Wrought In Flesh
The Vollmagus and the Etched
Book 1
Corinne Price

Crae Vost
Losweau
Tabrasia
Nether Peaks
Plaitius
Frew Braxus
Silverstrand Port
Juvial Osk
Kreation
Wesvrau
Volkrau
Hentruk
Fortrentok
Tellalily Harbor
Hackveu
Tabrasia Sanctuary
Orkstcad
Tresvus
Tabrius
DryftGrim
Platius Spire
Nether Grove
Krostrct
Charprin
Hazel Gryph
Trclusk
Bolorich Pinnacle
Brontcnux
Krcb Bay
Crass Wood Harbor
Habor Vcjtuus
Lotrijs Vos
Tjistux Frew
Suntallow Crcst

PROLOGUE

The creased leather of the grimoire felt like flesh under Sybil's fingertips. Pliant and rough as though alive beneath her touch. She tried not to let the creeping revulsion tap its sharp fingers up her spine. Hard enough to ignore with the smell that drifted off the pages. It reeked like the fetid, greying waters behind the charnel house.

Oils had been brushed on the cover to tamp the harshness of time, giving it a slick feel. The dust clung to it, particularly abundant in the sharp corners of the embossed title lettering. *Nachtite Volt Maeger*. She didn't know what those words meant, but that was a good sign, right? It was mystical. Unknown. Anything this mysterious had to be worth the punishment if they were caught.

Quinn had stolen it for her days ago. It radiated warning heat, like fire, and her instincts screamed not to touch it. But there was an underlying voice that whispered. It made the blighted, forbidden thing so tantalizing.

At barely sixteen years, most still saw Sybil as a child. The lack of whatever magic she was supposed to inherit had left a hollow pit inside of her. Now, a storm sparked and swirled in its place, filling the void. How could the daughter of a powerful warden be born without magic? Without worth? Just a useless *leertek*. Now that emptiness was filled with the anxious thrill of what awaited her between the pages of their stolen treasure.

"I need to cast a circle." Quinn gestured towards the grimoire still cradled to her chest.

Quinn cast magic with an enviable confidence. He only had to touch his fingertips to the floor. Dust and debris circled around them before collecting into an imperfect circle. His grin went lopsided as he blew his dirty blonde hair off his face. Years of watching him work, yet she still felt a sense of awe seeing how naturally his magic came to him. Jealousy was always there, whispering its callous remarks. She had learned to ignore it, focusing only on the dimpled smile he would routinely send her way after each success. A silent search for her approval, though he never needed it. He had two years on her, but his practice with his craft made the gap feel like decades.

"Then what?" she whispered, pressing her lips together to still the tremor. He didn't need to tell her what was next. They'd gone over it for hours, rehearsing every step with precise, measured focus. Yet, speaking helped her solidify their purpose. Maybe it made the fear less real.

Quinn's fingers laced in hers, holding the book together. Embracing her eased her trepidation. His inky black eyes met hers, searching and waiting for her plea to stop. Sybil bit her lip, subtly pulling the book closer.

"What if we wait?" she asked. "One more night. The moon isn't right, it isn't full." An old wives' tale. Still, those sharp nails of fear that tapped along her spine made the most ludicrous rumors believable.

Quinn's brows twitched to a frown before softening. He let go of the book, putting his hands on her jaw, thumbs beneath her chin, tilting it up to him. An old habit, but it worked. The familiar motion melted her heart, loosening her hold on the stolen tome. Like always, he smelled of the minerals he worked with, the rich, barest twist of loam in the air.

"Sybil, it is a great injustice that whatever deity looking down on us made you a *leertek*. With this book, we finally have a way to correct that. To make all your dreams come true." He pressed his lips to hers. "But, whatever you decide, I am here."

When he had snuck through her bedroom window weeks ago, his body vibrated with excitement. He'd broken the harsh rules dictated by the Wardens to tell her what he had learned. His panicked elation was contagious, the hope spreading with every quickly sputtered word. An ancient book, full of taboo rituals. One promising magical gifts, without the cost of life or limb. He told her that he could get it. Only for a night, of course, it wouldn't *actually* be stealing. Told her that he would do anything for her. Deep down, no matter what happened, he just wanted her to be happy.

She'd tried to hide it, but it was clear he could see the hurt etched on her face every time he called the earthen elements to his fingers. Heartbroken every time those around her cast magic with nothing more than a flick of their fingers. With every touch of his skin on hers, her worry melted away, dissipating between them. Whatever course they took, he would be there for her.

"I'm ready," she said, releasing her tight hold on the book. Sybil let out the smallest shudder and opened her eyes. "I trust you." The words were laced with a sweet surrender. She *did* trust him. To the ends of Crae Vost. After all, he was the boy who had held her hand through it all. Who had picked her up whenever the world brought her down.

Quinn's teeth flashed at her as he laid the book across his lap. "Cast a circle of mineral, then ignite it," he said, more to himself than to her. "As the circle burns, I recite the words."

Sybil had watched her father cast his magic. No matter how effortless he made it seem, there was always a slight strain to his face. A focused tension only she had noticed. If Quinn believed it to be as easy as a quick spell, he was a fool. She'd never say it, but she leaned closer anyways, watching Quinn flip through the pages of the book.

So close. Just a few more minutes and she would no longer be an outcast. A failure. Not fated to be just a *leertek* that mucked stalls for the rest of her life. She would be a powerful mage and finally make her father proud. Make *Quinn* proud.

She'd spent the last four nights dreaming about what the gift would become. Control of the earthen elements with geomancy like Quinn? Able to bend the flow of water to her will with fluidicity like her father? Or would she mend the flesh with sarcomancy like...

She shuddered, her thumb absently running along the scar on her palm. Healers were revered, and she would be blessed to be given that gift. But that was the one magic she prayed didn't wrap its teeth around her core.

Quinn grabbed the flint, the movement pulling her back out of her spiral. He held the match above it, ready to strike.

"We don't have to," Sybil said, pausing his momentum.

He smiled. "Yeah. We do." He struck the match.

Minerals and dirt that should never burn on their own ignited instantly. Sybil felt a heavy breeze whirl around the enclosed room, leaving behind harsh shivers. Unnatural in the small space, but with magic like this, she hadn't expected anything less.

Quinn tried to hide the shaking in his fingers when he blew out the match and discarded it. His throat bobbed as he turned his attention back to the book.

He was the one that was supposed to be strong. A warden-in-training, learning to defend the nation from threats both at their borders and beneath the mountains. Yet Sybil found her hand wrapping around his, squeezing it in reassurance. He responded with a slight shake of his head, refocusing himself and bringing the book closer.

In spite of her heart thundering beneath her ribs, Sybil leaned closer to the tome. The inked lettering blended into nothingness the longer she stared at it. An illusion that made her eyes burn. Enchanted so only the one who held the book could decipher the words.

"Are you sure you can do this?" Sybil asked, for what seemed like the hundredth time. Quinn chose not to answer. Instead, he cleared his throat and began.

"*Hark, nachtus creed. Metun crosh ligitus,*" he started, his voice growing less shaky with every syllable. Sybil's fingers curled inwards. The room seemed to shift around her, like the walls were breathing. The darkness crawled across the wooden boards towards them, held back by the flickering candles. Their minimal light tried to fight back, though the shadows made it falter.

An odd scent wafted through the small room. Cinnamon mixed with ash. The sharp, sweet spice punctuated by the acrid, bitter accompaniment of discarded fires. An odd combination she wouldn't soon forget.

"*Tredintus klarken hitsten. Jorsetris, flet,*" he continued as the room began to shake. The twisting darkness started to stretch out over the barrier of the light. Harsh shadows cast along the dented, cracked flooring. Twitching, blackened vines tested the light before swallowing it with every shuddering lurch forward. Its tendrils wrapped around Quinn's limbs, though he didn't so much as flinch. Sybil could only watch on, frozen in terror. It wasn't supposed to be like this; there wasn't supposed to be this much darkness. The inky blackness coiled up his legs, slithering around his torso and looping through his arms. It curled around the hand she held, but it avoided her skin like it sensed poison.

"*Voidkin, nachtborn.*" The words slipped from his mouth like water. "I welcome you." His eyes were glazed, faraway. Not even seeing the jumble of ink on the decaying, frayed pages.

Something was wrong. She knew those words, and had heard them on cold, dark nights around the fire light. Stories of monsters told to children. Warnings of things dragging you off into the night. But only *stories.*

Sybil jolted back to herself. She gripped tightly to Quinn's arms, her nails digging into his skin. Panic threaded through her veins.

"Quinn, stop. You need to stop." She clutched his face in both hands, straining to tear him back from wherever he had drifted. The light slowly returned to his eyes, her terror reflected back through the dark pits of his pupils. The smell was harsher now, the cinnamon a bare background to the swirling ash that stung her sinuses, the only sense that wasn't dulled. The darkness muted the room. Quinn's voice felt so far away. But that smell. Pungent and forceful. Eviscerating the rich dirt scent that once clung to Quinn's skin.

His mouth opened and closed a few times, his breath coming out in ragged gasps. The darkened tendrils had now encircled him, shadows pressed tightly to his flesh.

"I... I love you." His words choked out of him. He blinked a few more times, heavy and slow. "I'm so sorry... I... I fucked up,"

His screams shattered the muted haze. The flaming circle caved in, a purple-black hole opening within. The cinder smell flared through the room as though a fire were burning beneath the abyss. A shredding sound raked from the hole, tearing at her ears. Somehow louder than the boy in her clutches. More of the horrifying tendrils reached out from within the abyss. They grasped him with their thousands of clawing arms. Dug into his flesh, tearing away at the skin as they dragged him from his seat.

The chasm had become a cavernous mouth of flailing arms and grasping fingers. Their blackened, oozing flesh leaving imprints everywhere they touched, the wood beneath them slick and oily. They tore against Quinn, shredding through his skin with every grating pull. Sybil couldn't hold on. The tendrils pulled at her limbs, her muscles burning with the effort. She dug her nails into the flesh of his arms, leaving red trails as the darkness tore him from her grasp. The scratches were nothing, barely noticed in the growing pool of blood as the shadowed limbs ripped him open.

Half his body disappeared into the abyss. His mouth formed the start of her name, but was struck down into silence as the last grasping appendages tore him from beneath her nails. The chasm sealed without a sound, leaving behind only a scorched ring.

Sybil sat in silence, her ears ringing a high, nauseating tone. Blood splattered across the floor and up the opposing wall. Her arms hung limp where Quinn had just been, her fingers coated in blood, his flesh lodged beneath her nails.

For a brief moment, she felt nothing, her mouth hanging open as her mind stayed blank. A hollow emptiness sat in her gut that made her feel both weightless and heavy. A single thought crossed her mind. One she should have heeded the moment he told her it would be easy.

All magic has a cost.

ONE

The wax seal stared up at Sybil, even as the paper around it crinkled in her fingers. Thick and red, it depicted a cloak shrouding the faceless head of a soldier. The warden emblem. The wax mimicked fabric, pooling along the symbol's edges. Stamped in a hurry, no time to be delicate and precise.

Sybil hadn't meant for her hands to collapse inwards, crushing the envelope. Something about the way the messenger's forehead dripped with sweat made her back prickle. He wasn't afraid of the letter. He was afraid of *her*. And that only meant one thing: whatever was written on it was going to piss her off.

She broke the seal, decapitating the little red Warden. There was a satisfying tear as she shredded more than the wax under her nails. The folds of the paper were barely creased, the letter not clutched in the messenger's greasy palms for very long. The single page flipped open as soon as its paper cage was removed.

The missive was short, barely a scratch across the top third of the page. A request? No. An order.

See me immediately.

Captain Hertrin had taken the time to write, fold, and seal the letter. He could have sent his trembling messenger through the hallways of the Bastion to find her and speak the words himself. Instead, he chose extravagance. No doubt to remind her of her place.

A flare of heat coiled through her spine, contracting and seizing the muscles of her back. Before she could stop it, the flame of a nearby candle leapt to her fingers, engulfing the letter. The ashes floated down and scattered around her feet. A small yelp escaped from the shaking boy to her side. Her fingers twitched in his direction, the sudden noise rattling her.

She clasped her hands together, holding them tight to her chest, willing the magic back into her skin. The heat tempered as she closed her eyes.

Deep breaths.

When she reopened her eyes, the messenger was still there, looking paler than before. Clenching her jaw, Sybil forced a smile.

"Thank you, Frederique," she said, straining to speak through her teeth. "You are dismissed."

The boy bowed. He turned before straightening, his head still dipping forward. The off-centre twist tilted him further. He barely caught himself before he shuffled back down the hall.

Bronze leaves. She absently ran her fingers along the golden leaf pinned to her collar. Not long ago that leaf had been bronze. She shouldn't let her advancement overshadow all the hardships she endured as a fresh warden. Constantly reminding herself that she was very recently the awkward, sweaty, uncoordinated underling that stumbled through these halls.

She had almost made it to the Arcaneum before Frederique had called out to her. With so few hours free from warden duties, she'd carved out time to visit the arcane library whenever she could. Her plan had been to thumb through books until the candles became little more than puddles of wax and she was forced to drag herself home. And the captain had seen fit to tear that out from under her.

It would take her a lifetime to finish every one that lined the massive shelves. With even fewer days to visit, the size of it became increasingly daunting. Even still, she found herself solemnly eyeing the Restricted Area balcony.

Someday.

Once Frederique skittered beyond the marble column out of sight, she let out a heavy breath. With her palms turned up, she called upon the water under her skin, letting tiny pools accumulate in their centre. She then focused on the air around her hands, slowing it to a crawl, chilling it as it circled her fingers. Air was easy, an element just about every magic user could control. Using it to turn water to ice was not. She had been practicing it for the last few months. Her first attempt had made her collapse. Not unlike all the other pathetically easy magical tasks that caused her to sweat and shake uncontrollably. Tasks children could muster with a flick of their wrists.

When the skin of her palm had turned to a glassy finish, she pressed her hands to her forehead and let out a long sigh. The cold wouldn't completely stop the incoming throb in her head, but it could at least stave it off for a short while.

"That bad?" Killian's voice jolted her, his approach surprisingly quiet in the empty hall. The ice melted from her hand, trickling to the floor. It turned the ash of the missive to a milky swamp at her feet, muddying the marble floor.

"I'm sure it will be," Sybil said, flexing her fingers to bring the warmth back to them. "He sent Frederique."

Killian's brow arched up at the mention of his younger cousin's name. "*Really* bad then." Sybil nodded, stepping around him and waving her fingers to drag the puddle along behind her. A tiny floating orb of blackened water. It could make a new home in one of the extravagant planters outside the captain's office.

"What do you suppose he's going to say this time?" Killian asked, stepping in line with her and lacing his fingers behind his head.

Sybil just rolled her head on her neck, a subtle cracking pulling the tension from the vertebrae. "Oh, probably another overly practiced, long-winded speech about my potential, then a swift kick in the ass. I'll either get a week of guard watch with the bronze leaves, or get reassigned to the Kanal district," Killian winced, but she ignored it. She glanced over her shoulder, checking on the ball of ashen sludge floating along behind her.

"Guard watch, eh?" he asked, trotting slightly to catch up. "Sounds like some long, lonely nights." He was needling her. A tactic he used often when he could see her tipping towards the edge. Not to push her the rest of the way over, but to make her take a step back. A step back to strike him instead, of course.

"Oh, whatever will I do without your snoring to keep me awake?"

Garish, exorbitant décor burdened every single hall within this old university. Most were aware that it wasn't this spectacular in its academic days. Only afterward decorated with unnecessary lavishness when the Portcullis had taken over the building. What was once the epicentre of high learning for the continent of Crae Vost was stripped seemingly overnight. It returned to the living world as the headquarters for the country of Plaitius's hierarchal government. Had they not decided to keep the Arcaneum here, Sybil was sure it would have been completely razed. Probably something more ostentatious left in its place.

But why not relocate the Arcaneum to Bolorick Pinnacle with the rest of the powerful students of the Arcane? Sybil tried not to think of questions like that, knowing the whispers she heard in the streets. She was a Warden of the Portcullis. The last thing she should be doing is letting any pathetic rumors taint her. Not when they had dragged her up off the floor of her bedroom so many years ago.

Thick blankets wrapped around her while the room was seized and inspected. Soft hands of the Portcullis matriarchs with warm cups of tea. Calm words and quick comforts, ones she barely heard. Wardens had flooded her home, their white mantles appearing like a flurry of snow.

Quinn.

The captain's office was now in view, illuminated by the ominously placed chandelier that had been hung above the doors. Though it was identical to the many that preceded and followed the doors, it almost appeared to be enchanted to glow just a bit brighter than its neighbours. That, or Sybil had just been down this hallway so many times that that specific chandelier gave her pause. The latter, she thought. Definitely the latter. He wasn't showy enough to waste the coin on an enchanter just to create an aura of intrigue around his office.

But he is showy enough to send a messenger across the Bastion with a pointless, stupid, handwritten note.

When they approached the door, she tried not to let Killian see the nervous dust-filled air that wrapped through her fingers, her magic once more spiralling out of control. She took the flare of energy and turned it on her small follower. She flicked her fingers and threw the ashen puddle through the air towards a planter. Just out of reach of the pot, the ball swerved. Invisible fingers wrapping around the puddle and deflecting its path. It smashed against the wall instead, an inky stain splattered against the blue and silver wallpaper. The smudge spread like a tainted sunrise.

Sybil whirled on Killian, his hands still held aloft from his cast spell. The smile spread across his face. Sybil shoved him, fighting her own smile. "Ass." She struck him again on the arm, a cry as he clutched it in a mockery of pain. The buildup that had imbedded itself within the muscles of her back started to loosen as Killian burst out laughing. She could feel guilty about the stained wall later. For now, she had to stifle her own laughter as she frantically motioned for Killian to quiet. Whether the captain could hear them being foolish or not was up for debate, but she'd rather not find out.

His laughter ceased, his tone dropping. "You know I could ask my grandfather to waive it this time." It was a sincere offer, but that didn't stop the creeping smugness that came whenever he spoke of his family.

Nothing but a pair of legacies, she'd heard people mutter when they first got together. Killian had been unperturbed, but the comments infuriated her. The only thing worse than those whispers was the follow up about *her* father. About the reason he retired from the wardens in the first place.

Sybil's thumb ran along the scar on her palm. "Or, you could let me fight my own battles,"

"I'm serious. This is the eleventh time you've been to the captain's office in the last six months. This could be it for you," Killian said, wrapping his arms around Sybil, resting his chin on her head, his breath rustling her hair. He'd called the colour *decaying wheat*, a term he thought would be endearing, but made it seem like her hair was rotting.

She tried not to think of that as his arms squeezed her close. "I can make one visit to the estate and have this completely forgotten."

Sybil pressed her hands to his chest, building the space back between them. His blue eyes regarded her, brows pressed back. "You know I can't let you do that," she said, pushing further away until his arms dropped to his sides.

"Then, tell your father. I'm sure he would have a heart to heart with Hertrin and get it all sorted out."

"*Captain* Hertrin," she corrected. "Marten doesn't need to get involved. It was barely an incident."

"It was property damage," Killian said.

"*Barely* property damage." Sybil shoved him again, smirking as he stumbled, the thin white leather of his warden mantle twisting in his legs. It drew her attention, her nose crinkling. His mantle was lopsided, the leather straps on his left leg pulled tighter than the right. With a shake, she straightened her face. His mantle wasn't her problem. Now wasn't the time to let it bother her.

They could stand out here for the rest of the evening, hiding away until Captain Hertrin left the Bastion. It'd delay the news she was trying to be casual about, but she'd be back here in the morning with the captain even more furious.

She turned back to the embossed door. She could draw out every filigree line of this gaudy door off memory by now. The increasing frequency of standing in front of it never made it any easier to raise her hand to the wood and knock. Her fist would hover, a barricade between her flesh and the gilded paint.

Deep breaths.

She barely had a chance for her fist to strike the wood before the call to enter rang out from beyond it. Too quickly for her to get her bearings, but enough to give her hands one final shake. Sybil cast a sardonic smile in Killian's direction before pulling open the doors and stepping into the office.

Whatever paper the captain had just set on the teetering pile in front of him was grabbed in the breeze of the opening doors. It was carried off his desk and deposited onto the floor a few strides away. He still held his quill aloft, the ink dripping onto the wood of his desk. A heat spread across Sybil's face as she picked up her pace to grab the paper off the floor, but her hands betrayed her. A sharp gust of wind left her fingers and gripped the paper, whipping it up and into the nearby fireplace.

"Leave it," the captain sighed as she picked up her pace to save the paper from the flames. He gestured for her to stand across from his desk. "Please." Her cheeks felt hot as she watched the errant paper vanish into ash.

The doors slammed shut behind her, the noise making a thick pit grow in her throat, holding her words hostage. "Sir," Sybil stood in front of him, her fingers entwined, palms pressed to her diaphragm. The Warden Salute. One thing she could do right.

"Release, Wyntres," he instructed, lacing his fingers together. Sybil hesitated for a moment, appreciating the modicum of safety the salute provided. Hands pressed to a wielder's body were less likely to act of their own will. In the end, his raised brows won over, her hands dropping to her sides. "Would you care to explain what happened Strastag night?"

"I apprehended a thief," Sybil said, intentionally short.

The captain only sat back, rubbing his fingers against his temples. The firelight glinted off the impressive number of medals that adorned the sleeve of his white mantle, the obsidian leaf at his breast reflecting the fire light. "Wyntres, this is not the time to be clever with me. Tell me why I have reports of a balcony collapsing in the Habinare district."

"Because people that use enchanted rope to hold up their balcony should be ready to face the consequences."

"Wyntres," he warned.

She dropped her shoulders, lifting her gaze away from him to stare at the wall opposite, the stained glass a pleasant change from the judgemental stare he had levelled on her. "A thief ran past a woman out with her grandchild and stole her pouch. I gave chase and went after the criminal. He was a frostweaver and started to throw ice at me, endangering civilians. He struck me with two of them."

She dared a glance down to catch the captain's eyes flicking to the cuts in her mantle sleeve where the knives had sliced through the pale leather. She noted the slight nod and snapped her gaze back to the wall. "To prevent further injury, I used my surroundings to my advantage to apprehend the individual. I grasped hold of the nearby rope, and was able to tie the criminal's legs together, stopping him in his tracks and retrieving the stolen goods."

"So, you tore the supporting structure out of a shop's balcony to stop a petty thief?" There was no humor in his voice.

"Are we not obliged to serve the populace as their protectors?" Sybil asked, hoping for once to plead to a baser instinct.

"How much were the stolen goods worth?"

"It was a family heirloom, priceless—"

"How much was it worth?" His voice raised. Sybil pressed her lips into a thin line, squeezing her hands at her sides. The nearby fireplace had already started to flicker slightly, and she hoped that he hadn't noticed.

"Fourteen lok," she murmured.

"Fourteen lok. Little over a day's wage. Do you know what the cost of the balcony was?" Sybil didn't bother answering. It didn't matter. The captain let out a heavy breath. "I am running out of excuses for you, Sybil."

She bit down on her cheek, the familiarity of her given name meant as a loving gesture but burning her with disrespect and misplaced paternalism. It wouldn't be completely out of line to call him out on it, but the thin ice she was walking was already creaking beneath her.

"I am bound by the citizens of Plaitius to protect—" Sybil started the oath, only for the captain to slap his hands on his desk.

"Don't be ridiculous. You are bound to protect the city, not destroy it," he snapped, shooting forward in his seat. The outburst made Sybil flinch, the fireplace wavering next to her. The sharp, dismissive words stung, *especially* from him.

The captain caught himself, correcting his composure. He flexed his fingers in front of him, drumming them lightly on the wood. "Maiten Wyntres—"

"Is not here." Her tone dropped as she finally met his stare.

"—is respected long after his retirement," he paused, working his jaw across his teeth. "I understand the circumstances of that retirement were... unsightly."

Darkness. Screaming.

Blood. So much blood.

The captain started to twist the sleeves of his mantle between his fingers. His mouth opened a closed a few times. "What happened to Warden Vandryft was a tragedy, and..."

"We aren't here to discuss those events." She interrupted again. Her fingernails had started to dig into her palms, the pain grounding her from the swirl of contempt. The captain was struggling to toe the balance of familiarity and duty. Bringing up Quinn in hopes of solidifying some reserve of compassion was a poor choice.

"What has the Portcullis requested for punishment, sir?" She'd save him from himself, steer it back to the inevitable.

His jaw flexed, his lips twitching. "The Hauxin family wants to see you dismissed and removed from the Bastion."

Icy stone filled her chest, fracturing and cracking, tearing apart her insides.

She wanted to keep her head high, her shoulders tight as he spoke. Instead, her mouth ran dry, her throat filling with sand. "And the rest?"

"The rest are starting to see their side."

The families within the Portcullis held immense power, and a request from one of them could easily tumble into a request from all. Sybil wanted nothing more than to protect the people of the city of Hazel Gryph, a job her father had taken almost as seriously as she had. Yet at every step, her actions were being second guessed by some of the families that held their thrones atop the towers of the Bastion. Families that rarely stepped their polished slippers into the streets that she watched.

The fire behind her started to rise from its wire cage, the flames kissing at the edge of the mantel above. Hertrin's memorabilia and décor at risk of scorching.

"What are my options then? Kanal district? Night Guard? An increase in tutoring?" She had to tamp the shaking in her hands before it started to rattle to her teeth. "Please, sir. I can fix this."

The captain's jaw tensed, leaning forward on the desk to tent his hands in front of his chin. "That isn't the case anymore, Wyntres. Those options have been dropped." The fire inside her sizzled, replaced by the sharp sparks that started to crackle at her fingers. Zapping in tune with her rapidly increasing heartbeat.

It was as if he was holding her gold leaf in his palm, slowly crushing it in his fist. Everything she had worked for, destroyed in a split second. A swelling pain started behind her eyes, the pressure getting harder to fight. The smell of static and ozone filtered up from her fingers, the electricity making her braid fray and split on her head.

"You're being assigned to the Vinch district."

A weight dropped in her chest. Relief and despair all at once.

Vinch. Years she had spent fighting for her mantle, fighting for her place within the ranks. Fighting to be seen as more than just a name. Or even just as a blood tainted rumor. To succumb to the devastating, career altering district made her feel as though a scream was welling up in her throat, threating to pour out of her lips.

The Kanal was the lowest of the low, home to all types of criminals. A sanction that no Warden actively chose to be assigned to, knowing their hours would be fraught with activity. The Vinch district, however, was its polar opposite. Usually assigned to the older, more senior members of the wardens that had not excelled beyond their station. Complacent to spend their final years helping the elderly, issuing noise fines, or enforcing magic curfews. A reward for decades of service as they chased their twilight years. A graveyard for the ambition still held tightly in Sybil's heart.

But she was keeping her leaf.

And that was better than nothing.

She needed to get out of here. She needed to let out that scream that was burning the back of her throat. The hold on her magic was only growing weaker.

"Sybil, I am sorry—"

"Understood, Captain. I'll report for duty first thing in the morning at the Vinch district office." She pressed her pained palms to her torso, using the salute to extinguish the final flare of sparks against the leather of her mantle. "May I have my leave?"

The captain frowned, clearly expecting an uproar, a burst of emotion. Maybe even her all too typical flood of uncontrolled magic. Clearly not this. Not a calm, complacent response. He nodded, gesturing towards the door with his outstretched hand, keeping a level gaze on her as she spun on her heel and marched out.

"So, what's the verdict? I didn't hear any yelling or thunderstorms. That's good, right?" Killian asked, the doors shutting behind Sybil. She pressed her back to them, letting her weight fall into the wood, not caring about the pressure of the handle in her spine. She was vaguely aware of the ice that shot out in fractals along the ground beneath her. A heavy release of everything she held tight. Small, quiet. Better than a sudden torrent of wind. Or something worse.

The captain could hear them, there was no doubt about that, but she needed a moment before leaving the Bastion to go home. Needed a moment before she faced the streets of Hazel Gryph surrounded by the people that feared her help. She had to breathe, the throbbing in her head had hit a crescendo, making her vision start to waver.

"Vinch," she finally choked out, her face buried in her hands. She didn't need to see Killian's face to know what it looked like. The hefty pause was enough.

"It's not a dismissal," he said, his hand resting on her shoulder. Sybil dropped her hands, looking up to will the tears away that brimmed along the lids. "Come on." He grabbed her hand, hoisting her to her feet. "Let's get you a stiff drink."

As incredible as that sounded, she needed something else first. "I'm going to Groth's."

Killian let out a heavy breath, his hands slapping against the rough fabric of his trousers. "I can help you through this too, you don't always have to go to *her*."

Sybil shook her head, knowing that too many more words and the tears would come. Or the flurry of magic. Neither would look good leaning against the captain's door in the hall of the Bastion. "Let's go."

"I'm not going to that filthy, disgusting place. Come on, we can go grab a drink, take a load off, and then you and I can go home and relax."

Her lip curled up, flinching at his words. To talk so coarsely about her second home hurt. Her hands suddenly felt very cold. It took a moment for her to realize that they had started to ice over. She gently shook them, trying not to draw too much attention as she warmed them up. "It's not disgusting, just don't brush up against the walls, or benches, or people."

Killian shook his head. "You can see Maex yourself. Maybe I'll meet you at Nostramus later if I'm still feeling up for it." He groaned, turning to leave.

Anger flowed out through her fingers, her magic coiling with frustration. It acted on its own again, wrapping around a nearby plant. Sybil reached out for his hand, an absent apology already atop her tongue. The pot went flying, the roots and dirt tearing from the soil as the pot clattered against the marble floor and shattered. The plant slapped into Killian's chest, showering his mantle in a coat of dirt, leaves and mud.

"Great," he snarled, attempting to pat the dirt off and only smearing it into the leather. "Just fucking great." He cast a last sharp look her way before stomping off down the hallway. She watched him as he left. As her eyes followed him, she caught a few other wardens staring at her from across the hall. They quickly averted their gaze, jumping back into whatever conversation they had been pretending to have. As though they hadn't been watching the entire spectacle.

She instinctively dropped her eyes to their collars, hovering over the bronze pin. A sneer reflexively settled on her face, but not at their training status. Instead, at the memory of her own time in the barracks. Every quiet moment flooded with the hushed onslaught of rumors. No doubt they would rush back to the barracks and fill the rest of the newest members of the Wardens in on 'the chaos mage' and all her latest theatrics.

Yeah. Just fucking great.

Two

Raekin didn't feel it anymore. The weight on his hips, the heat against his skin. None of it sunk in the way it used to. Wasn't sure if it ever did. She was warm, soft in places, vicious in others, but none of it reached him. His body went through the motions, performed the part, while his mind floated somewhere else entirely. Somewhere quieter. Somewhere dead to the waking world.

It wasn't about desire. Just duty. A performance that they re-enacted, nothing more.

His cock was nestled tightly between Varena's thighs. Though she slowly rocked her hips back and forth, he was barely hard. He'd lost himself in the glowing stalactites that hung above. His body reacted out of habit, not want.

She slid her hands along his torso, her fingers stalling and drifting along his inks, scars, and burns, delicately running along the muscles that years of work had carved into his body. Her skin was a match to his. Tattoos and scars carved like a map of her pain. A reminder of why their masters had called them "Etched".

Varena came to a rest at his shoulders, one hand sliding up to his neck, fingers curling under his jaw to force his gaze up. The other playfully curled in his long dark hair. His orange eyes flicked to hers, sharp and bright against the molten yellow burning back at him.

"Where are you right now?" she cooed, brushing her lips along his jaw.

The black ink lines across his nose wrinkled as he smirked. "Anywhere but here."

She fought to keep her face steady, but he caught the flash of rage tightening her mouth, darkening her already fiery gaze. Lowering herself against him, she pressed her forehead to his, her lips parting in a slow, deliberate sweep that yanked his attention down.

"I was told," she whispered, grinding her hips harder against his lap, a groan rasping up from deep in his throat, his eyelids fluttering, "that Tazec would make a suitable mate for me as well. Maybe I should go wrap myself around him instead."

He unlaced his fingers from behind his neck, cupping her jaw with one hand, gripping her hair with the other. Her eyes half lidded as she pressed her breasts into his chest. The pads of his fingers, calloused as they were, traced the inked and branded marks that decorated her face. Runes like a crown along her forehead, their sharp points drawing lines through her brows and across her lids. The line that ran from the centre of her lip to the top of her sternum curved as she cocked her head.

"Tazec is half the man I am," he rasped. That deep, buried part of him still felt the sting of her words. His hand releasing her jaw to drift to her back, pulling her hips into him, revelling in the sharp exhale that escaped her mouth. "But it would not surprise me in the least to hear that you already had him."

She hissed through her teeth, her nails digging into his flesh, palms pressing into his skin. A warmth drifted through her fingers, morphing into searing heat. Flesh melting beneath her touch, all but liquefying under her hands. Raekin roared out, gripping her arms and throwing her off him. Varena slid across the rough dirt on her bare ass, catching herself before rolling down the embankment of the nearby crevasse. The glowing lichen of the cave gave just enough light for him to see the surprise on her face as she glanced over at the oppressive depth of the drop.

"Bastard! You could have killed me," she shrieked, shifting to her knees and slowly backing away from the fissure.

"As if you deserve any less," Raekin said, leaning back to look at the mottled, disfigured flesh on his chest. The runes inked and scarred there were warped but not destroyed, the skin red beneath them. He winced as he ran his fingers along the damaged skin. Sarcomancers were healers, pillars of the community to the above ground. But down here, they were demons. Twisted, sadists with a penchant for destruction. Unsurprising he found himself forcibly paired with one.

"Should have melted right to your heart and ripped it out myself," Varena snarled, getting to her feet.

"And what do you suppose Naz'tak is going to do to me when he sees what you've done?"

"Served you right, bloodwhore—"

Raekin was on his feet. He flicked his hands towards her and she was flung backward into the wall. There was a sickening thwack as her head connected with the dirt. He closed his fist, coughing erupting from her throat as blood dribbled down her chin. When she tried to clutch at it, chunks of the cave wall shivered loose. Tendrils of earth curled and hardened over her wrists like cuffs of stone. He stormed over to her, his teeth flashing. It was hard for him not to enjoy the trembling she tried to hide as he bore down on her.

"What were you about to say? I didn't hear you," he growled, his hand twitching against the hold his magic had.

"I called you a bloodwh—" she started but was interrupted by another burst of coughing. She spat blood onto his damaged chest as he drew more of it into her lungs, drowning her with her own body. Coughs turned to gasps as she struggled beneath his hold, the air escaping her in horrid, wet, bursts.

"Sorry, Varena, didn't quite catch that," he asked again, leaning closer until he was sure his face was all she could see. He released her slightly to let her get a breath.

"Nothing," she whispered, her voice raw with the effort.

He should've killed her. Let her fall into the fissure and disappear into the dark.

But he didn't.

Because the moment he did, he'd be alone again. And right now, even hate was company.

Raekin grinned, dropping his hand and releasing her, the wall giving way from her limbs at the same time. She collapsed into him, and though he caught her, he immediately pushed her back against the rock. "You know better than to say that shit around me, don't you?" He gripped her face in his hands, pressing his thumbs to the bottom of her chin and tilting it up.

Varena nodded, locked on him. Her hands were free, and all it would take was one touch from them for him to be doubled over in pain again. But before she could shift a finger, he could have the wall devouring her, her cries smothered as her body was crushed. From the trembling under his grasp, the sharp movement of her throat as she swallowed, that threat wasn't lost on her. No point in feigning brutality if nobody believed you could actually do it. Not like she hadn't been witness to it herself on enough occasions.

He held her head in his hands, enjoying the slight fear in her eyes. There was a sickening feeling in his gut every time he got pleasure from it. Knowing how fucked up it was that something like this made him feel anything but disgust. The thrill of her fear twisted something inside him. Not disgust, and not horror. Something darker. Before he could stop it, the familiar ache ignited.

You're no better than them.

Just another monster.

You can't become them.

Raekin traced his hand from her jaw to her cheek, then tangled it in her hair. He pressed his lips to hers, silencing the grating voice that dragged its claws across his mind. The sharp tang of salt lingered on her tongue. His teeth raked across her lip, the soft moan escaping her throat making his blood heat. He lifted her leg, wrapping it around his hips, enjoying the warmth that drifted off her centre. The kiss was broken as he pulled her hair back, forcing her to look at him again.

"Never, ever talk to me like that again. Understand?"

"Never," she whispered, her lip trembling in the soft blue glow. The tremble was stopped as he captured it with his mouth, pulling her closer into his body, feeling the pulse of her blood quicken beneath her skin. The rush spreading through him like cold fire through his veins. He loathed her, but a command was a command.

There was always a stillness after the chaos. Not a peace, just an absence. That heated, slick energy that crackled between them faded as their moans echoed in the cavern. Varena laid her head on his lap, absently rolling stones into the fissure across from them. Soft cracking as they ricocheted off the walls until the sound drowned out into the depths. For now, rested like this, he could ignore the unclean feeling that lingered on his skin.

Raekin laced his fingers back behind his neck and relaxed against the wall. His gaze was fixated once more on the glowing lichen that coated the stalactites. Some of it detached and shimmered in the air as it drifted to the ground to die. He liked this section of caves. It was peaceful. This was the farthest into this section he had ever brought anybody, his own escape in the darkness. Varena had earned this much of his trust. But not enough to see the places he called his.

They hated each other. But hate was easier than grief. Easier than guilt. At least when she was near, he didn't have to hear his own thoughts. The silence scared him more than their fire ever did.

The pull at his neck had started a few minutes ago. A gentle itch that the rolling of his shoulders wouldn't quell, radiating from the centre of the rune carved into the top of his spine. A chain etched into his skin his masters could tug on whenever he was needed. The pain was manageable, for now. Time would only make it spread until that itch became a burn, then a searing heat that lit up his skull. The only thing that would diminish the pain would be obeying the call.

He should have savored the stillness. Instead, he had let it slip through his fingers.

"Do you feel it?" Varena whispered, drawing lazy circles on his leg. An odd softness that always bristled Raekin's back, but he leaned into it regardless. Something neither of them would admit to, but something they both needed.

Raekin nodded. "Time's up." He shifted her off his lap. "We're needed."

"What does he have you hunting now?" she asked.

Raekin just shrugged. "Doesn't matter. He's hungry."

THREE

The blacksmith shop was a short walk from the Bastion. One that Sybil knew very well. The oppressive oversized gates of the Warden's Hall were still visible from the store front. They peeked over the rough shakes evenly nailed to the buildings of the Habinare district.

Smoke still billowed out of the chimney even in the late hour. The cobblestones that led up to the thick metal door were blackened with soot. Stained from the many footsteps leaving the smith.

The smell of the fire that raged in the central forge always filled Sybil with an internal warmth that felt like home. Trelusk used to be the place where she felt most at home but had since lost its luster. Now, it only reminded her of the darkness. She found the smithy was a welcome replacement. The clanging of the hammers, the buzz of the magic warping metal. Angry grunts and curses from the smiths as they crafted their plethora of blades and steel. Even the ashen smell didn't bring on any dark memories like it usually did.

"Sybil!" A voice called from within one of the many plumes of sparks bursting forth from an anvil. "Business or Maexantrius?"

"Maex this time, Groth," Sybil called back to the shop's owner.

Five years ago, the first time she had entered the shop, Groth hadn't acknowledged her. No happy, albeit grating and coarse shout to her as she stepped up to the counter. Instead, she'd been met with animosity and sneers. Back then, she'd felt meek and pathetic hovering in the door. She had been there to collect an order for the wardens, a beginner sent on a rudimentary errand. Hauling an armful of weapons from here back to the Bastion was no easy feat. The gravity of it was not lost on her.

She had tried her best to stand at attention while Groth peered down at her over his bulbous nose. She had been too nervous to meet his eyes at first. He appeared hefty, but his bulk was intimidating, the sheer size of him taking up her immediate view. He only grew larger as he crossed his arms over his broad chest.

It didn't help that she had approached the counter curling in on herself, her voice barely audible above the smashing hammers and crashing bellows. She had to repeat the order three times before he heard her. Nowadays, she suspected he heard her all along and just enjoyed watching her stumble and stutter through her words. Sybil had contemplated turning tail right then and running back to the Bastion. That was until he sent his apprentice into the back to fetch the steel.

When the dark-haired girl appeared through the smoke of the shop, Sybil was smitten. She held several of the blades aloft behind her head, floating gracefully through the air above her with mineralist magic, a common sight in a smithy. What brought Sybil's attention was the blades curled up in her other arm. Or rather, where her arm should be. Instead, a metal prosthetic had been affixed just above her elbow, the blades balanced in its clutches. The material was spotless, the craftsmanship exquisite. A true master had made the appendage, and the girl controlled it seamlessly with her magic.

The girl laid the blades along the counter, flashing her bright teeth at Sybil. A chunk of tightly wound curl had dropped out of her head band.

She used both hands to adjust it, and Sybil watched in awe at the delicate, graceful way the metal prosthesis moved to expertly shift her hair back into place.

Whether Groth had been the instigator, or not, Maexantrius had been the one to serve her whenever Sybil came to the shop since.

The memory faded, dragging her back to the present as Groth's familiar shout cut through the smoke. "Maex. Sybil is here." She heard the telltale shout of her friend emit from that same cloudy haze, a beacon for her to find through the building.

Groth had hung a sign across the chain dividing the smithy from the customers reading 'no entry'. Sybil had long since ignored it. Couldn't be bothered to care about the soot that coated her hands after she re-clipped the chain in place either.

Most of the smiths paid her no mind as she walked through the building, though some would tip their head to her, even fewer would raise two fingers in a half-hearted wave. She wasn't that uncertain girl anymore. A welcome presence among the wolves.

Maex was settled back at the far end by the forge. Her dark skin cast orange by the embers within. Sybil rarely spoke when Maex was working, her friend usually too focused to really hear her. Instead, she walked to the back wall, grabbed a hammer, and set it next to Maex's anvil.

When Maex pulled the straw-yellow metal out of the forge and set it down, there was barely a spark of surprise to see her hammer already waiting for her. Sybil leaned back against the wall, then pressed her hands to her ears as Maex struck the metal.

"Sickle for a farmer in Charprin," Maex said turning the piece over in her gloved hands, then returning the curved blade to the fires of the forge, the glow slowly returning to the blackened steel. Maex tapped the edge of the forge three times with the tip of her finger, leaving little prints in the soot. Sybil went to grab the hammer, but it lifted and floated through the air and returned to its hook on the wall. She scowled, but Maex's back was still turned, paying her friend no mind as she magicked the tool back to its home.

"Doesn't Charprin have a town smith?" Sybil asked, knowing full well they did. Also knowing that Maex had been dismissed from their shop a decade or so ago. She let the words cut as she grabbed hold of a bucket, leaving the stone walls behind to fill it with oil from the stash of kegs in the yard. When she returned, Maex was leaned against her work bench, the hot metal tempering on top of it next to her.

"They want *good* tools." Maex narrowed her eyes. "Not weak, dull, cracking tools". As soon as Sybil placed the bucket on the ground by her feet, Maex submerged the metal in it, the steam billowing around them. She drummed her fingers along the workbench. Counts of three.

She brought the curved metal over to the grinding stone and started hammering on the foot pedal. Her metal arm rested closer to the wheel than the flesh one. It could withstand the heat and sparks, and she used it as a brace against the wooden cross-board to lean against. She went to gingerly press the sickle blade to the stone when she was shoved from behind. The blade dragged hard against the fast-spinning stone, shortly followed by her arm, throwing white sparks into the air.

"What the shit, Corbin?" she shouted, whirling around at the shop's newest apprentice. The smashing and hammering started to falter, a bare minimum of quiet settling over the shop.

"Sorry, Maexantrius, didn't see you there," he said, taking a step back, his eyes wild, arms full of scrap iron. There was a heavy gouge through the centre of the sickle, a chunk sheared right out of it. But what caught his eye was the scrape that ran from the edge of Maex's elbow to the middle of her forearm. The grinding stone had carved right through the delicate filigree she had painstakingly etched into her prosthesis. He swallowed hard. "*Really* sorry. You can fix it, though, right? Just meld in some more metal?"

Maex snarled and Sybil had to hold her tongue from laughing. "Magic is a crutch, Corbin. If you build things only expecting you can fix them easily every time you make a mistake, what's going to push you to be better?" Sybil watched the young boy open and close his mouth, his eyes taking in the harsh stare of his superior. "Remember that next time you think you can just 'meld in some more metal'." Her mocking tone hit the mark, the boy flinching away from her.

"Yes, ma'am."

"Go clean out the ducting and make yourself useful for once."

Sybil watched the boy scamper off, holding her tongue until he was out of earshot. "That's an invigorating life lesson coming from somebody who sold their arm for magical ability," she tutted, crossing her arms.

"Yeah, well... I was a good blacksmith before that. Now I'm an amazing one." Maex shoved the sickle back into the forge, abandoning it for the time being. Her fingers ran the length of the forge, drumming along them as she let out slow breaths. She unlaced the leather apron from around her waist and haphazardly flung it onto the nearby workbench. "If he's so keen on just using magic to fix all his little fuck ups, he can go join the cretins in Charprin then." Maex's eye twitched slightly as she ran her fingers along the gouged metal of her arm. She would never forgive Charprin for turning her away because she had been a *leertek*.

Maex let a heavy breath through her nose before turning back to Sybil. Her face softened. "Isn't today 'Arcaneum day'?"

Sybil shook her head, the earlier events coming back to her as the distraction and ease of the smithy slid away. She could stay in this place helping Maex build for days if she wanted to. If she had been better with metal warping, she might have done it permanently. She hadn't even been able to consciously control the minerals in the dirt, let alone a full billet of metal.

"I saw the captain today."

The background noise of hammers, bellows and grinders had risen back to its loud hum once Corbin had scampered off, but Maex still glanced around the shop at the rest of the smiths. She stepped around Sybil, leading her out the back door. Though the other smiths turned a blind eye to Sybil's stained white mantle, they would always see her as a warden. She appreciated that her friend gave her a semblance of privacy when they talked about the goings on in the Bastion.

Apart from the oil kegs, the yard housed a pile of coal, stacks of billets, a few haphazardly constructed metal benches, and a locked shed. The coal was delivered once a week, the billets every other, though that was almost double the deliveries since Maex had transferred here. Last Sybil had heard, they were looking to up the order again. Not surprising, with smaller towns seeking delivery from Hazel Gryph now.

Maex slumped down on one of the benches, avoiding the chunk of sharp iron that jutted out from the corner. Projects made by every apprentice they took on. Maex's was the only one built without any magic, and the only one that wasn't a safety hazard. Which was why it was displayed proudly at the front door.

Maex tapped the fabric of her pocket on her oversized breaches three times, then reached into it, pulling out her tobacco tin and the pipe. More than once she had dropped it into the fires, unable to rescue it. She still claimed her pocket was a safer place than within grasping distance of the rest of her colleagues. 'I love them, but they're thieving snakes," she'd said.

Sybil ran her thumb along the flint clasped to her belt. Sparks shot up from her nail as she struck it, her magic grabbing hold of them. She twisted them between her fingers until they burned brightly, like a candle atop her thumb. "Is it about the balcony?" Maex asked, dipping her head to let the tobacco burn.

"I was trying to grab his bootlaces," Sybil said, shaking the fire off her hand. "That stupid rope shouldn't have even been there."

"But you didn't tell them that, right?" Sybil shot Maex a sharp look. "How bad?"

"Vinch," Maex visibly flinched.

"Yeah, that's bad. Permanent?"

"If the Haixens have anything to say about it."

"Did you talk to your father?"

Sybil rolled her eyes, slumping further into the metal bench. "I figure I'll go to Vinch in the morning, and I'll be the perfect warden. I'll do everything I need to, and after a few days, I'll talk to the captain and beg to get assigned elsewhere."

Maex laughed, her pipe swirling smoke into the air as her body heaved. "Try in a few months instead. But it's not a bad plan. Just try not to destroy anything else in that time," Maex shoved Sybil playfully, catching the hint of a smile back at her. She took another puff of her pipe, her face solidifying. "What's Killian think of all this?" The sharp tone in her voice wasn't lost on Sybil.

"He thinks I should talk to my father too," Sybil said, leaving out the added 'because he's worried I'm slowly destroying the Wyntres name'. With the purse of Maex's lips, it wasn't hard to see her mind went there anyway.

"Well, if your plan of keeping your head down doesn't work out, you might want to take a trip home to Trelusk."

Home. That town hadn't felt like home since…

Maniacal, panicked scrubbing. Desperate to get his flesh from under her nails. His blood forever inked into her hands.

Maex lifted her boot, tapping the pipe on her heel before grinding the ashes into the ground, the black soot lost to the stained stone. "Listen, I do have to finish that sickle. I really think you should send a letter to Maiten. At least tell him about the reassignment. He'd want to know. He loves you, Sybil, you can't hide this stuff just because you're worried about what he'll think."

That wasn't the reason she wouldn't write, but Maex didn't need to know that. "Maybe," she muttered. Maex stood from the bench, giving one last twist of her back, the cracks ripping through her spine. She tucked her pipe and tin back into her pocket, giving the coarse fabric three taps.

"Hey, Nostramus later?"

"I'd love to, but not tonight," Sybil answered.

Since Killian's initial offer, the harsh, bitter taste of ale had practically encompassed her mind, sinking deeply in the buds of her tongue. Shedding the mantle, ducking into the dim underground of the tavern and swallowing back her frustrations sounded pleasant. It sounded like just what she needed. Then she could drink her fill, try and forget about the reassignment, devolve herself to the point where she could no longer feel her own skin. Maybe start performing party tricks for the *leerteks* at the tavern that idolized her spectrum of skills, make a few extra lok.

But then she would wake up in the morning, her head pounding, her mouth sticky and putrid. She'd roll over and haphazardly lace up the front of her mantle, the scratchy fabric rubbing her dry skin raw. She'd show up for the first day haggard and barely functioning, go through the motions. Try to keep herself upright as the previous night pulsed through her temples and threatened to pour out her stomach.

The idolization of those nights was always worth so much more than the night itself. It was easy to forget about the 'after' when all you could think of was the beginning. That first warm sip sliding down your throat, fogging your mind to everything that had wrapped its shadowed claws around it. Yet every time, without fail, she would wake up not only feeling terrible physically, but that nagging voice would be whispering in her ear for the rest of the day.

What are you doing? Why are you wasting your chance? Is this what he would want for you?

For once in her life, Sybil wanted to face a horrible day with her mind intact. Show up early, ready in uniform. She would be the best Warden that they had seen in years. No matter what, she would give them no reason to dismiss her. Let her show the city of Hazel Gryph that she could be better. She just had to try.

S ybil's shoulders dropped with relief when she saw that Killian's boots weren't thrown haphazardly at the front door of their row house. Even the seemingly constant smell of fresh bread had faded from their small home. An odd hobby for someone of Killian's status, but one she usually revelled in. Just not today. Today, she wanted to wash the day off and be done with it. She didn't have the energy to go through a long talk with half-hearted apologies right now. There was enough clogging her thoughts without adding that emotional stress.

The upstairs bath was adjacent to the bedroom. The clawed tub filling most of the room, leaving just enough for the vanity. The taps creaked and groaned when she turned them, the threads long overdue for a thorough cleaning. The water that poured out of them was blessedly hot. Not needing the expensive runes carved into the faucet like some of the other small houses. The Bauers had gifted them access to the city's steam power, running tightly along their water line. A gift she had worried about accepting but was thankful for years later.

Stripping out of her mantle and the rest of her uniform was always an exhausting process. Undo the laces on her boots, loosen them from the bottom of her knee to the top of her ankle, then kick them off back through the door of her room. Six buttons on the mantle itself, two metal buckles snapping the leather straps around her thighs, one golden pin clasping a third strap across her collarbones. Then she'd slip the long white sleeves off her arms and toss it onto the cracking, stained salmon tile. Three buttons on her tanned vest, and it joined the mantle. The linen shirt under it all had been dipped in a flame-retardant ichor, but that only seemed to make the itchy fabric more uncomfortable against her bare skin. Two buttons on the trousers, the black leather pooling on the tile before she shoved them back against the wall with the ball of her bare foot.

The ice knives from the thief in the market had taken slices out of her mantle, but she'd neglected to tell the captain that she had felt their bite through her skin as well. Two unequal, mottled lines ran up the back of her forearm, the cracking scabs fighting to seal over. A report to the Bastion sarcomancer to seal them up would have meant a fuller investigation with the potential for a 'reprieve from duty'. Neither of which Sybil could handle right now. Not with the precarious way the sword of finality was dangling over her future.

Like every other school of magic, sarcomancy was in her veins. She should be able to press her hand to the wounds, sealing them back up like any other healer. The courage to try had only swelled up once, in Trelusk, nine years ago. A small cut up her thigh from training. When her hands warmed against her skin she was sure the wound would heal. Instead, the flesh had parted, ripping open like torn fabric. Her screaming had brought her father to her, his face pale in panic.

Maiten had stitched the skin back together, not wanting to take her to the town sarcomancer and risk questions about her magic. His hands shook as he did, the needle and thread wavering and fluctuating in their depth and spacing. The left-over scar was large, grotesque and uneven, a constant reminder of what she couldn't—and shouldn't—do.

Even now her hands trembled uncontrollably as she hovered them over the cuts running along her skin. That memory and the flood of pain seared into her skull. Blood was a frighteningly close second to the things she struggled to overcome as she moved through the waking world.

Every Warden was given free runes by the city enchanter. All of them in place for a particular reason, especially those inked to keep the Wardens safe while they protected the city. And there, on Sybil's arm, clear as day, the wound from the frostweaver had cut through the ink of not one, but two runes. The black ink had fizzled and spread through her arm like muddy water, the once solid lines dissipated and barely recognizable. The telltale sign of a failed enchantment.

Shit.

They'd carved their way through a few vanity inks she had opted to get, small designs that looped around her wrist and up her arm. Not runic at all in nature, but pictures and drawings she loved or found meaning in. Those could be fixed with some lok and free time, but the others would require a visit to the wardens enchanter, Preskilla. And she was very vocal about her distaste for re-dos.

There was one more option, though. If she could figure out what they were, maybe Ethissa could fix them. A talented artist and a master enchanter, the woman that had raised her when she was no longer able to stay in Trelusk with the lingering panic attacks. Ethissa would tut her tongue at her but still take her in and imbed the inks back into her arm. After all, she was the one that had done the vanity pieces, what was one more favor? She just had to tell her what they were.

She narrowed her eyes, bringing the smudged marks closer to her face, trying and failing to discern their meaning. Two lines and a curved hook. Six dots and a diagonal line. Footsteps and... *shit.* She cursed to herself, running her hands along the damaged runes. Loud footsteps she could deal with in Vinch, but the other was escaping her. Captain Hertrin and Preskilla had wanted her to get so many of them, she was struggling to keep track after all these years. She should have been paying more attention when she got them. *Idiot.*

Whatever the rune was for, she wasn't going to figure it out standing naked in the bathroom squinting at it in the dim candlelight. She'd either figure it out later, or she'd have to wait until she crawled out of the Vinch district and swallow her pride to talk to Preskilla. Either way, she'd survive.

Her personal ritual came next. Every night before washing the day off, she would bring her fingertips to her hip. There, nestled against her hip bone and drifting down the crease of her thigh, was the first rune to ever be carved in her flesh. Scabbed on, crooked and decrepit. The dark ink had seemingly been burned into her skin. Appearing on her like a bad dream, no memory of its creation. Sometime between the hollow pit that devoured Quinn, and the shaken, gasping breaths she was finally able to take when the wardens left her house.

A wobbling line, two lines branching off from its centre and reaching upwards like a three pronged 'Y'. Curled, mirrored lines to either side, and one cutting the piece in half horizontally. An upside down, five-pointed star at its crest, seemingly random lines that radiated outwards of the star and bled through her flesh. Compared to the warden tattoos, it was junky and crooked, almost done in a hurry instead of the careful precision of a master of their craft.

A gift from the Void Born.

The Void Born were the creatures that had torn open the floor of her room, ripped and shredded her best friend, dragging him through the black ichor and swallowing him whole. They left her sitting in his blood, his final breath echoing through her head. Imprinting her with their mark, and the chaotic magic that she now struggled to control. Still red and raw from being carved into her skin. A deal struck and sealed before she had a chance to understand what, exactly, she had levied up for collateral. Or whom.

She kissed her fingers, then pressed them to the cursed rune, the pressure radiating pain into the bone of her hip. A pain that made her feel alive, feel grounded. With her eyes closed and her lips pursed, she let out a long breath, the air circling around her head, cooling itself.

"Thank you, Quinn, for everything," she whispered. The words were there, just as they had been every night, but the meaning fluctuated so often. They were impossible to get out at first, her guilt weighing them down, and holding them tightly to her chest. Then they became easy. Fluid and purposeful, every uttered word from her heart. Now, they were forced out again. Couldn't be sure she meant them anymore. Would Quinn even be happy to see her faltering like this, failing at every turn? Would he think his death was worth the shiny gold leaf situated in the crumbled pile of white leather?

She swallowed the lump in her throat, chasing the nagging, pained feelings and threading them back into her mind.

Children and teenagers alike ran around the country of Plaitius casting spells from their fingertips as easily as blowing their nose. Fire bursting from the thermacists, dirt erupting from the earth by the geomancers. The fluidicists crafting intricate water works, botanomancers growing plentiful crops and dangerous carnivorous plants. Sybil struggled to bring the magic she wanted without the others flaring in defiance. The discipline and time that comes with a birthed magic escaping her.

She was a vollmagus, a moniker few bothered to call her. Instead, opting for the slur of 'chaos mage' to really bristle her back. But the sentiment was fitting, no matter how badly she wished it weren't.

But tomorrow would be different; had to be different. Sybil had spent enough time screwing around, trying and failing to help every Hazel Gryph resident that she happened upon. No more. She would be a model Warden in the district of Vinch tomorrow, no matter what it took.

She had to.

FOUR

Ktharheim's narrow streets were a gauntlet for Raekin and Varena. Varena moved through them like prey. She kept the hood of her cloak tied tight to shroud her face, her head kept down. It stayed locked on the uneven dirt covered path in front of her feet the duration of their walk. It wasn't a secret that she wanted to go unnoticed, but Raekin made that impossible.

Raekin moved through the streets like a challenge. He never wore his cloak. Wouldn't conceal himself from the Void or the Etched. He walked with purpose, his head held high. Not high enough to welcome the ire of a prideful Void Born, but enough that they could see.

Though most of his body was a messy patchwork of scars, burns, tattoos, and runes, his face had been left mostly untouched. Sharp black lines that ran across the bridge of his nose, a rune beneath his left eye, and crooked, malicious designs up the right side of his temple. It took the right light to see most of his scars, and there was little of that to go around underneath the mountains. The visible ones were worn like medals. It was obvious who he was, even from afar.

He heard the whispers, caught the murmurs of spit-laced insults not meant for his ears. Only spat when his back was turned, knives pointed at it wherever he went. But they would cower when he turned their way, scampering back to their shadows. They'd seen the massacres he could bring. Saw the death that sometimes followed in his wake. No one dared raise their voice loud enough to garner his anger in their direction.

But his bravado was all just a show.

They had all been through the same torture, some worse than others. He'd watched friends and enemies alike have their skin torn and branded. He knew who the real enemy was. All his sadism and malevolence was for the other Etched. For now, he would accept their hateful stares, the resentful glances as he traversed the city. This was his burden to carry.

At the very back of the city was the Uldspire. Named after some long dead fool named 'Uld' who'd heard the word in passing and claimed it. Thought it was fitting without bothering to ask what it had meant. Inaptly named as the building was squat and stretched out immensely in either direction. Carved into the rocks by geomancers, its foundation predating even the oldest Etched memories.

"I *am* sorry," Varena whispered from below the hood of her cloak, her last opportunity for her voice to go unnoticed in the expanse of Ktharheim. As they passed under the oppressive arched entrance of the Uldspire, the raw hum of the city snuffed out, leaving only their hurried footsteps along the halls. Even after all these years the walls tightened and shifted as Raekin walked through them. As though they could remember the blood he had spilled.

"You aren't sorry. Not yet," Raekin snapped back at her, his words echoing loudly against the narrow stone passages. His chest still burned, and he had to stop himself from touching it. He'd looped his pack across it, snapped the armor straps as close together as possible. That didn't do much to cover the burn. Even in the dim torchlight, that damage was apparent. The less attention he could draw to it, the better.

If she had been any other sort of sarcomancer she would be able to undo the damage she caused. Never able to grasp what so many sarcomancers had mastered, she was only able to eviscerate. A dangerous weapon for the Void. A useless fucking partner as far as Raekin was concerned.

"Just keep your mouth shut and let me talk," he snarled again. There were days he wanted to step back and throw her at Naz'Tak. But even Raekin had his limits.

Not of cruelty, but what he could live with after.

Raekin swore he could hear the clicking of Naz'Tak's talons before they even reached their master. When the scaled beast came into view, he felt no surprise to see sharp, ebony claws tapping their incessant beat on the polished stone table. The other hand held a thick book, sharp lines dug into the spine from the tight grip.

Naz'Tak didn't lift his head when they entered, only ceased the movement in his long, gnarled fingers.

"Raekinblod. Sarcovarena. I called well before your arrival," he said, his tone slick and guttural. Every word he said was slow and methodical. Paced out to draw the listener in, make note of every syllable that dripped from his fanged mouth. "But I suppose you have an excellent excuse?"

"No, sir." Raekin said. He'd played this game before, knew the rules were always twisted out of his favor. No answer would be good enough. Every word from him would be combed through, inspected and turned back at him. *Take the punishment and move on.* It was easier than trying to fight, and he had become an expert at picking his battles.

Naz'Tak let out a heavy sigh. He folded over the page of his book, closing it with a snap and gently placing it on the obsidian tabletop. Treated with such delicate care as one would treat a child.

The torch sconces affixed to the wall behind the beast lit up his iridescent, partially scaled skin as he turned. Light filtered through the webbed fins that ran from his temples to the nape of his neck, illuminating the veins that ran through them.

When he finally looked up, his eyes darted to Raekin's chest, his lip curling in disgust. They slid their way along his torso, slow lines from chest to stomach to the hem of his pants. Even in the dim light, Raekin could see the way his pupils shrank to narrow slits. The vibrant orange flaring around the sharp line of black.

"Does this lack of excuse also include a reason for the mess you have made of your skin?" Naz'Tak stood, sharp eyes darting to Varena. The fins that ran up the length of his upper arm turned from deep purple to vibrant hues of turquoise and sea blue as the light twisted behind him.

When he took over the Void, he had requested a place within the Uldspire for conversation to be had amongst more exalted members. An odd request, but the room was built regardless, housing the obsidian table and the respective chairs that encircled it. It had, however, been a last-minute addition and they hadn't quite bothered to worry about the size of the table.

As Naz'Tak took a few steps forward, his bulk shoved against the chairs, their stone scraping and shrieking against the rock. Varena made a quiet noise from behind Raekin's back. She was a few fingers shorter than Raekin, but next to Naz'Tak, she was miniscule. It was a common sight, their master's shadow bearing down on them, encompassing them and swallowing the light. Raekin had adjusted to it. No longer dreading that darkness. Varena had not, and even now he could feel her heart racing in her chest.

"An accident, sir." Raekin shifted as slowly as he could to shield Varena further with his back. He may have hated her, but he was only a monster when he chose to be. Now, the bigger monster was before them.

Naz'Naz'Tak ran a hand along Raekin's jaw, his sharp claws lingering on his chin. "I don't recall telling you to use your 'artistry' in your rutting." His lip curled up in a half mockery of a grin, one opalescent fang glowing in the faint light. Raekin had to fight not to swallow against the grip as Naz'Tak slid his hand lower, resting it against his collar. He left his eyes level, unmoving against the slits reading his face. "I do, however, recall how I feel about being lied to." His master's gaze once more snapped to the cowering sarcomancer.

Raekin tilted his head, slow and deliberate. He already regretted the tactic before his mouth opened. But it was something to pull the attention back. Away from *her.* "If you wanted me silent, you would have done it already." Naz'Tak stilled. Just for a second. Just long enough for Raekin to feel the shift in the room. The challenge was there, sharp and glinting between them. The air felt thick. Stagnant. The moment before a storm. Raekin knew better than to step back, knew better than to show even the barest flinch. But still, his fingers curled involuntarily, a pathetic imitation of claws. He had no weapons here.

Don't move. Don't speak. Don't breathe.

When Naz'Tak's eyes flared to life, Raekin braced, inhaling deeply. The clawed hand wrapped tightly around his throat. Naz'Tak let out a low grating rasp as he shoved Raekin against the wall, his head slamming into the rock. For a moment the room swam in darkness, twisting back to itself in a foggy haze. Sharp points punctured through the flesh of his neck. The pain was barely felt. The world was blocked out around him. Only the choking pain of his spine grinding against his throat and the sharp, orange eyes burning through him.

Where is Varena?

Raekin was disgustedly aware of her silence. Though his vision was blackening, the room fading to narrow points, he could see her. Or rather, sense her. Curled into herself, averting her eyes as he took *her* punishment.

He hated her silence more than her cowardice. Because he knew it too well, knew it had been him on more than a handful of occasions.

Raekin reached for his magic instinctively. He felt it wrap around the thick, black blood that flowed through his master's veins. Before he could get a grasp, the runes that they had bored into his skin flared to life. Like acid flowing through his body, the poison carved into his skin radiated through his flesh, his muscle. A dark emptiness filled his soul, a part of him being cut away with sharp shears. His power became a numb limb hanging limply from his body. There, but disconnected, the pain obliterating it. With every flail, the rune at his neck seared into his spine, agony lancing up his back and into his skull.

Don't panic. Don't panic. Don't panic.

He gasped against his master's hold, his heartbeat so loud in his ears. His lungs screaming for just one ounce of air. He would breathe in the acrid, toxic gases that seeped from the fissures at this rate, his chest just needed to fill. Raekin clawed at the hands around his throat, his nails useless against the leather armor that wrapped up around Naz'Tak's wrists. Even more useless against the thick, scaled skin.

When Naz'Tak finally let go, Raekin slumped against the wall. With his throat released, his lungs struggled to fill. Unable to inflate as he gasped for breath. The dread still hovered around him like a thick smoke, but he didn't let his eyes drop from Naz'Tak's. He could feel the slow trickle of blood down his neck, pooling into his collarbones. It would have taken barely a second to cease the bleeding. He didn't dare, only using what little energy he had left to straighten himself against the stones.

"Do you understand what an insult it is to me that my property returns to me damaged?" Naz'Tak's nostrils flared, eyes casting quickly to the still cowering Varena. She'd stepped away, her back pressed to the far wall, her cloak brought back up tighter to her face. Raekin felt his face grow hot as he followed Naz'Tak's gaze. The rage only flickered briefly, the light reflecting off her wide eyes and the wet streaks that lined her face.

"It won't happen again, sir," Raekin said, his voice a creaking whisper.

Naz'Tak snapped his attention back. Raekin knew the strike was coming, but bracing for it only allowed him to stay upright. The back of Naz'Tak's hand at least, his claws not raking skin from his cheek. "If I ever see any more marks mar this flesh that I haven't put there myself, I will personally rend your skin from your bones, Raekinblod." Raekin only nodded, not letting his stare fluctuate anywhere but his master.

Naz'Tak stepped back, crossing his arms over his broad chest. "Leave us," he said, his head cocking towards Varena. Raekin saw the slight nod from under her cloak, the tiniest bow as she turned to the archway. Before she could fully leave, Naz'Tak snatched back her hood, lacing his fingers in her hair and dragging her backwards. She cried out, her hands leaping to her head, her magic no doubt already struck down and lost to her. Raekin winced, knowing stepping in would only make it worse for her.

"This isn't the first time I have had to undo the damage you have caused, Sarcovarena," he hissed, wrenching her head to his so he could speak in her ear. "If this happens again, I will tear off your flesh and use it to patch up his." He jerked the long claw of his thumb towards Raekin. The words loomed in the room as he held her tight for a moment. Then, he shoved her, a grin twisted up his lips as she stumbled out with a muffled sob.

"Pathetic," Naz'Tak muttered, turning his attention back to Raekin and leaning his bulk against the stone. "If she had not been such a fine specimen, I would have flung her into the fissures the day I was cursed with her." He pressed his thin, cracked lips into a line. "You better make keeping her worth it soon, Raekinblod."

Worth it. As though she was nothing more than a womb. Raekin's back bristled. There was a long list of horrible things the Void had called their pets. Objects weren't out of the range, especially since the Void saw them as nothing more than tools. That didn't stop the heat that burned through his chest.

Naz'Tak let out a heavy sigh as though the act had taken a toll on him. "'The Hag' needs another tome." Raekin clenched his fists. The Hag. As if she needed a title when every whisper in Ktharheim already carried her weight. Naz'Tak spoke of her like she was just another tool in his arsenal. Though she was human, her moniker had remained. Rumors and myths surrounded her, passed down through the whispers that traversed the dark corners of Ktharheim. 'The Hag' was all anyone dared call her, Raekin included.

To the Void Born, names had power. Their utterance could bring on curses to those that spoke them and those that bore them. They contracted their own names, hiding them from all but those they trusted the most. The Etched didn't deserve the respect of shortened, altered names. Another show of power to remind them just how little they were worth.

"She says the tome is in Hazel Gryph, in that Arcaneum again, of course. You'll be going out immediately with Hirnstitch and collecting it."

The words barely registered in Raekin's head, his thoughts still on Varena. Her cowardice. A drip slid off one of the stalactites above him, landing on his shoulder and slithering down his arm. The water had an icy chill to it, a stark contrast to the humid oppressive air between them. He hadn't realized his gaze had slipped, lingering a half second too long on the wall beyond. It was yanked back to his master, the wicked grin slashing a thin, curving line up his scale flecked face.

"You're thinking too much, Raekinblod," Naz'Tak said, his voice like crushed embers. "That's a habit I should break."

Raekin kept his face neutral, though his fingers twitched at his thighs. "Are our thoughts a threat now?" The words shot from his mouth before he had a chance to grasp them back, lying heavily between the two. He curled his fingers, tightening them in his palm to halt the trembling as time stretched, the oppressive quiet a dull ache on his shoulders.

"If I truly wanted to silence you, I would have cut out your tongue. Just like you said." Naz'Tak cut through the tension, his claws flexed idly, a slow curl of blackened bone. "But your voice is only worth removing if it carries weight. You'd do well to remember that."

The statement settled between them. Raekin kept his expression unreadable, but the truth was clear. They didn't silence opposition; they let it wither under their gaze, suffocated by its own helplessness.

Naz'Tak flourished his hand, like he could wave off the comment. Raekin's outburst temporarily dismissed, though undeniably held tight in the back of his master's mind. As were most things he planned on using for his benefit. "You have one week. Bring me whatever else you can fit in your pack, as usual."

"Of course," Raekin said.

The Void Born had always ruled through blood. Every leader before Naz'Tak had clung to power for as long as their blade kept others at bay. But Naz'Tak was different.

He was well read, methodical and calculated. An oddity among them. Though the Void couldn't reach the surface, he had gotten his hands on books early, absorbing one after another through his years. This gave him a wicked advantage to the competition around him. Naz'Tak had never needed the brute force of his predecessors to rule. He had watched and waited as others bled themselves dry. When the time came, he took what he wanted.

Raekin wasn't sure when exactly Naz'Tak had first laid his eyes on him, but it sealed whatever plan he twisted into place as soon as word got around about his power. Raekin had been purchased by Hon'Gar before he even left the Alpstraum. His skin still raw and red, wounds still actively bleeding. The rune at his neck made movement almost impossible for months after that. But his new owner cared little for the pain, only bristling with excitement over having won the great prize of a geomancer *and* a bloodweaver. A tool and a weapon.

Weeks went by of nothing but anguish under his new master. The likes of which were only slightly overshadowed by what had happened to him in the Alpstraum. Until, of course, Hon'Gar was slaughtered. Raekin had seen the remnants of that first kill. Hon'Gar's throat still hung in Naz'Tak's quarters, rotted and dried. A trophy of patience.

When Naz'Tak had tangled his fingers in Raekin's hair, forcing his head back to look at it, something twisted through his gut. Both a show of benevolence and a reminder of what his cruelty could achieve. When Naz'Tak held him there, his eyes glued to the barbarity, his master had run his cracked lips along Raekin's neck. Whispering promises of freedom and sanctity in his ears.

Naz'Tak won the ownership of not one, but four Etched with Hon'Gar's death. The geomancer and botanomancer were quickly dispatched to work in the mines and fields respectively. Varena and Raekin, however, were immediately brought under his wing. A sarcomancer and a bloodweaver. He had his army.

The murder and subsequent overthrowing of the then leader, Yak'tinar, was easy once he had them. He'd been the third longest running ruler that the Ktharheim had seen and had protected himself well. Dozens and dozens of Etched at his control, able to be thrown like fleshy shields at whomever came his way. But against Varena and Raekin, it was a massacre. The halls of the Uldspire had been red for weeks afterwards as the blood seeped into the stone.

Once Naz'Tak had his throne, he gained access to 'The Hag'. Capable of unlocking powerful, ancient runes for the Void, and fluent in the world above ground, she was a prized possession. The Void had no magic of their own, but every one of them was gifted with incredible enchanting power. Able to easily carve runes into anything they got their hands on, and they had a particular affinity for flesh. With her and his mercenaries, he was able to gather books from every corner of Crae Vost. He utilized them to build up the city of Ktharheim until it thrived. But he wanted more. He wanted the surface; he wanted freedom. And he was going to destroy anything that got in his way.

"Keep Sarcovarena in mind when you watch the days tick by. One week, Raekinblod. Remember what happens when she isn't kept useful." A quiet, but noticed threat.

"I'll be back sooner than that," Raekin said.

Naz'Tak stepped forward, taking Raekin's jaw in his hand once more. "I know. And I know this wasn't your fault," he said, brushing the raw skin on Raekin's chest. A slow caress, almost loving. He rested his head against Raekin's, his bright eyes closing as he let out a slow breath between his teeth. Raekin felt his stomach twist. He forced his body to remain still, to stay upright. The touch was calculated. Everything Naz'Tak did was. Every caress a cruelty. Every breath a reminder of what he could take, just to watch him flinch. The swinging pendulum of Naz'Tak's emotions was impossible to predict. Doing nothing was safer than ever expecting anything of him. "I do not enjoy hurting you, pet."

"I know, Nazenitak," Raekin replied, trying to keep his voice level. He watched his master bristle under the name, his breath coming out faster. Though he couldn't grasp hold of the dark blood, he could feel it beating in the monster's enlarged heart. The thrumming pulse racing under his scaled hide.

"Raekinblod," Naz'Tak seethed through his teeth, pulling his head away. "Under other circumstances things would be different between us." He ran a claw along the seared flesh, his brows twitching as they moved along his chest. "A travesty that that curse between your legs exists."

Raekin swallowed, hoping it wasn't noticeable. Balancing along the edge of conjuring his master's rage, his lust or his admiration was like walking along the sharp edge of the fissures with his eyes covered. One wrong move, one wrong word, and he would teeter over. Whether it was towards the safety of solid ground, or tumbling into the depths was impossible to know. Though no matter which way he fell, the consequence of the tumble would likely end in the dangerous walk starting once more.

Naz'Tak straightened, rolled his shoulders and cleared his throat. More than once he had voiced his disgust with his attraction to Raekin, slighting it as a disgrace and an abomination. Raekin was lucky this time he didn't take it out of his flesh in retaliation.

"'The Hag' says this book brings us one step closer to the key to what finally unshackles our chains, Raekinblod." Naz'Tak's eyes once more fell between Raekin's legs. "Having you and that bitch produce me a brood would be a great treat, but I would be willing to forgo that if you aren't successful." His lips twisted again. "I can find other uses for you instead." The implication left intentionally vague, as all of Naz'Tak's carefully worded threats.

Raekin held his stance. "You have my word," he murmured. Someday, he would make sure it held the weight that Naz'Tak feared.

FIVE

First day, and already Sybil was ready to conjure ice and shove it through her temple. She'd started at the crack of dawn, the chilled air of the Dimming season making her wrap her mantle even tighter around herself. At least in other districts you were busy enough that the year-end cold was barely noticeable. Not here.

Most of the morning was spent walking from one end of Hantro Street to the next, noting how many different coloured buildings she saw on the trek. It was three. Beige, grey, and white. Oh—and one red building, an incredibly exciting palette change.

It wasn't until she felt a sharp pain and noticed the blood soaking through the sleeve of her mantle that it registered just how bored she was. Absently picking at the slices on her arm from the fight on Strastag. With a quick lick of her finger, she scrubbed the blood away, turning her attention back to the placid, monotonous street.

As the sun started to crest over the tops of the idyllic, manicured buildings, it had cast the district in an ethereal, pinkish glow. The beauty was only highlighted by the silent, cozy streets. A stark contrast to the Kanal district. Like its name suggested, the district ran along the canal. Just across the waters from the Bastion you could see the tops of some of the more dilapidated buildings. When the sun hit the city just right, they even gave off a foggy, green glow, the abundant moss that seemed to blanket every surface reflecting the bright light.

That view from a distance was the best the district had to offer. Due to the westerly winds, the smell of whatever was dumped in the canal wafted over the district. A smell that only those in desperation would live with daily. Emaciated people, children without shoes, families left out in the cold. It was hard not to feel for those people, wishing she could do more.

"How many old ladies have you arrested so far?" Killian said, stepping into line with Sybil. She was miserable enough, she didn't need him wagging his tongue at her too, regardless if he thought it took the edge off. He'd worn his mantle even though he wasn't working. Except that he had left the straps on his thighs and collar loose. It shouldn't have bothered her as much as it did, but with every pendulum-like swinging of the dark leather her jaw tensed.

"Oh ha, ha," she groaned, lacing her hands behind her back, hiding the marks on her arm.

"You're just jealous of my wit." He grinned.

Sybil shoved him, watching him stumble over his own feet on the stones, narrowly missing a low hanging sign for the nearby flower shop. "Don't you have something better to do today than bother me?"

"I don't, actually."

Sybil rolled her eyes, turning away from him. "I would appreciate if you let me work." She turned her back on him, starting her umpteenth patrol of the street, but paused. Her shoulders slumped as she saw the quick motion of several people quickly averting their gaze. She should be used to it by now, but it still stung.

The steady slew of negativity started to flow through her again. A wicked voice taunting her, telling her all the things she tried to keep snuffed away elsewhere. Regrets tinged with fears. Anxieties and self-doubts masquerading as truths.

Not today. Please, not today she thought, pinching the bridge of her nose.

When she opened her eyes, Killian's sardonic grin faded, leaving only softness. "I'm sorry. I know it's hard, I just... want to help."

She flapped her hand, waving him off. "It's fine, I'll be fine. Can you please just—" she started, but a warmth on her wrist stopped her.

The runed stone of her bracelet started to heat, drawing her attention, and she released a heavy breath of relief. She pressed her fingers to the stone and closed her eyes. The message played through her mind like an internal whisper.

Investigation request. East Groten Street. Second floor of Juniper Landing. Door 2B. Mr. Donavin Maisonneuve.

Finally.

Killian knew the look, the sudden silent freezing of a Warden. Her eyes had likely fluttered under her lids, the ghostly whites peering out through the gap. The Warden's report system was very difficult to get used to. The first few times that she pressed it, she felt as though somebody was massaging her brain with icy cold hands, their digits covered in thorns.

When she turned her direction due east and started off towards another street, Killian didn't say a word, just followed silently behind. Sybil was aware that whatever disturbance she was headed towards would most likely be an unruly pet or a magic user practicing too loudly. Anything was better than walking back and forth for hours.

Juniper landing was a short, stout building compared to its neighbours. Only two floors to its body, the roof cased in shadow from the structures that towered over it. Grey door, grey trim, grey accents. Like someone had just poured overcast skies in their plans. The front windows were fogged and battered age eating away at the panes. The stairway leading to the front door was swept, though the stonework was cracked and faded.

Sybil pushed open the door, then followed the stairwell to the upper floor. The wood panelling on the floor had indents and scuff marks from vigorous travel. The dark forest green paint felt overwhelming and daunting no matter how chipped and scuffed it was.

The second floor landing was cleaner, less foot traffic to sully the flooring. More dust touched the molding, fingerprints pressed into sporadic spots, lines of it cleared away from low hanging sleeves. Only two doors on this level. There was a poorly made, wooden '2' hanging from a single nail next to one of the doors. The 'B' was leaning up against the wall, the upper swoop snapped in two.

Killian leaned against the wall, out of sight, as Sybil raised her knuckles to knock on the wood. Barely a blink passed before the wood was torn away from Sybil's raised fist, a gust of wind rushing out with it. Rose petal scent and strong incense followed, overwhelming her. She had to scrunch her nose to keep from sneezing.

"Warden?" Sybil heard, the man stepping through the haze of smoke that billowed out his door. A long black cloak flared out through the haze, settling neatly around his skinny, knobbly, and rather bare legs. A spindly beard hung down from his chin, wrapped around itself and tied tightly with beige cord. His brown eyes were wild as they drifted from the base of Sybil's mantle, flying across her torso and ending at her hazel stare. An empty patch of skin sat at the top of his head, the hair circling it in a ring, though it was thin and frazzled. Had it not been for the static-filled air that made it curl and flex around his face, it would have hung down to his shoulders.

"Donavin Maisonneuve?" Sybil asked, pressing her hands to her diaphragm in salute. Out of the corner of her eye she saw Killian slap his hand to his mouth, stifling whatever laughter was seconds away from escaping.

"Thank goodness you are here. It is a travesty what is happening downstairs. You need to get down there quickly and arrest that man!" He lifted his hands to the sky, his voice floating in and out of octave as he bellowed.

"What can I help you with, sir?" Sybil didn't drop her salute, but leaned forward, trying to catch a glimpse of the man's residence through the smoke that seemed to permeate his existence.

"My neighbour. Downstairs and across the hall. You passed him on the way up the stairs. Something wicked is happening behind those closed doors."

"What makes you say that?"

"I can *sense* it." He chewed his lip, diverting his gaze to the wood flooring. He hesitated, his eyes darting between each of hers, thinking as he did. Finally, "There's a smell."

"A smell?"

"A smell."

"I didn't smell anything, Mr. Maisonneuve."

He shifted his lips from one side of his face to the other, his eyes narrowed at her. "You have to bring it to you."

It took her a second to understand exactly what he was saying. When she did, she dropped her salute in a huff and laced her arms across her chest. "You pulled the smell out of his residence with air magic."

Red flushed his cheeks. "I know, I know. It's illegal, immoral and, frankly, perverse. I understand that I can face repercussions for it. Believe me." He strung out the e's elongating the word as his hands danced circles around the air. "Please, you have to know that I wouldn't ordinarily do that, I just knew something wasn't right. Go down there, talk to him yourself, you'll smell it too. Blood and rot, it's all over his home."

Sybil bit her lip. The warden in her would arrest the man for openly admitting to breaking the law with invasive magic. But the rational side of her felt a sense of pity for him. He'd come to her and poured his heart out, knowing he would be prosecuted for openly sharing this information.

"You can't seriously be thinking of listening to this gas mage," Killian groaned, stepping away from his spot on the wall. Donavin straightened, his eyes wide, his face burning red.

"Aerokineticist, sir," Donavin said, crossing his arms over his chest. "And who are you? I should have you reported for that slur."

"Oh, really? The gas mage that openly admitted to breaking the law is going to put in a complaint?" Killian laughed. "Sybil, leave this loser to his pathetic conspiracies. This is a waste of your time."

Sybil's back bristled. How many times had she had 'chaos mage' spat in her direction? With just as much poison as was laced in Killian's snap of 'gas mage'? She didn't have anybody to stand up for her when the slurs were hurled her way. Things might have been easier if she had.

Her fingers curled into a tight fist as she swallowed back the memory of spiteful voices. "Downstairs on the right, correct?"

The smallest grin flickered across Mr. Maisonneuve's lips. "That's correct, ma'am."

"Sybil," she corrected. "I'll take a look at your neighbour." She punctuated it with another salute.

"Thank you," he hesitated, the wrinkles crinkling along his eyes, "Sybil."

"You're being ridiculous, you know that, right?" Killian asked as they descended the stairs. "The man is clearly losing his mind. Indulging his delusions can't be healthy."

"We're sworn protectors of the populace, Killian. Denying him is denying our duty." The oath's words slid off her tongue easily. It made a fresh surge of nausea tickle her throat at how pathetic it sounded, but it felt good to needle Killian even in a small way.

"And if Hertrin hears about this?"

She cast a look over her shoulder. "Why would he?"

She had promised to be the perfect warden, following every rule laid before her, no deviations. Barely six hours had passed and she was already bending the rules, and only to spite Killian's patronizing words. She should have dropped it, should have given the man a fine for intrusive magic at the very least. Not be about to question someone without a modicum of evidence except a 'weird smell'.

"Hello?" The man that answered was a half a head taller than her. His blond hair crisscrossed around his head haphazardly as though he had just woken up. Beneath the vibrant blue of his eyes hung large exhaustion bruises that dragged his eyelids down into the heavy bags. His cheeks were gaunt, his lips a faded pink, burgeoning on grey. They half twisted up in greeting, though it seemed strained, a fight to control the muscles.

"Hello. I'm Warden Wyntres. There has been report of a strange smell from your residence, I've been asked to investigate."

Without a hint of direction, his head drifted upwards, landing on the door to Donavin's residence. A sneer flickered across his face, tearing the smile away, but only for a moment. "Mr. Maisonneuve has reported me at least three times now," that false smile stretching his cheeks. "He doesn't like my cooking. I've travelled here from Losweau, our dishes contain different spices."

Sybil dropped her shoulders, dread spreading across her skin. Of course it was this simple. The thick Losweauian accent cementing it. It wouldn't be surprising in the least if it followed with a complaint to the captain about being harassed. Not hard to figure out what young, gold leaf Warden had been the instigator. *Idiot.*

She'd have to beg for her job. Shit, she'd probably have to use her father's name. There was a burning sensation on her hip at the rune. Imagined, but it felt so real she had to stop herself from rubbing the spot. If she lost this, she lost everything. His death would mean nothing, all her effort would be pointless.

"We understand, Mr...?" Killian asked, placing his hand on Sybil's lower back, easing the tension that had torqued through like a twisted thread. Regardless of the arrogance, he was able to satiate her so quickly. The person she could lean on, look for when things were falling apart. And right now, she hated it.

"Tendos," the man replied, his hand drifting to the edge of the door as he readied to close it. "If you'll excuse me."

"Of course, sir, we'll be on our way." Killian started to direct Sybil around, turning her away from the door.

A creeping feeling started at the base of her neck, working its way up into her skull. It spread across her scalp, making her hair feel light and tingly. An itch started to burn through her head, under her skin and deep between her ears. She rolled her shoulder in an effort to shake the feeling away, but it did little to satiate the unsettling twinge.

Then, so softly she wasn't entirely sure she heard it, "Help. Please, help."

It sounded as though it was spoken through a wet towel. Her head tilted to the side. It wasn't until it sounded again that she realized she wasn't actually *hearing* anything. She stopped herself, ignoring Killian's hand pushing her onward, focusing only on the voice that didn't seem real.

"Killian," she whispered as she turned away from the door. "Do you hear that?" He didn't reply, only raised an eyebrow at her. That was enough of an answer.

Sybil's eyes bulged, snapping to her arm. Beneath that fabric, two runes had dissipated into her skin. One for softened footsteps and the other...

Intrusive voices.

Spinning on her heels, she faced the man. She took a lesson from the upstairs neighbour, unleashing a small gust of air. It swirled around the residence before returning back to her. The smell hit her like a wall. Metallic, sticky, and far too familiar.

Blood.

The man must have seen it in her eyes, must have understood the gravity of what just happened beneath his nose. His pallor deepened, his cheeks sucking in as he took a stumbling step back from her. He tried to slam the door closed, but Sybil caught it with her magic, splintering it into pieces in its frame. The shattered bits burst outwards into the residence and down the hall.

Sybil had meant to lightly grab hold of the fabrics of his clothes, but her magic went further. She couldn't be sure what exactly it had sunk its teeth into but it threw him heavily backwards. He struck the wall hard. His head lolled pathetically as he slumped to the ground. She didn't have time to care. Not about him, or the surge of well-placed magic she had always dreamed of having. The pleading, horrified voice was still echoing in her head.

He lifted his hand lazily, his words barely mumbles above his breath. "I needed the practice. Only practice..."

"Killian, get the captain. Now," she barked behind her.

"What are you—" he started.

"There's a neuroweaver here," she said.

"Are you going to be—"

"I'll be fine. Just get help."

With a soft squeeze of her arm, Killian turned from the door and took off running towards the street.

"Anybody! I need help!" The neuroweaver's voice was clearer now as she passed the entrance and walked through the residence. Louder. A young woman. The connection was still strained. The woman was either a weak mage to begin with or...

Sybil couldn't think like that. The woman could still call out with her magic, she must still be okay.

She tore through the residence. Mr. Tendos uttered faint, weak cries as he came back to his senses. Each of the small, ancient and weathered rooms of his abode was quiet. No other occupants, no tucked away secret corners. Dusty boot prints were left in her wake as she trod through every room.

Nothing. She started to doubt that Tendos was the origin of the frightened cries. Her doubtful voice whispering in tandem with her racing heart.

Until...

A tattered rug was draped across the floor. One of the few things that wasn't covered in a fine layer of grit or dust. She gripped the edges and ripped it up. Beneath it, one of the boards wasn't nailed to the floor, lifting slightly at its broadest end. The boards on either side were loose as well, the opening more obvious the more Sybil stared at it.

The boards opened up to a ladder leading down into darkness. A sharp scent of blood and rot wafted up. The voice was barely whimpering now, a slight cracking and separation of the words as what Sybil hoped was the woman's magic dwindling. How long had she been crying out into nothingness to be heard?

Sybil cast a last glance over at Mr. Tendos, who had curled in on himself, bawling like a child. Whether he ran or not no longer mattered to her. Killian was getting the captain, or at the least more Wardens. This place would be crawling with them soon enough.

A hard pit blossomed in her throat as she stared down the opening. She hadn't realized her hands were shaking until the boards in her grip started to rattle.

The darkness started to morph and shift before her eyes, taking on a purple hue. The ladder swirled like a whirlpool, quickly replaced by slow moving tendrils of inky ichor. They crawled up over the edge of the floorboards, some morphing into gnarled, crooked hands.

They flooded over her skin, their icy touch burning through her leathers and into her flesh. A scream was hammering in the back of her throat but it was sealed behind her teeth. She could hear a groaning, chaotic yelling below now, puddles of inky ooze fluctuating and bubbling in time with the voice. Why was the voice deeper? Why was it screaming like that? Was that her name? Why was her name punctuating the shrill scream?

She clasped hold of the shaking wrist, digging her nails deep into the skin. The pain grounded her, centred her. Sharp crescents imbedded in her flesh to force the nightmares back to where they came from.

Not now. Not real.

Slow, methodical breaths, that was what Ethissa said. *When it feels like the darkness is surrounding you and you have no way out, remember to breathe.*

The pit under the floorboards solidified itself, the darkened tendrils vanishing. Disappearing back to the recesses of her psyche where the nightmares hid. Waiting for their chance to twist her mind again.

The voice was still calling, but it had wavered back to the weak neuroweaver's. Their pleas started to become fewer and further between, the volume dropping below the barest whisper.

One last long, drawn out breath. Sybil struck her hand along the flint of her belt. Her magic struggled to grasp hold of the sparks, her mind wavering with every failure. This had to work. She couldn't face the darkness blind, couldn't trust her own mind to hold her together. Biting into her cheek until she tasted copper, she was finally able to pull the flames to her hand. As soon as it burned bright enough to fight back the shadows that mocked her, she descended the ladder.

The dark, soft, moist mud at the base of the ladder swallowed the bottoms of her boots once she stepped off the last rung. A grunt and a curse escaped her lips as she lifted them from the swampy basin. Whatever layered the ground clung tightly to the soles.

All noises of the outside world had halted once she entered the hole. The only response the squelching of her feet in the mud. The darkness was all around, its shadows grasping at the light that twitched in her palms. It shook and shivered, threatening to collapse and let the darkness swallow her. Another long breath to stabilize it. A flood of rot permeated her nose, her lungs, and her eyes. Burning each of them in turn.

She lifted her hand up, letting the light burn brighter, taking in the small, dank hole. It was barely the size of the room above her, but her head almost scraped the ceiling. Precariously carved, most likely an unskilled geomancer taking on a side job to make the pit.

Sybil lifted the flame upwards, squinting into the darkness to see further ahead. As she did, her other hand slapped across her mouth stifling a scream. Bones were clustered along one side, piled haphazardly in a clump against the wall. Another mound was next to them, and as she took a few daring steps towards it, her stomach rose into her throat.

Skin.

Stacked in heaps, like discarded jackets.

Sybil gagged under her hand, the force making the light at her hands dim and sputter. For a moment, the lights crept over the pile, the shadows making it seem alive.

"Please, somebody hear me," the voice called, much clearer now, and loud in Sybil's ears. It tore her away from the nightmare before her. A woman was tied to a post that had been driven heavily into the ground. Her body was pitted with slashes and gouges. The rags that barely wrapped around her body were dishevelled and torn throughout her torso, matching the scars and wounds that riddled her body. Completely soaked and stained with blood.

Blood.

There was so much of it. Clinging tightly to the woman's body. Her tattered clothes. Her ragged hair. Sybil's gut twisted tightly, squeezing with everything it had. None of the training she went through would have ever prepared her for this.

Sybil swallowed what she could, wiling her stomach to stay put. The flame tried to ebb, fading ever so slightly as she approached her. The ropes bound the woman's hands behind the post, her wrists raw from the friction. Sybil reached for the blade on her belt, fingers shaking as she struggling with the hilt. With a slow breath between her teeth, she brought the blade to the ropes and sawed them. The flame at her fingers kept trying to die, but with every shimmer of light, Sybil stopped, refocusing the flame. All the while the woman cried, soft noises from her throat, inaudible words.

The rope was slick with blood, the fibres slipping and fraying under the blade instead of cutting. They finally snapped away, the woman falling to her knees in the mud. Sybil was quick to react, closing her hands around the flames, and wrapping the woman's arm around her shoulders. Her boots sank deeper, leather straining as the muck tried to pull her under.

"Can you walk?" Sybil asked, trying to keep the shaking out of her voice.

"I think so. Please, just get me out of here," the woman croaked, clutched tightly to the leather of Sybil's mantle.

As soon as Sybil stepped through the door of the building, the woman dropped to her knees and let out a cry. She stared up at the sun, arms open in greeting as she took it in. Sybil didn't have time to help her to her feet, to move her further from the house. Sarcomancers ran over, taking the wounded woman in their grasp, their hands already pressed to her torn and shredded skin. Tears were pouring down her face, inane mumbles bubbling past her lips.

Aerokineticists had built a barricade of wind around the block, the pressure and the noise acting to keep the events within the walls quiet from the outside world. So many wardens were running around, some towards the house, others around the barricade. Sybil could barely focus on them, just tiny, warbling, white dots flitting about in front of her.

"What happened?" Killian asked, running up to her, three more wardens trailing behind him.

"Will she be okay?" Sybil started before she collapsed onto her hands and knees. "There's so many bodies down there." Her stomach couldn't hold on anymore as the adrenaline and panic burned it up her throat and out onto the stones under her. She coughed and sputtered, spitting the last of the taste off her lips. By the time she was able to look back up from the mess on the ground, the rest of the wardens had run off into the house.

Killian had dropped to his knee, his hand on her shoulder, gently rubbing it, careful not to touch the spots that were splattered with blood and mud. She barely felt her legs moving as Killian hoisted her up, directing her to a nearby step. Someone had brought her a hot cup of herbal tea, but she couldn't find the energy in her weak arms to lift it to her lips.

When the setting sun reflected off a set of badges, Sybil's heart dropped.

"Hertrin," Killian said, standing up to greet him.

"*Captain* Hertrin," Sybil whispered her correction. Her gaze was unfocused in the distance, barely cognisant to the chaos unfolding around her.

"Bauer, you are dismissed for the night," the captain said.

"Sir, respectfully, absolutely not. I'm not leaving her," Killian said, his arms wrapping tighter on her shoulders.

"It's fine," Sybil whispered, not looking to either of the men. "I'll be fine."

Whatever reason the captain had for wanting her alone couldn't be good. But she felt numb, as though everything around her was moving too fast for her to get a grasp on. She was stuck in stasis, watching the world turn around her, unable to do anything about it. She should have been terrified, should have felt unending remorse over her job. She couldn't. She just felt empty.

Killian tipped her jaw towards him, a silent question on his face. She returned it with a slight nod. A further assurance that she was fine. Though she was the farthest from fine she had been in a decade.

Killian accepted the nod, pressing his lips to her forehead. With a quick salute to the captain, he left them, already shouting at the aerokineticists to lower their barricade.

She expected the captain to command her to stand. It was a wonder she didn't immediately leap to her feet the second he had walked up in the first place. Instead, he sat down beside her, his perfect, bleached mantle spreading out over the dirty steps. He rested his elbows on his knees, knotting his fingers into each other.

She felt as she had ten years ago. Helpless and terrified, the end of her own world about to cave in and crash into her. Though her father had been the one sitting next to her, his arms around her shoulders. And she had been the one in tears, screaming.

When she was younger, she had imagined her tragedy as a bucket. Quinn's death had filled the bucket up almost to the top. Every subsequent, awful thing after added to it, but nothing was enough to breach the rim. Today, the bucket was overflowing, the thick black ichor of her horror pooling around her and soaking into the ground. Quinn was supposed to be it. It wasn't fair.

"Are you alright?" the captain asked, turning his head to her.

She bit her lips to keep them from trembling as she swallowed. "Is the woman going to be okay?"

"She is. You got to her just in time. She's at the infirmary being treated, but her outcome is looking positive."

"How many?" Sybil asked, knowing she didn't need to clarify.

A heavy pause. "Twenty-six," he said. She took a long sip of the tea still held in her shaking hands. Cold now, but it was something other than the burgeoning scream she could feel in her chest. "Fourteen are identifiable. They'll evaluate the rest when they are able to get them back to the Bastion."

Sybil let out a heavy breath, the air stuttering through her lips. *Twenty-six people.* It was sheer dumb luck that it hadn't been twenty-seven. She could live with that.

The silence between them was too heavy, too thick. This was it, the final conversation before everything fell apart. Waiting would only make it worse. "I know why you're here." Another sip of the tea to help push her emotions back to her gut. "The Haixens are getting what they want, right?"

"Wyntres, don't be ridiculous. You stopped a killer today, saved who knows how many more lives. That woman gets to see another day because you did the one thing no other Warden had bothered to in Vinch." Sybil wrinkled her nose at him. "There were twelve different complaints put in. Every Warden that went to investigate wrote it off as a minor annoyance and ignored it. Only three other Wardens had even spoken to him themselves, but they brushed it off. Because you took the time to do your job, that woman is alive."

"She was a neuroweaver. That's how I knew."

"But you have—" He started, but she rolled her sleeve up, showing the damaged runes.

"I didn't want to get in any more trouble," she laughed out through her nose. "Moot point now, I suppose."

"What does that mean?"

"I told you, the only reason that I knew was because I chose not to report the injury and she was able to speak to me through my thoughts. It was—"

"I swear on my wife's grave that if you finish that sentence with 'luck' I will shove you off this step," the captain grunted. "Sybil, you have always gone against the grain with every step of your Wardship. You need to know that I hated the punishments I had to lay against you. It's so rare to find somebody that genuinely cares about the people around her and wants to do better, especially within the ranks. I never wanted to tear that spirit away from you, but there's only so much I can do. Do you have any idea of how proud I am of you for using your bullheadedness in the right way for a change?"

"So, I'm not being permanently dismissed?" She should have been more elated, but the energy just to turn and face him made her head grow foggy. Spoken as if she was asking the weather. "Can I come back to the Bastion full-time?"

The captain tucked his lips into his teeth, glancing around the area, waiting until prying ears were out of range. "I'm sure the Bauers want to tell you themselves, but I can't see any harm so long as you pretend to be surprised. They'll have an official ceremony, but you won't be just a Warden anymore." The corner of his mouth ticked up, the closest to a smile she'd ever seen. "Congratulations, First Command Warden Wyntres."

SIX

The molhund was already saddled, the leather straps biting into the thick fur of its belly. Raekin was trying to buckle his armor as quickly as he could. The beast paced in place impatiently, claws raking deep lines into the dirt, loosing sharp, guttural grunts. It snapped its teeth against the bridle, braying as it thrashed its stubby neck side to side.

The beast's pointed nose twitched when Raekin got close, the tentacle-thin appendages at its tip writhing through the air. Raekin didn't bother looking into its eyes, the black pinpricks lost in fur. Decorative buttons, more ornament than function. The molhund sensed the world by air, by scent, by the pulse of things moving beneath the earth. Each twisting tendril tuned to a world unseen by the beings that rode them.

Raekin stepped into the stirrup and swung up into the saddle. The shields along its sides clacked against his armor as he adjusted, pulling the padded guards into place to protect his calves. Not that it would stop everything. The last time he'd ridden through the lower tunnels, a rock the size of his thumb had embedded in his leg. The scar served as a constant reminder not to underestimate the power in those claws.

He stroked its neck, the coarse grey fur flowing under his palm. "Easy, Trotter." The name was hardly suiting. The beast moved like thunder, all claws and speed and torn up debris. A gift from Naz'tak. A freedom wrapped in teeth.

Trotter reared slightly, stamping harder. Another molhund emerged from the shadows behind them. This one was darker, its rider a welcome sight to Raekin.

"Oh, look. They gave the muck they scrape from the stables sentience." Raekin called out, his lips twitching upwards. Trotter betrayed his cold indifference, stomping against the ground and trying to draw close to the other beast.

The torches lit up the Etched's crooked, gapped smile. His own mount rearing his head up in greeting. "Only being that can stand being near you. Besides, I hear that you can't do anything on your own, and you need somebody to hold your hand."

"I know how clean your hands are. I'd rather be thrown in the Alpstraum than hold yours," Raekin glowered at his friend. Hirnstitch burst into laughter, the outburst cracking Raekin's stoic composure, his own laughter echoing in the cavern. Raekin shook his head, letting the noise ease the atmosphere.

Moments off the post in the Alpstraum were rare, and the crowded space where the Etched were corralled was sickeningly muggy and suffocating. The only brief comfort then was Hirnstitch's once-bloodied face.

Sharing a pile of rags and straw to sleep and quiet conversation in the dark. Isolation inside the Alpstraum had become a second skin. Hirn was the first person he had been able to grasp on to once the blindfold and wires were removed.

As a neuroweaver, his powers weren't as sought after. He spent less time in the Alpstraum than most other Etched, but that didn't mean he was spared. Hirn's face had been carved with thick, haphazardly drawn streaks from the line of his dark hair, through his brows and down along his cheeks. Burn marks littered his body, some wrapping around his arms, up his back, ending at a grotesque necklace.

When other Etched had broken into meek, horrified, quivering mockeries of themselves, Hirn had defied his masters. When he broke, he buried the resentment and rage. He refused to let the horrors of the Nether invade his mind, instead focusing solely on what he still had. His mind, his sight, all four limbs intact. Though a few fingers had been removed from his left hand. The positive, cheerful outlook made him unbearable sometimes. It also made him impossible to hate.

"You ready? Naz'tak gave us a week," Raekin said, turning his molhund to the west. Trotter scrambled slightly on the wall; his heaving bulk difficult to manoeuvre in the narrow tunnel.

"Of course," Hirn shouted as he slapped his molhund's flank. The beast jostled, his hind leg bucking against the tunnel, wall sending dust filtering down. "Surprised Naz'tak waited so long to send us back out again."

"The Hag has a request of us." Raekin shifted his weight again, rotating in the saddle to glance behind him as Hirn caught up.

What The Hag had told Naz'tak and what she was actually looking for were drastically different. A secret only her and Raekin shared. One they had been discussing in private for the better part of the last five years. Hirn was the only other being that knew.

Raekin felt the grin stretching his cheeks. He knew what hope got him. That knife was ruthless, cutting deep, but it was hard to ignore. "Those scrolls we brought her from Losweau? Took her a while, but the

Hag was finally able to decipher them. This might be it, Hirn. This might be *the* book."

Hirn's face lit up, his pale orange eyes vibrant. "Is she sure?"

"Of course not. But she's getting close,"

Raekin had slipped away to meet her, even though Etched were forbidden. He'd listened to her talk of power and its cost. Of mistakes made and prices yet to be paid. Distant prospects of tearing down the chains that bore down on all the Etched beneath the earth. Ideas that sounded maniacal, but through her croaked, ancient voice they came through clear and real.

She didn't ask him to trust her, that wasn't her way. But she had wanted him to believe something. She wanted him to believe there was still a way out. That all he had to do was keep his mouth shut and do as she asked. Trust was a rare commodity, but with The Hag, it was disturbingly easy to trade.

Raekin's fingers twitched, the need to run his hand along the nape of his neck burning through them. The need to trace the sharp lines of the grooved rune was a grating itch in his chest. He shook the temptation off, using the motion to reach for his hair. He unwrapped the tie and looped it back up. The cold cave air was blissful against the close cropped hair at the base of his scalp. Naz'tak initially refused to let Raekin cut his thick, dark hair, but the oppressive air in the caves made it unruly and warm. The shaved off lower half was a compromise, allowing him the brief reprieve from the heat.

Hirnstitch shifted on the back of his mount, the leather creaking. His grin stretching the scars and inks that ran down his face. He nudged the beast along, coming to stride beside Raekin as they started off down the Plaitius tunnel. Naz'tak had been feeling benevolent one day and spoke to Hirnstitch's owner, granting him his own molhund and the freedom to join Raekin. Another gift to Raekin, and another that could be ripped out from beneath him. Another pawn Naz'tak could use against him at a moment's notice. Another idiocy to add to his list.

He often found himself thinking of Varena whenever they travelled to the city. She had never seen it, a freedom Etched like her were never granted. The pang of sympathy in Raekin's chest was quickly swallowed.

Hazel Gryph. The city hadn't grown much beyond its slow crawl outwards. Their greatest accomplishment the removal of the kennels that once lined the city streets. Tainted pathways for refuse. Thankfully, especially for Raekin and Hirn, the city had commissioned underground drainage tunnels years before their time. These offered quiet access to the city above via maintenance hatches. Their biggest benefit to the Etched was the thin walls that separated them from the underground tunnels the molhunds would travel. A quick rip of the wall, and they had a perfect place to wait for the world above them to fall asleep.

With Raekin's sense of heartbeats, and Hirn's sense of thoughts, they had yet to be caught. A few patrols of Wardens or the occasional construction crew sauntered through. These led to a few close calls, but nothing worrying. Nothing ending in bloodshed.

"What happened with Varena?" Hirn asked, after a few oppressively quiet beats.

"You promised you'd keep your neuroweaver shit out of my head, Hirn," Raekin snarled.

"Don't need to look in your head to see the melted flesh, dummy," Hirn said.

In front of the shields on either side of Raekin's saddle were two conical shaped straps built into the thick hide. Formed to fit the two torches he had lit once Trotter was saddled. Raekin's black tunic had been stretched along his chest, his pack strap pulling it. Just enough to expose the tattered, marred flesh Varena had left. Brightly lit by the flames meant to guide them through the tunnels.

"I made an observation, and she took it personally." Raekin mumbled with a hefty breath.

"About?"

"How unsurprising it would be to find out she was fucking Tazec." Raekin didn't have to see him to know Hirn would cringe at the comment.

"That's harsh, even for you." Hirn muttered.

"And mutilating me was justified?"

"No, not justified. But not surprising."

"Not surprising because she's a psycho sarcomancer that can't control herself? Or not surprising because she'd tear the flesh from my bones if it meant she was given a few extra blankets?"

There was a heavy sigh from beside him, barely heard over the slow crunching of the dirt beneath their beasts. They'd had this argument before about any number of other Etched. As much as Raekin was doing what he could to earn them their freedom, he still saw the majority of them as parasites and snakes. Any one of them would toss him into a fissure if it meant they got to take his place as Naz'Tak's pet. If they only knew what that title brought with it.

When Hirn didn't respond, Raekin worked his jaw, letting the pain sizzle out the heat in his skull. "You think she's different," he said flatly.

"I think she's as desperate as the rest of us, but she isn't dangerous."

"Desperation *makes* people dangerous."

"So does pain. I don't think she would be so quick to turn against us as you think."

Raekin turned in his saddle, eyes sharp, teeth clenched. "You don't know her like I do."

Hirn didn't look away. "Maybe not." A pause. "But I know you. And you would be stupid to protect somebody you fully thought would slit your throat for her own gain."

Raekin mulled the words over between his teeth, trying not to let the seething out through his lips. Raekin had watched plenty of people burn. He'd lit the match himself more than once. But Varena? He'd had ample opportunities to let the fires consume her. Yet he had stood in the path of the flames every time. He wasn't sure what made her different. Maybe it was their shared master, their shared fear of the things he did to them.

That didn't matter. Whatever deep seated need he had to shield her from Naz'tak's wrath wasn't enough to forgo the suspicion he felt towards her. He'd follow Naz'tak's orders and keep her close. Keep forcing his primal instincts forward, even when his mind fought back.

Varena could rot in Ktharheim for all he cared. If this book truly was their salvation, it would only be a matter to time before he could forget she ever existed. All they had to do was reach the Arcaneum and find their moment to break in. As Hirn would say: "easy-easy."

SEVEN

The buzz behind Sybil's promotion didn't wait long to start its rampage throughout the Bastion. The whispers and eager words passing from one set of lips to another, overtaking the oversized halls. It wasn't unusual for there to be some sort of grand celebration after something as massive as the apprehension of a killer. Except, there was an odd quiet that surrounded it. It brought out even the quietest of wardens into the flare of gossip.

Sybil wasn't a stranger to murmurs at her back. They'd spew words laced with spite and disgust. Not intended for her ears but always making their way to them regardless. What she wasn't used to was the hushed tones of admiration and awe. It was difficult to adapt. Her shoulders would absently crawl to her ears every time they were audible.

"Excited?" Killian asked, spinning lazily on the stool he had dragged from the kitchen to the bathroom.

"Trying to be," she mumbled, undoing the buttons and adjusting the thigh straps of her mantle, hoping to pull it straight. The idea of the members of the Portcullis having their attention fixed on her filled her with a sickening mix of thrill and dread. If the heads of the nation saw any discrepancies in her uniform she would be mortified. She let out an exasperated sigh, dropping the leather. "You could help, you know?"

"Oh, like I could have helped in Vinch?" he grumbled.

Her fists clenched tightly at her sides, abandoning the half-done buckle on her right leg. "Somebody needed to get more wardens, so you *did* help. How many more times do I have to tell you that?"

"Oh, am I getting a promotion tonight as well?"

"There was nothing stopping you from ignoring me and barging in the house yourself."

He narrowed his eyes at her. "Just being a good soldier."

Sybil turned from the polished glass of the vanity, meeting his gaze outside the reflection. The sharp shock on his face did little to deter her. "What is your problem? I thought you were happy for me?" She crossed her arms over her chest, wrinkling the vest and undershirt in the process. The static was already building between her fingers, the candlelight flickering.

"That wasn't... I didn't mean..." Killian raised his hands in surrender, crinkling his face. He left the stool to wrap his arms around her shoulders, soothing the magic back into her veins. "I'm sorry. I *am* happy for you. It's just... hard. I promise I'll be on my best behavior tonight." He backed away from her and held her at arm's length. When he smiled, she could smell the faintest liquor on his breath. His grandparents would be there tonight, but he would never admit that their presence rattled him.

As softly as he could, he lifted his hand to the fabric at her chest, steam pouring from his palm before he ran both hands down the clothing. When his hand reached the bottom, the wrinkles had miraculously flattened themselves. "Better?"

"Thank you." She forced a smile, though it felt weak on her face.

All of this was meant to be different. There was supposed to be a group of children she would save from a rampaging fire using only the water from her hands. Or she would end a famine, growing fields of corn and wheat under her palms. Maybe even rescuing a member of the Portcullis, fending off a group of radicalized mages. Even though they were stupid, childish, idealized fantasies, she had secretly dreamed of them. Not this...

There'd be no blood, no crying woman ripped and torn, barely clinging to life. There wasn't a pile of bodies, each one a reminder of a person she couldn't save. The screaming...

I love you. I'm so sorry. I fucked up.

It wasn't until Killian carefully pulled her hands out of their grip that she felt the pain. The scar on her palm was rubbed raw as the memories flared back to life in her skull. She shook her hands out, ignoring Killian's concerned look to return to the mirror.

"At least that creep can't practice on any more innocent people," Killian said, resting his chin on her head. Sybil shuddered.

That's exactly what I'm trying not to think about, asshole.

Sarcomancers didn't get a lot of experience with their craft, and with the growing number of them, it was hard to stand out. Not that that made it excusable. Ripping a woman apart, only to seal her back up again was barbaric. Judging by the half-closed wounds, the scabs ripped open, and not fully sealed, he was shit at it.

There was a pulsing at her hip, a pressure she was used to. An anxiety-ridden tremor that seemed to flare up with her magic most days. Others, it acted of its own will, reminding her of its existence, whether she wanted it to or not. The feeling of a grating itch beneath her flesh. If she peeled it back, the horrors of what had happened would be etched into her bones. The inks of the rune that tainted her hip would have spread through her very marrow, soaking deep in her soul. Forever poisoning her blood with the reminder of the nightmares she witnessed. She resisted the urge to touch it, instead lifting her hands and staring at the inks that wrapped around a few of her fingers.

"Killian, do you ever... does it ever feel like... Your runes..." she paused, scrunching up her face as she fought to find the words. "Can you feel them? Like when you don't touch them?" She winced. It sounded ridiculous out loud.

Killian peered at her through the mirror from the top of her head, brow raised. But there was no mockery. Just the small, tired smile he always wore when she didn't know how to say something quite right.

"Yeah," he said quietly. "One of them. Sometimes." He shrugged, looking out at the street. "Usually in crowds."

Sybil twisted her head, staring up at him. "Which one?"

"The one my grandparents made me get," he said with a shrug. "That 'protection' one."

Her gaze dropped to his shoulder. "The one that hurt?" Killian didn't answer right away, just a slow nod, his smile fading slightly. "Does it work?"

He let out a quiet breath, almost a laugh. "No idea." He cleared his throat, taking his arms away from her shoulders, shifting slightly as though shaking the conversation off. "I'll meet you down at the hall." He pressed his lips to her head before ruffling his dark hair in the mirror, adjusting his own jacket once. "I want to get to Frederique before he starts too heavily into the wine."

He paused in the frame of the door, fingers drumming lightly on the wood, then looked back at her over his shoulder. "You'll be okay?"

Sybil nodded. Killian's lips twisted just enough, before stepping into the bedroom. She followed his movements in the mirror before he disappeared from sight. When she heard the telltale click from the door down the stairs, her shoulders dropped. She hadn't been able to spend time alone the last few days, every shadow like a living entity, palpable and chaotic. Killian had been there, soothing her back to sleep, lighting the candles to chase away the reaching abyss. Yet, this moment of quiet tranquility was a needed change. A placid moment before the commotion she would endure.

The dreaded image of her evening loomed over her. Surrounded by people, shaking hands and offering their congratulations. Commendations that she didn't believe she deserved. Her stomach twisted on itself, rising through her throat as she pictured their ecstatic faces. She should be revelling in it, not staring at her reflection as though it was a stranger wearing her skin.

She rubbed her eyes, harder than she had meant to, the stars chasing her hands as they dragged down her face. Her cheeks looked gaunt, the dark circles around her eyes pulling the hazel inwards. What she wouldn't have given for a full night's rest. Anything to return any sort of glow to her lifeless looking skin.

One last adjustment of the mantle. A quick cringe as it shifted back lopsided. Then finally, a few more pins to hold the collapsing roll in her hair.

Good as it's going to get.

Sybil's magic had finally vanished back into her skin during the walk to the Bastion, but she could feel the acidic tang of it trying to flare back to life. Though the doors to the hall were closed, she could hear the muted uproar of people beyond them. She pressed her hands to their wood, running her thumbs along the intricate moulding, grounding herself. Filigree laced through the embossed texture. Like the captain's door, though these climbed at least thrice as tall and doubly as wide.

One deep breath in, then a push, and the roar of the voices flooded her ears. It was tinged with the soft twinkling of music, the band having set up at the far corner, quietly filling the lack of silence. Thankfully, the noise was enough to drown out the creaking of the door that screeched through Sybil's ears. Only a few heads swivelled her way, most of them so enthralled with hearing their own voices, they only tossed her a short nod before turning away.

Sybil released the breath, the air fogging as it was chilled around her. She pressed her teeth together hard, willing the magic back into her veins.

Breathe in. Breathe out.

The room was a sea of white, interspersed with flecks of colour: the few guests not of the Wardens. Of all the mantles she could see in the cacophony of people, only a few of the heads were mildly recognizable. It wasn't worth trying to nudge through the crowd to verify. Instead, her attention was drawn to the banquet tables.

Tall flutes filled with bubbling liquid covering their surface, stacked a dozen or so high. They were being topped up by a fluidicist leaning lazily against the wall. The fluid would shoot upwards out of the bottles and perform circles and swirls in the air for the onlookers. It would then gently land itself atop the pyramid, perfectly level to all its neighbours. The growing crowd would clap quietly, showing their amusement before snatching a glass and resuming whatever had been paused while they went for another drink.

As Sybil tipped a flute to her mouth, draining the glass in one breath, she scanned the room. It was a strange feeling to know that so many people had gathered in such a small space to see you, and you knew so few of them. It felt as though each step had to be calculated, as though every person was watching her, critiquing and judging. Hyper aware of every muscle twitch, every twinge in her skin.

The nerves in her back started to untangle as the wine did its work. She had gone mostly unnoticed, leaning casually at the far end of the tables. Tucked discreetly into the corner by the immense windows that overlooked the courtyard. Those that left the warmth of the hall to peruse the balcony barely noticed her, their hands already gripping flints or flames licking from their fingers. Outside was starting to swell with the heavy smoke from an assortment of pipes and rolls.

She followed a couple of older wardens with her eyes, their wives laughing raucously as they stepped through the glassed doors. Her sights froze on the stone head that jutted up just over the railing of the balcony. Had the statue been turned around, it would appear to be peering into the hall, leering in on the ceremony.

Kreb Bolorick. The savior of Plaitius. Ender of Wars. Master Enchanter.

Slaughterer of millions.

Maybe that was the intention when they erected that gaudy statue in the courtyard. Make it seem as though the great bearded hero was watching over the wardens. A reminder of what they were serving for. What would happen if the peace wasn't kept.

Trumpets sounded as the large doors at the entrance opened once more. The gathered people went silent. The band switched tunes, a softer harmony whispering through the room. Two by two, the Portcullis entered, a soft pattering of applause filling the silence that had lingered for a moment.

The Bauers led the group, Justinia and Stewart, both of them with their hands clasped and their heads held high. Their extravagant purple and gold cloaks flowed silently behind them on the polished wood. They each wore circlets that wrapped delicate wires and milky white gems around their heads. Enchanted so tiny puffs of steam twisted out of the golden wire.

Justinia's gaze drifted over the crowd before it landed on Sybil. Her face stretched upwards, the lines around her eyes crinkling. She poked her elbow into her husband's ribs, directing his attention. They both nodded softly to Sybil before turning their attention away.

Though three of the nine families were missing, trailing along at the tail of the other five were the Haixens. The circlets that rested on the top of their heads had been adorned with crisscrossing wires resembling stitches. Atop the centre, directly above their brows, was a stained glass teardrop, one half white, the other red. The Plaitius symbol for officially recognized sarcomancers. The two of them overseeing the group as the governing heads. The matriarch had long, dark braids that entwined into the circlet, running down her shoulders and ended at her hips. The patriarch was shaved bald, the sharper edges of the circlet digging into his scalp.

They walked through the hall towards the stage with their heads held high. Their dark eyes not casting over the crowd, but centred on the far wall, narrowed ever so slightly. They held their shoulders back, their long, draping, black robes sliding along behind their feet. Just their presence was laced heavily with power, and it had little to do with their towering height. Power wept from every pore of their skin, and they held it like a weapon. Besides their unnecessary distaste for Sybil, she still felt a creeping desire to cower whenever they were near.

The Portcullis continued through the parted crowd towards the opposite wall. A stage had been erected years ago, the scuff marks along the wood already becoming visible from the traffic. After the Portcullis had taken their places, Captain Hertrin ascended the stairs, standing at the end of the line next to the Haixens. His arms crossed into the salute. He held stock still, though Sybil detected the slightest waver to his upper lip.

This wasn't the first time he had stood on that stage with the Portcullis. But it was the first time he had done it for somebody he had recommended for watch years prior. Whether it was pride or nerves that rattled him, Sybil couldn't be sure. Whichever it was, she felt a swell of gratitude for the old man. Grateful that he would be the one to stand beside her now.

There was no pause for any typical grand gesture to begin the ceremony. Once Captain Hertrin stood steady, his gaze landed on her. The crowd all swivelled to follow suit. Lingering there between the fluctuations of quiet whispers.

A heavy weight dropped in her gut as the sea of white started to separate, a pathway beginning to emerge between her and the stage. The rest parting like reeds as she trekked forward. She had to mentally stop herself from licking her lips, already knowing they'd be red and raw by the time she made it atop the platform.

The music was still quietly playing, but that didn't muffle the hushed comments quite enough. Her hands absently went to scratch at the wound across her arm, a silent wish that she could silence her footsteps as her boots clacked against the polished marble flooring. Another

Portcullis refinement. No need for silver embossed walls and crystal chandeliers when the room wasn't meant to be the focus of attention.

She wrenched her arms back to her sides, folding them tightly against her torso. *Focus, Sybil. One foot in front of the other.*

It wasn't until Stewart Bauer grabbed hold of her hand that she realized she had been running her middle finger along her palm. That familiar crease of damaged skin acting like a ground. Her finger was crushed awkwardly against her palm as the Portcullis patriarch grasped it in his large fingers.

Justinia Bauer threw away the formalities. Her cloak billowed out as she wrapped her arms around Sybil, pulling her tight. When she backed away, she held Sybil's shoulders, her eyes twinkling, creases building at the corners.

"We're so proud of you," Justina mouthed before dropping her hands and clasping them together.

This was the closest Sybil had felt to family in years, and it was a surreal feeling. She made a mental note to tell Killian later how grateful she was for this. For him.

She passed the next three, each accepting her bow gracefully. The patriarchs shook her hand or saluted her back. The matriarchs only nodded, their hands tightly gripped together, bodies rigid.

The Wetenstos family dropped their hold on one another, their brown furs shifting to drape along their arms. Their smiles seemed genuine, the patriarch gently gripping her chin to pull her up from the bow. They each grasped hold of her hand, shaking it, whispered thanks threading past their stretched grins.

The Bauers had always regarded her with such warmth because of Killian. She hadn't expected it from the head family of Plaitius's trade routes. The matriarch let out a laugh, her voice like bells in the wide hall as Sybil stood there slack-jawed. Sybil's face flushed, dropping her gaze as the woman once more thanked her. A quick glance to her right and she caught sight of the Bauers. Justinia's smile replaced with a tight lipped scowl as the other woman clapped excitedly for her.

Finally, she came to stand in front of the Haixens. Whatever animosity that lingered for her seemed to hold steady as their eyes narrowed at her approach. The patriarch gave a gentle bow in return for hers, but it was stunted, only the slightest bend. The matriarch, however, said nothing, just continued to stare down at Sybil as though she could see through her skin to the taint below.

Sybil felt like a fool for hoping that they would at least acknowledge that what she had done was a good thing for the city. She wasn't sure what had brought on this unwelcome hatred, but could only assume it had something to do with the rampaging rumors about the 'chaos mage'. Wild magic such as that could only spell trouble for the healers of Plaitius.

The captain stood, still saluting. Sybil mirrored him, her own salute a little wobbly after the parade of power she had just endured.

"Release, Wyntres," he said, dropping his own arms. She followed suit, though tucked her hands behind her back, standing as straight as she could with the shivering that bled through her spine.

His voice was loud, commanding over the crowded room. A voice that had years of practice ricocheting off expansive walls to breach the ears of a multitude of listeners. "Due to your recent exemplary service in the name of the Wardens, the Portcullis, and the nation of Plaitius, we thank you."

"Thank you, sir," Sybil attempted, though her voice was meek and pathetic next to his. A whimper that would barely reach the first row of onlookers.

"To commend you, we, in the presence of your peers and leaders, award you the title of First Command Warden. Congratulations."

The clapping erupted from the room as Captain Hertrin bowed to her. He pulled a thin box from his mantle pocket, presenting her with her new pin. Her silver leaf. The metal glinted in the bright lights of the hall. A flush of warmth rose through her body as she stared at it.

The captain undid the gold leaf from the straps on her collarbones, the leather falling lazily against her chest. At the thought of her mantle once more losing its symmetry, she made a face, though quickly corrected it when she remembered the eyes still on her. His hands shook as he pulled the straps back together. The captain clipped on the silver leaf, leaving the shoulders of the mantle a touch too loose.

When he stepped away from her to join the rest of the room in their applause, she glanced down at the pin. Almost mirror finish and so clean. There was one just like it at her home in Trelusk, shoved away in a drawer and hidden from the world. It was tarnished and worn, having been clipped and unclipped a hundred times. She used to marvel at it, never expecting that she would have one of her own.

She would appreciate its worth more than her father ever did.

"What did you feel? What was it like!?" The woman shouted, the flute in her fingers tilting dangerously towards Sybil. Sybil knew this woman, one of the younger cousins of the Wetenstos family. Claimed she was a writer, documenting stories that she had her family publish for her, scattering the sheets to the city for any who felt so inclined to pick one up and read it. Already light in her senses, tiny hitches punctuating the ends of her sentences. She may have been grasping for a new story, but Sybil wasn't sure she would remember anything that was said. If the rumors were true, she would make up her own story regardless if she got the truth or not.

"Horrible, actually," Sybil said, twisting her own empty flute in her fingers. It was the third glass of sparkling wine she had finished, though quite a bit slower than the first two. Didn't stop the warmth that bloomed in her belly. "There was so much blood."

The Wetenstos woman curled up her lips in a sneer, clutching her glass to her chest. "Gross."

Sybil could feel the words bubbling up through her throat but caught them before they released. She badly wanted to tell this woman that that was the reality. There was no point in trying to sugar coat it into some elegant, fantasy novella just because of her sensitive readers.

Instead, "My apologies." She smiled, tilting her flute towards her, feigning the sudden surprise at the empty glass. "Goodness, I've run out. Excuse me."

She rolled her eyes as she brushed past the woman, quickly drowning out the unintelligible half-shouts as the woman tried to goad her back.

That anxious energy had faded after she had stepped off the stage. A few slaps on the back from her peers, a few whistled cheers. Once the attention was off her, the night was easy. Just another gathering of the Wardens. No longer the celebration of her nightmare.

After grabbing another flute and tipping it to her lips, she glanced around the hall, trying again to find somebody she knew. Captain Hertrin seemed to be in a very intense conversation with the Bauers, his hand pressed to his mouth as he leaned towards them, his nodding over-exaggerated. Sybil found herself wondering if she had ever seen the captain drink. Wondered further if she could goad him into more. It would make for some good stories when she reported to him next, watching him attempt to hide any embarrassment as she asked for her assignment.

The crowd seemed to ebb and flow around her. She had to stand on her toes to see over the shifting, moving mass. She hadn't seen Killian from the stage, but he was here somewhere. She meandered through the hall, nodding quiet thanks and gently pushing through elbows. Finally, the dark, swept back brown hair showed itself on the outer balcony. Killian was motioning dramatically to a crowd of people, expelling some wild story. Her lips curled up as she stepped through the glass doors towards him.

"—so even after I'm begging her to listen, she's still fighting me, saying that it's pointless. It wasn't until we went to leave and walked by the door that I knocked, so she didn't have a choice." Killian's voice echoed loudly in the dark night, bouncing off the glass windows. "The creep comes out, and he just reeks like blood. He's twitching and shaking, and just *looks* guilty, you know? So, she goes to apologize to him, and tell him we didn't mean to disturb him. But I stop her and tell him that we need to investigate his house. He snaps, starts to try to run, but I grab him and just throw him against the wall. Sybil is just standing there, dumfounded. I tell her to watch him while I go get help. Next thing I know, she's strutting out of the building with that woman."

"Wait, why aren't you getting your silver leaf then?" A voice chirped in the small group.

"Political bullshit." Killian hiccupped, pouring a slug of wine into his mouth. "Can't have a Bauer take all the credit. It's just good to know that serving in the Wardens has meaning. Thankfully I was there to help, or—"

"What are you doing?" Sybil said, the heads of the people snapping to her.

"Sybil, love. I was looking for you," Killian said, stretching out his arms to her.

"What the Nether were you telling them?" She stepped back from his embrace. Her breath came out in sharp bursts of frozen air. Several of the gathered faces flushed as they started to disperse from their half-formed circle. Though they moved away from their clump, Sybil was acutely aware of them still standing around the large balcony, their ears no doubt still twisted in her direction.

"You know, just... sharing the story of your heroism," he sputtered out with a choked laugh. His eyes were red, struggling to open fully. She knew the look, knew the state he was in. That didn't stop the burning in her gut.

"Oh, really? Didn't hear you mention the part where you called him a 'gas mage' and tried to get me to leave."

"Oh, come on, it's just theatrics." His pseudo-apologetic grin was lopsided. "Besides, you know you never would have done any of it if I wasn't there. You would have been way too afraid to knock on that lackwit's door if you didn't have me as back up."

The words hit like a blow. She *had* only knocked on the door because he was there, but it was spite, not bravery that brought her fist to the wood. The tinge of truth only stung more.

Sybil stepped back, her face heating. "Excuse me?"

"Come on, you know you saw it when we were still bronze leaves. I don't mind that you rely on me so much, I think it's kind of sweet." He lifted his hands to grip her shoulders, stumbling a touch as he did, and she flinched backwards, baring her teeth.

"Don't touch me." Her patience unwinding like an errant thread. It showed its face in the wind that whipped around them, carrying dirt and dust with it. It stung her eyes, but she blinked the pain away.

"Be realistic Sybil, it's not like this is totally new. You rely on people, it's just who you are. It's nothing to be ashamed of."

A beat, her face feeling like it was on fire. "What are you saying?"

"The *only* reason Hertrin got you that medal," he nodded towards the silver on her chest, "was because of your father. You wouldn't even be wearing that jacket if it weren't for him."

"Maiten didn't do *shit* to get me where I am," Sybil snarled. The wind kicked up harder, sharp pains glancing through the fingers of her empty hand as the debris twisted and sliced between them. The vast air around her kept the sparks at bay, but she was able to grab so much of it that it was slowly becoming a torrent.

Rage flooded through her chest, the glass in her hand heating as the wine started to bubble and boil. It shattered, the shards clattering at her feet. Drinking had been a mistake, but it was one that stayed dormant in the back of her mind until now. Her teeth bit hard into the sides of her cheeks as she willed the heat to ease back down, but it fought her with every breath.

Killian leaned in, glancing awkwardly at the people that were pretending not to listen. He stumbled slightly, the crunching of glass drawing his attention to the ground. His face twisted as though he couldn't figure out where it came from. "Sybil, cut it out."

The wind died down, barely a whisper coiling around her. A barrage of insults filled her lungs, ready to unleash their toxic needles at Killian. Small movement caught her eye with the calming of the storm around her. The balcony had gone silent, every head focused on the two of them. No doubt revelling in watching the chaotic Vollmagus lose control. *Again*.

She wouldn't let them have that victory. Wouldn't lower herself back to the pathetic 'chaos mage' that Hazel Gryph assumed of her. "Go fuck yourself, Killian," she said, just below her breath but with enough bite.

The acidic burn laced through her fingers and up through her arms as she clamped down on her magic. She had to press her tongue tightly to her teeth to keep from wincing. The pain helped, pushing her to turn away from him and return to the interior of the Bastion.

There was no point in waiting for a retort, whatever he said would only fall on deaf, fury filled ears. For now, she just needed to get away from him before she did something she'd regret. She could come unravelled the rest of the way in the morning.

The thrumming of her blood raged through her skull, blocking out the noise of her feet stomping on the marble floor. She couldn't be sure if anybody had heard the outburst on the balcony, but most of the crowd seemed still enthralled with themselves. Her steps led her back to the table of drinks. She ran her teeth over her lips and thought better of it.

A chorus of laughter made her swivel her head back towards the balcony. The crescent of people had formed once again around Killian, one of the other wardens having said something apparently hilarious. A few of them peered over their shoulders at her, quickly averting their gaze. One of them even rested their hand on Killian's shoulder in a comforting gesture.

Pain burned through her jaw as her teeth creaked under the pressure. The barracks would be swarming with the rumors before the clock even hit middle night. The poor Bauer that came to a head with the 'chaos mage'. Twisted by the words Killian wove into whatever bullshit he was feeding them. Truth meant nothing. Her name may have had sway years before, but the Bauer name was still held high. Grovelling, Void-licking disgraces. Clinging to whatever they could that might get them a taste of his legacy.

She needed a distraction. Preferably somebody that wasn't so easily swayed into boot licking. No longer corralled into a conversation with the senior Bauers, Captain Hertrin was now surrounded by other high-ranking wardens. Their laughter could be heard throughout the hall. Louder and more boisterous than the cacophony of voices. Her heart sank. She couldn't ruin this for him, not for her own petty bullshit.

Watching him only brought on another heavy weight in her chest. In a room full of people that had just applauded her, it was sickening to think just how alone she felt.

There was one place where being alone was a thing of beauty. Where the crass voices and narrowed stares didn't reach her. Her own safe haven. A place where she could drown herself in books to mitigate the hatred that seethed in her skull.

The Arcaneum.

EIGHT

Sybil barely noticed herself leaving the Bastion. One minute she was seething, the next, she was in the courtyard, her breath fogging in the icy Dimming air. Her mind so clouded with the rage of Killian's dismissiveness she could barely focus on her feet moving her forward. But once that burning freeze gripped her lungs, her fury ebbed.

The Dimming season was reaching its frozen finale. Frostide was descending on them, likely within a few days. The surrounding gryphire trees had already turned to skeletons of themselves, but soon the Hazel Gryph lake would freeze. The days would waver to mere hours, the twilight stretching long.

The decay that came with the Dimming always filled Sybil with a sense of ease, but Frostide brought an unnatural calm. Though darkness was an unwelcome invader in her life, the long nights of Frostide weren't. The moonlight reflecting off the vibrant snow caps casting the world in its own ethereal brightness. Scaring the shadows and lurkers of the night further into their crevasses. If only it attacked the ones in her mind so easily.

Until then, Sybil had to make do with the torches that glowed around the perimeter of the courtyard. Her feet carried her to the east, past the barracks. The stout, elongated building not as extravagant as its westerly neighbour. Sybil could map out the interior of the building with her eyes closed.

Directly in front of her, however, was what she knew her feet had been leading her towards in the first place. The Bastion's great cathedral-like centre: the Arcaneum.

The last remaining element of the Academy still left untouched. The Arcaneum towered above its neighbouring buildings, only surpassed by the spire of the Bastion itself. Though a hall connected the Arcaneum to the Bastion, it appeared as its own stand alone. Great metal and stone arches were inlaid with ornate, complicated stained glass, and covered the majority of its surface. The roof peaked at a sharp angle; the top shingles decorated with metal adornments scaling along the ridge. Its great doors still held the original wood and paint, its surface flecked with scrapes and chips. A protest against the Portcullis's modern ways.

Sybil started faster in the direction of the building, the chill nipping at her fingers. She was stopped in her tracks as another shadow bore over her. The absurd size of the bearded statue of Kreb Bolorick now loomed, his arms outstretched, hands extended in front of him. A grimoire in one, the supposed lifesaving quill in the other. The sun-faded beard looked more warped and warbled up close than over the railing of the balcony. A grotesque reverence overseeing the courtyard.

From the ground, the statue appeared to be painted in blues, greens and purples. It wasn't until her focus was directed upwards that she saw the reason. The moon was reflecting off the intricate window in the dead centre of the main pillar of the Bastion. Its iridescent glass tinted and stained obscuring the interior. Most likely owned by one of the Portcullis families. Maybe one who admired Kreb Bolorick and wanted to have a nice view of his absurd statue. A monument to the death of thousands.

Sybil's history with sacrifices had made her bitter and cold to Kreb Bolorick. She saw herself reflected in the hollow eyes of the carved stone. Kreb Bolorick would never get the chance now to right his wrongs. If it took to the end of her days she would do what she could to not be given the same fate.

With a scowl and a grunt, she continued on past the statue. The alcohol was trying its hardest to warm her extremities, but by the time she reached the steps of the Arcaneum her teeth were chattering. The doors creaked as she pushed them open, stumbling slightly on the stones as she did.

The Arcaneum had a unique smell, one she wished she could bottle. Dust and mothballs, with a lingering of petrichor. Most people equated it with death. Sybil equated it with peace, a place where she could finally breathe.

During the day, people were usually flitting about, many of whom would bar certain areas from visitation due to impromptu research. Ropes or stacked chairs to protect their space. Sometimes even vines by the more skilled botanomancers. In the encroaching darkness of the night, in the dim light of the wavering candles, only silence greeted her entrance. Sybil's little reward to herself.

She stepped forward towards the library but, even as she took a deep breath of the emptiness, she paused. Her head slowly turned towards the arching stairs to her left. Immense doors with thick metal bars running both horizontally and vertically across the glass.

The Restricted Area.

The runes that ran along the edge of the doors, burned and engraved into the wood, were enough to ward any person off attempting to enter.

Though those that tried quickly found the doors were sealed tight, only opening to specific conditions.

Today, Sybil finally met those conditions.

The glassed doors opened wide as she approached, reacting to the new pin that was clasped across her collar. Sybil beamed at the gaping doors, swelling with pride. She ran her fingers along the indented runes on the door as she passed. Absently noting each curve and mark, memorizing the entrance. Her heart fluttered in her chest like tiny wing beats between her ribs. Everything else that ravaged her mind melted out as the scent of ancient papers filled her senses.

Much like the lower level of the library, the Restricted Area was a mass of shelves. Overwhelmed and bowing under the weight of years of taboo knowledge, or artifacts and grimoires too dangerous to be held by civilians. Every scrap of danger, secrecy, and forbidden knowledge now hers to claim.

Except, she could barely see past the first set of shelving. There was no reason for the candles to be out. For any of the lights for that matter. Their enchantment could withstand the most horrid storm, and the flames would still flicker.

Unless they were extinguished on purpose.

The petrichor and moss smell was suddenly overwhelmed and snuffed out by something stronger. The haunting memory that tangled into the scent's miasma flooded through her nose. It tainted her sinuses and burned into them. Her blood ran cold, an icy frost settling through her veins.

Cinnamon and ash.

A tightness formed in her throat, her feet refusing to move. She was back there again, ten years ago. Curled up on the hard wooden floor surrounded by blood and ichor. Screaming for help, screaming for *him*. *That smell.* Never had the two scents tangled together since that day. The cross of spice and death so unnatural and horrid. Yet here it was, ten years later, circling around a room forbidden to all other than a select few.

Her throat closed tightly, halting her breath. The memories pulled her down into the darkest pits of her mind, snuffing out the light inside her.

It's here.

It's back.

The Void.

The shadows moved, growing sentient. She blinked, and they had hands. Teeth. Their nightmarish limbs reaching for her. Tentacle-like appendages growing from the shadows. Raking at her skin, tearing at her hair. Grasping for her with their chaotic whispers.

Not real. Not real, she repeated, letting out the breath she had been holding. She dug her nails into the palm of her hand. It brought on a sharp stab of pain.

Just enough. It forced the shadows to slither back into shape.

A heavy thud as something dropped to the ground. Her attention snapped to it, her mind whirling.

That was real.

The window on the far wall shone bright moonlight down into the deeper sections, but not enough to illuminate beyond the darkness of the aisles. Better than the oppressive void that had encapsulated itself in the entrance.

Another thud, then a shuffling of pages, followed shortly by a book being tossed out of the aisle. It landed with its spine up, pages crinkled and folded on the gritty flooring. Then another landed beside it, the aged cover cracking. Sybil cringed. It would take weeks to fix those, if they were even repairable.

She crept closer, letting the moon light her way. There was a loud creak under her foot and she cursed herself once more for not fixing her runes. Thankfully, she stepped in tandem with another book being tossed. They seemed to be systematically thrown in rapid succession.

A few more steps and she would be at the head of the aisle. She took another, prepping for the next tome that came flying out of the darkness. Except it never came. The wood beneath her boot groaned, uncomfortably loud in her ears. The shuffling papers stopped, the rustling stopped. Just silence.

Flaring alarms and curses rang through her head. She had one shot to leap around and catch them by surprise, and even then she had no idea what sort of magic would cascade out of her outstretched hands.

No fire. Anything but fire.

On the brink of stepping around the aisle, she lifted her boot, but froze. The air caught in her lungs mid breath, trapped between her ribs. A horrifying sensation as she became hyper aware of her heartbeat in her ears. It had been racing, but now it felt wrong. Like someone was holding it, squeezing it, slowing the beat unnaturally. Like it no longer belonged to her. A foreign entity within her chest now controlled by the nightmare that hid within the shelves of the Arcaneum.

The room spun and blurred around her. Sharp pinpricks started to bloom beneath her skin, making it itch from the inside out. *Something* held her, yet nothing touched her skin.

The word came to her like a curse: *Bloodweaver.*

The realization raked through her thoughts. It was impossible. How many times had she been told the slightest hint of that magic was to be snuffed out? Sarcomancers could rend the flesh from your bones, but it worked through touch. Bloodweavers needed only to sense the beat inside your chest to grab hold. They were feared, so they were *erased*.

She had trained against sharp gales of air, roaring fires, and flooded terrain. Grasped the concept of hand to hand, blade against blade. Excelled at every one. But this... this wasn't something they could ever train for. Couldn't protect yourself against a war raging within your own body. A parasite crawling through her veins and attacking under the flesh.

Move. Fight. Something. Anything.

Sybil uselessly tried to flex her fingers, to move even the smallest joint. Her body fought back, every muscle feeling as though it was made of stone. For a second, she was weightless. She wasn't floating, nor was she falling. She simply... was. There was barely time to register the movement before she was fully airborne, the window rushing towards her.

There was a crack as her skull ricocheted off the glass. A spider web of splintering erupted from where her head struck. Her hands instinctively went up, air swirling around them. It faltered and faded into nothing as the room teetered dizzyingly around her. Her hair had fallen out of its roll, cascading down her face. A wet line dripped down her forehead, trailing from her cheek to her jaw.

A tightness wrapped around her chest again, followed swiftly by a burning through her lungs like acid. She started to cough. The iron tang that coated the inside of her mouth only served to further her panic. She desperately tried to breathe in against the pain and pressure crushing down on her.

A shadowy figure stepped out from between the bookshelves, his hand outstretched. He closed his fist, the crushing sensation magnifying. He stepped further towards her, the moonlight illuminating the black ink that traced across his nose and down his cheeks. The reflection in his eyes burned like orange fires. His jaw was tight, his sight fixated on her. As he pulled his hand back towards himself, the searing pain doubled. Blood pooled in her lungs, smothering her air. Drowning her.

The world around her was blurry. Fogging and darkening at the edges. But she couldn't look away from the figure towering over her.

A hallucination brought on by death. She squeezed her eyes tight, but when they opened, it was still there. This is what she'd always feared would happen at the end when she faced down the Nether. Nightmares that tormented you with their poisonous visages. Echoes of things that didn't exist. *Couldn't* exist.

The chorus of screams that told her it wasn't real started to shout into her ears. Barely heard over the pounding of her slowing heartbeat. Until that small twist of the figure's mouth indented his cheek. Something she had tried so hard to hold on to the memory of, but it had been lost for so long. The runic tattoos and scars couldn't hide that smile.

No. Not him. It can't...

She forced through what felt like a final breath. Blood spat from between her lips as her voice fractured like the glass behind her.

"Quinn?"

NINE

Raekin's hand froze, trembling on the precipice of tearing the blood from her chest. They threatened to finish what they started but faltered.

That name.

He'd almost forgotten it. It hadn't been uttered in a decade. Buried deep and left to rot. Safe with the rest of the things that could still be used to break him. It pulled at him like the chains carved into his neck.

Why was this Warden still alive? His grip on her life waned, his fingers uncurling. This weakness, this hesitancy. This wasn't the version of him that had survived. He should have shredded the blood from her veins the second he felt her in this oppressive room.

So why did he hesitate?

The Warden sucked in a ragged breath. Too sharp and painful; a rattling guilt gnawing at his spine. One that he'd thought had been buried long ago. Then the coughing started, wet and desperate, blood flecking across her lips. Her head lolled backwards, now illuminated by the moon. No longer just a faceless warden. Raekin felt a vice tighten on his chest.

He staggered back. This wasn't possible. She was in Trelusk. She shouldn't be here. She shouldn't be wearing *that*.

But it was her. The faint tremor of her lip, the way those all too familiar hazel eyes took him in. They never strayed from his face, and he could match the gears turning behind them to his own. Shock. Terror. *Recognition.*

In the Alpstraum, chained to the posts, everything you clung to was ripped away. Torn from your flesh with every cut, every brand. Stone, steel, claws and bone used to carve you into something new. Something to be used.

Raekin always wondered if he would have gotten out of the worst of it. If he had just let them break him down to nothing. His gifts had made him a prize, but defiance made him a target, a competition between the worst of his captors.

He wouldn't let them hollow him out. No matter how many times the needles pierced his skin, or claws tore through flesh, or scalding metal etched his skin, he refused. Because he didn't want to forget *her*.

There was a short time where he resented her. Blamed her for the pain he endured. Long, dark, lonely nights twisted the mind. Where it should have funneled him further into the dark depravity, he found a light. Whatever happened, she was safe. That was enough.

As the years went on, as his plans morphed, his ambition outgrew survival. He wanted blood. Revenge. He needed to thrive, needed to destroy those that tried to destroy him. Even as these things contorted and changed, she lingered like a phantom. Always haunting his every move.

Sybil shifted, her breath still fighting to catch up with itself. On shaking, unsteady arms she started to lift herself. Her foot slid, dropping her back to the hard floor. It connected with a discarded book, shoving it across the wood.

The book. The Etched. Their freedom.

Raekin lifted his hand again, once more curling it into a fist. Sybil went rigid. Her head slammed back against the sill of the cracked window. She croaked and gasped, her hands clawing uselessly at her throat where Raekin held her.

This was bigger than her. Bigger than his recessed softness. She could stay in the back of his mind for the rest of eternity, but that didn't negate the fact that he had a job to do. Countless Etched relied on him, needed him to make his own sacrifices for their own good.

He wouldn't leave another girl abandoned as the person she loved was ripped from their life by the demons under the mountain. Even if it meant destroying this one.

His grip tightened. He only had to think of the spikes for her blood to take that form. Razors running through her veins. Her feet started to kick, small cries burrowing their way from her chest. It would hurt, but it would be quick. She deserved quick.

With his arm extended, it drew his attention out of the corner of his eye. Four lines ran along his forearm. Once deep, painful gouges, now nothing more than a shinier shift in pigment. Barely noticeable under the runes and other scars that marred his body. But he saw them. He remembered them. *Felt* them. The lasting memory now drawn on his arm in parallel gouges.

She had tried so hard back then to hold onto him. Her nails biting into his skin and tearing him open. Nothing compared to the pain of the darkness peeling apart his flesh as it dragged him to the Void. Sybil pleaded with him using only her gaze. A mirror image of the expression now plastered on her face, desperate to hold on to what she was losing. Terrified of the horrors out of her control.

"Shit," he snarled. The magic snapped away. She collapsed, gasping. He didn't watch. Didn't dare. She'd survive. She was strong. Stronger than him, apparently. Not even a quick glance back as he slipped through the broken window.

He scraped the putty he'd smeared over the protective runes off the sill. A silent thanks to The Hag for her odd collection of magic. The drop to the stones was far, almost too far. He faltered for a moment, pain shooting through his knees.

Don't think. Don't look back. Just run.

Whatever event Hirnstitch had eavesdropped on must have been finishing up. White warden mantles and extravagant cloaks and gowns started to trickle into the courtyard and out into the surrounding city. Loud voices and uproarious laughter masking the sound of his heavy breathing. It made his back bristle, the noise like ceramic run over metal. Pitiful, pathetic people of the city, wasting the freedoms they were given. Completely ignorant to the darkness. *Disgusting, blind morons gallivanting about.*

He pressed himself up against a wall, closing his eyes and pinpointing the beating hearts that surrounded him. Most of them calm, some fluttering with excitement. But no fear. He was hidden. For now.

He slid along the walls, pausing to feel out the area. Once clear, he shifted from one shadow to the next, keeping his back to the bricks. The grate was only another block or two away, tucked down a back street. He'd escape back into the tunnels, regroup with Hirn.

It wasn't the first time he had skittered around Hazel Gryph's darkest corners. But it was certainly the first time his heart had raced so fast his limbs went numb. All Sybil had to do was raise alarm bells and every single one of these drunken fools would be searching for him.

He stepped around the side of the shop to duck behind the next. As he did, hushed whispers dragged him quickly back.

Shit.

A warden and his partner, their steps unsure and crooked. Arms looped around each other's waist; their weight heavily propped on one another. He'd been too focused on the visceral noises, not on the ones that thrummed in his head. Seconds away from being discovered. It'd be a shame if he spared Sybil's life only to tear away this young, inebriated couple's.

Too close.

The couple was gone, their stumbling stride scraping the loose dirt denoting their departure. He turned in the direction of the alley, picking up speed. The end was near, the grate so close.

A crackle shuddered in the air around him, a shifting in the atmosphere. He froze, the feeling not entirely foreign to him, but the mixture of it was uncanny. A chill swept up from behind him, the exposed skin of his back freezing.

Sybil stood at the end of the road, a few steps away, her body wavering heavily. Blood coated one side of her head, lines of it drawn down her cheek, dripping to stain the bright white leather of her mantle. There was a flare in her eyes, an unsettling mixture of contempt and grief.

Magic flared around her in fits and bursts. Water rose from her skin, freezing in the air before falling back to the ground as rain. Sparks crackled in her fingers, zapping to the ground then cascading up the nearby stone walls. The nearby fire lights flickered, the fires leaping out of their metal cages, swirling around her and returning to the lanterns.

You finally got it. You got everything you wanted.

Raekin watched in awe as the power flared, multiple elements battling for their position at the front of her focus.

She lifted her arm, ice and water fighting at her fingertips, one after the other. Icicles formed, then melted down her forearm. The magic surged, the static flaring in knots of white fire around her hands, the water solidifying and shooting towards him in sharp, icy daggers. They hovered in the air for a moment before melting, the water splashing harmlessly in the dirty street.

Her hand shook as she held it up, her cheeks growing red in the dim light. Then her eyes rolled back, her knees giving out beneath her, hands slapping hard on the stone. The breath coming out of her lungs in sharp, coarse gasps. The magic around her sizzled for a moment, dying out in the air.

Sybil started to lift herself up with her arms, the effort making her elbows wobble, threatening to buckle under the weight. Her eyes met his again, that soft pleading etched on her face. She reached her hand out again, this time palm up. Stretched open and needy.

Raekin stepped towards her, his fingers twitching up before he even realized it. His hand lifted slowly. Just enough that her breath caught. Then he clenched his fist and dropped it back to his side.

Don't.

Too close. Too real. All the horrific things had to stay in focus, had to remind him what was important. She had to stay a shadow, a memory. Nothing more than a sharp hiss on the wind. Let that part of him be slaughtered once more with her pleading eyes.

Dropping to one knee, he pressed his hand into the stone. It rumbled beneath his touch, the rocks fluctuating and morphing in a line towards her. She watched in horror, too weak to scramble away as the shifting stones reached her. The ground opened beneath her hand, swallowing it. The rock reformed around her wrist, binding her to the road.

Raekin let one side of his lips twist up, looking over her one last time. The last thing that he wanted was to walk away from her. Leave her scared and alone all over again. But he needed to. Couldn't let himself falter.

Yet this time, it hurt so much more.

By the time he reached the grate, Raekin's lungs were acid, threatening to burn through his chest. Only a block away but the whirlwind of his magic and fear made it seem like he ran the length of the city. The ladder leading down into the tunnels was no longer a few meters, but hundreds, thousands of rungs appearing out of the darkness one after another. Each descent dragging forth another regret, another panicked, screaming voice in his ears.

What have you done?

The feeling of her blood under his hands.

What have you done?

The horror etched on her face.

What have you done?

That ragged cough as he tore the life from her veins.

When his feet finally hit the stones of the tunnels, the weight of the night settled hard in his stomach. A momentary pause within the panic that let his mind sprint to catch up. It only lasted for a moment before a lilting voice shattered the muted calm.

"Did you get it?" Hirnstitch beamed, stepping to stand underneath the ladder. A smear of blood ran beneath his nose.

Raekin shook his head, glancing up at the metal disc of the grate. It twisted and warped, the thrum in his head making his vision waver. *Too much.* "No, I didn't."

"What!?" Hirn twitched forward, fingers curling tightly at his side. He stopped himself, letting out a slow breath before adjusting himself. "It wasn't there?"

"I was interrupted," Raekin snarled, drumming his knuckles against the brick. "They weren't all at that event."

Hirn muttered a curse. Though he could track the thoughts of those above ground, it was doubtful he would know someone would leave early. Even then, he had no way of letting Raekin know once they were apart, not gifted with the common neuroweaving trait. It was a gamble they always made once they had an initial clear path. It was up to Raekin to remain vigilant once on the surface. And in the event of a stray set of eyes landing on him, they both knew what their orders were.

"But they're dead, right?" Hirn asked. Raekin didn't have to respond. "You left a witness?!"

"There wasn't supposed to be anyone there."

"So, then you kill them. What in the Nether happened? Did they run?"

Raekin walked past him. The centre of the city's runoff channel wasn't the place for this. Not so close to the grate. He couldn't be sure how long until someone came upon Sybil and freed her. She hadn't seen where he went, but options weren't unlimited. Their whispering voices below the city would be a screaming beacon.

"Did you get a good look?" Hirn asked, jogging to catch up. "We can go back up, try and find them. I'm sure they're thinking about you right now. We just pinpoint on that, and *boom.* Rip them to shreds before they get a chance to tell anybody else." His feet sent water cascading up the back of Raekin's pants. The icy cold on his heated skin making prickles crawl up his spine.

"No," Raekin said, pressing his teeth tightly together. "We wait. When it's clear, I'll go back for the book."

Hirn laughed, shaking his head, sending sprinkles of water off the damp ends of his hair. "Sure, whatever you say." When Raekin didn't respond, he stopped. "You're serious? Have you lost your mind? We can't wait, that's moronic. We had the perfect opportunity. How did you, of all the Etched, let it get away?"

Raekin could feel Hirn twitching feverishly beside him. The air around them getting thick and hazy, growing polluted with the heady mixture of their anxieties. Raekin swatted the feeling away, casting a sharp glance at his tremoring partner.

"Deep breath, Hirn. We wait. That's it."

"We need to go back." Hirn stepped in front of Raekin, his hands shaking beneath the overly long sleeves of his tunic. "Who knows how long until the next opportunity? We go back up there, and we kill the waste of skin that made the mistake of seeing you." He stepped back, cracking his neck. Hirn's jaw shuddered for a moment, his lips twitching before the muscles solidified. "I'll start looking now. We can find them, it's not over. Easy, easy." A half-convincing smile stretched over his face, but Raekin could feel the fear lacing through his veins.

"It was her."

The recognition was slow. Hirn's brows slowly raising and pinching as the words mulled their way through his head. His mouth opened and closed a few times, whatever he was trying to get out stuck solid at his teeth. He started to pace, his hands tangling in his dark mess of hair. Raekin reached out to rest his hand on Hirn's shoulder. Meant as a comfort, but too quick, too tight.

Hirn jolted out of his grip. He leaned against the slimy wall of the sewer, running his hands down his face. The air started to deviate, separating and soothing. With every deep breath Hirn took in, the atmosphere evened out. When everything felt clear again, Hirn stood up, brushing his hands off on his ragged pants.

"I get it," Hirn said, rolling his shoulders, letting his face relax, colour flowing back to his inked cheeks. "If it was my sister I would have done the same thing. You have to see how stupid this is, though. If she tells somebody—"

"Then we'll know. You can keep your mind open, see what happens. We do what we came here for. We get the book and we get back to Naz'tak. Nobody has to know she saw me."

Hirn shook his head, his focus drifting off. "What if we get to the deadline? We can't go back empty-handed and if we're late..." Hirn swallowed hard. He absently ran his fingers along the stumps left on his hand. Raekin found himself once more wishing he had never dragged Hirn into this nightmare with him, regardless of the privileges it carried.

Right now, that deadline held every one of their lives on a spike, just teetering and ready to fall. His, Hirn's, even Varena's. She was too tightly clutched in their claws, no doubt Naz'Tak's first target if they missed their week. He couldn't think of that. He had to focus on what he could control, not on what *might* happen to her while he's gone.

Raekin grabbed Hirn's hand, squeezing it gently. "We won't be late. I'll find a way, I promise."

"I know you will," Hirn said, his smile trying to return to his face, though it never reached his eyes. Raekin's gaze flicked to his lips, lingering half a second too long. Hirn exhaled sharply, stepping closer. Too close. Raekin's fingers twitched, his jaw tightening, but he didn't step back at first. Not until he caught the flicker of recognition in Hirn's eyes. He hadn't let himself think about that night for months, but now...

He shoved the memory away before it could take hold. Hirn was speaking again, voice light, but stern, carrying them both away from past dangerous territory.

"If we don't fix this, Naz'Tak is going to find out about her."

"I'll deal with it if it comes to that."

"They won't just kill her. They'll make her wish you hadn't been a coward tonight."

The truth of it was a bitter poison. One he'd need to swallow every time he doubted it. Keep telling himself that it wasn't *her* that kept him going. It was the *idea* of her, and nothing more.

"Then I guess I better make sure they never find her."

Ever.

TEN

The fading voices of those wandering in the night had vanished, leaving Sybil alone. Alone, cold, and furious. She raked her free hand through the blood-crusted mats of her hair. Her fist tightened, the pain reawakening the numbness that had frozen her thoughts.

He was right there. He can't do this to me; this can't be happening again.

The thought of his unsettling irises made her flinch. Was that even Quinn behind them? She had to shake her head roughly to chase the thought away, willing the nightmares to leave the backs of her lids. Every breath she took was shaky and erratic. Her muscles contracted as she forced them to slow, her frantic heartbeat refusing to follow suit.

She had to get the fuck out of the street.

Once her breathing slowed enough that she could cast her magic, she had to pass the next hurdle: casting *specific* magic. Her chattering teeth made it next to impossible to concentrate. The magic kept trying to mitigate it, stealing the fires from within the sparsely lit torches and wrapping it around the fingers of her free hand. It scorched the mantle, the protection of the leather only doing so much to keep the fabric beneath intact. Every time the flames licked her skin she would spew pointless curses at the stones, slapping the fires away.

Finally, the rock started to rumble under her touch. Not enough to fully release, but enough to lessen the squeeze.

With one foot braced on either side of her arm, she leaned back and pulled. Her hand came out slowly, her skin being grated and raked on the stone as it did. She bit her lip, moving the pain somewhere she could control.

A last, brutally agonizing pull, and her hand broke free from the stones. It was raw and red, rashes and cuts littering the surface. Her fingers were pruned, the backs dry and cracked. She balked as she stared at it. In her panic, her magic had flared up in aggravating, belligerent ways.

With a few clenches of her fist, she worked the feeling back into the skin. She'd been pulling the water from her flesh, pooling it beneath the stones. Sheer dumb luck it hadn't frozen beneath the frosted ground. Couldn't afford an emergency run to the infirmary with frostbitten digits.

Time hadn't been on her side. The sky had taken on a pinkish hue at the horizon now, the sun trying to wake the world up. A soft calling of birds echoed from the trees by the Bastion, a taunting, grating song to her ears. The beauty of the dawn serving as a warning. He'd trapped her there, leaving with that smirk on his face. Intent on vanishing into the darkness while the light unravelled around her.

There'd be a few stragglers at this time of morning, but at the very least, she had the waning shadows to hide the blossoming, red stains. She pulled the hood of her mantle up, wrapping it around her head. Though it was matted with her blood, it could still swallow her face in its leather.

There was no clear path Quinn had taken. She had watched him continue down the alley, disappearing around the corner. The wind had taken that sickly sweet, death-marked odor away. There were Wardens that specialized in tracking. Ones that could use their magic to feel differences in the ground or touch the blades of grass that stretched between the stones. Sybil hadn't excelled anywhere close to that, not even grasping the concept when she was given sterile, confined tests. Attempting that magic while chasing a ghost was just another waste of time.

The sun had breached the skyline, the pink hues brightening to oranges and yellows. Time was up. She could already hear the shuffling and motion of more early risers starting their day. She needed a bath, or at least a good dunk in a barrel. Anything to cover up the mayhem that she'd been through. Her first thought was *home* but risking running into Killian made her stomach rise in her throat. She needed to be alone. Hidden from everybody until she could... sort something out.

Alone, or at the very least, with somebody that she could trust. And that someone just happened to live a few streets down from the Bastion.

Her legs ached with every step, but Sybil forced herself forward. The streets were waking now. Shopkeepers hauling carts onto cobblestone, couples stepping to their balconies to take in the morning air. She kept her head down, hiding the bloodstained fabric as best she could, ignoring the way it stuck and pulled against her hair and skin.

By the time she reached Maex's door, it took every effort to lift her arms to knock. Once. Twice. Then over and over until the wood rattled under her fist, the exhaustion being drowned out by the dread. She switched to alternating between hands. The wood started to splinter slightly under her assault, slivers embedding themselves into her skin.

The pain was nothing compared to the headache that had trickled into her skull.

She'd started slumping against the door frame, her knocks sparse and heavy by the time it opened. Maex's hair was tied loosely on her head, the silk wrap drooping lower on the one side like a candle sat in the sun. Her half-lidded eyes took a moment to blink away the confusion before they settled on the shaking figure at her doorstep.

"Sybil?" The foggy rasp to her voice lingered only a second before Sybil's frantic, frazzled state sunk in. Her eyes widened in panic as they fell on the darkening red of the blood soaking the mantle's hood and trailing down the shoulder. "What the fuck happened?" Her voice fractured, and she reached forward for a moment before flinching away, as though unsure where to grab hold.

"It's just... I need to bathe. I don't have time, he's getting away." Sybil's voice was raw, her throat still burning. She didn't wait for a response, only pushed passed Maex's half-stretched arms and stumbling through the open door.

The kitchen sat in the awkward middle light. Too dark for comfort, too bright for candles. The creases and scuffs in the wooden cabinets spreading unusually long shadows along their surface. There was a single bowl, and a single spoon set on the counter, their contents drying along the rims. Two cups on either side of the table, chairs pulled haphazardly back. A nagging sensation crept through her skull, but the urgency quickly shut it out.

"We need to take you to the infirmary. Do you know what the back of your head looks like?" Maex said, gently shifting Sybil's hair, coaxing winces as it pulled her raw scalp. Sybil shrugged it off, the touch sending shock-like shivers through her body.

"I said I'm fine!" Sybil snapped, tearing herself out of Maex's reach. There was a sharp waver in the air, that acrid blend of static and acid settling in the room. Not enough to grasp hold of anything around her, but Sybil still felt that vicious pull of her magic. Maex must have felt it too as her shoulders jolted towards her ears briefly.

Sybil ignored it, a sharp breath between her teeth to ebb back the flare of power. She started on the metal buckle across her collar. The pin was new, its clasp not having been opened and closed hundreds of times, the latch still tight. She grunted, the numb coldness of her fingers only furthering the sharp pains that flared through her wrists.

Maex grabbed her struggling fingers, squeezing them tightly to minimizing the shaking. She lifted the leather, her metal arm clicking on the buckle for only a second before it came undone. "You need to slow down and tell me what happened. Were you attacked? We can go get the captain; he can start a search. Do you want me to get Killian to take you to the infirmary? Is he at home?" There was a pause, a darkness settling over Maex's face. "Did he do this?"

Sybil looked up to see the pleading in her friend's eyes. It barely registered to her as she spun on her heels. Her heart was beating so rapidly in her chest it felt as though everything around her was moving in slow motion. There wasn't time for the rest of the world to catch up with her.

"No, not Killian," she said, moving her attention to the leather straps around her thighs. "We can't talk to the captain either. This can't leave this house, Maex." She bit down on her cheek to still her hands. It only brought that iron taste back to her tongue, followed shortly by a surge of nausea.

"Sybil, you're really starting to scare the shit out of me. Can you just stop and tell me what's going on?"

Sybil stood up, abandoning the straps for a moment. She ran her hands through her hair, her fingers sticking and pulling against the dried blood. "It was Quinn. He's alive and he's… something's wrong with him. He tried to kill me and then didn't, and then did again, and then… we have to find him." Words spilled from her like liquid before she dropped back to the ties on her legs.

There was a beat of silence. Her coarse, sharp breaths the only sound punctuating the air. Then a soft sigh. Maex dropped to a squat, resting her flesh hand on the arch of Sybil's back.

"Sybil, that wasn't him. You know it can't be." Her voice was low, a gentleness to it as she ran her hand along Sybil's back. "Please, we have to go to the captain. Can you remember anything about the man who attacked you? What magic did he have? What about runes?"

"He was all screwed up." Sybil tore her hands through her hair again, her voice rising to a frantic shriek. "But I know what Quinn looks like."

"It was dark, you've obviously hit your head. If you just—" Maex started to try and lead her to the table, but Sybil yanked her arms out of her grasp.

The table started to shake, the wood scraping on the floor. "It *was* him." She shoved Maex away from her. "You of all people should know I'm not—" her voice hitched in her throat. Memories came in flashes. Of shadows crawling towards her, tendrils reaching for her. Tracing their icy ichor across her flesh. She shook her head. "I'm not crazy. I *saw him*."

Maex narrowed her eyes, searching Sybil's. She ran her teeth over her lips. In all the years since the incident, Maex had been the only person Sybil had trusted with the truth. She was the only one that knew where Sybil's magic came from and at what cost. And who paid that cost.

Finally, "Do you know where he went?"

Sybil shook her head. "It was somewhere by the back streets of the Bastion. He disappeared around the back end a few hours ago. I just need more time too look and—"

"The streets around the Bastion are immense. If he's had hours to navigate through the city, he's probably *outside* the city. You can run around all day searching every damn corner but I'm not going to let you kill yourself doing this."

"But if I don't—"

"I don't give a shit, Sybil. You aren't chasing ghosts and shadows all over the fucking city. You're going to sit the fuck down and tell me what happened."

The shock in Sybil's system was starting to dissipate the longer she stood still. It evaporated into the air leaving her nauseous and shaken. Lifting her legs became painful, her knees cracking with every step of her swollen feet. Every rash and scrape littered along the backs of her hands from the stone trap started to pulse and burn in time with her thrumming heart.

With an exasperated breath, Sybil started from the beginning. She went through everything, every detail she could remember. The story flowed out like rancid water. Poison tainting each sentence. The pain seeped in, no longer dulled by panic. Each recalled horror punctured her mind.

Maex sat patiently watching her pace back and forth across the kitchen. Sybil alternated between tangling her fingers in her hair and picking at the skin on her nails. By the time she got to the end, the room was spinning. She collapsed down in the chair, one hand going back to her hair, the other dragging sharp lines on the wood under her grip.

Maex didn't say a word. Just stood up from her seat. Sybil could hear clanking around the kitchen but couldn't tear her eyes away from the surface in front of her. Exhausted and frustrated, thoughts swirling through her mind but none solidifying. It felt locked, frozen in a black abyss of nothingness. Nothing except that visceral image of his rage.

Where has he been all this time? What happened to him? How can he use blood magic? Why did he attack her? And... why did he let her live?

Another clang as a mug was set down in front of her. It was brimming, a hot welcoming vapor drifting off its brim. Its calming peppermint scent swirling around Sybil as she stared at the leaves dancing around each other under the steam. Maex's own cup was clutched in her fingers, a metal finger tapping lightly on the clay. The tone was a soothing ring in the quiet room. It swallowed up the harsh sound of Sybil's coarse, grating breaths forced through her burning throat.

"We need to tell Captain Hertrin," Maex said, taking a sip of her tea. "He can help. Send scouts or something."

One look at Quinn's scarred, inked skin or his unnatural, piercing orange stare and the wardens would have their weapons tearing through his skin. Especially if he used bloodweaving. Sybil couldn't let that happen. She had to know... all of it. She needed another chance. She needed to do it herself.

"No wardens. We need to go after him." Sybil said, shoving her cup away from her.

"You're being stupid. You don't even know where to start." Maex gripped hold of Sybil's hands again, ignoring the mug full of tea teetering towards her.

"We track him. We can—"

"Sybil, stop. You can't do that, and you know it."

"Then what—" Sybil started.

"Ethissa," A small voice said behind her. Sybil stumbled out of her chair, a ripple of lightning running the length of the table. It burned a short, crooked line along the wood. Sybil hissed past her teeth as the heat from the scorched wood snapped backwards through her fingers.

The girl that hovered in the archway to the staircase shrieked at the outburst. Sybil tried to wipe the tingling out of her fingers, but it embedded deep in her skin. Her eyes caught sight of the unsightly scar that now ran the length of the table. She ran her hands down her face, pressing tightly into her eyes.

I need sleep, I need to get control back.

I can't sleep; I have to find him.

The startled girl's short, dark curls were frazzled like a halo around her head. One side of it squished and flattened to her scalp. Her oversized rounded glasses sat crooked on her prominent nose, the frames having bent months ago. Sybil was sure if her wage hadn't gone towards countless pages of script paper and ink, she would have fixed them.

The short tunic she wore hung low, but the girl still tugged uselessly on the hem to cover up her bare thighs. The fingers that gripped the shirt were stained with a multitude of dark inks. They matched the runes and tattoos that ran up and around the girl's legs. Intricate designs on some, others mere flecks of lines and dots, their use lost to Sybil. But most likely known to the apprentice enchanter who bore them.

"Tilly's here," Sybil said, her eyes dropping to the discarded cups on the table.

Two cups. Idiot.

"When is Tilly not here?" Maex asked, cocking her eyebrow.

"How much did you hear?" Sybil groaned, slumping back into her seat, avoiding looking at the damaged wood.

Tilly glanced awkwardly at the floor. "I mean... I heard yelling and I thought... I just wasn't sure what was happening and..."

All of it, then.

"What about Ethissa?" Maex asked, steering the conversation back.

"Ethissa has been around forever, she's seen decades' worth of strange things." Tilly said, shifting under the gazes levelled on her. "And she has all those weird books in the back of the shop that we can't read. I bet she'd be able to at least point you in the right direction."

"That might not be a bad idea. She was there that night, she might know something else." Maex stood from the table, stepping around Sybil towards the stairs. She ran a finger under Tilly's jaw, tilting it towards her and pressing her lips to it. "You work today, yeah?" Tilly nodded sheepishly, her face burning bright from the kiss. "That's easy then. You can tell Ethissa we're coming. See if she can start digging up some of those dusty tomes while we make Sybil look less like a murderer."

"Thank you," Sybil whispered, though her throat felt like it was slowly closing.

With a fair deal of coaxing, Sybil was able to convince Maex to let her bathe alone. Sybil knew her friend was worried, but right now, she needed a moment. She could feel the teetering of her body as she ascended the stairs. Maex's hand held her steady on her lower back, but her pride had taken over, leaning on the railing instead.

It had taken an immense effort to strip off her mantle, her fingers still shaken and numb. She'd almost called out to Maex, but with a groan through her clenched teeth she was able to finally release the clasps. It peeled away from her flesh like a second skin, discarded in a pile in front of the door.

Maex had heated water, and though the warmth was swirling around the small room and kissing her tender skin, Sybil couldn't bring herself to step in it yet. She leaned on the vanity, her gaze locked with her reflection. Staring with such an intensity like she needed to see it, needed to ground herself as her skin stopped feeling like it belonged to her. Deep, dark purple rings had swelled around her eyes, though they were interspersed with red flecks. The pins had fallen out of her hair long ago, the blood holding it tightly as it dried. A splattering mix of *decaying wheat* and darkening blood tangling it up in an array of rolls and knots on her head.

Much to her dismay, no matter how hard she tried, her gaze still dropped to her hip. The rune remained unchanged, a permanent brand of Quinn's death. A death that never happened. She tried closing her eyes, but the rune had burned itself into the backs of her lids. That creeping dread started to trickle in the longer she stayed silent and still. Her fingers pressed over the mark, an old habit, a reassurance. Except there was nothing left to reassure her. It was a lie. It had always been a lie. With a shuddering breath, she covered the rune with her hand.

What the fuck happened, Quinn?

Then, pain; sharp and sudden.

She sucked in a breath, fingers jerking away, but the damage was already done, her hand coming away wet. The blood dripped slowly down her hip, following the delicate curve of the rune. The cut was too perfect, too intentional, but she hadn't meant to do it. She hadn't even thought about it.

A sharp laugh bubbled up in her throat, bitter and humorless. Sarcomancy. She had spent ten years forcing this magic down, willing it into silence. And in the end, it only needed a single crack in her composure to remind her who was really in control. A decade worth of focused, levelled breathing, repeated mantras and alternate outlets all obliterated in one moment. Was this all it would take for her to completely unravel?

Her fingers curled into a fist before she even realized what she was doing. She turned, slamming it into the wooden boards with a force that rattled through her bones. Pain flared up her wrist, but it was a pain that was hers. Something she could still feel.

Something she could still control.

ELEVEN

Sybil sang pointless, childish songs at the top of her lungs as she bathed, no doubt to the utter horror of Maex's poor ears. It seemed to be the only way to stop her fluctuating emotions from wreaking more havoc on Maex's house with magic. Every panicked thought was banging on the closed-in walls of her mind. Their incessant rampage threatening to buckle Sybil the rest of the way over the edge.

Maex lent her a pair of baggy trousers and a loose-fitting tunic. Her mantle couldn't be worn in the bright daylight until the stains were gone. Which would more than likely be permanent on the bright leather.

Nobody was quite sure when Ethissa's shop had appeared. One day, it just *was*. Nestled neatly between the decrepit tearoom and a herbologist. Over time, the entrance had flourished, blossoming into its own entity. The trove of oddities and relics that were bolted to the sill dragged eyes immediately away from the neighbouring shops. But all the whimsy in the world wouldn't stifle the faint humming of magic permanently etched in the shop's bones.

Ethissa's name was written above the shop in exaggerated swoops and lines of ink. Each letter was wrapped and decorated in symbols from her home country, few of which she had taught Sybil the meaning of. Their mystery matched the sketchbook of scattered lines, dots and curves that decorated the door. Runes Ethissa had engraved herself. Just pushing on the door made Sybil's skin feel a rush of energy and static, like it was testing her with just the touch.

Sybil was hit with the scent of the incense that burned from the back of the shop. A heavy air hung at the top of the room, fogging the steel lanterns that dangled from the roof, their dim light barely kissing the traffic worn floor.

Purples and blues hung in heavy tapestries across most of the walls. The few bare spaces held shelves that were threatening to collapse under the weight of the many relics and ingredients that floated or sat in bottles and bowls across their dark wood.

Alchemy was known to most as a farce magic, but that didn't stop the masses that flowed in and out of the doors searching for a cure to whatever ailed them. None of them were privy to the secret behind all her magical mixes: nothing more than runes carefully engraved inside the bottles. The mystique that she cultivated around her smoky shop was enough to garner her a trail of intrigue and mystery that made whispers follow her wherever she went. This, of course, delighted the old woman.

Tilly was already leaned against the counter. Her hair had been run through with oils since Sybil saw her, smoothing out her tight curls. A fresh blouse adorned her torso, tucked haphazardly into a rough-hewn skirt that trailed down to her ankles. There was a brush poised in her hand above crinkled parchment. Her wrist shook slightly with trepidation as she went to press the ink into the paper. At the last second, she adjusted her grip, moving the brush further up the half-finished rune. The burn marks that littered her dark skin were most likely her reason for hesitation.

Enchanters had to either research symbols through trial and error or be passed along knowledge from others. Since trial and error usually resulted in maiming or death, few were truly willing to experiment in the magic. Which was why apprenticeships were so sought after: let somebody else do the experimenting and coast along behind them.

Ethissa wasn't like that.

She wanted her apprentices to respect the craft. Learn and accept the dangers on their own. Her previous attempt at a protégé had lost all his hair, almost cut off his fingers, and changed the composition of the wood on the counter, making it burn through flesh with a single touch. He quit shortly after that, and that was when Tilly was taken on.

As they approached the counter, a nearby talisman hanging from a string started to swing. It would hover momentarily over the metal symbol etched on the stone placard. Then it would spasm, fluctuating between all the other carvings, before hovering back over 'metal' only to resume its flailing dance shortly after.

The sudden movement drew Tilly's eyes, narrowing at the device as it twitched on its little string. The distraction shifted her attention just enough that her shaking hand dipped low, the brush touching the page lightly. The half-finished rune erupted into ash, the paper following soon behind it. A sharp shriek burst from her lips. When Maex and Sybil caught her eye, she jumped, then let out a curse as her face burned red.

"Didn't hear you come in," she said, her small voice catching. Tilly glanced solemnly at the remnants of ash atop the counter, twisting her mouth back and forth. Sybil wasn't a stranger to Tilly's attempts at enchanting. She had a few damaged, incomprehensible runes on her legs from letting Tilly practice. They were mixed and mottled into the more professional ones Ethissa had added after. A free of charge service for letting Tilly potentially mutilate her.

"I'll go tell Ethissa you're here," Tilly said, sweeping the ashes off the counter and onto the floor.

"You told her why we're here?" Sybil asked as Tilly blew the rest of the mess off the surface.

"I tried to." Tilly shrugged. "I think she understood that you wanted to talk to her. You know what she's like. I don't think she heard a word otherwise."

Tilly went to turn from the counter, but stopped, narrowing her eyes at the brush. She readjusted how it was lying on the counter by the tiniest degree. Seemingly satisfied, she pushed through the purple curtains behind her, but not before casting a sideways glance at the brush before the curtain took it from her sight.

The shop seemed to come alive as Ethissa dramatically pushed back the fabric moments later, Tilly close on her heels. Ethissa barely looked a day over seventy, though she was approaching her thirteenth decade. She'd had her hair trimmed short, what little length pulled tightly into a tie at the nape of her neck, the whites and greys vibrant against the dark inks that ran along her temples and down to her jaw. The tattoos continued down her neck and disappeared into the collar of her long silk robe. With every step it swished open, showing off the silk slippers that hugged her feet.

Though a yawn tried to split her lips apart, Ethissa held it tight. A spark lit her eyes as they met with Sybil, widening with excitement. She danced her fingers in the air as she stepped up to the counter, pressing her elbows to the wood. "Sybil, my sweet girl. What brings you to brighten an old woman's day?" She narrowed her gaze, mischief flashing across her dark irises. "What am I fixing this time?"

The missing magic of the runes had faded so far to the background, Sybil had completely forgotten about it. She ran her lip between her teeth as she decided whether to show the woman. Her runes weren't important. Getting answers was. Before she could choose, Ethissa snatched up her arm and pulled back her sleeve. The damaged runes had almost bled completely into her skin at this point, their meaning lost to her flesh.

Ethissa only let out a heavy breath, tutting then roughly turning Sybil's arm over. "Come to the back, we'll set you in the chair."

"There's something we need to talk about," Sybil said, pulling her arm back and glancing quickly around the empty shop, pausing on the still closed door. "I don't have time."

Few people were remaining after the Tabrasian-Plaitian war. Ethissa's gifts had kept her going all these years, leading her to be one of the oldest people living within Plaitius. Maybe even all of Crae Vost. Countless runes engraved into her own skin that only she could craft. They held her body together like hundreds of stitches constructed of ink.

"We have nothing but time, don't be ridiculous." With a quick spin of her slipper, she vanished back beyond the curtain before Sybil could protest. Tilly shrugged her shoulders, then turned to Maex, abandoning her runic practice.

Multiple bottles of inks, salves and cleaners lined the far wall of Ethissa's room. Most people overlooked the symbols and marks as nothing more than spell craft, but clever eyes could see it for what it was. It was an art form, and Ethissa was one of the masters.

Candles were strewn about the room, casting the fabric-draped chair in a soft glow. A rolling shelf was tucked next to it, its lip tucked neatly beneath the arm rest. Atop it was an assortment of different sizes of magnifying glass, each a different thickness and curve. Ethissa's needles were already on display. Each one was laid out on the leather strip atop the shelf, equidistant from one another, their placement measured and precise. Sybil winced as she stared at their sharp points, already remembering the feeling of them puncturing her skin.

"Sit," Ethissa ordered, her back to Sybil, rummaging through an assortment of bottles.

"Can you just stop for a second?" Sybil stepped towards her, reaching out, only for Ethissa to wisp out from under her hand and shuffle to the other wall.

"In a moment." A sharp snap back, followed by more clattering as Ethissa jammed a few bottles underneath her arm.

Sybil pressed her teeth tightly together, her patience twisting and pulling into a tight line before it finally snapped. "Quinn is alive."

The clattering stopped. Ethissa's fingers stilled over the bottles, but she didn't straighten right away. Instead, she ran a hand along the shelf, thumb tracing the ridges of an old vial.

"Hmm." The sound was noncommittal, but the way her shoulders stiffened betrayed her.

Sybil waited. The silence stretched too long. Finally, Ethissa sighed through her nose and straightened, but her hands were slower, more careful now. She grabbed two more vials and turned back to the chair, her gaze levelled on the floor.

"That's all?" Sybil growled as the woman started to gently place the bottles on the rolling cart. "Hmm? Not 'How do you know?'"

Ethissa dropped her small shoulders, her head craning up to the ceiling as she let out a heavy breath. "Just sit. This seems like a much longer conversation that I don't feel like having standing and flailing into the air." She finally looked at Sybil, and for a split second, Sybil swore her gaze dropped to her hip.

The movement like a sharp chill along Sybil's spine. Ethissa knew of the rune's creation, knew of the anguish that followed when Sybil woke with the ink. But the quick, almost purposeful way Ethissa narrowed to its location made her back bristle.

"You know something, don't you? Did you always know he was alive? Do you know what happened to him? Do you know why he's all messed up? What about the bloodwea—"

"Goodness, Sybil! *Twaheind, ab ain mod toil!*"

Sybil flinched at the phrase so often used against her as a child. A Frew Braxian phrase, which she always found odd coming from the mouth of someone from across the seas. Far, far away from the nation of Frew Braxus. *Two hands but one mind works.* Or, as she had so politely explained years ago: *Shut up small child, I can't focus on everything at once.*

Sybil let a sharp breath squeeze through her teeth, speaking from between her clenched jaw. "Can you please tell me what you know?"

"Sit."

Ethissa had only grown more stubborn with each of her thirteen decades. A truth that had infuriated Sybil throughout her young life. If sitting in the stupid chair was what Ethissa wanted, she'd be more likely to abandon Sybil entirely than let her mind be changed.

With a hefty eye roll, Sybil dropped into the chair. Ethissa kicked the lock and the chair fell back, the footrest springing upwards, stretching Sybil out vertically. Her fingernails instinctively gripped the wood of the rounded ends of the arm rests. They dug into the perforated indents marred and shaped by hundreds of clients' nails. The toughest of Wardens would flinch at the touch of the needle, no matter how much they claimed otherwise. Sybil was sure Ethissa got some sort of sick elation out of watching grown men squirm.

Sybil pointed at the blurry, blotched amorphous blobs under her flesh. "That one was for quiet footsteps and—"

"I know. I always know," Ethissa muttered, her fingers dancing over her assortment of needles, not bothering to follow Sybil's finger. Seemingly satisfied, she plucked one up from the leather. With one hand, she popped the cork on the vial filled with swirling black ink. Held up to the light, you could see the traces of ground-up minerals and herbs Ethissa mixed. She insisted they made the ink more potent, but it sounded like more hogwash.

After dipping the needle into the ink, she swirled it a few times. With thumb and forefinger, she pulled Sybil's skin taught. There was the slightest shake to them as she carefully brought the needle to the skin, hesitating for only a moment before starting.

Every muscle in Sybil's body tensed, pain flaring through her, radiating from the sharp needle. The room was silent, so much so she swore she could hear it as it broke through her flesh. It pierced through the first layer, imbedding the ink below as though her skin was just another amorphous liquid.

With each press of the needle, the ink settled, then spread. A fine line tracing through her veins as the magic of the runes merged with flesh. When the needle was removed, the line was complete, the capillaries of ink solidifying and darkening. The decorative tattoos that wrapped around her legs and across her back had been painful, but nothing compared to runes. The magic felt like liquid fire travelling beneath your skin and flooding through your veins. A brief warmth that swelled to a searing heat.

The wood cracked and popped under Sybil's grip as she tightened her fingers on the pommels. "Will you tell me now?" she seethed through tightly clenched teeth, using the words to pull her mind away from the sensation that carved through her spine.

Ethissa stopped her movements, hovering above Sybil's skin. She blew out between her lips. "You're sure it was—"

"It was him. He attacked me, but I don't think he recognized me. Not at first. Then he ran and... I lost him."

Ethissa pressed her lips into a line, her eyes narrowing in on the rune she was constructing. The tremor in her fingers had vanished, her movements more fluid. "You think I know why he is alive?"

"You were there after, you saw what was left of my room." Sybil hissed through clenched teeth. "If anybody knows anything about what happened that night, it's you."

"And Maiten," Ethissa corrected.

"My father won't talk about it." She forced her eyes open, rapidly blinking away the foggy sheen. Ethissa's focus left her work, drifting down Sybil's body, landing on her hip again, fixated on the layer of clothing that hid the first rune etched on her body. Sybil opened her mouth to say something, but Ethissa pressed the needle in once more, almost too far, rattling her and evaporating the thoughts.

"I was there," she started, readjusting her seat. "By the time I got there, Quinn was gone. Nothing left of him but the massacre on the walls and floor."

Sybil bit her lip, wincing. "Then how do you explain what I saw? You know things that the rest of Crae Vost has forgotten ten times over. Tell me, Ethissa. Why do you seem not even slightly surprised that he is alive?" The shortest pause, but Sybil could see the way Ethissa worked her teeth over her lips. The heavy weight settled on her shoulders. "You knew..."

"Other people have vanished like Quinn. Hundreds even. But you span those numbers over decades, and nobody really takes notice."

"Wait, this has been happening forever? And nobody has done anything about it? Does anybody else know?" Sybil jerked forward, her heart racing. Ethissa had to pull her needle back, glaring through her brows until Sybil lay back in the seat. "I know, I know. *Twaheind, ab ain mod toil.*"

Ethissa shot a sharp laugh through her nose. "It hasn't been happening *forever*, impatient whelp. When the war ended, everyone was too busy celebrating to notice. We had won, Kreb had done the impossible."

"Killing thousands in Tabrasia. I know."

Ethissa tsked through her teeth, and gave a sharp shake of her head before continuing. "The disappearances were slow at first, but it started to pick up after a few months. Mages would go missing, vanishing seemingly into thin air. Not a trace left behind. But only mages, never *leerteks*. A lot of them were promising pupils, their magic not having fully formed yet before they disappeared."

Ethissa straightened, rolling her shoulders before continuing. "Years went by, and the numbers were never plentiful enough to garner attention further than a select few of us that started to connect the dots. 'Oh,' they'd say. 'They were just accidents.' 'They were just Tabrasians fleeing persecution.' But we knew better. As time went on, fewer and fewer of us remained that even remembered the war. Soon I was the only one left. And the only one that had seen this pattern."

"What changed from the war then?"

"As I said, Kreb had done the impossible. The magic that was cast to destroy the Tabrasian army was beyond any enchanter's capability, even the great Kreb Bolorick. Nearer the end of the war, Kreb had become desperate. Maniacal even. Spouting off about the Void and the Nether. We had joked before, sure, but I never thought it'd be taken seriously."

"The Void was what we thought killed Quinn. You think they were involved in the ending of the war?"

Ethissa shrugged her shoulders, then wiped the needle off on the hem of her skirt. "We know little to nothing about the creatures that reside in the mountains." She let out a heavy sigh, pushing her stool back from the chair and crossing her arms.

"Kreb was desperate, but I never thought it would result in such drastic measures. Callous, careless twit."

"It still ended the war. Besides, he was killed right after. It couldn't have been malicious."

"Bah. Kreb's death was too easy a punishment for such a thoughtless spell," Ethissa spat. She glanced up at Sybil through her brows. She flapped her hand, chasing the thought away. "I was doubtful too that the Void had anything to do with the disappearances. Just a fantastical story. That was... until you described what happened after Quinn foolishly read from that book."

"What do you mean?"

"Shadowed arms grabbing hold of him? Pulling him through the floor? That doesn't sound like a cautionary children's tale to you? Why would he be dragged through the ground if he was just a sacrifice to be slaughtered?"

"You think..."

"I think that the Void has been taking powerful mages for decades. I don't believe that they killed Quinn. I think they took him."

Sybil felt her blood run cold. The Void were kept as a horrifying story, one to scare even the unruliest of children. But they always ended the same: the Void are trapped in the Peaks. We are safe. They can't get us.

The runes and scars that marred Quinn's body, the hate in his eyes before he recognized her. A nightmare etched into his skin like a scary story come to life.

And she had let him hand himself to them like a fresh piece of meat.

"He's been down there for ten years," Sybil choked out. Her hands started to shake, her stomach twisting tightly in sharp knots. "What have I done?"

"We aren't going back to that dark place again," Ethissa said, reaching across to rest her hand gently on Sybil's thigh. "Quinn was a powerful geomancer. Who knows how long they had their eyes on him."

"Bloodweaver," Sybil muttered.

Ethissa's face paled, a stark contrast to the dark ink. Her fingers shook, the needle barely held between her knuckles. "What did you say?"

"He's a bloodweaver. He—"

"Tsst!" Ethissa started to look around the room, her eyes wide. She stood, tossing the needle into the nearby bin. "We do not speak of these things within the gates of the city." She snarled.

"But—"

"But nothing. Even *my* walls can grow ears."

"What do I do?" Sybil hated how small her voice sounded. "How do I fix this?"

Ethissa turned, putting her vials away and rolling her needles in the leather strip. "Nothing. You forget you ever saw him." Her eyes fluctuated again to Sybil's hip, lingering a little too long. "We all want answers, but there are some questions that shouldn't be asked. You don't know what they would invite in. You say he ran when he recognized you? Then you know that's what he would want."

Sybil grabbed Ethissa's arm, pausing her cleanup, making her face her. The woman stood over a head below her, yet Sybil always felt like a child in her presence. Ethissa had been the only one that had been there for her, trying to hone the frantic powers that had suddenly been thrust on her overnight a decade ago.

She'd given her elixirs to calm her nerves and tamp the magic back down; she'd engraved runes on her that would help heighten her focus and soften her reach for the power. Ethissa had hidden her from the rest of Trelusk for weeks after Quinn's so-called death. She had helped her work through the overabundance of emotion that wreaked havoc in bouts of elements shot from her fingers. Sybil owed a great deal to her, but this wasn't something she could just let go, no matter how much she respected her guardian's words.

"I need answers. Something. You didn't see him, Ethissa. What they did to him. It was—" She shook the image out of her head. "I can't just walk away."

Ethissa turned, staring at the dim light that filtered in through the sheer fabric of the curtain draped in front of the tiny window. Her age suddenly vivid on her face, the secrets and mystery finally catching up to her and weighing her down. Sybil had never seen her look so frail, so tired. Thirteen decades was a long time to live, and only a fraction of it was known by the rest of the world. Wars, isolation, refuge. Ethissa had lived through it all. Sybil only knew a drop of her life beyond the tiny shop in the centre of a dying street in a busy city. A guilt had always clawed at the back of her neck from not learning more of her caretaker's life.

"Quinn was a good boy. He could have been..." Ethissa's face flushed again as she brought her hands to Sybil's face. "I can't give you the answers you want, love. Not here. But I might know where you can get some."

TWELVE

The air in the sewers was thick with damp rot, the scent of stagnant water and mildew clinging to Raekin's lungs like an infection. It wasn't the filth that suffocated him today, though. It was the memory of hazel eyes, haunted with a crushing mix of fury and fear. Every time he blinked, they were waiting on the backs of his lids.

He'd done what he needed to do. He knew that. He just wished that she wouldn't be so prolific at possessing his thoughts. Even now, though he told himself not to care, he wondered: was she okay? Did someone help her?

And did she just go back to pretending he was dead?

"Still thinking about her?" Hirn asked.

Raekin didn't bother looking up from the greenish, blackened spores. "You said you weren't going to pry into my head," he snarled.

There was shuffling, enough to draw Raekin's waning attention. Hirn lifted himself off the dank ground, crossing his arms. "Do you really think I had to look in your mind to figure that out?"

"Have you heard anything?" Raekin said, ignoring the needling and noting the small smear of blood under Hirn's nose.

"Arcaneum is crawling with wardens while they clean up *your* mess."
He narrowed his eyes. "Maybe we'll get lucky and there will be another
chance this century."

"Once night hits, I'll go up there and find you something to keep
you busy. In the meantime, go fuck yourself if you're so bored." Raekin
meant for it to sting, or at least make a mark. But Hirn didn't so much
as flinch.

There was a heavy pause before Hirn spoke. His eyes narrowed, his
voice sharp. "Are you with us?"

"What kind of moronic question is that? Of course I am. I already told
you this changes nothing."

Hirn rubbed his jaw, the runes on his cheeks twisting with his skin.
"Sure, sure. But now you know. She's here. Just out of reach, right?
What's stopping you from going up there and checking in? Have some
torrid affair wrapped in nostalgia?"

"Give it a rest, Hirn." Raekin shifted his back on the wall, lolling his
head back to stare at the stained stones above.

"Are you going to admit that you've been thinking about it?" His
tone darkened. "How easy it would be for you to get distracted for just
a second too long?"

Raekin snapped his gaze down. "What are you getting at? You think
I'm going to do something idiotic to risk everything? Just for *her?*"

Hirn shrugged, stepping away from the stones, kicking his foot up
lazily. "You already did once." Raekin felt the heat rise in his face.
Hirn stepped forward again, tipping at his waist with a shit-eating grin.
"Maybe you'll get lucky, and you can fuck her before Naz'Tak tears off
her skin."

Raekin reacted before his thoughts could fully form. One moment Hirn was goading, the next he was grunting as his back hit stone. The crack of the impact echoed through the tunnels, sending loose debris tumbling from the damp ceiling. Raekin held his forearm to Hirn's chest, pressing hard against the softer bones. He didn't need to, though. He could already feel his magic gently threading through Hirn's veins. He held him there for a moment, feeling the control. The power.

His magic surged and flexed beneath Hirn's flesh, twisting and turning through the fluid that flowed with each beat of his heart. A single twitch of his wrist. A thought. All it would take, and he could wrap the arteries around his friend's bones, snapping his ribs into shards. He didn't need to touch Hirn's flesh to tear it apart. Blood obeyed his command like a hound on a leash.

But Hirn didn't react the way he should have. He didn't flinch, didn't shove back. He just tilted his head, and smirked. Raekin's hands on him. The damp air. Hirn's back pressed against the stone. Too similar.

Something cold slithered down Raekin's spine. Not fear. Something worse. *Recognition.* The icy touch clung to his skin, sharp as it had been *that* night. The distant crackle of a fire flickered in his mind's eye, shadows dancing over a face he knew too well. The feeling coiled around him, tightening. Then, with the acrid sting of magic, it pulled him under. The past slammed into him like a fist.

It had been months ago now. Raekin had known it would be a mistake the moment it happened. He had gotten too close. Hirn's laughter, Hirn's smile, Hirn's optimism. It had been intoxicating him for years and in such a lonely world, it had been near impossible not to lean into. Years spent chained to the same nightmares had built up strong bonds, coaxing Raekin further down a path the Void would kill him for. More likely worse.

Times were bleak. Everything had started to look hopeless. The Hag hadn't come up with their next step in months. Naz'Tak started to take out the frustration on Raekin. Every waking moment spent in dreaded anticipation of what creative punishment his master had imagined for him.

Hirn and he had finally been given a minor reprieve. A stint to the outer villages of Frew Braxus to steal supplies. A temporary escape, but one that was vital for Raekin to take a breath. He was frustrated. Terrified. Furious.

And Hirn was there when he needed him.

The cave walls dripped with condensation, the scent of wet stone clinging to the air. Shadows flickered over Hirn's face from the campfire, twisting the sharp angles of his jaw into something softer. Hirn had told him he would be there for him. Told him everything would be alright. Always in that tone that could satiate the biggest cynic. When Raekin acted, it was a rash, impulsion taking over logical sense.

Raekin slammed Hirn against the rock, the impact sending a sharp thrill through him. Their bodies collided, heat against cold stone, breath stolen between them. Thoughts abandoned him as his lips crashed with Hirn's, a clash of desperation and hunger. His hands ran through Hirn's dark hair, fingers tangling in thick strands. Pulling him closer as if to anchor himself in something real. The rest of their wretched world could burn. All except for the feeling of their skin together. A stolen ember in the frost that had encircled his soul.

Hirn had stopped him. A slow, deliberate press of fingers to Raekin's chest. Gentle but firm. Breaking his heated, passionate and utterly thoughtless abandon.

"Don't," Hirn had whispered, his pale orange eyes filled with the twisted flames from the dying fire. Not a hint of the unrelenting passion reflected at Raekin. Just cold pressure.

It stung at the time. Every half cast glance after feeling like treason. It wasn't disgust that built the gap between them, only a new outward honesty Raekin had wished he'd kept to himself. The kiss had been impulsive. Maybe stupid. But the moment Hirn had pulled back, had made it clear he didn't feel the same, Raekin had buried it with everything else.

He'd buried it deep. Locked away in his mind. Hidden until he caught sight of the sharp grin on Hirn's face as he pinned him to the tunnel walls beneath Hazel Gryph. A knowing look that felt like fire scorching his skin. Hirn's smirk widened.

The memory wrapped around his throat like a noose, his breath choked. Raekin's fingers twitched, a surge of power coiling under his skin, demanding release. For a moment, he swayed between instinct and restraint, heat crawling up his spine like fever.

Then he let go. Staggered back, shaking off the weight of it. Revulsion twisted in his gut. Not at the memory. At how effortlessly Hirn had used it against him.

"You're a bastard," Raekin muttered, voice hoarse.

Hirn tilted his head further, watching Raekin like he was studying him, waiting for him to put the pieces together. He rolled his shoulders, dusting himself off, looking obnoxiously unbothered. "Huh." His voice was light, thoughtful. "You really never learn, do you?"

Raekin clenched his jaw so hard his teeth hurt. "Shut up."

"Jump in headfirst," Hirn said, lilting and amused. "Act before you think. Feel everything all at once." He made a soft clicking noise with his tongue. "Still throwing yourself into things like you don't know how to stop. Especially things dictated by the brain between your legs."

"Shut the fuck up, Hirn." Raekin warned, already feeling the tunnel walls swelling as his power gripped hold of the stones.

"So, tell me: does she know?" Hirn's grin changed, shifting into something dangerous. "Does she know that when you love, you don't stop? You just fall hard, like a reckless idiot?"

Raekin's fist twitched, just a fraction of an inch, but enough that Hirn caught it. His smirk sharpened like a blade. Raekin exhaled, forcing the fury that was burning through him back down. Forcing himself to be still, be level.

"That's what I thought," Hirn chuckled, tilting his head back.

"You have no idea—" Raekin stopped. He'd been so preoccupied with Hirn's bullshit he hadn't been keeping a sense out to the tunnels around them. Now, trying to calm his own heart, he felt more thudding nearby.

He didn't have to say a word, only a single look to Hirn and they were both already moving. Raekin put his hands on the wall, breaking open the stones and shifting them back from the dirt beyond. The noise was violent and racked through the sewers like an earthquake, but it was their only option. The molhunds were back at the entrance to the nether tunnels. No way to reach them without colliding into whatever beings were approaching their small hideaway. It was hide or kill whatever morons decided to take a leisurely stroll through the underground.

Hirn stepped through the gap in the stones first, and after a quick glance back, Raekin followed. The childish bickering ending immediately as they squeezed into the small space, silencing themselves as they listened beyond the walls.

The noise was enough, whoever was out there was running now, their heartbeat racing. Except they were running towards the noise.

Wardens.

He counted the heartbeats, matched them to the growing noise of footsteps. Not just a random patrol, there were four of them. If a single one of them was a geomancer they'd be able to figure out what happened in a second.

"What the hell was that?" A voice called out from just beyond the wall. Raekin reached out with his magic, feeling each of them. They'd feel a chill, then a strange creeping sensation travelling up their spine, but nothing more. At least that's how Hirn had described it. How it felt when he threaded his magic through Hirn's blood, hovering in stasis and waiting to grab hold.

"A carriage on the street above?" Another voice, a woman. "Look at all the debris. These tunnels are crumbling. We shouldn't even be down here."

"Agreed," A third voice, shaking and croaking. Raekin could feel them shivering. "This place gives me the creeps. Let's get this sweep done and get out." Raekin eased his grip off, letting the tension go.

"Hold on, we were given an order. These sewers have been up for decades. They aren't going to crumble right this second. We should at least look around." The fourth, a hint of Losweau accent. Raekin quietly cursed the owner. There was shuffling of steps, some assured, others quiet and careful. Then, "Why are there so many footprints down here?"

Raekin's pulse raced. He pressed his hand to the wall, preparing to tear it down. He could take hold of their blood without seeing, but it was risky. Grab the wrong blood or not grab enough of it and allow them to run. It'd be easier, quieter, and quicker if he put eyes on them. The stone trembled lightly under his touch, the minerals liquefying and solidifying in rapid succession. He'd tear down the wall and tear out their throats in three quick beats of his heart.

Like tying the laces on his boots. Taught, but ingrained so deeply in his muscles he barely had to think to do it. His fingers twitched against the rock. The veins would tighten; the oxygen would stop. They'd collapse to the ground, clawing uselessly at their skin. He felt it start. Just a twitch, barely anything. He stopped himself. Forced the breath through his teeth. *Not yet.*

"This place is a cesspool of transients. Come on, Giordin. There's nobody here."

There was a silence, a beat where all Raekin could hear was the thudding in his own chest. The four outside pulses fading to the background of his mind.

"Fine. But we aren't going back up, we have to at least be able to *say* that we searched everywhere," the Losweauian said.

Raekin let out the breath he had been holding, his head swimming as it caught up. Their footsteps vanished into the silence, followed shortly by their heartbeats. He waited another few moments before letting the power flow from his hand. The rocks shifted and twisted, opening the small hole in the wall. He tumbled out of it, taking in a deep breath of the stagnant tunnel air.

"Are you done being a piece of shit?" Raekin asked over his shoulder, trying to steady his racing pulse.

"For now. Better me than Naz'Tak, right?" Hirn beamed. "Are you done brooding?"

Raekin cast him a sharp look, but let it go. He could see the red stains now massively smeared over the lower half of Hirn's face. "What did you hear?"

"Not much. They got orders to look for a rogue mage or something. They're nervous, though, I could barely get a straight thought out of any of them," Hirn chuckled. "One of them was holding in a fart."

Raekin rolled his eyes. "Anything useful?"

"Not really. Unless…" Hirn squinted an eye, staring up at the ceiling with the other. "They were thinking about who gave them the orders. Have you heard of 'The Bauers'?"

THIRTEEN

"You can't be serious," Killian said, standing abruptly from the bed and running his hands through his hair.

He'd barely spoken, barely moved, while Sybil spilled the entirety of her past. All the secrets, all the unanswered questions coiled tightly on her psyche. Only retorting when she told him exactly why she needed his help to unravel them. But the request was where he drew the line. "Even if all of that is true, what you're asking me to do is treason."

"Only if they find out," Sybil stood, moving into his eye line, pleading with him. "It will only be a few days, I promise."

"You expect me to drop to the feet of my grandparents and request a hiatus without cause? My family will be furious. *Hertrin* will be furious."

Sybil gritted her teeth. "You were willing to beg them when you thought I was going to be stripped of my rank, how is this any different?"

"Because you are asking to go find out about what happened to a previous lover that..." He glanced around the room before lowering his voice, "*stole* a grimoire and cast *illegal* magic. That isn't just asking them to forgive a small mistake. The Portcullis has executed mages for less."

The secrets that circled around Quinn's disappearance were tethered to her soul. Every second that passed they seemed to unravel, scattering into the ether. A decade had passed with her guilt weighing her down and crushing her spirit; not even saving a life had mitigated the pain. If she could have some sort of finality that went beyond Quinn being shredded to pieces, she might finally feel whole again.

Those answers were in Trelusk. A half a day's ride if she pushed her horse hard. But even then, she couldn't leave her station so abruptly. Not without a good reason. And any mention of Maiten would only bring about more questions. Which was why she was now grovelling at the feet of the man whose grandparents could enforce anything with a flick of their jeweled wrist.

"Please, Killian." She gripped his shoulders, tiny sparks dancing between her fingers as her magic threatened to pour out of her again. "I've spent the last ten years trying to make up for his death. I need to find out if what I've done was worth whatever he's been suffering instead."

Killian ran his hands down his face, looking anywhere but at her. "And what if you don't get the answers you want? What if you realize that your... gifts are worth nothing compared to what has happened? What if whatever you find out isn't worth putting your life at risk? *My life* at risk." He dropped his arms and shifted out of her grasp. His gaze hovered on the window of their bedroom, distant as he took in the fading light. "What would my life be worth to you? Would you sacrifice me to the Void to make yourself captain?" For a moment, surprise flicked across his face, almost taken aback by his own words. With a quick shake, it was gone.

"It wasn't like that."

"Wasn't it?!" The volume made her flinch, her shoulders curling into her neck. "You let him die for power, what's stopping you from doing it again?"

"Killian, you know me. *Us.* You can't seriously believe I would—"

Killian's voice dipped lower, rawer. "I can't believe I trusted you." The words stabbed, and that should have been enough. Should have been the final strike. He scoffed, stepping back like she was something filthy. "I told you everything, I gave you everything. All this time together and you couldn't even trust me with this. With any of it."

Sybil's stomach twisted. The air around her crackled, ice threading through her fingers against her will. It lanced up her wrists, crawling along her veins like frostbite. Her breath hitched sharply. Cracks spiderwebbed beneath her feet, splintering outwards. Killian's hand twitched towards his mantle, fingers brushing the dagger at his side. That snapped her out of it. She clenched her fists, forcing the magic back down. The ice shattered, melting away like it had never been there.

"I'll lie for you," Killian said, letting his hand drop from the blade. He adjusted the collar of his mantle, not turning to face her. "You can go to Maiten and get your answers. But... Don't expect me to wait around for whatever version of you comes back. I'll get your shit sent to the Bastion."

"Killian—"

He held his hand up. "Don't." The air hung heavily around him as he searched her face. He opened his mouth, but thought better of it, only shaking his head once more before disappearing from the room.

"That smarmy little twat said that?" Maex asked, pulling a little too hard on the strap of the saddle bag, the leather stretching and creaking from the pressure. Thankfully that bag only contained spare clothes and the blankets for her pallet. It could take the strain, but Sybil still winced. She didn't bother responding, just threw her bedroll atop the back end of her mare and strapped it to the saddle.

Maex had finished loading the other saddlebag with supplies, being gentler on the strap that held the food tight to the horse's back flank, though her face didn't hide the fury-laced hurt. Sybil could feel the thick air of disapproval that swam around her friend's head like smoke. She was thankful for the help but could do without the constant barrage of unsaid judgement that came with it.

"To have the gall to insinuate you got your magic from some personal vendetta. How old was his uncle when that crook enchanter murdered him to pass along the power to Killian?" Maex snarled.

"Hey!" Sybil hissed. "Keep your voice down."

"It's true, Syb. Just because his uncle surrendered his life willingly, doesn't make it any less unspeakable. It wasn't like you *forced* Quinn to read that book." Maex's face softened as it met hers. "I'm sorry, I didn't mean—"

"It's fine." Sybil said, barely above her breath as she finished off the last pack.

Maex let out a heavy breath. "Is there anyway I can talk you out of this? You could even just wait until tomorrow. Get a night's sleep."

"I'm fine," she muttered again. She tugged the fresh mantle's leather strap tighter. Only one more left now, the blood soaked one headed for an incinerator. Watching Maex take it in the ragged bag felt like she was watching part of her be torn away to be burned. She tried not to add the pain of it to the already overflowing bucket inside her.

Sybil turned her attention to the road out of town. The light of the day barely winked above the treeline. The encroaching darkness didn't matter. Her mind had been made up the second that Ethissa had told her to ride to Trelusk.

Exhaustion was a demon sitting on her shoulders and making her legs wobble under its weight. Sleep or no sleep, riding through the night would be hard, not just on her horse, but on her body as well. The muscles of her legs and back weren't made for long rides anymore. If she left now, she could be in Trelusk by morning. She'd owe Metronome a week's worth of treats, but hopefully the old girl could manage it.

Metronome was her personal horse, gifted by the stable master in Trelusk when she was relocated. She was barely past a colt, but Sybil had loved the mare the second she laid eyes on her. Other Wardens had to use Bastion horses, needing to adjust their riding with every trek, relearning their horse's quirks and personalities. She was even more thankful today that the brown mare was in her care. It saved her an awkward request of a warden-commissioned horse for the trip. Another hurdle that could have led to a mess of uneasy questions.

Sybil had grabbed a riding cloak to wrap over the clean mantle. One of the thicker ones to help stave off the chilled air. The fur-lined boots were old, but the leather exterior was mostly intact. Her knees would be facing most of the cold air as they ran, and she would have to rely on the cloak to stay wrapped around her to protect them. If only she could have unlocked the secrets to her past *after* Frostide was over.

She slid her foot into the stirrup and hoisted herself up, landing harder than she would have liked on the leather saddle. Metronome shifted her weight, her head flipping back and forth in annoyance. Otherwise, she only stamped her hooves a few times in impatience, already used to Sybil's awkward mounting and shifting stride.

"I'll be back before you know it," Sybil said, looping her hair into the dark hood. "Killian said he could get me a few days, so I'll have to be back before then anyways."

"Bring back answers," Maex said, gently patting Sybil's leg before stepping back away from the mare. "And please, for my sake, don't do anything stupid."

Sybil twisted her lip back at her friend, then clicked her tongue and Metronome was off.

The air was more frigid than she had expected for the end of the Dimming, not quite late enough in the year for it to be biting so hard on her cheeks. As soon as the horse picked up to a slow canter, the wind wrapped its icy fingers through her hair, pushing the hood right off her head to get a better grip on her skull. She could readjust it when they slowed to take a break. For now, she just bit her lip, squinting into the cold air that carved tears down her face. She barely noticed. Her thoughts were already ages ahead, racing faster than Metronome beneath her.

Would she find anything in Trelusk? Would it even matter? Killian's words still echoed in her skull, louder than the howl of the storm. *I can't believe I trusted you.* She clenched the reins tighter, ignoring the sting in her frozen fingers.

The night deepened, swallowing the road in darkness. Frost clung to Metronome's coat in brittle shards, crackling every time the mare shifted. The wind had started as a harmless whisper—now, it howled through the trees, rattling their bare branches like bones. The first flakes of snow were light, almost playful. Within minutes, they thickened, turning the air into a swirling, blinding wall of white. It was too early in the season for such a hectic snowfall, but Crae Vost wasn't known for keeping to a proper schedule. Sybil's teeth had started chattering long ago. The gloves protected her hands, but they had frozen in place. They creaked stiffly as she tried to straighten them out from their grip on the reins.

It took several tries to flick her flint enough that she could grab hold of the flame. Metronome only glanced back at the light, shaking her mane. Another warden horse used to its rider's magic. The wooded hills passed alongside her, barely noticed as she focused on her magic. She'd only ever used the air for warmth once before, but even then, she was barely able to hold it. A few hours still from the crest of the sun, they needed something. The heat from a fire may have been stronger than heated air, but the magic always threatened to take off into an out-of-control forest fire. She couldn't risk it, her aerokineticism would have to suffice.

Sybil pulled the flame back into her hands but held the warmth it left behind with her will. The heat swirled around her arms, tapering off slightly, almost dying before she was able to grasp hold of it again. The shaking in her hands spread, no longer from the cold.

The heat spread down her body, wrapping around her ankles then spreading to Metronome's ribs and out towards her neck and flank. The mare never slowed, her hooves pounding in time with Sybil's racing heart. Red hot pokers drove themselves into the soft tissue within her head. Searing light flaring behind her eyes. *Push through.* Once it was wrapped around them both, she could let it hang, and the pain would subside with it. She just needed to go a little further.

Like a heavy weight, the magic teetered at the tips of her fingers. Wavering with every plume of icy air that escaped her lips. The strain made the pain in her head intensify, flashing lights at the corners of her eyes, her vision tunnelling in. Only her fingers and the grasp on the hot air kissing her skin left of the outside world as her mind swam.

Just a little more.

A wall of heat blasted outwards, violent and untamed. The frost on her skin vanished in an instant, steam rising in angry tendrils. The ground hissed beneath her, ice turning to sludge in the span of a breath. Metronome slid to a halt, then reared back, hooves kicking wildly. Sybil barely managed to keep her seat, her muscles locking with exhaustion as the magic drained from her in one massive, uncontrolled pulse. The light vanished immediately after, taking the heat with it. The burst of magic left behind a soft moisture that the frozen air immediately grasped onto and added to its freezing grip.

"Void be damned," she groaned, dropping her head back and staring up at the dark sky. The shivering in her fingers and jaw started again, though the rest of her body shook with the sudden massive expanse of energy.

She glanced back the way she had come. The wind had slowed her down and she couldn't even be sure how far she was from the edge of the city. The blizzard was picking up with every second. It hadn't quite gotten bad enough to obscure her vision, but if it kept up this pace, it wouldn't be long before she was lost in it. Even the road had started to blur into the white expanse, barely seen against its grassy neighbour.

There was a nearby skiff of trees that could hold back the worst of the wind for the night. It'd have to do. There was no way she or Metronome would be able to keep moving as the wind picked up and threw slivers of ice their way in the darkness. She slid off the side of Metronome, clutched the leather of the saddle bag as her legs threatened to give out on her. With the cloak pulled tight around her face, she led the horse towards the trees across the winds. Metronome leaned gently against her shoulder, the mare's warmth and size a nice protection from the onslaught.

Her fingers were frozen. The ties on the bags turned into complex puzzles as she tried to undo them to get at her supplies. With a few stuttered curses, she opted to grasp a few of the ties in her teeth and tore at them to get them loose. Finally, she tossed the bedroll onto the ground, followed shortly by the extra blanket. The trees indeed provided enough coverage from the wind, but that didn't stop her from staring out at the gusts that blew by with disdain.

With a great deal of effort and strain she was able to strike up a small fire. Metronome sauntered over, her heavy breath throwing Sybil's frozen bangs off her face. Sybil ran her hand down the horse's muzzle as the mare dropped beside her. The extra blanket would have been nice, but the added weight of Metronome would be enough. She laid the wool over the horse and shifted the bedroll closer, sliding into it and shifting closer to the mare.

The 'what ifs' came fast and cruel, stealing her attempts at sleep. If she had rested earlier, she would have had the strength to warm the air. If she had left earlier, she would have missed the storm. If she had run to Trelusk the moment she saw Quinn, she would have her answers by now. If she had practiced more, it wouldn't have taken such an effort to cast her stupid little spells.

If I had just been content with my stupid little leertek *life, Quinn would have never been taken.*

FOURTEEN

Twenty Years Ago

The air smelled of moss, wet stone, and iron. Sybil's fingers pressed tight against her palm, but the blood still slipped through. The warden behind her kept shoving his hand between her shoulders, urging her forward. He was rambling about keeping the wound held high, but Sybil was more focused on watching the red make tiny rivers on her skin. She narrowed her eyes at it, willing it with all six years of her might to change course. To lift. To obey. Nothing.

She'd overheard her father talking about a powerful sorcerer that had the ability to turn his blood into sharp, deadly arrows. After trying and failing to control the elements, this *had* to be the magic that hid deep inside her guts. But no matter how hard she concentrated, or how hard she held her breath, the blood continued to drip down her forearm. It left a small trail behind them as the warden rushed her towards the Trelusk barracks, his frustration shown with every hurried shove.

He had found her down by the river alone, with her caretaker nowhere in sight. A tradition for the young girl, slipping out from under the watchful eyes as soon as she had a chance. They'd told her not to go out on her own, pressing how dangerous it was. She never listened, vanishing each day to explore somewhere else in the forests surrounding Trelusk. Today, that wandering had led her to the river.

A sharp stone lay next to the river's edge, and with it came an idea. If she could only *see* the life that flowed through her veins, she could surely control it. She only meant to press lightly into her palm, but the algae covered rocks betrayed her, denying her a clean slice. As soon as the rock touched her flesh, her foot slid down into the waters. The sharp stone plunged into her hand, the fall tearing it across her palm in an arc. She cried out, tossing the rock and sending a splatter of blood into the air around her.

Her pulse stuttered. Excitement, then something deeper, sharper. The scent of iron curled in her nose, thick and metallic. She barely noticed the way her stomach twisted at the sight of the blood hovering and trembling. But then, gravity won, and it fell to the water. Though when she tried again, it didn't budge. No miraculous dance of blood, it only started to fill the centre of her palm, overflowing off the sides of her hand.

That was when the Warden found her, blood splattering the front of her dress, her bare feet soaked and muddy. Everyone in town knew who Sybil Wyntres was. They also knew where to take her whenever she was found wandering alone. To the captain of the Trelusk Wardens: her father.

"Fetch Maiten," the Warden barked once they reached the edge of the barracks. A younger warden took the call and ran inside, leaving her to stand uncomfortably while the disgruntled man tsked and scoffed.

The loud clang of the Trelusk Tower bells pulled her attention away from the warden at her side. The same time every day, but when she was this close it always made her jump. In the direction of the bells, she caught sight of movement in the nearby garden. A boy was standing within the trellis, slowly stacking rocks without touching them. The Warden didn't notice as she stepped away from him, drawn by the boy's fantastical magic.

He didn't seem to be stacking the rocks in any particular way or order. Just grabbing one with his magic from across the small garden, bringing it over to him, and placing it at the top of his pile. He'd tilt his head one way or another, seemingly satisfied, before turning and lifting another. Sybil didn't speak, just sat on the low fence. Her blood had staunched its seemingly never-ending flow for the time being as she cradled her hand in her arms.

The boy had started to move dirt to the base of the pile, filling in the cracks between each of the stones. It drifted across the ground like veins and rivers, flowing from the soil that housed the plants around the garden. The boy barely had to move his fingers to make the dirt slither this way and that, his eyes fixated on each of the trails as they moved around his rock pile. She glanced at her own hands, frowning at them. *Useless.*

"What are you building?" Sybil finally asked. She expected the boy to start at her voice, but he didn't flinch. Instead, he let out a breath, tossing his dirty blonde hair off his face.

"A fortress, obviously," he said, grabbing another rock with his magic and floating it towards his outstretched palm. He turned it over in his hand, inspecting it thoroughly, but then tossed it back out of the garden and out of sight before grabbing another.

"What kind of fortress?"

The boy shrugged. "A rock one. The rocks back home were a lot better though. These ones are too jagged." He finally turned to look at her and his dark eyes narrowed. "You're bleeding." He stepped towards her, gently taking her hand in his and turning it over to look at the cut.

"It's fine. Barely hurts," she said, sticking her chest out, trying her hardest not to flinch at his touch.

"You're pretty brave." He smirked, "for a little kid."

"I'm *very* brave. I didn't even cry," she beamed.

The boy smiled at her, two little dents appearing in his cheeks at the corners of his lips. Sybil couldn't help but notice them, such an odd thing for a face. Nobody else's did that when they smiled. "I'm Quinn." He stuck his hand out, an old gesture from an older world, but Sybil knew what it meant. Even noticed how he held out the hand that would grasp her uninjured one.

"Sybil," she smiled, grabbing hold of it. His hands were already calloused, strange for somebody so young. "And I'm not little. I'm six." She jumped off the fence, wincing at the pain in her hand, and trying to hide it from the boy.

"Well, I'm eight. So, you *are* little." He peered around her, and she followed his gaze to the Warden that had brought her over, now arguing with the younger one he had sent inside. Their voices were hushed and didn't make it over to the garden.

"I haven't seen you around before. Did your parents move here?" Careful not to disrupt the pile, Sybil stepped around it and inspected each of the rocks. Some of them were still hanging precariously in the air, floating under invisible strings.

The rocks shuddered a little bit as he turned to face her, but didn't fall. "No. They're supposed to be making me a ward. Whatever that means." A couple of the stones dropped, tumbling and rolling away from the pile.

"Oh." Sybil whispered, digging her toes into the ground. She knew what a ward was, and she wished she hadn't brought up parents.

"I don't think I want to wait anymore. I'm probably going to leave."

Her shoulders slumped in time with the corners of her lips. "Are you allowed to leave?"

Quinn shrugged. "They can't stop me."

Trelusk wasn't known for its younger population, and this was the first boy close to her age that she had met. Most children lived in Charprin to be closer to the school. It would have been nice to at least have somebody that she could go to the river with. He could have built her a bridge across it with his rocks, and they could see what was on the other side. If he really was to be a ward, he wouldn't have a lot of time to play. But anything was better than the cranky old Ms. Cordival that scolded her every day.

"What magic do you have?" The question spat from Quinn's lips so fast, Sybil could barely catch it. In Plaitius, asking that question was considered rude. A politeness she appreciated since it spared her the awkward silence that followed.

She hesitated for a moment, her teeth worried at her lip. The boy didn't frown at her or cross his arms as if comparing his own to whatever she had. Just a tilt of his head, a curious, wide-eyed look as he waited for her to answer. "I... uh... don't have any yet." Her voice was so quiet, but it felt like she was screaming about her deficiency.

But Quinn just shrugged. "Okay. Are you here to get your hand fixed?" he asked, moving past without pause. No flinch, no pity. Not a quick cover-up for embarrassment. Just a natural pivot as if it didn't matter in the slightest.

Sybil stared at the wound, now scabbed and crusty, the blood hardening in the lines of her hand. "Yeah. The town sarcomancer works here, he'll mend it back together." She made a face, curling her upper lip to her nose. "He's gross though. Gives me the shivers all over."

Quinn scrunched up his face, glancing behind her once more. The wardens had gone inside, leaving the two of them alone in the garden. She could see the gears turning behind his dark eyes as he looked past the barracks and out into the forest.

"I could wait at least a little longer. Just to stop him from being gross," he muttered, shuffling his feet through the dirt. "If you want..."

"Like a guard?" she asked. His face lit up to match hers.

"I can use the ugly, jagged ones if he makes you queasy." Quinn twisted his hand around, pulling a few of the rocks towards his palm. One overshot, sailing past his reach and disappearing into the underbrush of the garden. He muttered a curse that Sybil had only heard the wardens say, and she had to bite her tongue from giggling.

Kneeling, she sorted through a few stones scattered around the garden path. She plucked a few of the less jagged ones and stepped forward to hand them to Quinn. He beamed down at her, gently taking them from her hands and flying them towards his fortress, balancing them at the top.

"Sybil!" Maiten stepped around the low garden wall, racing towards her before clutching her hand in his to inspect the damage. His brows knit together on his head; lips pressed into a tight line. His hands were almost twice the size of hers, enshrouding them in their grip. "What happened?"

She dropped her gaze to the ground, fighting back the trembling in her lip. He wasn't mad *at* her, but at six it was hard to distinguish between worry and anger sometimes. "I just wanted to try..." She glanced up at him through her brows, water flooding her eyes but not quite tipping over the edges of her lashes yet.

Maiten let out a heavy breath, curling her hand tighter in his, then pressing his lips to her forehead. The gesture filled her eyes the rest of the way, drops flowing down her cheeks. She no longer cared about pretending to be brave. She was scared and just wanted her father to hold her. He turned around, the Warden that brought her over standing at attention, his salute still held as he awaited his orders. "Go get Warden Nostene, please."

At the name of the sarcomancer, gooseflesh broke out all over her arms, ice tracing down her spine. The tiniest whimper slipped past her lips. A small hand wrapped around hers, a gentle squeeze steadying her. She saw her father's brow tighten, a slight movement to his mouth, but it was interrupted as the nearby door to the barracks slammed against the slats that ran along the outside walls.

Warden Nostene stepped around the perimeter, resting one leg on the small fence of the garden. He flashed his yellowing teeth at them. Long greasy hair hung down over his face, tracing thin lines along his hollow cheek bones. Even standing at a distance, Sybil felt the harsh sting of the scent that wafted off him.

"Well, little lady, what did we do this time?" His voice was like oil, seeping through her pores into her flesh. It slithered through her and made her throat tighten, the tears shrivelling up on her face. The small hand wrapped around hers squeezed tighter, draining the shivers out of her, the trembling vanishing with the reassuring hold.

Maiten stood, lifting his daughter's hand up so the sarcomancer could see. He tutted under his breath a half-hearted laugh looping through the air, the thick taint of his breath permeating the garden. She tried to hold it back, but she sniffled, the noise audible enough for the smile on his face to falter just a bit.

"Don't cry. We'll get this fixed up and it'll just be a bad memory." He grinned, showing off the chunks of tobacco between his teeth. Leftover remnants from the stash that seemed to be permanently imbedded in his lower lip. Sybil held tight to her new friend's hand, the warmth that emanated off it feeding her bravery.

Nostene's fingers traced the wound too slowly, lingering at the edges before sliding over her skin like he was testing it. Sybil clenched her jaw, forcing herself not to pull away. She had been here before, knew what he had to do to seal up her cut. He had to tune into the skin that surrounded the wound before he could close it, every sarcomancer did. Even the fancy ones in the big city. That didn't make her feel any better. The touch was never fully clinical, always slightly *off*.

"You know," he started, "I think you may have the softest skin I've ever worked with." Sybil felt her flesh flicker and crawl as he spoke, her eyes dipping away from his. She looked up at her father, hoping to see the disgust reflected in his eyes as well. Except his attention had drifted outside the garden, back towards the barracks. Fully unaware of the sarcomancer's tone.

The ground rumbled beneath her feet, the stones skittering around her shoes. Whether Nostene noticed it or not, she couldn't tell, but she felt it. Felt the growing heat and tremors that rattled from Quinn's hand. The way the ground seemed to be shifting towards him.

Nostene's hands closed tighter around her palm. The wound started to grow tiny tendrils from the edges, wrapping around themselves and knitting into a weave. Other children would close their eyes tight and turn their heads away, but not Sybil. Her eyes were wide, taking in every turn and twist of the skin under the sarcomancer's hands. What she wouldn't give to have that kind of power, to be able to undo the damage humans inflicted on themselves and wrap flesh back together, rewriting the past from their skin.

"Wait!" Sybil called out, the realization clicking into her young mind. The warden paused his work, though the strain and annoyance was written in the scowl on his face. "Can you leave a scar?"

"Sybil..." Her father's voice dropped to disappointment burgeoning on weariness.

"Why on Crae Vost would you want to leave yourself with such a hideous mark?" Nostene asked.

She glanced over at Quinn, as though he could reason with them for her. But instead, he just solidified his stare and nodded, the only declaration she needed. "I want to remember it." For once she didn't drop her eyes from the intense stare of the Warden's. A heat settled behind her ribs as he narrowed his gaze at her; a challenge.

Nostene looked away first, turning to Maiten, waiting for his response. Maiten just shrugged, his attention not truly on the interaction. "Fine," Nostene conceded, pressing his thumbs once more to the flesh of her palm. The strands continued to weave themselves together, but this time, their hypnotic dance was interrupted along the way, a dark line following them as they closed themselves. They worked faster now. The delicate way they spun the flesh was no longer needed. Nostene pulled the muscles of her palm back, inspecting his work and let out a heavy breath. "Shame. No boy is going to like this mark on a pretty girl like you."

"I like it just fine," Quinn barked, suddenly drawing the attention of the older men. Nostene scowled, ready to retort, but Quinn spoke first. "You're done, right?"

Nostene's face burned red. Ready to snap, spittle ready to fly. Maiten held up his hand, gesturing back towards the barracks. "Thank you, Nigelle. You're dismissed." Sybil could hear him huffing all the way back to the door, slamming it once more against the slats. She stifled a laugh, knowing it would only garner a scolding from her father for impoliteness later.

Quinn stepped around her, grabbing the scarred hand in his and spreading it open. "I'm so jealous. I can't wait until I get battle scars." He beamed at her, flooding her cheeks with heat. She'd never had anybody jealous of her before, not some poor girl who hadn't grown into her magic yet. Especially not an older, more talented child.

"Who might you be?" Maiten asked, dragging their attention back to him.

"Quintaine Vandryft, sir. I'm your new ward." Sybil let his name float through her head like a leaf on a river, slow and steady but almost magical in the way it drifted in her thoughts. That was, until she looked at her father's face. It drained of colour, his eyes wide. She'd never seen him like that, and it made her veins feel like they were heavy and full of ice.

She frowned at the way his hands twisted together. The way he kept glancing above their heads as his mouth opened and closed. The words seemingly stuck on his tongue. Maiten Wyntres was the bravest man she had ever met. Brave enough to lead all the other brave men in the town. Yet, this was the first time she had ever seen him frightened.

"Of course. I... uh. Warden Moniqure can get you sorted. I'm—*we* are happy you made it here safely." The captain started to fidget with the buttons of his cloak as his eyes darted between each of them. His hand hovered at Sybil's shoulder, as if he meant to rest it there, but didn't. Instead, he adjusted his cloak, fingers stiff. "Sybil, don't you think it's time you were getting home?"

"Yes, *sir.*" Sybil mocked, dragging out the word, following Quinn's lead. Her tone hinted at rebellion, her smirk cementing it, but nothing quite sharp enough to sting.

"Come on, Dev— er, Quintaine. I'll introduce you to Warden Moni\'que." Maiten turned away, his white mantle flaring out.

Sybil took her chance, standing on her tiptoes to whisper into Quinn's ear before he stepped away. "You're not leaving, then?"

Quinn's smirk softened. He leaned in, voice barely above a breath. "Not until I get more scars than you."

Something shifted. Something invisible, something unspoken, settling between them like an unbreakable thread. Sybil's fingers curled into her palm, pressing against the fresh wound as if she could trap the moment there, keep it inside her skin forever.

She looked back down at her hand, marvelling at the pink skin that traced its way up the centre of her palm, interrupting the natural lines that creased the flesh. Nostene called it hideous, but she had never seen anything more beautiful in her life.

FIFTEEN

Sybil woke to a burning sting on her cheeks, the frigid air biting against her bare skin. The sun lit her lids, illuminating the latticework of veins like fractured glass. She wiped a gloved hand along her lashes, the soft leather tearing away the frozen crystals sealing her eyes shut. Her fingers were stiff, practically creaking as she tried to bend them in the gloves.

A layer of snow had settled on the clearing over night. Metronome looking like she had been dusted with sugar, her dark fur sparkling like glitter. The shifting of her stomach the only crack in the stillness. The corner of Sybil's lips twisted up as she stared at the slumbering beast, her dry skin tightening harshly at the movement.

Packing up took some time, most of it revolving around her working the feeling back into her limbs. They'd grown numb and useless on the cold, hard ground, like rigid branches of a tree. Once she was seated back atop the mare, she was finally able to let the stupidity of the night settle. Rushing from the city in an extravagant burst to make up time had been foolish. She could see it clear as the day in front of her now. Quinn waited ten years, he could wait another day or two.

She peeled her glove back slightly and stared at the faded pink line across her palm. Strange how its origin had filtered into her dreams. It was a memory she thought of often, so desperate to hold on to the fading strings of it as time passed. The scar was an anchor, tying the memory tightly to her hand, holding it when the rest of her thoughts seemed to be slowly shrouding in smoke.

There were so few memories of him that stayed solid and clear. Now, the remaining shreds of him still living in her mind were being twisted into this new grotesque iteration. Those nightmare orange eyes. His face contorted with rage as he controlled her blood as easily as he had stacked those rocks. That couldn't be the last memory she would have of him. Having him screaming for his life while being ripped from her world had haunted her every waking moment, but having him abandon her freely somehow felt all the more painful.

When Trelusk breached the horizon in front of her, the sun had filtered through the thick blanket of clouds and managed to thaw her frozen skin. Now, the light was making every effort to disappear. Night was on the edge of her sights, whispering its warnings into her ear of the darkness to come. She'd slept too long.

Metronome had slowed her stride; grunts bursting past her lips every few meters. Sybil's exhaustion matched the horse's, her thighs and back aching with every shift of the saddle. The skin at the ridges of the fur-lined boots had rubbed raw and no amount of adjustment of the leather was slowing the ache. When she saw the wooden buildings peaking through the trees, her whole body slumped heavily into the saddle.

A quaint town, the few people that still wandered in the dirt streets were quickly making their way home for the evening. She struggled to make sense of the changes she saw in what was once her home. A large number of new buildings had been erected near the outskirts, the town's footprint expanding northward. The butcher had built an extension to the corner of his shop, the extra runed walling suggesting a cold room. The town hall had more shrubs planted around the wooden fence, which had been remade at some point, its once crumbling structure now standing tall.

All of it left a sour taste in Sybil's mouth. Granted, the expansion was a welcome sight, but all the growth made her heart ache with remorse. She shouldn't have stayed away for so long. A fresh Warden lived a busy life, but not so busy that penning words to paper were out of grasp. Maiten could have told her before, perhaps softening the blow that came with seeing what the distorted image of her childhood had become.

But her grief had been heavy. She couldn't bring herself to carry her father's too.

Though the barracks were the heart of the town, it hadn't been the place to find her father in years. Maiten's house used to be on the outskirts of town. Now it was surrounded by other small huts and cottages, his land slashed in half. Smoke billowed out of the chimney above and Sybil pretended to be relieved to know she wouldn't have to go searching for him. It was tainted though, that voice in the back of her mind reminding her that he hadn't strayed far from home since retiring. Curling in on himself and letting the guilt swallow him whole. Guilt that wasn't even his to own.

Sybil dismounted Metronome, running her hands along the horse's legs, gingerly lifting a hoof to inspect it. No ice built up, but the rocks and dirt were caked into the shoes. Sybil silently cursed herself, making a mental note to request new ones when she got back to Hazel Gryph.

She patted the horse's shoulder, whispering her thanks as she tied her bridle to the railing of her father's balcony. There used to be a hitch post driven into the ground, but now it lay on its side. Nature had claimed it a long time ago, the wood barely seen under the overgrown grass.

Maiten Wyntres had been unkind to his body in his lifetime and now relied on a cane to move. Even with the assistance, his movements were slow and calculated. If anybody asked him what he thought about that, he would swiftly tell them that the pain was worth the pride that came with serving one's country. Sybil knew better. Years of watching her father, idolizing his every movement, had given her a keen insight to Senior First Command Warden Maiten Wyntres. Lingering glances along old medals and weapons. Outside eyes could see it as longing, but Sybil saw it for what it was: disgust. As she aged with her father, she saw what once looked like sadness devolve into anger. At what, he never shared.

Sybil knocked on the door. As soon as the dull thud echoed behind the wood, she realised how foolish it was. This had been her home as much as his and acting like a guest only furthered the ache of distance that had grown between them. The scent of moth balls and long-settled dust hit her as she pushed the door open. The house was silent, though the quietest whistle could be heard from the kitchen. She followed the noise past a set of discarded, dusty boots and down the hall with tipped-over portraits. The noise was a kettle on the stove, close to announcing its readiness. Sybil pressed her brows together, but shifted the kettle to another burner halting its attempted scream.

"Father?" she called out after blowing out the flame on the stove. Dread started to dig its sharp fingers around her shoulders, making her heart race in her chest.

When silence was her only answer, she ventured into the living room, only to find her father fast asleep atop a sofa. His cane seemingly discarded without thought on the wood flooring next to him, a hat falling across his face. His mouth open below it, soft snoring rattling up his throat. Sybil granted herself a moment, smirking at the state of her father, hands on her hips as she watched him.

She grabbed a nearby pillow off an adjacent couch and whipped it towards him. There was a sputtering and flailing of limbs as he started. "You know, you aren't supposed to set the kettle before you go to sleep," she said, crossing her arms.

He narrowed in on her voice, the surprise lasting as long as it took to recognize his daughter leaning against the door frame. The confused anger morphing quickly as his face brightened.

"I'd wake up for it, I just closed my eyes," he lied, rubbing the sleep off his face and rolling to sit on the couch. He blinked a few times and focused on Sybil, his hazel eyes taking her in.

"Sure you were. Is that why there are burn rings on the bottom of the kettle?"

"Did you come all the way out here to nag me?" Maiten stood from the couch, reaching his cane with great effort and wobbling as he rested his weight on it. Sybil couldn't help staring at him. He wasn't a geriatric old man; he was barely in his fifth decade. The creases along his lips and the ones that crafted paths between his brows seemed to deepen in the years. Her father's life had continued in the background of her own. Somehow she had always expected it to stop, hovering in a time all its own, only restarting when she returned. Nobody could outrun it forever, she just hadn't realized that it was catching up with him so quickly.

She found herself struggling with what to say, chewing on the edge of her lip. Niceties felt as though they were too light for the time that had bridged between them. Yet an excuse for her absence was too difficult to muster. This heavy gap that settled between them was new, their once easy relation dissipating as a wedge was driven between them by distance and time. She had so many things to tell him, yet they all stuck on the tip of her tongue, held tight by her own teeth.

She should have softened the start, eased into the conversation. As the seconds stretched, she couldn't hold it in any longer. The question broke loose, raw and unfiltered.

"What happened to Quinn?"

Maiten's face fell, the bags under his eyes sagging with the strain. He shifted on his cane, supported his leg, then stepped forward. "The kettle should still be hot," he said, shuffling past her, his steps punctuated with a click.

Last time Sybil was here, Maiten had pulled the tea from the kettle with his magic, effortlessly pouring it into each of their stained, chipped cups. Now, he poured it from the kettle by hand, his arm shaking under the weight.

The tea strainers were old, bits of rust flaking the old metal wiring. Regardless of their age, they were quality and Maiten had always kept care of them over the years. Sybil could point out the patched holes off memory, the tarnished metal being a staple in this house. A strange thing to be sentimental about, but it wasn't the only thing in this house held together with homemade stitches and glues.

The repairs seemed to have been neglected lately. Bits of tea seeped past the strainer's tiny cage now, dotting the top of the steaming water like drifting motes in the sky.

The rich black tea was sprinkled with spices, warming her nose as she leaned into the cup, letting the hot steam melt the shivers from her fingers. Since the incident, cinnamon had been banned in their house. Maiten was the only one she knew of that could make spiced tea without it.

"How are you doing these days?" Maiten asked, blowing on his tea. The scent off his own cup wafted over to her and she wrinkled her nose at the trace of liquor that meandered with it.

"I—" She paused. The easy question softened her for a moment, but the reality of her trek lingered with the sharp sting of the cold wind on her cheeks. He was stalling. "What happened to Quinn?" she repeated.

He flinched slightly. "Sybil—"

"Something weird is happening in the capital and I need to know," she paused, lying to ease the tension, letting her exhale swirl the steam around her fingers. "Please."

Maiten set down his cup, spreading his palms out flat on the table. He shook his head back and forth, eyes focused on the window just beyond Sybil's head. This wasn't an easy ask. She had wanted to forget that horrible night, but so had he. Quinn had been his ward, his responsibility. He'd taken it hard knowing that as soon as Quinn had left his care to start as a warden, he had done something so reckless. Maiten left Hazel Gryph as a top officer years before Quinn came to Trelusk, seemingly out of the blue. He took his legacy with him, leaving nothing more than a name. It wasn't hard to see that he had hoped to leave something more than that with Quinn.

"I heard you screaming. I didn't even know he was here, I figured he was back at the barracks... *like I told him to be,*" he scoffed, his voice taking on that paternal tone. "You both knew the rules, and he bloody well knew that he wasn't allowed to leave the Bastion until he completed his exams and he—"

"Papa, stop. That isn't what I'm asking. What else do you remember?"

Maiten let out another heavy breath, dropping his hands to clasp on his lap. "Blood, Sybil. The room was covered in it. The walls, your bed... the *ceiling*. I thought it was yours at first," he paused, picking at his nails. "And you wouldn't stop screaming.

"I finally got you to tell me what happened. Well, not what happened. You just started yelling his name and crying. When I finally figured out you weren't hurt and that the blood was his." The rattling in his hands started to shake the table. "Then I saw the book. It was still flipped open and the pages were stained red. It didn't take long to put two and two together. I got you out of there as fast as I could and got a hold of Tomtin. He went to the barracks and they were here within minutes. Nobody found a trace of Quinn."

"And Ethissa? She was here too."

He nodded. "Gave you one of her tonics that put you to sleep. I was so worried you were going to hurt yourself with all that screaming and crying."

Sybil stared at him, glancing between his eyes. Mirror images of her own, their only difference the age that dragged them down. She'd heard this story a million times, over and over again. He burst in, he grabbed her, they left. The guards swarmed in and did what they did, and the next time she had the courage to step foot on the worn wooden floors of her room, they were spotless. Only the faintest outline in the grain where the circle had burned. A constant reminder of what she had done.

"What if Quinn wasn't killed? What do you think could have happened to him?"

Maiten tutted, clucking his tongue against his teeth. "Sybil, there was no way he could have survived that. There was too much blood."

"But what if he did?"

His face darkened. "Stealing from the wardens is a crime in and of itself. Stealing magic texts and using the illegal magic to summon forth the darkness is *treason*. If he survived the Void, the Portcullis would have slit his throat. The second he opened that book up, he forfeited his life." Maiten reached across the table and grasped Sybil's hands in his. A gesture he had used so many times before, but it felt patronizing in this moment. "That isn't your fault."

Sybil pulled her hands out of Maiten's. "I need to see that book."

Maiten's jaw flexed. "Digging up all these bad memories won't bring Quinn back, love. It's only going to hurt you."

"Papa, this is important. Something... happened. I can't really explain, I just need to see the book. Maybe there's something in there that will explain what—"

Maiten slammed his hands on the table, his teacup rattling on the scored wood. "I will not let you sacrifice yourself to the same fate as him because of your guilt."

Ice burst forth across the table beneath Sybil's hands. It wrapped its fractal patterns around the cups and skated across the surface of the liquid. She tore her hands from the wood, her skin frozen to it, hisses seething past her teeth.

Maiten jolted backwards slightly, but the fear in his eyes only lasted a moment. Quickly cascading to wonder as he stared at the twisting veins of ice. His mouth dropped in a silent 'oh', his fingers twitching towards it absently.

Sybil let out a slow breath, refocusing herself. "I'm not going to re-enact the ritual, Father." She leaned forward, looking deeply between each of his eyes, drawing his attention away from the wild surge of magic. "I just need to know. That's all. Please. If you've ever trusted me before, trust me now."

Why she didn't just tell him the truth, she couldn't be sure. Maybe it was in the memories of how often he had looked at her with exhausted disdain when she screamed of the monsters in the dark. How she would call to him in the night, begging him to help her when nothing but shadows awaited his frantic search. To him, Quinn would be nothing more than fantasies in the dark that warped her mind. And this would only be another nightmare that haunted her.

She could see the internal battle happening; could see him fighting between warden and father, protector of one and protector of many. She may not remember most of that night besides the horror and the tremors that it left her with on the darkest of nights, but he did. He saw the blood that coated the walls, saw the shredded marks of nails along the floor.

Maiten's jaw flexed under his skin, his fingers absently picking at the skin on his palm. "They locked it away. You won't be able to access it..." His gaze trailed to her mantle, focusing on the pin as he frowned. Something clicked in his expression, his eyes drifting from her collar to her hands. She quickly pulled them out of their grip, stopping the incessant trail she had absently been tracing along her scar. "You got your silver pin."

"I... did," she mumbled, the room suddenly feeling too warm and too small.

"That's fantastic, Sybil." He stepped around the table, his arms outstretched. He made it a step before he wobbled, his legs betraying him as he grabbed hold of the surface.

Sybil didn't so much as flinch to catch him, her lips only twisting up in a sneer. "The cane or," she nodded towards his tea, "your drink."

Maiten's face burned pink as he stared down at his hands. They trembled slightly, and he curled his fingers to tame it. He didn't have to say anything, that was enough for her.

"I'm going to see that book, Papa. And then I'm going back to the city." She gently grabbed hold of his arm to steady him, then reached down to pick up his cane from the floor. She wanted to berate him, but she felt a pang in her chest. If she had come back sooner, maybe he wouldn't be in such a state. "You need to take care of yourself or I'll start sending Ms. Cordival over here to babysit you."

"You wouldn't dare," he laughed, the joke easing the tension back from between them. He let her lead him back to the couch.

His hair was fading from the top of his head, but she still smoothed it back. Maiten caught her arm as she went to walk past. "Please, Sybil. Please don't get yourself killed. Those memories aren't worth your life, and neither is anything you can dredge up from the pages of that book."

She frowned at him, trying to read the sharp look in his eyes. A glint of silver caught her attention to the side table in her periphery. Atop it was a flask, the lid hung half open. One that used to be locked away in a cabinet. Her arms wrapped around Maiten's shoulders, carefully grabbing hold of the flask and slipping it into the pocket of her mantle. It wouldn't stop him, but maybe, *just maybe,* it would slow the dregs of time.

"I'll be safe, Papa. I promise."

The late hour meant that the barracks were relatively deserted. Only a bored-looking Warden sat at the wood slat that ran along the length of the entrance, absently tossing a Lok between his fingers. He was young, and judging by the boring station he was charged with he probably hadn't even taken his exams. And much too young to know who she was.

Her heart thrummed in her chest like a caged bird as she stepped up to the slat. "Quiet night?" she asked, trying her best to angle her body so the dim light reflected off the metal of her pin. She'd seen the captain use a similar tactic.

There was a flicker of pride in her chest as the man jolted to his feet, his salute striking his abdomen a bit too hard with the flare. His voice came out pitched and forced. "Sir! Uh... ma'am."

"Sir is fine." Her smile stretched her eyes, her heartbeat pounding away. "I need to access the Northern Hall."

The young man frowned, his salute faltering slightly. "That's restricted, ma—sir."

"Pardon?" Sybil lowered her tone, the falsetto meant as a warning, but it only pitched her voice awkwardly. Sweat coated her palms, her teeth clenched too tight. The dirt around her feet started to swirl ever so slightly, a silent prayer for it to go unnoticed by the twitching Warden in front of her.

His eyes darted to her pin, then back up again. "It's just that... Marshal Gresk has to authorize entry, and he never mentioned a visit."

Sybil brought her hands behind her back, doing her best to stand as tall as she could in the tiny entrance. The boy stood a head taller, but he still cowered at her stance. *Fresh meat.* It was fun seeing it from the other side for a change. "Marshal Gresk has requested I investigate a peculiar book. If you would like, we can interrupt his family's supper and drag him down here to tell you himself..." A bold lie.

"No, no, please don't do that," The boy visibly paled at her request, standing from the bench and reaching for the ring of keys he had tied to his mantle belting. Figured, the artifact that ruined her life was protected by nothing more than keys and a trembling boy who wouldn't see facial hair for another few years.

Keys were archaic, but it wasn't as though Trelusk had a plethora of enchanters available to rune the door. The number of things were was locked away in these barracks paled in comparison to bigger towns like Charprin, and next to Hazel Gryph it was a farce. It wasn't a wonder to see why they hadn't bothered with proper security. Any mineralist worth their salt would be able to twist the lock to their whims. The local blacksmith was so overwhelmed with work, it was doubtful he would have even thought about trying. Besides, he wasn't fortunate enough in his younger years to learn to read, so the fifteen or so books would have been wasted on him.

The young warden shut the door behind her, muttering something that could have been an apology. Sybil didn't bother asking him to repeat it. Was too focused on his small chamber.

Though the barracks may not have had the most extensive collection, there were still a few odds and ends that would have left Sybil in awe on any other day. But not today. Today, she was focused on the embossed spine of a particular book. The indented lettering was faded, but the second she laid her eyes on it, it was like a beacon in the small room. Just seeing it made a hard pit form in her throat.

Her hand reached towards it absently like a child staring at a bright flame, unfamiliar with its sharp bite. The call was a dangerous one. It begged her to rip open the cover and tear through its pages, devour its secrets. She ran her teeth along her lips, her tongue tasting like copper.

Everything thus far had pulled her forward. Her body moved while her mind lagged behind, either refusing or unable to wrap itself around what was happening. Yet now she faltered, staring at that black leather, horrifying images of blood and blackened tendrils flashing through her thoughts. It was just a book, but to her, it was so much more. A passageway to the memories of the nightmares that haunted her even in the waking hours.

She brushed her fingers along the spine first, the skin-like texture prickling her flesh into bumps. Though they were clammy and jittery, she willed her fingers to grip the book, pulling it from its neighbours. The sound was grating on her ears as leather slid past leather. It seemed so much more aged than it had before, the dents and scratches deepened since the last time she had laid eyes on it. The cover seemed as though it was seconds away from cracking, its spine separating from the pages beneath.

A single table sat in the centre of the room, the chair tucked under its surface old and weathered, dust collecting on the seat. Sybil placed the grimoire atop the table, her hands on either side of it, fingers spread as though the surface could keep her from succumbing to the fear. It helped to calm the shaking, but her heartbeat hammered in her ears. She regarded the black leather, an empty void staring back at her from between her thumbs. Though all she had to do was open it and spread its pages, she couldn't bring herself to take the weight off her arms as she leaned over it.

"Whatever you decide, I am here."

His voice floated through her skull, the memory grasping at her from so far away. He'd been so sure of himself that night, so sure that everything would be okay and this would be the only thing that would ever make her happy. If she could only go back and tell him that it was okay, that everything was fine. That she was fine living as a *leertek*, she didn't need magic. So long as she could hold him again.

She hadn't realized that she had started crying until the wet drip landed on the black leather. It spread along the wrinkles and lines of the ancient leather, soaking into it.

Sybil wiped her eyes with the back of her hand, standing up straight and taking in one final deep breath before grabbing the cover of the book. She bit down hard on the inside of her cheek as she flipped it open.

The first page held a single rune. The centre was an 'X', its lines sharp and pointed like spears. On either side were two black crescents facing away from the intersection of the cross. At the top, pointed downwards towards the same intersection, were two arrows, their narrow points driving towards the 'X'.

Definitely not one she recognized, but it wasn't what raised the hairs on her neck. Inked above the 'X' was an upside-down pentagram, bleeding ink lines radiating out from it, fading into the yellowing, stained pages of the book.

Just like the one etched into her hip.

The book thudded as she dropped it. Her hands shook, a heavy wind swirling out from the tips of her fingers, panic shaking her magic. She had inwardly known that she would find something that would give her pause. She just hadn't expected it to be so clearly drawn out in front of her. The pages of the book started to flap, all of them rustling in front of her with the sharp breeze she created. As they flipped, her hand froze in midair, her eyes fixated.

In the centre of the book, clear as day, two of the pages were a dark red. She slapped her hand down, stopping the wind's torrent. Quinn's blood stained the paper in violent sprays. It had been smeared, as though haphazardly wiped away, but it did little to fade the stain. Her stomach twisted hard, a knot clenching it tightly. Of course they wouldn't have been able to clean it off, but it never occurred to her that it would still be trapped in the pages. The history of the massacre forever tainting the tome.

She tore herself away from the book, pressing her hand against the wall, taking in gasping breaths as she tried to slow the panic that threaded through her nerves. The rising nausea and bile threatened to escape past her teeth and she bit down on it, willing it back.

This wasn't over, she still had to find answers. And if they were anywhere in the book, they were on the last page that Quinn had read. She shook herself, working the ice out of her skin. With one final exhale, she dropped her hands back over the book, forcing herself to stare at the bloodstained pages.

Blank.

When Quinn had held the book, the words had been gibberish to her, only showing themselves to the person that held the book. But there was still ink on the pages. Now, there was nothing but the red smears.

Her brow furrowed as she choked down the nausea and flipped to the next page, still stained with red, still empty. And the one after that. She picked the book up off the table and started to flip frantically through it. Every page was blank, only the centre pages showing any difference, with their echoes of Quinn's final moments.

Her stomach twisted again. A roaring sound filled her ears, drowning out everything else. The pages blurred, her vision swimming as the weight of it settled in. She had come all this way, and there was nothing. No answers. No explanations. Her hands trembled. She swallowed hard, forcing air into her lungs, but it didn't feel like enough. Her fingers curled into the hard cover of the book, desperate for something solid. Something real.

"What is going on?" She flipped through the book once more, to no avail. With a twist of her wrist, she closed the book, once more taking in the cover, verifying it was the same. As though the blood wasn't enough of a tell.

She flipped the book open once more, staring at the rune inked on the first page, narrowing her eyes at it as if it would leap from the page any second to reveal its secrets. But nothing about the dark lines spoke to her.

Sybil might be a vollmagus—gifted from the Void with a touch of every kind of magic, chaotic and unstable, but powerful—but even the most gifted of them couldn't hold a candle to an enchanter's abilities.

That powerful ability was exactly what Sybil needed right now.

Sixteen

Hirn and Raekin had barely said two words to each other since the wardens had left the sewers. Raekin couldn't be sure if he was more furious with Hirn or himself. For the bullshit Hirn had spewed, or that he was letting it sink in. Every second that passed turned his anger inwards, twisting like a blade. He hated that Hirn was right. Hated that some sick part of him was even humoring the idea that anything would distract him. That hatred had started to overshadow his fury at the way Hirn had gone about proving his point.

He needed to think of something else. *Anything*.

He cracked his knuckles against his thighs, resisting the urge to press his fists into his eyes just to feel something sharper than frustration. He'd hoped for a better way to pass the time than staring at the backs of his eyelids. Or at least hoped he wouldn't have to do it for long. But as the day turned to night, then back to day again, the commotion above them never faltered.

The longer they waited, the slimmer their chance became. The window before Naz'tak called them back was closing with every second. They needed something. A break. A gap. A reason. Because the last thing Raekin wanted to do was run in there blind and start killing wardens. But if he had to, so be it.

When the muffled ringing of the bell rumbled through their underground haven, Raekin couldn't sit in silence any longer. Every loud crash of their metal felt like Naz'tak's claws gripping tighter on his throat. "When was the last time you checked?" He slid his back further down the wall as it started to go numb from the stone, the third and final ring sounding from above.

"I don't know, an hour? Whenever that bell thing made its ding-a-ling last time."

"Clock tower, Hirn. So, two ding-a-lings last time?"

"Yeah."

Raekin cracked his eyes open again, rolling his head in the direction of the grate. He had noticed the steady beat of footsteps thinning out earlier, but never silencing. It wasn't surprising, then, to see that the streets above had gone dark, save for the few lamps still lit. He must have slept without realizing, the hours passing by around him unnoticed.

"When the tower makes four *'ding-a-lings'*, check again. It'll only be another hour or so after that that we lose the darkness as our window."

"A couple *more* hours? I'm not sure I can stand another second with your moping, let alone a day if we don't get our chance. It's killing me."

"I'm going to kill you if you don't—"

Hirn shot up, tearing Raekin's thought from him. He rocked onto his toes beneath the grating, his fingers gripped the bars to peer through the gaps.

Raekin jolted to his feet, a breath already locking in his chest. "What?"

Hirn didn't answer immediately. His head tilted, shoulders going rigid. Then, "A bunch of those wardens just took off."

Raekin's pulse spiked. That could mean anything. Could mean nothing. "They left the Arcaneum?"

"I don't know, I just saw three of them running."

Three. How many had been keeping watch? "Well, don't just stand there gawking," Raekin snapped. "See if there's anybody left inside."

Hirn let out a dramatic sigh, but his irises vanished into the back of his skull. Raekin stepped back slightly, watching as the veins beneath Hirn's pale skin pulsed faintly. The blood running from his nose was expected. But the slow line of red dripping down from his left ear?

Not good.

Raekin's teeth clenched. "You've been checking too often, you idiot." Hirn wouldn't hear him. Not when he was deep in the trance, his mind too far away. But that didn't stop Raekin from muttering it anyway. He resisted the urge to slap his friend, pulling him from his magic and stopping any further damage to the twit's brain. He couldn't lose him, but they couldn't miss their chance.

"I think they're gone," Hirn whispered, blinking rapidly as his eyes refocused.

Raekin's stomach twisted. *Think.* That wasn't certainty. His hands curled into fists. "That's all you got?"

"Hey, focusing on your own thoughts is hard enough," Hirn muttered, wiping the blood from his nose. "Try listening to someone else's."

Raekin felt the heat rise in his face. Had seen Hirn get distracted far too many times in such crucial moments. "I get that, but this is—"

Hirn cut him off, voice slurring slightly. "All whispers and belligerent garbles. Brief snippets about a rogue mage, but that's all I can get."

Raekin stilled.

"They're far away, though." Hirn ran his hand down his pants, smearing them with red. "No idea how much time you have."

"Shit. Okay. I'll be back."

Raekin turned to leave but hesitated. He exhaled sharply, gritting his teeth. "Your ear is bleeding. You need to be more careful, moron.

"Awe, you do care." Hirn grinned, rubbing the blood from his ear with his dirty sleeve. "We'll kiss and make up when you get back." Raekin tossed a rude gesture behind him before scrambling through the tunnels towards the grate nearer the back of the Bastion.

Rogue mage could mean anything. Or it could mean nothing. If they were getting the wardens to converge on a target, there was no telling how long they would be gone from their stations. They could be running to the other side of the city or running to the next street over. He'd just have to focus and make sure nobody snuck up on him this time.

She can't see me again.

The rocks and chunks of debris that would have made him stumble or roll an ankle flew out of his way as he tore through the sewer towards the ladder. He'd open it back onto the street behind the Bastion, then it was a quick jog towards the Arcaneum and up through the window. It'd be boarded up or, more likely, sealed with brick, but that wasn't enough to stop him. He could be in and out in ten minutes if he was lucky and the book was easy to find. He hadn't even found the damn thing when he was interrupted before, but at least he had a starting point in the shelves.

Raekin moved like a shadow through the twisting alleys, keeping close to the walls, where the lanterns flickered weakest. The night was cold, a dry kind of chill that crept beneath his flesh and settled in his bones, but he barely felt it.

The city wasn't fully asleep, it never truly was. Voices still carried from distant taverns, laughter drifting between buildings. But this deep into the district, the streets were empty enough that every footstep sounded too loud. Every breath too sharp. Every shift of fabric too obvious. He exhaled slow and even, shoving the discomfort away.

He wasn't used to Hazel Gryph's streets anymore. The buildings were too clean, the stone too smooth, the scent of it all wrong. He had spent too long underground, where everything was damp and stale and rotting. The difference clawed at his nerves, set his teeth on edge.

As expected, the window of the Arcaneum had been closed off, stones roughly mortared into place around the sill. An even easier hurdle than he was expecting. He could climb up, delicately rest his hand on the rocks and silently remove them from the sill, but that would take time he didn't have. Instead, he held up his hand, careful to grab hold of the barricade and only the barricade. He cracked the boulders loose from the mortar with his magic. They took a chunk of the window with them, the brick work shattering under his touch and falling away. He paused for a moment, listening intently around him. His jaw felt like it was going to crack as he lowered the stones the rest of the way. Holding the heavy weight steady and slow was almost more than he could handle. Once they were safely on the ground, he paused once more to listen to his surroundings before approaching the wall.

The footholds Raekin had made previously had been broken away by whatever concerned builder had sealed up the window in the first place. But with a few tugs, Raekin pulled stones loose from their neighbours, extending them out just enough to get a handhold.

The cold wind whipped around him, hastening his climb as he ascended the building. When he had climbed this the first time, he had had time to look out over the city and marvel at the size of it. This time, he made the mistake of turning skyward and it knocked the wind out of him. He had almost forgotten how many stars there really were up there.

Something he had taken for granted when the sky was something that wasn't constantly shielded by a heavy layer of dirt.

There was no time to revel in the soft kiss of the wind, or the vibrant lights that shone down on the world. Not this time. In and out. Get the book, get back to the Peaks.

At the top of the climb, he scanned the frame for the rune that protected the window. A curl of his lip when he saw the wood was bare, no longer burned with an engraving. Either forgotten, or never known about, it was gone. One less thing to worry about.

His arms shook as he breached the sill. Both from the magic use and what it had taken to scale the wall. Sitting in the tunnels for so many hours shouldn't have taken such a toll on him but it felt as though his body had already gotten accustomed to the placid waiting.

The Restricted Area was still dark, enchanters not yet being called to relight the candles. He shifted to drop off the sill, but froze. Something. A noise. Quiet and distant, but he swore he heard it. Raekin hesitated at the window, fingers twitching against the ledge. The silence pressed against him, thick and unnatural. It felt... wrong. He slid through the opening, landing with barely a whisper. His pulse pounded against his ribs. After several beats of silence, no echoing heartbeats matching his own, he continued to breathe and crept to the shelves. That sharp scent of petrichor infiltrating his senses, helping the nervous panic ebb slightly. A smell he had always cherished. So much more pleasant than the spicy sting of the fissures.

There had been ample time to go through most of the shelves the last time he was in here. The interruption happening after he'd sorted through a large chunk of them. It had crossed his mind that if he hadn't gotten fed up and started tossing books Sybil may never have seen him. None of this would be happening, then...

He shook his head hard, knocking the thought away.

Concentrate.

Starting where he left off, running his fingers along the spines, reading out whatever titles were printed there. Most needed to have the years of dust brushed off to make them legible, but it only slowed him slightly.

First three shelves held nothing but old tomes on ancient magic that nobody would bother attempting to practice anymore. Grimoires housing knowledge that was common in this day and age. Pointless for the mages of the Arcaneum to bother keeping locked up. Doubtful there was ever anybody ambitious enough to go through these and sort out what wasn't useful anymore.

Book after book. Useless. More outdated texts, more grimoires long since replaced with modern teachings. He gritted his teeth, forcing back the creeping frustration.

Stay calm, keep looking.

Two rows later and his fingers stopped, hovering over a cracked spine; its leather worn thin. He barely caught the title beneath the grime: *Wachae Jyst Enchanting*. His heart jumped. This was it. Against his better judgement, he opened it, thumbing through the pages, regardless of the clock ticking its urgency at the back of his head. It wasn't exactly a wonder why the tome hadn't been picked up. It was written in Frew Braxian. Raekin had a limited understanding of the language, but even then, most of it was lost on him. Enchanter garble. Just what The Hag needed. Just what *they all* needed.

"There you go, you old crone. One ancient tome. As requested." Raekin smiled to himself as he slammed the book shut, immediately regretting it when the dust burst into the air and filled his lungs. As he struggled to keep his coughing fit silent, he wrapped the book up in one of the silk table runners, excitement thrumming through his chest.

A sharp pain slammed into his skull, his vision briefly disappearing to nothingness before contorting back to him. The silk-wrapped book fell from his hands, vanishing into the shadows. He tried to reach out, but heavy fog in his head made the room spin. A foot in his side, twisting him over. Instinct took over and he stood, whirling on his attacker. Steel whistled through the air, a blade flashing in the dim light. Raekin barely moved in time, the tip of the knife kissed his ribs, a sharp sting blooming across his side. Too close.

A fist came from nowhere, colliding with Raekin's jaw. His head snapped sideways, a burst of white-hot pain flaring behind his eyes.

He spat the blood from his mouth and struck back, magic already curling in his fingers. The ringing in his head made everything around him spin. His magic grabbed hold of the first thing he could sense, ready to tear the blood from their body. Stabbing pain jolted through his side. The muscles in his back seized with the shock, holding him immobile. When they released, he immediately coiled over, a groan raking past his lips. He pressed his hand to his side. His fingers came away soaked. The superficial slice from the blade was now torn open, ripped apart by his own blood, chewing through him from the inside. Muscle tearing like wet paper.

Idiot. Wrong blood.

Something blunt was rammed in between his shoulder blades as he fought to overcome the pain. He was forced to his knees. A rush of memories flooded through his mind, further clogging the panic that had already swelled through him. How many times had he been in just this position before Naz'Tak tore his skin again?

Red burned through his vision. He didn't think, only acted. Raekin's leg shot out, connecting hard with something solid. The attacker stumbled, a sharp gasp breaking the silence. Before they could shift away, Raekin twisted. He brought his heel up and slammed it into the side of their knee. The joint gave with a sickening pop. They crashed to the ground, hands clutching uselessly at the injury. He could see the white of their coat now, that familiar leather of a warden mantle.

For a split second he hesitated, his fight held back on the edge of a blade. A vice crushing down on his chest. A trick of the dark?

Is it her? Please, no.

The warden groaned, their deep, masculine voice snuffing out his thoughts. Raekin leapt to his feet, driving his heel down into the warden's ribs. He felt a disturbing elation as they crack beneath him. The warden screamed, but it was choked and stuttered, barely echoing in the darkened room.

Raekin dropped to his knees, gripping the Warden's face in his hand, clenched tight around their jaw. Raekin leaned in close. "You could have just run..." he whispered through his teeth. His hand wrapped around the man's throat, but didn't squeeze. Only gripped hold of his blood, pooling it into the man's jugular. He flooded the artery, feeling the man uselessly squirm under his grip. The blood swelled tightly around the man's windpipe until, with a short, muffled crunch, it collapsed.

The warden's body was still warm beneath his palm, chest rising in one last, shallow breath before stilling completely. Raekin exhaled, slow, watching as the final traces of life drained from the man's open eyes. He should be gone already. But he wasn't. Not yet.

His fingers twitched as he stood. Once, twice, before he curled them into a fist, pulling his hand back as if burned. He'd done this a thousand times, in a thousand different ways.

When did it stop being an order and start being just... him? His choice? And since when did that bother him so much?

He stared down at the white mantle, noting the silver leaf brooch clasped at his collar. A sharp pang stabbed his heart. He couldn't help wondering if Sybil knew the man. What she would feel when she heard of his death. And for the first time in so many years, he felt the tiniest hint of remorse.

Raekin landed hard in the tunnels, his breath ragged from the fight, from the climb, from the whole bullshit week.

He took a moment to steady himself, hands braced on his knees, then pushed forward. He'd held the blood back in his ribs, the wound still hanging dangerously open, only slightly covered by the sliced tunic. He'd have to stitch it up when he got a chance but for now, he could keep it from bleeding out. In a sick turn of the tables, he always hated controlling his own blood. Made him feel nauseous and the chill it left felt like the icy hands of death itself. Didn't help that he'd have to push out the violent reminder that this is exactly what all his victims felt.

Hirn was still waiting in the shadows, hunched over like he was trying to fold into himself.

"We live to see another day," Raekin chuckled as he strolled towards him, the book clutched tightly in his fingers. "There was only one straggler. Don't worry. I got rid of them, it won't be an issue this time.

Thank the malicious deities that that rogue mage picked tonight to be a problem." When his friend still refused to answer, he stepped up to him, grabbing his shoulder and turning him around.

Hirn's eyes were still rolled in the back of his skull, the lower half of his face painted red with blood. Both ears now had small streams trailing out of them, running down his neck.

Raekin had seen men bleed to death, others that had their brains hemorrhaging out as they struggled to stay alive. But not Hirn, it couldn't be Hirn. If he went too far, there was nothing Raekin could do to bring him back.

With a quick slap to the side of the head, Hirn's irises snapped back into place, levelling on Raekin. A sharp breath blew between Raekin's lips, the relief like a burning ember. He expected a quick retort, a burst of anger for the hit, but Hirn just stared at him slack-jawed.

Hirn's mouth moved, but no sound came out. His breathing was shallow, his fingers twitching uselessly against his lap. More blood dripped from his ears, staining his collar dark. Raekin's pulse spiked. "Hirn." He shook him, roughly. "What the fuck is wrong with you?"

No answer. Hirn's mouth opened, but his throat bobbed uselessly, as if the words were caught somewhere too deep to reach. His fingers twitched at his sides, useless, shaking.

Raekin gripped his friend's shoulder, shaking him hard. "Hirn. Look at me. Why the fuck were you under so long?"

Hirn's lips parted, his voice little more than a breath. "It's the..."

Raekin didn't realize he was holding his own breath until his lungs ached. "The what, Hirn? Spit it out."

Hirn's eyes finally lifted to meet his. Wide. Bloodshot. Terrified. "The rogue mage."

Raekin's stomach twisted. "What about them?"

Hirn swallowed, but it barely seemed to work. His throat bobbed once. Twice. The words fumbled at his lips, trapped somewhere deeper. Struggling with some internal fight.

Raekin's grip on Hirn's shoulder slackened. For a moment, the air between them was silent. "Hirn. Who's the rogue mage?"

SEVENTEEN

The light that shone behind the city gates as Sybil approached was almost obnoxiously bright. What should have been a beacon in the darkness guiding her home became more of a growing taunt. A reminder that the trip hadn't solved anything. A quick dig of her heels and Sybil urged Metronome to pick up to a gallop to reach them. Sybil dropped her body to run her hand along the horse's neck, whispering appreciations over the stomping of hooves, grateful the mare could keep up the pace to get them back before dawn.

She tapped her front pocket for the hundredth time, feeling the hard weight of the book. It was still there. But with every jostle of the horse, she swore it had fallen out and was buried somewhere in the snow. It would have been better to have jammed it in one of the saddlebags, but she had leapt on the horse so quickly, she didn't have time. If her father caught her taking off in the night without saying goodbye, he'd ask questions she didn't want to answer. Ones she didn't have the time for. She could apologize and explain herself later.

She had to get back to Hazel Gryph.

Hunger and lack of sleep made her feel almost delirious and hollow. A strange sensation as she urged Metronome to the stables outside the city gates. Instinct was the only thing steering her forward now, the logical side of her mind having been burned as fuel to propel her forward the last leg of the journey.

Only one of the stable hands was up this late into the night. On duty to collect the horses of the few people that were daft enough to be out after dark this late in the year. As soon as Metronome came into his sight, he was on his feet, opening her stall and kicking some of the hay around. Sybil thanked him profusely for dealing with the tack, tossed him a few dozen lok for his efforts. The metal coins clanged against the flask in her pocket as she retrieved them. It barely registered as she turned on her heel and started towards the centre of the city.

Though Ethissa's shop was closed, Sybil still struck her knuckles against the glass of the door. Just like the rest of the woman's life, Ethissa's residence was shrouded in secrecy. Sybil had always assumed she lived at the shop, her hours strange and hectic. The glass rattled and echoed through the shop, but the interior was still. Empty.

The clock tower that looked down over the city read a quarter after three. Sybil let out a silent, choked yell in the direction of the door as though it was the cause of the late hour. Quinn could be leagues away by now, but that wasn't what raked its sharp nails down her spine. The wicked, twisted hold the book in her mantle pocket had on her made her ready to throw it into the sewers and never look at its slick, black leather again. The sooner she could get her answers and be rid of its daunting weight the better. She needed those bloodstained pages to never taint her life again.

Sybil let out a long breath as she relaxed her arms into her body. The heat had already started to spread to her forehead, crackles of static jumping between her fingers as tiny torrents of wind ripped around them. Standing outside the shop losing her mind wasn't going to help her get anything she needed. The shop would reopen in the later morning hours, and she could come by again and get her answers. The nightmare in her pocket would just have to wait.

The idea of getting off her feet for a moment filled her heart with desire. A hot bath, a warm meal, and a comfortable bed. Then she recalled the last conversation she had had within the confines of what was once her home. Killian had said enough, she wouldn't be welcome. She hadn't had the chance to mourn the loss of him, let alone what that loss took with it. In her half-awake state, she found herself missing that stupid smell of fresh baked bread the most.

Now, late into the night, she had to figure out where she would sleep.

She just needed to let her breath catch up with her body, let the ache in her ribs settle into something manageable. The thought clawed at her, heavier than it should have been. Every muscle trembled beneath her, and the simple act of staying upright felt like a fight she was barely winning. If she sat, she might not get back up. Wasn't sure she even wanted to anymore.

The stone archway of the Bastion hung over her head, its overwhelming size paralyzing her. She'd walked the whole way without thought, her feet carrying her somewhere familiar. Her mind never quite settling on any specific thing. Hundreds of different thoughts were drifting in and out of her skull, fading to smoke before they could solidify. It wasn't until she saw the arch that she was even able to focus on her surroundings. She wasn't sure what had led her there, but deep down, she was glad to see the ugly buildings.

Bumps prickled up her spine as she stood there lost in thought. wardens were a noisy bunch and there was always somebody on patrol. Yet for the duration of her internal turmoil, not a single white jacket had crossed her path, not a single voice echoing out from the brightly lit courtyard. In fact, she became aware that she hadn't seen *anybody* since leaving Ethissa's shop. Like the entire city was holding its breath.

Something she had never witnessed in all the years living here.

She turned. *Tried* to turn. Her coat didn't move with her. The fabric beneath the leather stretched tight, pressing into her shoulders like a second skin.

A thin voice behind her. "Don't fight, Sybil."

"What are you doing, Victor?" Sybil asked, recognizing the botanomancer's magic. A talented mage with an affinity for flax and cotton. He was a favorite among the higher Wardens, quickly excelling and receiving his gold pin before most others in his training year. Though it was suspected he used his magic for more nefarious activities. The higher-ups always seemed to turn a blind eye whenever the whispers started.

"I'm sorry, Sybil. We've been instructed to take you to the Underkeep," Victor said, his hold on her mantle loosening ever so slightly.

"On what grounds? Whose orders?" Sybil snapped, her voice too high and sharp. "Who's *we?*"

"Don't be a bitch, Sybil, you know why." Another voice, a snivelling aerokineticist named Kohl that she had surpassed years ago. Who never forgave her for it either.

"The Bauers have placed you under arrest on the grounds of practicing illegal magic." A third voice, Hann.

"What could they possibly..." She started but the ice crawled up her neck as she realized. For a moment she doubted it, but his name wormed through her thoughts too clearly. "Killian." She'd trusted him.

She had given him everything he needed to ruin her. So naive to hope that he wouldn't. He'd been so furious. Even if he didn't tell his grandparents the full truth, any piece of the story she shared was enough to condemn her a hundred times over.

Sybil bit down hard on her lip to keep it from trembling as the weight of what was happening started to settle. Her knuckles started to burn with the pressure she held in her fist to keep any errant magic from drifting out of her skin. Now was not the time to be threatening in any way. They already sounded nervous enough beneath their bravado.

"Victor, come on, you know me. This has to be a mistake. Just let go of my clothes and we can talk about this."

"Don't you dare, Victor," Hann shouted, but before he could get the words out, Sybil's sleeves released from her arms.

She turned slowly, clasping her hands on her torso in salute. The gesture did little to satiate the fear she could see on the three men's faces. Victor clutched onto her clothing once more, just at the edges and only the lightest grip. A small swirl of air had started to whip up the dirt around Kohl's feet, his legs spread and anchored. Hann's fist was raised in the air. Four metal shards hovered above his hand, twisting, ready to be thrown. They each stood several feet away from one another, a semicircle around her. She knew this stance well. Standard warden defence: Mages throw wide. Never give them one target.

"Don't do anything stupid, Sybil," Kohl snarled, the wind flaring out the bottom of his mantle. He took the slightest step back from her. She was sure he was trying to hide it. They'd sparred years before. She always had him up close, but when he got the range, he could hold his own for much longer than she could.

She didn't move her hands from her stomach, but straightened. "Come on, guys. This is clearly a misunderstanding." Her voice flickered the tiniest bit, but she held it together. "The Bauers wouldn't have me arrested."

"Apparently you've been dabbling in some pretty messed-up shit. That's why you left the city," Hann snorted, adjusting his stance. "Wouldn't surprise me. We all know about... what was his name? Warden Vander? Vendir? Whatever. We all heard how you murdered him, tore him into scraps and shreds until there was nothing left." He smirked, the flash of his teeth sending a fresh wave of heat through Sybil's skin. "First victim of the 'chaos mage'."

She should have let the comment go. Should have ignored the slur, kept her composure. Her exhausted mind acted before she could grasp hold of it, the fury dictating her movement.

Her hands were up before she could take a second thought, a yell barrelling out of her throat. Though she went to throw the air around him and knock him off his feet, her magic had other plans. Several windows in the Bastion burst out from their sills, the glass raining down on the courtyard. A handful of shards rushed towards Hann. He barely had to move to avoid them, her control on the glass pitiful and chaotic. His magic was far more controlled, the metal reacting easily to his flicked wrist, shot like arrows across the courtyard. She reached up again, her magic listening and three of the four metal shards superheated and dropped to the ground. The fourth sliced into her shoulder, embedding molten metal in the muscle.

"Piece of shit," she snapped, clutching her shoulder, the hot metal burning her hand as she tried to tear it from her skin. Kohl was whipping up a heavier wind, effectively blinding her as she shielded her eyes from the onslaught. Her mantle started to constrict around her again and in a flurry of panic, she flung her hand out. Stones flew out of the tornado and vanished out of sight. A cry sounded from beyond the dust and the hold on the fabric was dropped.

Hann appeared through the gust first, his fist already raised. Sybil moved fast, dropping low as he went to strike. He overcompensated, twisting awkwardly and stumbling on his own feet, vanishing back through the dust. Sybil dragged her foot along the stone, slamming it hard into the blinding wind, elation warming her as she felt it connect. Hann cried out, the whipping wind hiding his collapse. Sybil straightened, squinting against the onslaught of debris that tried to slice through her eyes. Kohl was a coward, as usual, hiding beyond her reach. She tried to use her own magic to calm the whirling storm, but to no avail. The wind only sputtered and shifted, resuming its tight turns and tears.

Something hard struck her head, and she was knocked sideways out of the wind tunnel back into the calm courtyard. She went to stand, but a fist slammed into her stomach, twisting her back into herself.

"Stay the fuck down," Hann yelled, shoving her face into the stones.

Her whole body felt like it was vibrating, icy cold burning through her flesh as the panic consumed her. She tried to move her arms, but another blow was struck to her side. Trapped and pinned, her cheeks rubbed raw against the coarse path. Her magic twisted and contorted beneath her skin, mimicking her panic with its tantrum. It flared and burst at her fingers, up her arms, even sparking across her chest down her spine. But with nowhere to go, no immediate direction, it sputtered inside, sending burning lightning into her nerves, her body convulsing under the pain. The men gripped her tighter, bruises already welling beneath their harsh hold.

"Hey! What are you doing?" a voice called out. A familiar, grating, but safe voice.

"Captain," Hann muttered, stepping back from Sybil. She was finally able to open her eyes as the stars cleared from her eyes. Captain Hertrin was jogging towards them, stopping briefly to check on the collapsed body of Victor.

"Help," she wheezed, every breath burning through her already bruised body.

"She tried to kill us," Hann said, gesturing towards the glittering shards of glass that littered the stones. "We had to do something."

"And you've already made your point shoving her into the ground," Hertrin dropped to a knee, resting a hand on Sybil's shoulder.

"These fucks... attacked me first," she choked out. "The Bauers..."

"Get the cuffs, Kohl." Hertrin sighed, ignoring Sybil's weak voice. "That's all you needed to do."

"What?" Sybil whispered, trying to sit up, only for her arms to be wrenched behind her. "What are you doing?"

The captain sighed. "You shouldn't have gone to Trelusk, Sybil. You should have just taken the promotion and been done with it." He shook his head, leaning close. His voice dropped low, almost breaking. "I can't help you anymore."

Sybil's heart fell into her stomach. Metal was clamped around her wrists, then spread over her hands, still warm from the magic that formed it. His hand left her shoulder, and the warmth with it, as cold spread through her back. A bag was slid over her face, obscuring the captain's soft, pleading eyes from her view.

She tried to call out, to question it again, but another wind torrent was ripped underneath the bag, suffocating her voice in her throat.

"Is Victor okay?" Kohl said, though it was dimmed and faded as though he was leagues away.

"I'll take him to the infirmary. Get to the Underkeep. The Bauers are waiting," the captain said, his voice fading with every word under the shrieking storm in her ears.

She was hoisted to her feet, practically dragged across the stones as the wind pummelled her ears, twisting the world around her even under the dark hood.

The path to the Underkeep was a well-known route to the wardens but with her senses cut off she felt as though she was walking in circles. The pain rattled through her body as they descended a set of stairs, but she could barely focus on it. Could barely focus on keeping her feet landing one in front of the other. With every step she took, she couldn't help thinking that they should have reached the bottom already. Even functionally blind, the path seemed wrong. The moldy, soft moss smell was stronger, danker down here. Like rot permeated more heavily than she remembered in The Underkeep.

The men at her side stopped her once the ground levelled back out. The metal wrapped tightly around her hands was suddenly loosened, the shackles clanging and falling away. The windstorm whipping under the bag ceased, leaving only a high-pitched ringing in the silence. She was shoved hard in the back, stumbling for a few steps before the ground briefly disappeared beneath her feet. Her knees hit dirt with a crunch that rattled through her spine.

Everything inside her collapsed with the fall. It wasn't pain, but a sudden, crushing absence that burned from within. A hollowness that sucked the breath from her lungs and locked her bones in place. That thrumming undercurrent of energy she had lived with for so long vanished. A sickening drop twisted through her, like stepping off a ledge expecting solid ground only to find nothing beneath her feet. The space where her magic had been felt scraped raw, as if something had reached inside her and wrenched it out.

Her stomach curled in on itself. She had spent so long fearing what her magic could do, but now, stripped of it entirely, she felt... lesser. Exposed. *Weak.*

She tore the bag off her head in a panic. Bright torchlight immediately stung her eyes, forcing tight, long blinks to refocus. She could barely breathe as it was, but the smell of rot and decay burned her sinuses, raking out any hope she had of settling her gasping breaths.

"Why did you bring this with you?" The high, lilting voice startled Sybil. She twisted around, whipping her head to face the voice. Justinia Bauer stood at the edge of the dirt, the toes of her polished boots hanging off the lip of a stone ledge. Pinched in Justinia's hand and held like a diseased rat was the black leather grimoire. Sybil glanced dumbly down at the pocket on her mantle that was now torn open.

"Yes, we knew you had it. Please, just answer us, Sybil. We want to make this as quick and painless as possible," Stewart Bauer cooed from behind his wife, his voice warm and easy. He was leaned lazily in an archway. They weren't wearing their garish gowns or cloaks, replaced with dark tunics and trousers. Their finery stripped from them, only the circlets on their heads left to indicate their station.

Sybil's mind was trying to catch up to what was being said as her head swivelled around. The walls were stone, their surfaces cracking and pitted, mold and moss painting the divots and fissures. The pit she had been pushed in was a step below the ledge that ran the length of it. Heavily packed dirt was underneath her hands. Discoloured and mottled, spots of it riddled with growths.

In the dim light of the torches she could make out the runes engraved into the stones directly on either side of her. Positioned so that the stone ledge acted as a barricade line dividing the runed pit from the rest of the room.

The emptiness made sense. A makeshift magical cage. Common practice in the Underkeep. Except *this* wasn't The Underkeep. Not the one she knew anyways. The Underkeep had stone floors, a multitude of wardens on watch. Cells lined the walls, usually with at least a few people within them. A few grates were installed in each of the cells so the prisoners had some semblance of daylight. But this room was closed in, the only path to the outside world being guarded by the heads of the Bauer family.

"She attacked Victor," Hann said, drawing Sybil's attention to the far wall where Hann and Kohl stood at attention, glowering down at the girl on her knees in the dirt. "And kicked me. She needs to pay for—"

Stewart snapped his fingers, silencing the man. He gestured to his wife, urging her on. "We just want to know about the book, Sybil. That's all," Justinia said, her eyes soft, the light browns welcoming and patient. They crinkled with her lips, the surrounding wrinkles twisting delicately around them.

She had held Sybil so tightly only a few nights prior, brimming with excitement. A warmth that emanated with each gesture as she congratulated her. Such a matronly aura, vibrant and caring with every turn of her lips. Everything inside of Sybil was telling her to keep her mouth shut. Sybil knew it was pointless. They had the book, they had her. The Bauers had been her family, and in the thick of everything that was going on, she needed that.

"It was the one that Quinn used when he was killed," Sybil said, a harsh breath releasing between her lips. She rolled her legs out and crossed them in the dirt. The words fell from her, heavy, weighted, and bitter. A held secret that she had trapped between her teeth for so long, but it seemed to be escaping more frequently.

"This is the book you two used that night to enact that ritual?" Justinia dropped to one knee, holding the grimoire aloft. Sybil felt as though somebody had kicked her in the chest.

Had Killian kept anything she had said to himself? He better hope he never crossed her path again after this. She bit into her cheek but nodded her head, trying to not let her fuming at their grandson sprinkle on her face.

"Thank you for being honest, Sybil." She tucked the book under her arm, clasping her hands in front of her chest. "Why did you bring it back to Hazel Gryph?"

Sybil hesitated again, but only for a moment as the woman's lips twitched to a sad smile. "The book is blank. It shouldn't be. I was hoping I could get some answers..."

A pause. "I see. Was anybody able to give you these answers?"

Sybil chewed her lip, craning her head to look behind the matriarch. Stewart had his eyebrow cocked, excited curiosity mixed on his face as he leaned towards them. "No. I was going to try in the morning."

"So, nobody knows you made it back with this book?"

A heady chill ran through Sybil's veins as she stared into the bright eyes that seemed to be studying her. She couldn't answer, her mouth running dry as the questions started to drift more clearly through her head. The way they lined up made her skin crawl, the dissecting way Justinia's wide eyes measured every inch of Sybil's face. "What exactly are you asking me?"

"Does anybody know you are in possession of this book, or the contents of it? Does anybody know you made it back to town?" Stewart said stepping forward to stand by his wife.

"Sir, we followed her through town. She didn't stop anywhere but—" Kohl started.

Stewart raised his hand, silencing the warden. "That's enough, Justinia, I can take it from here," he said, patting her gently on the shoulder.

"Yes, dear." Justinia stood, shifting around her husband to take his place on the wall.

"We really do appreciate the cooperation, Sybil. Thank you for answering all our questions," he said. He was calm. Too calm. "Makes this next part that much easier."

Stewart circled his hands around one another as though forming an invisible ball with his fingers, a movement Sybil had seen countless times from their grandson over the years. The steam billowed out between his fingers as the air between his hands filled with water and then was subsequently heated. He was slower at it than Killian, the ball morphing in and out of shape. His mastery became clear when he flicked his wrists, and the ball of steam whipped out from between his hands. Sybil flinched, closing her eyes tight as she prepared to feel the scalding ball hurled towards her.

Instead, screams rang out from beyond the magical barricade. She snapped her eyes open as Stewart directed the steam, flowing it through the two wardens' nostrils and gaping mouths. Kohl and Hann's screams only lasted a moment before they devolved into choked gurgles. Aerated blood bubbled out of their mouths and down their chins. Their stomachs swelled while their hands grasped uselessly at their necks, trying to tear the scalding steam from within their throats. They both collapsed to the ground, rolling onto their sides, their cries coming out as wet gulps.

Watching them wither and shake on the ground felt like an eternity. Flashes of their faces laughing at warden events littered her mind, interspersed with the horror before her. Pink liquid poured out of their slack mouths onto the stones, flowing through the gaps and cracks. She stumbled back from the border of the dampener, her feet sliding uselessly on the dirt. It was the first time in ten years she didn't feel a flood of electricity through her veins as she panicked, an empty, mottled feeling clamping down on her heart. That swirling, messy, storm that lived in her core snuffed out and silent.

"Oh, goodness," Stewart said, wobbling on his feet before Justinia raced from the wall to catch him. His hands shook as he wiped his forehead, sweat beads dripping down from the garish circlet. A line of blood dripped from his nose, vibrant and red against the pale backdrop of his greying skin. He turned towards the door, vomiting beyond the archway. He coughed once, spitting into the dirt at his feet. His face was pale, the colour lost, but he still stood. "Can you believe I used to be able to do four people at a time?" He swayed again slightly, but Justinia held his arm tight.

"Why?!" Sybil finally screamed, her own insides still threatening to pour out. Her eyes were locked on Hann and Kohl, the pink puddle turning redder by the second as it spread and leached into the spaces between the stones. She waited for their breath, for something to show that they were still alive. That this was all a sick, twisted joke. This couldn't possibly be happening. Not from the family that had taken her in.

"Because we're old, Sybil. That's just what happens as you age," Stewart said, gently patting Justinia's hand and removing it from his arm.

Her face burned with the rage, the casual dismissal tearing her away from the still bodies. "Why did you *kill* them, you crazy, old bastard?!" Sybil shrieked, her voice catching and jumping. How long ago had she sat at their dinner table? Shit, less than a week ago and she had her arms wrapped around them.

"Yes, dear, why did we have to get these poor children involved in this messiness?" Justinia asked, flippantly waving her hand towards the corpses.

"Love, we needed somebody to get her down here, and our dear captain was too close to this." Stewart rested his hand against his wife's. "I'll get it cleaned up when we dissolve her. Wash them away into the pit, it's what it was made for. We can just say they died... oh, I don't know. We'll figure out something. We always do."

"Why are you doing this?" Sybil screamed, wrenching their attention back to her, tearing away the sickening adoring gaze that solidified between the couple.

"I don't know why you decided *now* was such a brilliant time to start going digging in places you shouldn't be." Stewart adjusted his tunic, wiping the dirt only he could see from its front. "This is what happens when you stick your nose where you shouldn't. You should know that as a warden, Sybil. Especially as such a highly decorated one." He crossed his arms. "Your father knew when to turn his head and mind his own."

"Knew? Knew what?"

"He knew that he wanted to protect you. Was smart enough to move to the country."

Move to the country.

Before the nightmares. Before the blackened abyss. Before the darkness consumed her every waking moment. Before all the secrets that she thought had broken him.

That didn't make sense.

Stewart stepped forward, his hand opening, the palm filling with water. "We'll inform everyone that you died on the road back. I'm sure your father will be devastated." He stared a moment at the swirl of water that refused to boil in his hand, brows furrowing. "Pity. Wasted my energy on *nobodies*. This is going to be much slower," he paused, a smile stretching across his face, softening his eyes. "But probably less painful."

"Please, you can't do this!" Sybil screamed. She reached uselessly for her magic, trying to call on anything to throw at the man, the emptiness crushing down on her. It'd been ten years since she had been this helpless. All she could manage to think of was the crippling image of Quinn. His body being sucked through the black void in the floor as his skin was carved and sliced. She'd been helpless then, and here she was all over again. A little girl, her world crumbling around her while all she could do was watch.

"Unfortunately, I can, and I have to." Steward said, lifting his hand. The water slithered from his palm like a serpent. The magic dampening runes didn't hold it back; it passed through the barrier unhindered.

Sybil slapped her hands over her mouth, closing her fingers around her nose as the water reached her. She held her breath. Pressed her hands tight, hoping to seal any pathways. But water was clever and slick, and moved easier than flesh. It snaked between the gaps and filled her cupped hands. It wormed its way between her fingers, up through her nose, through the tight line of her lips pressed between her teeth. Filling her mouth until all she could taste was the stagnant water.

The ground beneath her started to shake, rumbling a lone tone. The invasion of water halted, held steady between her cheeks as her tongue fought to keep it from sliding to her lungs. Stewart hesitated, his hands still held aloft, but his head swiveling on his neck as he searched for the source of the noise. The ground beneath her feet started to ripple and shift. She tried to scream but choked instead, inhaling the water as her feet were wrapped in dirt, the floor liquefying as it started to swallow her legs.

Stewart dropped to the ground, his mouth opening and closing in a smattering of shock and disbelief. He grasped uselessly at Sybil as she sank through the ground of the prison. The dirt devoured her, wrapping around her lower body and crawling up her torso. Stewart's wild eyes vanished as Sybil's head was pulled under, darkness swallowing her. Dirt and water mixing in her mouth as she tried to inhale. She could barely hear the curses that Stewart screamed as the soil encompassed her, suffocating her with its bulk.

Her dark, dirt-built coffin opened, and she briefly fell through seemingly nothingness. Blackness surrounding her, the air the only thing to greet her as she tumbled through the darkness. She landed on her hip, the ground below her hard and compact. The pain sent lightning through her skull, but it was barely noticed as her body seized, desperate to inhale.

Dirty water sputtered past her lips as she coughed, the last remnants of Stewart's magic escaping her.

Then, like the crack of distant thunder, she felt it. A slow, aching pull in her chest. A thread of warmth curling under her ribs. Then another. And another.

The flood didn't come all at once. It trickled, then surged, then broke over her in waves. Lightning shuddered across her knuckles, static snapping in her hair. The dirt around her shivered, wind kicking up dust. Pins and needles across the barricade of her flesh, her body struggling to grasp the magic.

Years of learning to hold it in washed away as she grasped uselessly at control. Like a spoiled child that had been neglected, the magic reared up dramatically as it flowed back into her. It spasmed and wavered before dying, only to then repeat its temperamental surge. Element after element rippling across her skin.

It felt as though she had been breathing in sand, her throat dry and rough, every movement and breath raking across the damaged flesh. Fighting to temper the wave of power that was surrounding her and desperately trying to fill her lungs, she was briefly lost to her own panic. She dropped to her knees, the pain in her skull making bile rise in her throat.

It wasn't until she was finally able to take a full breath that the smell hit her.

Cinnamon and ash.

It was overpowering down here, like a heavy cloth wrapped around her head, forcing itself on her. She stumbled trying to get to her feet, barely catching herself as she fell back to her knees. The flaring sparks that danced over her skin were sporadic, barely lighting up the dark space.

Little bursts of vision, taunting images of what was around her. She cursed silently, trying and failing to get a hold of her magic.

Her fingers felt numb and shook as she grasped for her belt. They rattled so hard, she struggled to find her flint. She dug into every fold and crevice, the small box seemingly lost to the confines of her dilapidated mantle. There was a tinkling of metal, followed by a soft clunk. The strong scent of liquor overpowered the cinnamon and ash. A reminder of her father's stolen trinket. She went to drop to the ground to feel for the flask when another flare of magic ripped out of her fingers, the static snapping in the air before the sparks settled. The liquor burst into flames, the dirt erupting beneath it as the darkness was snuffed out and the tunnel illuminated.

A choked gasp echoed against the dirt wall as she stared down the tunnel. There was a rustling and clattering of metal before two booted feet stepped out of the darkness and started towards her. Her body was paralyzed, unable to do anything other than stare as the figure emerged from the darkness. Too exhausted and empty to shift, or move, or run.

The figure's legs were covered in straps of leather, the scuffed and ragged boots kicking up plumes of dirt with each step. Sybil felt a yell burgeoning in her chest, but her teeth held tight. Her magic continued to flicker and burn between her fingers and dance along the dirt away from her. She wanted to direct it towards the figure, throw a gust of wind, sharp daggers of ice, even just grasp *something* to slow them down. But even as she lifted her hands, the pitiful little sparks only continued their dance. Never drifting more than a few inches from her skin.

The figure dropped to its knees in front of her, the light finally illuminating his face. His orange eyes were narrowed, brows heavy under the mess of black hair that hung over them. The scars and runes on his body lit up under the dying flames.

"Quinn?" His name came out of her mouth breathlessly, heavy as though wound up like a spring, the metal snapping as it released. His face softened as he lurched forward, grabbing hold of her shoulders and dragging her into his arms. The cinnamon smell faded as the earthy scent of loam overtook her, wrapping through her nose and sitting heavy in her senses. He tangled his hand in her hair, pressing her head to his chest.

His fingers curled into the fabric at her back, clinging tight, as if grounding himself just as much as her. He didn't speak at first, just breathed, chest rising and falling quickly.

A soft breath caressed her hair. His voice was lower than she remembered. Sharper. But it was him. "I almost lost you." Barely a whisper, raw with exhaustion and dangerously close to breaking. His arms tightened, just for a second, his breath coming out ragged and heavy.

Then, softer, his voice dipping into something that almost sounded like the boy she used to know. "Don't ever make me run like that again."

EIGHTEEN

Raekin wasn't supposed to care this much. Not anymore. Not after a decade spent scraping through the dark, learning to let go of everything that mattered to him. But the moment he saw Hirn struggling to tell him who the wardens were after, it all fell away. Naz'Tak, Varena, the Etched. None of it mattered anymore. Nothing except getting to her in time. He stopped thinking. Fuck the consequences.

He had been with the wardens long enough to know what they meant by 'rogue mage'. When he tossed the book at Hirn, he was barely able to get out that he would meet him back in Ktharheim as he fumbled pathetically to light his torch. He could deal with whatever punishment Naz'Tak dreamed up later. Hirn was more than capable of covering for him until then.

They'd take her to the Bastion, that much he knew. More than likely the Underkeep, but it was more runed than the Arcaneum and he was out of The Hag's mixture. He didn't know what he would do, he just needed to get to her. And time was already stretched thin.

Run. Just fucking run.

The first heartbeat snuffed out and his chest caved. But he didn't slow. The second stopped and he almost broke. By the time the third started to falter, there was nothing left in him but unadulterated terror. He'd ripped through the walls with manic abandon, tearing down the ceiling above, caution thrown to the dust. The flurry of dirt and stone tore the torch from his grip, engulfing him in darkness. When the body crashed down with the debris, he stopped breathing. He couldn't see her, could only hope it even was her. Only saw the static lined silhouette of the woman that had fallen from the ceiling. Twitching and convulsing as magic rippled across her skin. That should have been enough, a clear reminder of the last time he saw her chaotic magic in the back alley. When her sharp coughs echoed through the tunnel, the tightly wound tension in his body released.

It's her. Sybil. She's safe.

He felt as though a decade of weight had lifted from his shoulders. The empty focus that had levelled through his head didn't fade away until she was wrapped in his arms. A feeling he hadn't felt in years, one he had forgotten existed until he felt her sharp breaths against his chest.

She was shaking, her chest rising sharply against his. Breathless, struggling, but alive. She didn't lean into him, not at first. He felt the hesitation, the way she stiffened, like she was holding something back. But then her fingers twisted into the fabric of his tunic, and just like that, whatever internal crutch had been stabilizing her disintegrated. Her breath hitched. A sob cracked through her ribs, and she sank against him, her hands clutching at his torso, pulling him closer, as if afraid he'd disappear if she let go.

Raekin tightened his grip before he could stop himself. He shouldn't have. He should have let go the second he felt her breathing. Should have put space between them. Reminded himself why this was dangerous. But he didn't.

As time passed in the Alpstraum, most Etched slowly let go of the things they cared about, the anguish the only thing that filled their heads. Easier to lose those tiny shimmers of hope or joy to the darkness than to let them remind you of better things. Nightmares don't seem as immeasurably violent and abysmal when you forget that dreams exist.

Raekin hadn't. He had held on to his last scrap of humanity through to the bitter end and out the other side. His memories were the only thing they couldn't carve from his skin, and he wouldn't let the monsters take them. She would always be there, but he had snuffed out the desire to reach for her.

At least, he thought he had.

With her in his arms, every broken, buried thing came clawing back to the surface. The want tightening him in its clutches until it was the only thing that brought the pulse to his heart. Burning away the daunting whispers that tried to shake him.

"Are you okay?" he asked, not daring to let her go yet. She didn't answer, tiny, choked gasps emanating from where her face pressed into his chest. She was trembling in his hold, and he could feel the tears soaking into his tunic. The drumbeats in his head were starting to fade as he caught his breath. The excessive use of magic like a hammer to his skull.

He glanced up at the ceiling where she had fallen through. He had solidified the dirt behind her, but he couldn't be sure that they wouldn't burst through it at any moment. Any Bastion geomancer could already be on their way to tear through the barrier. He gently leaned back from her, unlacing his hand from her hair to press his finger under her jaw and tip it up to him. That blackened char in his chest started to heat as he took in the tear-filled hazel gaze. Exactly as he remembered it.

Exactly as he remembered *her*.

Her brow furrowed as her eyes darted over the lines and scars that traced across his face. Ten years had passed but he could still hear the cogs turning in her skull. Her damp eyes started to dry as her expression switched to uneasy curiosity. The questions that vibrated through her head threatening to rattle into Raekin's arms. A fight was running rampant on her face as she tried to answer them on her own.

"We need to get out of here. They'll come looking for you soon," Raekin said. His eyes landed on her shoulder, the once-white mantle stained with dirt and blood. The shine of metal caught his eye from within a blooming flower of red at her shoulder. He ran his fingers along the metal, a sharp wince scraping past her teeth.

Raekin grabbed tighter on the metal and tore it out of her skin. She screamed out, pushing back from him and clutching her shoulder. The metal was melted and morphed, extreme heat touching it before what was left of the sharp point had embedded in her flesh. He tossed it flippantly to the ground before standing and extending his hand to her. Sybil eyed it, her own still gripped tightly on the wound before cautiously accepting the help. Electricity shot through her hand as she grabbed his. He couldn't be sure if it was magic or nerves, but he let the sensation awaken the parts of him he thought had rotted.

"Are you hurt anywhere else?" he asked, eyes skating over the rest of her body.

"I'll be fine. But you—" He didn't wait to listen, turning away from her to start back out of the tunnel.

"Quinn, stop," she shouted, that name sending shivers through his spine. Every time she said it, he wanted to wrap her in his arms all over again. An ache blooming in his chest. He had to force himself to push it deep down where it couldn't bring those needs to the surface.

When she caught up to him, she wrapped her fingers around the scarred and etched runes on his forearm. She flinched back like he was a lit flame. His jaw clenched tight, not letting her repulsion imbed its nasty little teeth.

Of course she flinched. Who wouldn't?

"What—" She started again, but he pressed his finger to his lips.

Raekin turned again, knowing that if he started indulging her now, they'd be here forever, whatever answer he gave her only birthing two more questions in its wake. He barely even knew how to answer any of her questions. If he told her the truth, told her everything that happened, how quick would she be to turn any guilt inwards? He'd need time to soften whatever he was going to say, twist it until it was easy and comfortable. Wrapped in just enough truth to keep her from pulling the threads. A difficult line to walk. One he hadn't had to walk for so long, he wasn't sure he even still could. He needed time to think, and they needed to get somewhere safer.

"I have a place I can take you that's hidden." He reached down, digging through the sporadic mounds of debris in the dying light. "You'll be safe until I can figure something out." There, half crushed by a fallen rock. The torch at least had enough tallow still left on it to light. He brushed the mud off it, then cracked his flint, touching it to the fat. The growing darkness around them was driven back again as it ignited.

"Quinn—" Sybil started.

Raekin shook his head, grabbing hold of her hand and clenching his jaws to still the sudden fluttering in his chest at her touch. "We need to get out of here first. That was the Portcullis up there, right?"

"It was, but—"

"Then we need to not be here when they get someone to dig through the ground looking for you." He led her around the larger fallen debris on the ground. She tripped up slightly, catching herself as he pulled her along. He wanted to slow, to help her, but there wasn't time.

They'd double back through the eastern tunnel to get to the mol-hunds, back towards Hirn. He would be long gone by the time they reached the beasts. All the better. He could get to Trotter, and get her to the caverns. It gave him a modicum of time to figure out what he was going to do.

A sound, like something tumbling into a deep crevasse, echoed through the tunnels. Raekin stopped.

Sybil stumbled into his back but caught herself, her breath sharp in the stillness. She didn't speak, didn't have to. Just watching him with a wide-eyed stare. He was already listening, ears straining for anything beyond their own breathing. Silence.

Then, a sudden snap of energy licked across his skin. Sybil's magic. The charge passed from her hand to his, sharp enough to jolt him back to motion. He picked up his pace, driven by an instinct that told him to be as far from Bastion as possible.

"Where are we even going?" Sybil whispered.

He didn't answer, their footsteps filling the space left by her question.

They rounded a last bend, and, like the loyal creature he was, Trotter was waiting. No doubt already having sensed Raekin's return. The torches strung along the saddle were already lit, and Raekin let out a quiet thanks to Hirn. He reached forward to grab hold of the reins only for his hand to stop midway, a sharp cry ringing out behind him.

Raekin turned, already moving.

"What *is* that?" Sybil stepped around him to look closer at the beast. Raekin opened his mouth, ready to blurt that Trotter was friendly, that they'd be able to move faster. But before he could, she had stepped up to the beast. Trotter shifted momentarily away from her reach, but after a twitch of his maw, he nudged her hand closer. She brought her fingers above Trotter's nose, letting him run his appendages around them. "He's incredible." Trotter stepped forward, pressing his snout into her palm, the mud and saliva slathering over Sybil's skin. She didn't seem to mind as she ran her hand along the light fur, her smile stretched across her cheeks.

"A molhund. His name is Trotter," Raekin said, crossing his arms and stepping back to watch her. No hesitation as she moved closer, her hands skating along both sides of the beast's head. She laughed as he tried to feel her face with his tendrils, moving out of the way to run her fingers deeper through his fur. Even as the prehensile whiskers ran across the shoulders of her mantle, smearing the dirt into the fabric, she didn't flinch.

She turned back to Raekin, and her smile faded. He'd seen that expression before. One so close to it a common sight on the faces of fresh-captured Etched when they caught themselves in a reflection. On the ones who hadn't yet learned to stop wasting energy on fear.

She wasn't just looking at him. She was seeing what the Void had made of him. Disgust he could handle. This was grief. The realization scraped like a rusted blade against his ribs.

"What did they do to you?"

He didn't realize he'd turned away until his hands found the saddle straps, tightening them with slow, measured precision. Something to focus on. Something that wasn't the way she'd looked at him like he was a ghost of something she used to love. Flashes started to decorate his thoughts, regardless of how busy he tried to keep them. He clenched his jaw, squeezing his eyes shut. Years of training to lock those memories away, seconds to unravel it all with one single question wrapped in a mortified tone.

What did they do to you? What did they do to you? What did they do to you?

It deserved an answer. He couldn't give it. Not until it stopped tasting so tainted on his tongue.

Claws, needles. Knives. Hammers. Over and over. Carving him into something he no longer recognized. Didn't *want* to recognize. The Void had sculpted his flesh to their design, a complete disregard for the traumatic way they went about it. The fear and horror that reflected at him through her eyes was enough to bring all the hurt barrelling back. That nightmare was torn free of the dark place he hid the pieces of him too damaged to bring to light. They floated imperceptibly around him, sucking the air in the tunnels out. The other Etched all shared his experiences. They would never look at him with such distaste. This was new, and from her, it hurt.

He rolled his neck around, the cracking and pulling of his bones quieting the noise that vibrated through his skull. A sharp pain at the top of his spine, a harsh stretch at his scalp as he brought his chin down. A reset; the repetition silencing, normal thoughts flooding back through his head.

"We can talk later," he said, shaking the tension out and stepping back from the saddle. He dropped the last of the leather straps from his hands slowly, measuring each dent and tear through his fingers. Each indentation that slid over his flesh pulled a different torsion from the tight grip of his muscles.

"I didn't know it was this bad," she whispered, her voice only just audible as it echoed against the tight walls of the tunnel.

Raekin didn't acknowledge it. Just, "Hop on."

"We're riding him?" Sybil asked.

"Fastest way to travel the tunnels," he said. The pride faded quickly as her face dropped.

"You've been down here this whole time," she said, her voice trailing off.

He ground his teeth together, flexing his fingers a few times before answering. "I have." Before she could press, he grabbed her hand, helping her hoist herself up onto Trotter's back. She flinched as her injured arm adjusted her weight but stayed silent. When she slid forward on the saddle, he stopped her, his hand on her knee. "You can't ride in the front, too dangerous." He gestured towards the armor on his legs. It was riddled with nicks and dings, small tears throughout the thick plates. Sybil glanced nervously down at her own thin leather pants, then at the large claws that had started to paw anxiously. They left heavy tears in the dirt, the threat making its mark. Sybil nodded and slid back on the saddle.

Raekin grabbed hold of the horn, hoisting himself up to sit in front of her. He'd ridden with Varena at his back before. That was stained with fear and necessity. This was something else. This was familiar. An old comfort he had forgotten about, and his chest ached with the feeling of her thighs against his.

With the barest hesitation, Sybil wrapped her arm around Raekin's waist. When Trotter shifted, throwing his heavy weight around the wall to turn himself, the hesitation was ripped from her and she tightly gripped his torso. He winced, the wound from earlier stretching open further. He held the blood tighter, keeping it from trailing onto her arms. As the pain dwindled to a dull grating, he gripped her hand that pressed to his stomach. It had been meant as a reassurance, a soft gesture to tell her she was safe. Except, once he had hold of her, he didn't let go.

Trotter dug his rear paws in and took off. The dirt flew up around them as his claws tore through the earth propelling him forward. The shriek that sounded behind Raekin was lost to thundering paws.

He had no doubt that the sight of the darkened tunnels barrelling towards them would have been much worse than just the feeling of the beast thundering through the underground. At their current speed turns and forks would materialize out of the darkness so quickly it only gave the molhund fractions of seconds to dig his claws into the dirt and adjust his course. His rear would sometimes brush along the walls, sending clumps of debris tumbling from the ceiling. It had terrified Raekin the first few times, flinching as he prepared to crash catastrophically into the dirt. This was Trotter's world, though, and the great beast never slowed. Even as Raekin did.

There was another fortunate gift the speed gave. The noise that followed behind them as they travelled drowned out any chance of conversation. A roaring crunching echoing against every wall, muffling even Trotter's heavy snorted breath. The encompassing noise was one of the few luxuries he was allowed. It gave him his own space to either turn off his thoughts, or finally let the more complicated ones be the focus of his attention. Like a soothing earthquake.

He needed that focus now, the tight grip on his waist and the quick heartbeat a steady reminder of what was at risk. If the Portcullis had a death warrant out on Sybil, they would be on high alert all over Plaitius. She couldn't go back, not anytime soon. At least not without somewhere to hide. He could get her to Tabrasia, maybe even Losweau. But it wouldn't be before Naz'tak started the pull and the pain would be too much for him to do anything. He had to go to Ktharheim sooner than later to sort his own shit out before he could deal with hers.

It wasn't long before the tight grip on his waist started to falter, slipping away from his hip, a start, and then wrapping around once more. The cycle repeated, the weight on his back getting heavy before it jolted back up again. The feeling made his face flush. The beast was loud, but his run was even. A constant, rhythmic beat. That flare of magic before must have been too much for her. The steady thundering of paws lulling her slowly to sleep.

Raekin wrapped Trotter's reins around the horn between his legs, the molhund barely noticing the extra slack as he continued to run. He reached down, grabbing each of Sybil's hands in his. She pulled back at first, but with another small reassuring squeeze, she relaxed, letting him tuck them under the armor on his thighs. With her body secured, he felt it slump against his back once more, her head nestling tightly into the cavity between his shoulder blades.

The second her heartbeat evened out and ebbed, he felt it. Slow and steady. Safe. He should have pulled away, shouldn't have held onto the beat with his magic, letting every soft thud sooth him. Should have ignored the feeling curling in his chest like a slow-burning flame.

Instead, he reached back, fingers ghosting over the fabric of her sleeve, as if to make sure she was real. As if he needed proof. Sybil stirred slightly, her grip around him tightening even in sleep. He rested his hand on her thigh, the feeling eerily new yet so familiar. His throat ached. Her weight against his back shouldn't have felt like relief—but it did.

This was dangerous. This was everything he couldn't afford. She wasn't his to have and he wasn't the one that should be keeping her safe.

But for once, he let himself be selfish. As the tunnels blurred past them, a single thought settled heavily in his chest. Something he hadn't thought about for years.

Home.

Nineteen

Raekin hadn't slept properly in years. No sunrise, no sunset. Just exhaustion catching him when it could. Trotter's steady pace should have lulled him to sleep, but the slow breaths against his back chased that need away. His mind was too tangled in the questions he refused to answer.

Logic told him to turn north towards Losweau or Tabrasia, but he never adjusted the reins. He told himself it was temporary. Just long enough to make sure that she was okay.

His teeth ground together as the lie settled uncomfortably in his chest.

When the dirt gave way to stone, the pitch-black expanse they walked towards started to dot fluorescent blues and greens. Glowing spores clung to jagged stones like ghostly embers. A welcome nod to Raekin that he was getting closer to safety.

Trotter's thundering steps slowed, no longer drowning out the constant dripping echoes that surrounded them. His snout brushed the earth, drawn to the scent of lichen.

Raekin shifted awkwardly around to snap the extinguisher cap from its binding. The movement jostled Sybil out of her sleep. She pulled her hands out of his armor, and he felt her stretch on the saddle before looping them back around his waist. Raekin dropped the cap over the torches, the darkness engulfing them, but only for a few moments. The lichen growing on the stalactites grew more commonplace, the tunnels lighting up around them as they walked. Their eerie glow clung like a phantom to the sharp points of the hanging spires. Ethereal teeth in the never-ending mouth of a shadowy beast swallowing them hole as they traversed its tongue.

"What are they?" Sybil asked. The narrow stone walls grabbed onto her voice and threw it, reverberating it around the tunnels until it returned to their ears in a shout. The jolt told Raekin enough, her volume dropping as she leaned into his ear. "Shit, sorry."

"It's fine," he whispered back over his shoulder. "Bioluminescent fungal growths. There are hundreds of different spore variations down here. About a quarter or so of them glow."

"It's beautiful."

There would no doubt be a hundred more questions rattling around in her head. Always so curious, so inquisitive. The echo must have held her tongue. Or maybe overwhelmed by awe. Whichever it was, and against his better judgement, Raekin found himself wishing he could hear what she was thinking.

They passed close by a cluster of lichen that had grown low on the stone wall. Trotter slowed further, his nose dropping low, a long blue tongue flickering out and collecting it. He threw his head up and down, soft grunts emanating from his maw as his lips slapped together, the little appendages on his nose flexing and wiggling. Raekin tried to dissuade the behaviour, but as Sybil sat up to peer over his shoulder, he let the beast indulge itself.

"Where are we?" she asked. He could feel her twisting and turning in the saddle behind him, the enchanted way she spoke filled with wonder.

He paused for a moment, knowing the answer would tear away that mystique. "Below the Nether Peaks."

The movement behind him halted, fists tightening on the fabric at his waist. Then, a sharp laugh as her grip eased. "Very funny. I wasn't asleep that long." The laugh was forced, the edge to her voice tinged with uncertainty. Raekin's stillness was answer enough. "How?"

"Runes in the tunnels," Raekin said. "One under Hazel Gryph, one under the Peaks. The enchantment tears away what's in between. One step on one side, the next, across the continent."

"That's impossible."

Raekin shook his head. "Not impossible, just very difficult."

"But that would take… "

It would take an incredible sacrifice.

Seventy-six Etched were slaughtered in the crafting of the tunnels to Hazel Gryph, Raekin had been told. Thirty-four sacrificed for the capital of Losweau. Thirty-eight for Frew Braxus. Fifty-nine for Silverstrand Port in Tabrasia. Lives ripped away as though they meant nothing. Just to make trips to the major cities easier for the Etched given the privilege of travel.

The silence that rested after the thought was enough to tell Raekin that Sybil didn't need him to explain. She understood the gravity just fine.

"This is where the Void is?" she said, breaking through the heavy quiet. She rotated again, the saddle leather creaking beneath them.

"No. That's further towards the centre of the mountains. This is just a small corner on the southwestern edge. We won't be going anywhere near the Void."

"Where *are* we going?"

A smug satisfaction bristled up his spine, the corner of his lip twitching up. He turned slightly on the saddle. "You'll see."

A few more minutes and they rounded a tight corner that opened into a bigger cavern. Several more tunnels branched off it, leading in multiple directions. The walls splitting and diverging. Some appeared to have grown out of the stalactites and stalagmites themselves.

Raekin led Trotter down a tunnel to the right, the brightest of all of them. The further down they went, the more plentiful the clusters of fungi were, some portions of the wall almost completely covered. When he saw the collection of sharp rocks jutting from the wall, he gave Trotter a slight tug to halt him. The sharp rocks were aligned in such a seemingly random way, but Raekin had positioned them just perfectly. A marker for his secret hideaway.

He dropped off Trotter's back and went to his creation. Sybil's eyes were on him as he moved, memories flooding through him of all the times she had watched him use his magic. That awed fascination and envy that he had always loved. Even now, with her company, the magic flowed so easily from his hands.

There was a loud shuddering crack as the rock split down the seam he had built so many years ago, the halves yawning open between his hands. The stone scraped and groaned as the gaping maw flooded the already lit tunnel in new shades of colour. With a final crack, the stone slid into the place where Raekin had found it years ago.

Sybil's face was alight with the colour when he turned to help her off the molhund. She was so engrossed in the opening, she barely noticed as Raekin wrapped his hand in hers, guiding her off the saddle and onto the moist rock below. He gestured forward, letting her walk through first, leading Trotter in behind her. Her footsteps were slow, seemingly hesitant, but her hands stretched out around her, her head on a swivel as she took in the cave.

The almost claustrophobic nature of the tunnels made the great expanse of the cavern seem practically alien in nature. The roof stretching upwards, hundreds more stalactites pointed down at them, each of them coated completely in the colourful fungi. Greens and blues, even dark purples and deep reds decorated the ceiling like a multi-coloured, starry sky. It was only a fraction of the light that lit up the cave. An assortment of overgrown, bioluminescent mushrooms grew in clusters out of pockets between rocks in the soft loam. Moss coated the slick surface of the stones, its web of fibres coated in the bright speckled spores.

The warmth came from a pool of water at the far side of the cavern. Its surface reflected, distorted, and refracted the light around it making it appear as though it was alive. A trickle of water constantly poured from above, meandering through the cracks and fissures in the rocks. Likely originating from some lake or river that flowed through the mountains.

This had been his secret when he was granted access to the tunnels of his own free volition. The bends in the tunnels were too sharp, the Void never bothered to send anybody this far, much to Raekin's luck. He'd found it with the first use of Trotter without the overseeing hand of Naz'tak. Once trust had been earned, alleviating him of the tight leash and constant tracking. When he came upon the cavern, he knew immediately that he had to hide it. The Void enjoyed crushing what little joy or hope they could grasp onto. If they found this place, they would have it destroyed. So, he closed it behind him. He would reward himself with a visit on the rare occasion he was given a decently lengthy reprieve from his constant barrage of orders.

Once Trotter was clear of the opening, Raekin pressed his hands again to the stone, the cave once more sealed off to the rest of the world. He led the molhund to the space Trotter had claimed long ago, the ground soft and already torn up from his claws. The beast pawed and grunted in impatience as it waited for Raekin to start unclasping the leather of the packs that sagged under their own weight. The saddle would stay on, the chest and rib straps being loosened off. It was almost too heavy to lift when he had the proper stand to drop it on, let alone if he had to lift it up from the ground.

Before Raekin could finish, Trotter grunted, pawing at the ground once more before collapsing into the dirt, his long snout stretched wide in a yawn. He clicked his teeth together a few times before resting his head into the dirt, the tendrils still silently grasping at the air. Built for long distances, but that didn't help the fact that once that reserve was depleted, they were dead to the world.

It took an uncomfortable amount of time for Raekin to uncurl his hand from the tight grip it had held on to the reins. The shaking was hampering him while he worked at all the buckles of his armor. The sturdy, heavy pads were tossed into a heap as he shook the tightness out of his legs. He ran his hands down his face, pressing heavily into his eyes. It took a few extra blinks before he could fully open them again. His back cracked from top to bottom when he stretched it out, his shoulders following suit once they were rolled.

The pent-up energy that had propelled him through the tunnels became heavy and rested on his bones, the weight of it pairing with gravity to fight his ability to stand upright. The few hours of sleep he had gotten with Hirn hadn't been enough and that creeping exhaustion was getting difficult to keep from being overwhelming. That didn't stop the flood of thoughts from thundering through his mind. A menace he wouldn't be quieting any time soon.

Raekin turned his attention to find Sybil kneeling in front of the water, her eyes focused on the sparkling flicker that danced on the surface. It cast ethereal shadows and lights across her face, illuminating it in its own beautiful way. Raekin didn't move, only watched her. Completely still to an errant eye, but he could see the fluctuations and twitches in her face. She chewed her lip, her eyebrows wavering between relaxing and pressing into each other. Her eyes darted across the water, never settling anywhere for longer than a few seconds. Even from this distance he could see that, though her hands were clasped together on her lap, her thumb moved, tracing lines on her palm. Or more likely, just one single line. One he knew well.

He fought the urge to step towards her. Instead, going to the pile of myco-wood he had stacked the last time he was here. The phellrym mushrooms grew invasively in other sections of the Nether tunnels, towering over six feet tall, but oddly lightweight. The dead phellrym was particularly resistant to moisture once stripped from its roots. It stayed dry and brittle, ready to light with the smallest spark.

The first fire he had ever set in here had been watched carefully, though the smoke never lingered. Instead, it drifted upwards in a fine stream, disappearing into the dark reaches between the stalactites.

He started back towards the pack to grab his oil and flint, only to be stopped halfway as he heard a snap, then crackling behind him. Sybil held her hand over the wood, strain on her face as she spread her fingers wide. Her tendons cast sharp shadows along the backs of her hand. The wood ignited, sputtering, tiny flames sparking on the mushroom's stalks, threatening to go out. The fire reacted slowly, building up and fading repeatedly before the wood caught enough to feed itself.

Years of watching her in silent awe at others' magic, he'd never thought he would be on this side of it. She watched the flames like she had done this a hundred times before, and maybe she had. In the years he had spent bleeding under the mountain, she had grown into someone he hadn't expected.

The girl he had known was gone. So why the fuck did part of him still care?

"You're not saying anything." Sybil's voice broke the silence.

He exhaled sharply through his nose. "What do you want me to say?"

Her gaze flickered to his scars again. The muscles in her throat tightened. "I don't know. Maybe start with the part where you've been alive this whole time." She paused, her jaw flexing. "If you were beneath the city, why didn't you ever come find me?" The slowly winding string that had been straining between them finally reaching its limit, snapping in two in a sharp twinge. There would always be a pause in the chaos. A brief hiatus that would inevitably drag this conversation out kicking and screaming.

"We don't need to do this." He knelt down at her side, carefully adjusting the lit wood.

Her breath hitched slightly, barely audible over the cracking of the mushroom stalks. "I'm just supposed to pretend like I'm not the reason you're down here? That I wasn't the cause of whatever shit you've been through?"

"Stop." Raekin stood abruptly to meet her gaze. "Neither of us knew this was what would happen."

"But—"

"No, you don't need to do this. Look, I thought about this a lot while I was—"

Praying for death.

He paused. The speech he had rehearsed a hundred times over as they stampeded through the tunnels. Polished to a lie he could almost believe. Yet now, the misplaced placation tasted like poison on his tongue. All the words were pitiful fabrications, the reassurance and coddling only going so far to negate the guilt that ravaged them both. Everything was not okay, and trying to soothe her with his bullshit just felt wrong.

"I spent longer than I'd like to admit hating you," he said, voice quieter than it should have been. Sybil flinched. Her mouth parted. "Hating you for living while I was down here, being torn apart. Piece by *fucking* piece."

She sucked in a sharp breath, but he wasn't done. He had to say it. He had to rip the bandage off.

"I blamed you. Well, I *wanted* to blame you. But the truth? I did this to myself. I stole the book. I spoke the words. And all you did was trust me enough to let me." The hurt on her face tugged on his heart, but he knew pulling his punches would have done neither of them good. It didn't stop his need to not see it anymore. He stepped away, shifting over to the sleeping molhund, carefully running his fingers through its fur. Letting the touch anchor him.

"I loved you, Sybil, I just wanted you to be happy. If I had known this was what would have happened, I never would have stolen the book. But I didn't and we can't go back and make it 'un-happen'. It's over. Ten years is a long time. I don't hold that animosity anymore and I've come to terms with my idiotic decisions." He paused again, stepping from the beast to look down on her. "I'm surprised you haven't."

Flashes danced across her face as she held back her shoulders to meet his stare. She did her best to stand tall even though he towered over her. "I *had* come to terms with my idiocy," she spat. "I came to terms with the fact that I had been powerless that night. I came to terms with the fact that I had gotten you killed, that your bloodstains would never come out of that room. Off my *skin*. You were gone, and I was never going to see you again.

"What I *haven't* come to terms with is the fact that you have been alive this whole time, having who-knows-what done to you to make you look like—" she gestured at his skin, her eyes skating along the inks "—this. You were dead, I mourned you. I watched them light an empty pyre. You can't ask me to come to terms with something I haven't even had a chance to fully understand. I'm still trying to grasp the fact that you are flesh and blood in front of me. But you know what? *You* have to come to terms with the fact that finding out you were being mutilated for the last ten years to 'make me happy' is *fucking horrifying.*"

He couldn't stop the smile that stretched across his face as her voice raised, temper flaring in the small cave. Wild eyed, her cheeks flushing pink in the dim bluish light of the cavern, he felt like he was sixteen again. "You haven't changed a bit," he said, watching the fire in her eyes burn hotter.

"Haven't I?" Her voice cracked, the pitch rising with the volume. "Because I feel like I've done nothing but change." She sucked in a breath.

She shoved him, stumbling on her own feet as she did. He reached out, a habit, uncontrolled, and caught her arms before she could fall. There was a brief surprise on her face, the two of them hovering in a breathless suspension. Holding her, the touch almost too familiar. It lasted for an eternity before she tore herself from his grip, the muddied grime from his hands barely noticeable amidst the staining of her mantle.

"I had to learn how to live without you," she snapped. "Had to scrape myself back together while you—" Her voice broke. Her jaw flexed. Her fists curled tight at her sides.

He ran his hands up her neck, hooking his thumbs under her jaw, pausing the torrent he could see tearing through her mind. The movement was uncontrolled, a habit that had been shoved into the depths of his soul. Able to crawl out the second that familiar flash of her heated personality sparked to life. Unaware of it himself until his hands were pressed to her skin. The scowl on her face flickered to surprise for a moment before it sprang back. Though he could see the tiniest twist of her lips as she fought to hold on to it. She tried to tear out of his grip, pulling his hands from her face, but he held her jaw firm. He enjoyed watching the whirlwind of expressions flash across her face.

She had been his everything once. His first indulgence, too deeply etched to fade. He'd built a chasm between them, but some things still lingered. How quickly he would succumb to that temptation if he gave himself that chance. The distance between them should be insurmountable, and this truth gnashed its sharp teeth in the nape of his neck. Emanating from the rune carved into his spine. The one that reminded him he didn't belong in her world anymore.

And it was only a matter of time before the agony came to drag him back to his.

TWENTY

Raekin released her jaw before she could tear herself away, a sharp line of reddish dirt trailing up her neck. His fingers lingering just long enough to feel the heat of her skin fade from his own. Her reluctant, retreating expression faded fast. He stepped back, forcing air into the space between them. A second more and...

No.

He needed to say something. Something sharp, something to push her away before the moment could settle too deep in his chest. Before the words could form, her gaze dropped to his ribs, her body going rigid.

"You're bleeding." Her voice wavered, but only slightly. He followed her gaze, landing on the cooling blood on his side. It poured down from the gouge in his ribs, soaking into the shirt. He'd let himself get too distracted. His magic had shifted back to the recesses of his mind. The wound from the warden's blade no longer being held closed by his power.

A sharp breath hitched in his throat as her fingers traced along the tear in his shirt. He hadn't meant to jolt so suddenly, but her touch sent a warmth through his chest that felt too heavy. It made his heart stutter, the swirling twisting of nerves like snakes curling behind his sternum.

He wanted to hold onto that feeling, but at the same time, tear it from within and be rid of it.

"I'm fine," he said, pulling away from her.

She grabbed his tunic, pulling the fabric back, the forceful movement tearing it further. "You aren't. Quinn, this is really bad." His shoulders once more contracting tightly at the sound of his name.

He pulled the shirt from her grip, shifting away from her. "When was the last time you ate something?"

"Can you let me at least wrap it up? Or stitch it? Do you have thread?" She glanced behind him at the slumbering molhund. He did have thread. A needle too, but the last thing he wanted was her hands on him again. That touch too tender running along his skin. Too familiar, too safe, and too dangerous.

"Seriously, let it go." He let a half laugh through his nose. "I've had worse. I'll get you something to eat."

He started towards the bags, only for the ground to rumble beneath him. The dirt split open, cracking and splintering under his boots before wrapping around his foot. It was crooked, porous, and looked weak and easy to step out of. That didn't stop the thrumming in his veins at seeing his own mastered magic used against him. Sybil looked almost as shocked as he felt when he turned to face her. She quickly corrected her face, crossing her arms over her chest.

"Will you let me help you?" she asked.

His lip twisted up slightly. "Thread and needle are in the back bag."

He'd been right, his foot crumbling the stones with a sharp turn. She wasn't as skilled as him, but it was still an impressive feat. Especially from someone who had to learn their magic so late.

He grabbed the edges of the tattered tunic and pulled it over his head. It caught on the tie at the crown of his skull, the dark hair spilling out over his shoulders. The small, sharp inhale from Sybil made him wince, the vulnerability of his bare flesh dawning on him. She hadn't seen close to the worst of the damage that littered his skin. Not that he had either. Varena often traced lines on his back, softly whispering about the scars and runes there. He never let it soak in. Knowing about the damage wouldn't lessen the impact of it. He had the memories of the pain, and that was enough.

A slow breath between his lips as he dragged forward the courage to face her. Her eyes were wide as they darted over his body. Her lips had parted, her tongue pressed into her teeth, an eyebrow raised. He'd expected horror or fear, but he could feel her heart racing as she looked at him. Years of practice with bloodweaving, he knew there were several different things that could make a heart race, each having their own specific rhythm. This was one he knew almost as well as the harsh thrum of fear. "Sybil?"

"Yeah, sorry." Her face burned pink as she quickly and abruptly turned her attention to the thread in her hand. "I guess I just thought living underground would make you emaciated or something. Not..." she cleared her throat. "You were so scrawny. I assumed you'd always be like that."

"Is the great Warden Wyntres blushing?" Raekin cooed.

"Shut up," she groaned, flashing her teeth at him.

He laughed, and for the first time in a long time, it felt real, like it had risen up through his torso instead of just wicking out his mouth. Waking up emotions he had buried long ago. With a quick shift of the dirt, he dropped to the ground, leaning back so the wound was easy to see in the bright light of the cave. He could see faint traces of his ribs through the gouge, his power once again holding the blood back. It was bad, she was right. He should have looked at it sooner.

Sybil started to cross her legs, dropping to a squat before her mantle scrunched up around her thighs. She let out a curse, pulling the fabric around only for it to bunch up somewhere else. The blood and dirt had solidified where it dried, turning the leather into a heavy, rigid piece.

"Take off your mantle," Raekin said, reaching up to gently take the needle and thread from her.

"I will if you wipe that stupid smile off your face," she growled. He refused, letting his lip curve up as he watched her bend to work on the leather ties around her leg. Her fingers struggled as they tried to get a hold of the metal clasps.

"Want a hand?" Before she could protest, Raekin laid down the needle and thread, and shifted to crouch at her feet. He couldn't remember the last time he had touched his own warden mantle, yet every strip of leather and flash of metal seemed so familiar. He undid the belting that held the jacket to her thighs, his fingers lingering a little too long against the muscle that shifted under them.

Lifting himself to his knees, he undid the buttons of the lapels. The position brought her chest too close, his fingers trembling slightly as he swallowed against the lump in his throat. He had to force himself to focus on his task and nothing else.

He stood to undo the belting that ran across her collar but stopped. There was a split second where his eyes met hers, a second of hesitance that felt like time had screeched to a halt.

He was back there again. Fourteen years ago. Sitting across from each other in her bedroom. Cross-legged on the blanket Sybil had been gifted from her mother, the wool tattered and riddled with holes. His hands were sweating, and he held them tight to his knees, hoping she wouldn't notice. They'd known each other for six years at this point, but that didn't stop him from his seemingly endless anxious energy around her. It told him that at any second, she would finally realize she deserved a better friend than the orphaned ward that Trelusk had taken in.

That day, he'd been talking to the other wards about girls, which inevitably barrelled into talks of kissing. Some wanted their first kiss to be the most special thing in the world. The perfect place, perfect person. Some even claimed they had already had it, but Quinn knew better. He could see the way their lips twitched, or their eyes darted away when they boasted about it. Too prideful to admit to their own innocence.

At the time, Quinn hadn't bothered to think about a person or a place. Too busy worrying about how he was supposed to do it. Was it quick? Long? Was his mouth open, or closed? What about his eyes? Did he move first, or did they? His pulse raced under his skin as he envisioned every possible way he could screw it up.

Sybil had talked about it with some of the girls at the Charprin school. She didn't seem nearly as worried about it as Quinn when he brought it up, shrugging it off as if it was nothing. When he'd asked if he could try with her, the words had fallen out of his mouth before he even had a chance to catch them. He'd backpedalled so quickly, insisting it didn't even count because they were friends and friends didn't do that sort of thing and only if she really wanted to and they didn't even really have to do it and it was just a dumb idea and she should forget he ever said anything and he didn't want her to think he was gross and he was obviously just joking and—

Then she kissed him.

It was quick, over in a second, but it felt like the world moved around them. He'd left his eyes open, the surprise not giving him a chance to prepare, but he knew that felt wrong. When he was finally able to put two thoughts together, he was so ashamed that he hadn't made it perfect. Sybil just smiled. Said it didn't matter. It was nice, he was a good kisser. He always felt like she was growing up faster than him and watching her be so casual made his heart hurt. He'd said that it wouldn't count, but afterwards, he knew what an idiotic assumption that was. Sybil Wyntres had been his first kiss, and he would do everything in his power to make sure that she was his second as well. Then his third, his fourth, fifth...

"What happened to your eyes?" Sybil asked, rattling him out of their past. It tore his gaze away from where it had settled on her lips, eliciting a shallow lump in his throat.

Her question wasn't exactly out of the blue, but he had mostly forgotten there was anything unusual about his eyes. He hesitated to show her, but the tantalizing inquiry written on her face was hard to resist. With a slow breath, he pulled his eyelid down and looked up. Another soft gasp as the reddish black rune inked into his eye became visible. A pointless rune, its only purpose decorative, an addition to his master's adjustments to his body. A nightmare that the Void looked forward to with every Etched brought to the Alpstraum. Fun for them, but he remembered every agonizing second of its creation like it had been stabbed into his memories at the same time.

Pained horror took over the curiosity when he dropped his hand to look at her. It was obvious from her stare that she knew the dangers of such a rune, the list of repercussions so long no one dared test it. Having a completed rune there was miraculous, let alone one that stayed for years after.

"I can't believe you called me scrawny," he scoffed, changing the subject to rip the expression from her face. He refocused his attention to the leather strap across her collarbones. Once the leaf was unclipped, the straps fell to her shoulders. He stepped back, letting her shake the jacket off.

"You *were* scrawny." She dropped the mantle to the ground, the already pitted and stained white leather folding in on itself in the dirt, seemingly heavier than it was. He'd expected her to carefully fold it up, a strict lesson the wardens were adamant about. The strangest sensation crawled up his spine as his fingers twitched towards it, a deep-seated habit that still lingered there. One that urged him to pick it up, to fix it. The lack of care just felt like his old Sybil.

"The boys used to call you 'dust mite'."

"If only they could see me now," he said, flashing a grin. His smile quickly faded as her face fell, her eyes once more casting over his skin. This was the line he was walking. One unintentionally crass comment away from shattering the ease with which they spoke.

There was no point letting her dwell on it. He dropped back to the ground, repositioning himself in the light. Sybil sat, crossing her legs to face him, her knee brushing lightly against his. Her fingers shook slightly as she unwound a length of the thread and ran it through the needle eye.

The craftsmanship of the needle was barbaric and crooked. The point was nice and sharp, but the shank was bulbous and uneven. Still, it was better than some of the instruments the Void used to stitch up their pets.

Her fingers skimmed low on his ribs. It was hard to ignore the way her fingers skated around all the other scars and marks like they were poison. Afraid to touch them as though her skin would invoke the pain all over again.

Just below the wound, she paused.

"You still have this," she said quietly. Her thumb traced the half-faded, spiraled ink. Barely noticeable under the scarring that carved through most of the vanity tattoos he'd gotten before he was taken.

"Yeah, they missed it," he said, keeping his voice even, though his pulse drummed in his ears at the touch. That mark was the only one he had gotten that had any meaning. The others were carved by the wardens or inked for pride or rebellion. But this? He got it for her. Twelve years ago, quietly and without asking, back when they thought they still had a whole life ahead of them. He already knew what he wanted. He wanted her. All of her. This protected them, kept that night just for themselves. Protected their future.

Now, all it did was remind him of Varena. Of what they were being forced to do and what he was pretending would happen. Because the Void didn't know what the mark really meant. As long as it stayed a secret, every humiliating command they gave them was pointless. But he would obey if it meant he kept himself intact.

Another of his collection of lies he held like treasures. And it belonged to Sybil. Always had.

"This is going to hurt; I'm sorry," Sybil muttered, grimacing as she held the needle up in the light. She pulled the skin together, her touch so gentle and soft it almost hurt more. Her hand shook, the hesitation tight on her face. He didn't let his eyes falter from it, watching her take a slow breath through her teeth before finally pressing the sharp tip to his skin.

One stitch done, she looked up at him, her eyebrows dropped back in concern. Raekin just cocked his head, a silent question of her pause. She frowned for a moment, but went back to her work, shaking her head.

Had she expected him to flinch? To wince? To cry out? Maybe he should have. Let a touch of normalcy worm its way back between them.

"You were shooting sparks out of your fingers under the Bastion," Raekin said to pull apart the tension slowly knitting itself back between them. Her face twitched slightly, but her focus didn't falter. "Air may be easy but moving it quickly enough to generate lightning is very impressive. Stormweaver, right?"

She let out a quick breath through her nose, the crook of her lip twisting up. "With very little control over the storms, but, sure."

"Your geomancy needs work. You at least have a decent grasp of it, not needing to touch the ground."

"That's not exactly fair coming from you, is it?" Sybil raised an eyebrow, a brief glance up at him between stitches. "Are you profiling my magic?"

"Thermacist," Raekin added, already on his roll. "But with your impressive grasp of the air, that doesn't really surprise me all that much." He mulled it over in his mouth for a moment. "Four different magic classes if you count the aerokineticism. That's..." He paused, mulling it over as he frowned. "Incredible."

Sybil paused the stitches, chewing on her lip. "Not four," she corrected, shifting in the dirt.

"Five?" He scrunched up his face before the memory flooded back. "That's right. Ice. I guess I'm worth more than I thought." When she shook her head, he furrowed his brow. A stabbing cold had settled over his skin as he mentally worked through what few schools were left. "Six?" Even in the firelight he could see her jaw working back and forth, flickering shadows dancing across her eyes. Six should be impossible. Shit, even five was wildly unlikely.

Before she even said the word, he knew it was coming. No matter how badly he didn't want to hear it. A thin, breakable tether in the cave ready to snap as soon as she opened her mouth.

"I'm a vollmagus."

His ribs cinched tight, trapping the air between them. That all too familiar pain flared up at the base of his neck, the memories clawing up through his skull again, his mark making its presence known. He'd been coveted by a mass of Void Born in the Alpstraum. The cruel, malicious things that had been done there while his ownership was fought over plagued him more ruthlessly than the nightmares he'd endured afterwards. A talented geomancer was a luxury slave able to work the tunnels to their master's requests. But a bloodweaver was a walking weapon.

A vollmagus.

Master of all.

I never should have brought her here.

TWENTY-ONE

S ybil noticed the change immediately. Only moments ago, he had
been laughing. Those stupid dimples again. Gone, like they never
existed at all. Ripped from his face the second the word left her tongue.

The rocks scraped on the cave floor, Quinn's legs shifting under him.
He was no longer actively watching her work. A glazed-over stare at
the space just beyond her hands. That soft look replaced with palpable
unease. As she bit through the thread with her teeth, she let the silence
hum around them for a few beats. A silent challenge for him to break the
tension with an explanation.

With no words in thanks, just a final glance at her work, Quinn stood.
He raked his hand through his hair, retying the knot that kept it off his
neck. Looking everywhere, at everything. Everything except her.

"I have to... I need to leave," he muttered.

"You know," she started, wrapping the thread back around the needle.
"I've seen envy, I've seen disbelief. Hatred, even awe. But of all the ways
people have reacted to finding out what I am, I have never, *ever*, seen
anyone look as terrified as you do right now."

Finally, he looked at her, those eerie orange eyes meeting hers.

"What is it, Quinn? What aren't you telling me?"

The muscles in his jaw flexed. She had tried to ignore the way his smiles never quite reached his eyes. How he paused as though mulling over and parsing through his words. The constant way he deflected everything had reached its limit. There was no use hiding behind quips and sardonic remarks, because she saw him. Had always seen him. Whatever reason he had for treating her like eggshells he was carefully avoiding stepping on, she'd had enough. He'd broken her once, what more could he possibly do?

"We can talk when I get back."

This dance wasn't new to her. Maiten did it for years. Fill the silence with niceties or outright vanish to prevent anybody from bringing up anything too painful to deal with. That pain brought with it questions. Questions nobody wanted to hear, and certainly didn't want to answer. A breeding ground for animosity and resentment between her and her father.

Before she had a chance to argue, Quinn turned away from her, the vibrant light illuminating his tattooed back. It lit up the vicious damage along his shoulders, no longer hidden under his dark hair.

"What the fuck is that?" Sybil shouted. Quinn flinched at the outburst, his hand drifting to the back of his neck. No chance for denial, the attempted cover-up only solidifying her reaction.

The tension between them snapped like a band, ricocheting against the walls. Sybil grabbed a fist full of his hair and yanked him down and into the light. The grunt vibrated through her forearm as it pressed into his spine. Once the damage was twisted into view, dread stitched a net across her lungs.

Between the curved bones of his shoulders ran a jagged scar. It was thick and gnarled, the skin appearing to have been torn, not cut. Like someone had grabbed hold of the nape of his neck and the skin above his spine and pulled, ripping his flesh from shoulder to shoulder. The scar dipped downwards as it met in the centre of his spine. A twisted, toothless smile across his back. Large divots appeared across the top and bottom of the ragged line in unequal intervals. Stitch scars? Too large for any stitching material she had ever seen. Thick enough for twine, though. Or rope. She would have thought that too barbaric, but the disfiguring lines of the scar made it not seem so improbable.

The gruesome nature of the wound should have been enough to steal the breath from her lungs. But what drew her attention was above it. At the top of his spine, just above the centre of the scar, someone had inked a rune. Whoever created it had used too much pressure with the needle. The skin was indented and rough, the ink practically carved into his flesh. Though he had more inks than bare skin, this one stood out with its precision. Each line meticulously crafted. Perfect symmetry on either side of the bones in his neck.

The brutality of the rune wasn't what twisted her stomach. It was the familiarity. With the recognition came the panic swelling back through her ribs all over again. Identical to the horror she felt when she saw it the first time. Behind the cover of the *stupid fucking book* that started all of this.

She ran her hand along the scar, the bumps and ridges of it thick underneath the pads of her fingers. There was a slight tremble to his flesh as she traced the scarring, echoing a tremor through her own skin. When her touch went to the rune, Quinn jolted, wrenching his hair out of her grip.

"I can't stay any longer," Quinn said, grabbing his tunic off the dirt floor. Not even letting out the barest wince as the stitching stretched against his side while he pulled it over his head.

Sybil didn't move. Only followed him with her eyes as he approached the molhund.

"Why didn't you come back?" she said. Not a shout, but enough that it stopped him. The question hung in the air between them like an open wound, festering and rotting as the silence grew unfathomably heavy. But Sybil knew the answer. Knew it the second she had seen that rune on his neck. She needed him to admit it, to finally speak an ounce of truth.

There was the slightest shift to his shoulders. Maybe he knew that the answer was going to be the final crack. Knew that the truth would inevitably devour this fantasy they had hidden themselves in. She could pretend that she didn't see the horrific things marring his skin. Could even pretend that the last ten years had never happened, and nothing had changed. Act as though everything was fine. She knew, and he must have known it too. This was never meant to last.

"Quinn," she said, still choosing to ignore the way he flinched at his name. "Why didn't you come back?"

He turned. Slowly crossed his arms, his voice dropping. "Because I can't."

There it was. The foggy glass wiped clean. The images beyond had been distorted, but there was no use in acting as though there was nothing past the panes. The heaviness of tears started to blossom behind her eyes, but she bit down on her cheek, shoving them back. The air already started to spark against her knuckles; her fists clenched so tight she shook. That too familiar sting of ozone burning her nose.

"What did they do to you?" she seethed between clenched teeth. When he dropped his arms, the air crackled around her. "No. No more bullshit. Something horrible happened to you in the last ten years, I won't—"

"We're not doing this."

"And why not? I can't just ignore what I'm seeing. You aren't okay. Nothing has been okay for you since..." She swallowed. "I did this to you. I don't give a shit what you say. I did this, and I need to fix it."

"Do you think hearing about how the Void mutilated me is going to make it go away?" His voice rose around them like thunder. "Do you think making me watch you die a little more inside with every revelation is going to make this better? The nightmares I had to endure are something that I never, *ever* want you to witness, much less know about. The Void broke me, Sybil. Tore me apart, then stitched it all back together to suit their fucked-up needs. I had to live through it, why should I make you do the same?"

The cavern walls started to rumble. The tiny pools that filled the cracks in the stone rippling in time with it. A cold laced through her veins, an uncomfortable creeping sensation wrapping under her skin. Magic. *His magic.* She twisted her wrists to shake the feeling loose, but it only grew with every spite-filled word spat from his mouth.

"I'm not asking you to recount everything," Sybil said through clenched teeth. She could already feel her own magic flickering air around her fingers. She balled them into fists to halt it. "I'm asking you to stop pushing me away. Let me help you. That thing on your neck is... what? How they control you? A chain?" He cringed at the word, his lip curling up before pinching in a tight line. She didn't need any further answer. "Every rune can be removed. Every spell undone. If we could get to Ethissa, she could—"

"Don't you think if it was that simple, I would have done it already?" His words came out sharp, but he let out a slow breath and they softened. "Void runes are different, they're more complex. They don't just ink your skin. They rip open your flesh and carve into your muscles, your viscera. Your *bones*. I've tried to cut the rune away, but it will always return." He forced a breathy laugh. "I think they know every Etched makes the attempt. I'm sure they get some sick enjoyment from watching us mutilate ourselves for a change."

"Then we go deeper. We find a sarcomancer—"

"Sybil, in order to remove the rune completely, I have to remove my spine."

A sharp feeling of cold, stone hands wrapped around her heart, crushing it tightly. A twisted, macabre choice: succumb, or die. Her mind raced with all the options before her, ideas sparking in her skull. Every single one died out before it could bloom to anything useful. The enchantment an impossibility that shouldn't exist, but the existence of the Void was wrapped in its own shrouded mystery. She hadn't realized she had started pacing, her footsteps still silent, even on the gritty ground.

"There... There has to be another way. There has to be something. It can't be—"

"I've been trying for years. I'm sure others tried before me too."

The pressure in her eyes ached in time with the sharp sting of tears. It wasn't over, it couldn't be over. "You shouldn't be here. You should never have been brought down here. *Fuck*. I don't care that you read the stupid words. I was the pathetic *leertek*. I should have been—"

"Don't," Quinn snapped. "Don't even think that. *Nothing* is going to change what happened."

It was too late. The idea caught like dry tinder. "We... We talk to them. Let me bargain. Your life for mine. They want powerful mages, right? They'd be idiots not to take the trade."

"If you walk into the Peaks, they won't wait to listen to you." She could hear the strain in his voice, the placid, careful way he slowed each word down. Like he was right on the edge of breaking. "They'll grab you. They'll rip open your back and brand you just the same. I bled in that place for a decade, don't make it meaningless."

"Then we find another book. We make another pact, a different one. We—"

"Do you think I enjoyed them carving away my skin every hour of every day?" He shouted, arms wide. "I can't let that happen to you. The best thing you can do for me is get somewhere safe. Far away from me."

Sybil froze. White hot rage licked through her veins and burned her skin. A wind kicked up, fast and sharp. The once warm water that slid off the rock teeth above them started to cool. It froze and hung in the air, a swirling, unnatural blizzard whipping around the small cave. Sybil barely felt the cold on her bare arms, her body overheating with the fury that ran through it. The howling wind numbing her to everything except him.

Her thoughts rammed at the backs of her teeth as she clamped them shut tight, holding back the poison. She destroyed the life she had worked so hard for in an instant so that she could see him. There was nothing to go back to. At least with him, there was still a tiny tether left of her life. "You're gone for a decade, I finally get you back in my life, and you want me to just run away? Pretend you don't exist? Pretend that I haven't seen how you've been massacred for '*my happiness*?'"

Quinn stepped forward, the icy wind wrapping around his skin, reddening his cheeks. "I'm just trying to protect you, Sybil." His voice was low, patient. He reached towards her, but she stepped back. The swirling wind started to spark brighter at her fingers, the water in the pool rippling behind her.

"I don't need you to protect me, Quinn. I haven't needed you for ten years," she snarled. She lifted her hands, gesturing to the swirling storm made from her magic. "Does it look like I need your pathetic help?"

Quinn paused, eyes on her as if gauging the message. "You're right. You don't need my 'pathetic help'. You've clearly got a handle on yourself." The slowest smirk crawled up his lips. "You know what I think? I think all this chaotic magic needs a leash."

It wasn't shouted. Wasn't screamed. Just audible over the whirling wind. Quiet and dismissive, like it didn't mean a thing. It still tore through her memories, dragging forth every use of the slur either at her back or to her face. For a breath, she couldn't hear anything at all. Not the wind. Not the water. Just the echo of old voices. The words repeating in her head like an ever-increasing chant. The air around them shifted, and the storm shivered, stalling as though a beat in time had wavered. Her magic recoiling like it had been struck.

She waited. Only for a second, just long enough for him to realize what he'd said, for him to take it back. He stayed silent, just cold restraint and that slight curl to his lip.

"Fuck you," she spat. The blizzard spiked with the utterance of the curse. "Quinn may have been able to talk to me like that, but not you.

You aren't him." The ice swirled sharper, stinging her cheeks. "You're just some monster that crawled out of the dark wearing his skin."

There was a pressure shift. A twisting, heavy beat, pulling and pushing against the cavern walls. Quinn didn't speak, his chest stilling. He stared at her, stoic and unreadable. Not even the faintest tick to his lips. Then, slowly, he moved. The ground didn't shake, but she could feel it tighten beneath her feet. Like the cave was holding its breath.

He stopped just in front of her. Close enough to touch. His voice, when it came, was grating and deep. Clenched and controlled. "Say that again." His jaw twitched, fingers flexing ever so slightly, eyes wild. "Say. That. Again."

Another palpable pressure shift, the storm wavering as he towered over her. That orange gaze was too intense. Too measured. Though the storm flinched around her, she held her composure, tilting her chin higher.

"You like the cruelty, don't you? Like what they made you? Maybe because if you stopped hurting, you might just remember who you used to be." She lowered her voice, speaking from the depths of her chest. "Not this monster you've become."

The ground cracked beneath her feet. A sharp, echoing fracture. She stumbled, just a step, but he was already moving. Before she could speak again, one hand slid up under her shirt, palm flat to her ribs. The other coiled through her hair roughly, yanking her forward until their foreheads touched.

"You're so desperate to know what happened? You want to know what it felt like? What I went through? *For you?*" he hissed, voice shaking with fury. A pause as his eyes darted back and forth, searching hers.

"Fine." His grip on her side tightened, a heat spreading out from beneath his palm. "Then feel it."

Pain tore through her body. It ripped beneath her skin, bursting behind her ribs, twisting into her lungs, her spine, her throat. She gasped, choking on nothing. Her blood coiled in her veins like fire made liquid as sharp points tore beneath her flesh, raking unseen. Her scream stuck halfway out of her throat. Her limbs locked, frozen, out of her control.

"This is what it feels like," he seethed. His breath was hot against the thrumming beat in her temples. "To be owned. To have every part of you twisted and contorted while you fight uselessly against it. To be chained and shackled by nothing more than your own body."

"Stop. Quinn, stop—"

"No." His eyes locked on hers, the rest of the world fading to a blurry fog outside the vibrant orange. The pain intensified, her muscles contracting inwards as she fought to stay upright. She could taste iron on her tongue, and every sharp breath was fire in her throat.

"They didn't stop for me," he growled. "Ten years. Ten years of being rewritten from the inside out. Being turned into something I couldn't recognize. Didn't want to recognize. You say I enjoyed the cruelty when you know nothing about what cruelty is."

His magic flared beneath her skin again. Harder. Like her blood was a vicious parasite. A sharp, animal sound scraped past her teeth. Her knees buckled. But he didn't let her fall. She teetered off-balance, drowning in herself as her body fell limp and useless against him. Her hands fumbled at his chest but there was no leverage, no escape. Nothing to hold on to that wasn't just constant, searing pain.

"They'll use you," he breathed. "Carve you. Tattoo obedience into your skin. And you'll call it *sacrifice*. You'll believe it means something."

His voice broke. A crack in the restraint, but the rage remained. Quiet and alive. "Believe that everything you gave up made all the anguish worth it. And through all that, everything that you are suffering, you will be alone. Completely. Alone. You want this?"

His hand slid from her rib to wrap around her waist. Her weight fell heavily into his chest as she collapsed the rest of the way. The dirt scraped under her feet as her legs shook. He lowered them to the ground carefully, like she was fragile.

She crumbled between his outstretched legs, trembling. He cradled her, one hand at her spine, the other still curled in her hair. His voice was a raw, grasping thread as he leaned in. "I won't let you throw yourself into that, or give yourself away," he whispered. "Not to them. Not to me. Not to anyone. Ever."

She didn't speak.

Not even to spit back the vile poison that still lingered beneath her skin.

But she let him hold her.

Because even though he had shattered her, she didn't have to hold the pieces together alone. And that was more than he ever got from them.

TWENTY-TWO

S ybil didn't know how long she trembled in his arms. She only knew the pain had faded to a dull ache. Her blood was hers again and her body moved when she told it to. Her hands still trembled, but they were free.

Quinn's arms were around her, though a deeper part of her wanted to push them off. She wasn't sure he had any right to hold her like that anymore. When she shifted, he went still. He didn't apologize, didn't let go. He just held her like he was the only thing keeping her in one piece. After all of it, she let him, because his last seething words still echoed through her skull.

Completely. Alone.

When she finally gathered the courage to sit up and move away from him, she couldn't look him in the eyes. Terrified about what she might see if she did. Would she see Quinn, or the monster? The one that reminded her pain was always right there and that death could be more comforting than she would like to admit.

Instead, she unthreaded herself from his arms and went to the warm, rippling waters. They shivered slightly from the torrent that had ravaged the small cavern. An icy touch lingered on her skin, an aftermath from the blizzard. She untied her boots and rolled her pant legs up. The glass surface of the pool was broken once more as she slid her bare calves into the welcoming heat.

The water latched hold of the tension and rage, leeching it out of her skin. Even amidst the disarray in her mind her thoughts found time to settle. In this moment everything stood still. All her failures and mistakes made insignificant under the glowing lichen. A separation of the two people, who she was and who she was going to be. In this tiny space, the world stopped, where neither of them existed.

The sound of dirt crunching echoed behind her, allowing her to release the air she hadn't realized she'd been holding. She'd expected to hear the scraping of the rocks as the secret entrance was opened. An odd relief settled onto her shoulders.

He'd stayed.

"Don't ever do that to me again," she said, once she was sure her voice wouldn't hitch in her throat. It was still ragged but controlled.

"I needed you to understand," he said. Not an apology, not even softly spoken. But the truth. Finally.

"I do." The water shifted around her calves as she turned sharp eyes on him. Hurt, but not gone. "And I'll never forget it." His jaw tightened as his eyes flicked away, like he was bracing for something worse. But then he met her stare, unflinching. With a breath, she relaxed the muscles in her back, shifting over slightly in the water to open room beside her. An unspoken invitation, though she hoped the silence between them spoke volumes.

When he dropped to sit on the edge of the water, pants rolled to his knees, his arm momentarily brushed hers. Another icy chill followed the touch, but it faded quickly with the heat from his skin. The shivers up her spine weren't uncalled for, but the constant shifting of her emotions was bordering on exhausting.

What he did was... horrifying. The helplessness. The pain. It awoke something in her. A fear that she hadn't let surface. The problem was, it only made her realize that she should never have buried it down in the first place. The inks and scars on his body weren't placed there with care like hers but sheared into his skin with malice. It was obvious, but somehow, she hadn't let the weight of it fully sink in. Not until her body wasn't her own, her blood flowing through her like knives while she was left powerless. That was his rune. His chain.

"I'm dead in Plaitius," she said, her voice creaking. "The Bauers said they would spin that I never made it back from Trelusk." Sybil let out a soft curse, her heart tightening in her chest. "I feel like such an idiot for trusting them."

"You shouldn't. Most of Hazel Gryph trusts the Portcullis. They don't know the crooked side," Quinn said.

"You did?"

He shrugged. "Maiten had a deeply unsettling distrust for them. He never really explained why, but I could always see the disdain whenever they were brought up. He was a good man, so I believed him."

A sob choked in her throat. "I should have said goodbye to him." She stared up at the flickering rocks above them, willing the dam behind her eyes. "I'm going to miss him. All of them." She trailed off, letting her words float over the water.

Sybil Wyntres was dead. Those who loved her would be grieving. She wasn't a stranger to that pain. It had emptied her into a hollow husk, but she had pieced herself back together. She was never the same, but over time, she was whole enough. And they would be too. Someday.

With a sharp blink, she pulled her attention back to the cave. A glimmer of red caught her eye, slithering down Quinn's thigh and staining the water. "Your stitches," she said. He lifted his tunic to see that one of them had ripped open.

"Oh," he muttered. Sybil watched with awe as the blood suddenly stopped flowing, vanishing back into his body. He reached down, splashing some water to rinse the last of it off. When he turned his attention back to her, he frowned. "You're a vollmagus. Why didn't you just use sarcomancy to seal it?"

Sybil swallowed the memories back down before they could bubble up. "I won't use that magic." When he cocked his head, she just shook hers, letting the silence stretch.

Quinn's face softened, on the edge of sympathy. When the Trelusk sarcomancer had sealed her hand, Quinn was there. But he had also been there for every other wound the twisted warden had healed. Every uncomfortable, lingering touch from his calloused hands. All the conveniently timed run-ins when he thought she was alone in town. Even the shadow that lingered outside her house on late nights. His disappearance thereafter had always been a mystery, though Quinn never seemed that surprised.

"When did the bloodweaving start?" she asked. The lingering of his new magic still felt raw under her skin.

"I was sixteen. Went to dodge an attack from your father and accidentally grabbed hold of his entire body."

The confession felt like a slap to the face. *Sixteen.* Two years he'd hidden it from her. Should she have known? Should she have seen some hint of such a dangerous magic? "Why didn't you tell me?"

"Maiten made me promise to never tell a soul about it." He paused. "Especially you."

"Of course he did." She curled into herself, her arms dropping to her legs. "Maiten Wyntres: shrouded in secrets. Always paranoid of people. So distrusting he barely trusted his own daughter." The realization settled in her gut. "I guess he was right not to. He had been right about Killian."

"Killian?"

"I trusted him to care more about me than his stupid family name. I told him about you, and he turned around and told the Bauers." A bitter taste coated her tongue. "Probably spouted it all while sitting around their gaudy, fifteen-seat gryphire wood dinner table."

"*That* Killian?" Quinn's tone was sharp as though the name itself was a crime.

Sybil winced at the inflection. "Yes, *that* Killian." A decade was a long time, but guilt could still gnash its teeth. How guilty should she feel though? Killian wasn't in her life until years after Quinn's death. Besides, it wasn't like she had fallen into his bed the second they crossed paths.

The lapping water against Sybil's calves as she swung her legs punctuated the heavy quiet. There were a thousand things she wanted to say, a thousand things she wanted answers to. But her lips felt sealed, a glue of grief and guilt holding them together. She picked absently at the skin of her thumb, using the sharp feeling to distract her. Thoughts like that weren't getting her anywhere but a slope down into somewhere she shouldn't be. Not right now.

She tried to shake the fear that still traced the path his magic had left behind in her veins. It was deep, immovable. Shaped for him, reminding her just what he could do.

"Have you been able to bloodweave?" he asked, peeling back the decade-old curtain that settled between them, filling the cavern with his voice.

She scoffed. "I can barely control the air. Blood was never high on my list." She started swirling the air around her hand and directing it to the water's surface. The ripples fluttered and fluctuated under her invisible touch. After the focus started to feel like needles behind her eyes, her magic grasped hold, swirling the water in a small vortex. "Besides, I would have ended up in The Underkeep if I ever got caught trying."

"Come here." He turned, his one leg still dangling in the pool while he folded the other beside her. The vortex at her feet faded back into the placid water as she shifted to face him. It was difficult to keep her gaze on the eerie orange of his eyes. A flash of his fury passed through her mind again, his head pressed to hers, pain flaring through her veins. She swallowed it down, balling her hands into fists to steady the tremble.

Quinn reached for her fists, slowly at first. When she didn't pull away, he slipped his fingers between hers, loosening the tension. Her hands softened under his touch. Gently, he guided her palms to his neck, one on either side.

"Close your eyes."

She hesitated. She should still be furious. Still be shaken. And maybe, somewhere beneath her ribs, she was. But it was fading just a little. The way exhaustion softens a sharp edge, or survival makes space for something else.

She closed her eyes.

"Focus only on what you feel right now."

"Other than the rocks stabbing into my butt?" The quip came out easy, settling the nervous energy that churned in her stomach.

"On my pulse, brat," he chuckled. Her lips curled at the vibration of his voice under her grip. That laughter was as captivating to her as it had always been.

She did as he asked, concentrating only on the feeling of his skin beneath hers. After a few moments, she could feel the steady thrum of his heartbeat. Was this what he felt with his magic? A beat in the air around him that he grasped not through touch, but something ethereal. She shifted her thumbs until they were above his veins, the movement making his pulse quicken. Whether he meant to or not, he started to stroke the back of her hands slowly. The gesture made gooseflesh rise on her arms.

"Feel it?" His voice rumbled under her grip, the lingering tremor flooding her with a sensation she hadn't felt for years. "Imagine that pulse is a tangible thing. Something you can grab. Now, imagine your own pulse. Think of how it speeds up when you run or slows down when you sleep. How it seems to grow louder when you hold your breath. Imagine all of that. Try to match it to the beat under your thumbs."

"But what if I..." She snapped her eyes open.

His expression softened, face shifting as his lips curved. He leaned forward, pressing his forehead against hers. "If you hurt me, I'll deserve it."

He hadn't mentioned what else could bring her heartbeat thudding into her ears. The one that was currently tumbling through her rib cage and making her mouth feel uncomfortably dry. The feel of his skin, his breath on her face, the lapping water at her feet. Every nerve under her flesh felt like it had been electrified with the static from her fingers. Each sensation exaggerated and hard to ignore.

How many times had she lain awake at night enraged at herself for not spending more time memorizing every curve and dip of his face? Every day that passed the memory of it was waning, drifting into the ether like smoke. She had no way to hold on to it. Could only watch as that mental picture she had of him slowly disappeared until there was nothing left of him but a shapeless figure in her mind.

Now he was here, his face the only thing she could see. A fresh visage to graft into her memories. It had been this close only moments before, riddled with anger and hate. Now, the softness pulled at her. If she tried, she could squint just enough that he flickered back ten years again. The dark eyes, light hair. Inkless, innocent face.

That version of him was gone. It was time to let it fade the rest of the way.

She closed her eyes again, resting her head a little more on his, letting him take the weight of her thoughts. It was near impossible to focus on the beat beneath her thumbs as her own drummed through her torso. It was too loud, too heavy, like a storm beneath her sternum.

With every deep breath, the rapid pounding started to ebb, the rate slowing. But still too loud. She pushed on it again, willing it further to quiet. Her head felt light. An icy sensation flooded her extremities, threatening to break out in shivers along her spine. The beating in her ears dulled until it was barely audible. Each pause between thrums of her heart longer than the last. Almost silent.

Her head spun. A weightless, floating sensation overtook her, like she was slipping free of her own skin.

Then, nothing.

Twenty-Three

The cavern spun in a hazy mix of blues and purples when Sybil's eyes snapped back open. Nausea rose up her throat, choked down before it could spill over. Quinn was gripping tightly to her shoulders, holding her up while her head lolled.

The thrumming of her heart started up in her head again, louder and heavier, as though her pulse had been pulled into the base of her skull and turned to thunder. Air punched out of her lungs in sharp, burning breaths.

Then the ceiling above gave way. A torrent of water slammed into her, sudden and frigid. An icy crash that stole what little breath she had left. She lifted her arm in instinct, but the strength faltered, her hand collapsing limply into her lap as a numbness rolled through her limbs.

"What..." she started but she couldn't find the words. Quinn's eyes searched hers, though they were impossibly far away. Her brain felt like it was wrapped in a thick cloth, muffled to everything around her.

"Lie down." He put his hand to her back, guiding her to the rock. Her foot flopped lazily back into the water to join the other. Droplets sprinkled down from the lichen-covered stalactites, tapping their sporadic beat against her cheeks and forehead.

"What happened?" Her head started to clear, the details in the cave sharpening. Quinn hovered over her, propped up on his elbow. His focus on her was intense, never straying. The coarse ridges of his calloused hands still felt numbed as he wiped her damp hair from her face.

"You did it," he said, the tone too lilting for his heavily creased brows. "Except you grabbed hold of your pulse, not mine. I think you stopped it."

"I did?" Her voice was slurred and an octave too high. She couldn't quite grasp how she went from holding his neck to collapsing in on herself. "But I... I didn't *do* anything."

"You stopped your heart, you dummy," he mocked, though the laughter barely scraped past his lips.

She blinked. Her pulse was still fluttering, fragile as a moth's wings, but there.

"The water..."

"You grabbed it with your magic once your heart started."

"Chaos mage strikes again." She tossed a sleepy, half-hearted smirk in his direction.

Quinn's hands stilled for a second. Barely long enough to catch, but she did. Then he exhaled and shook his head. "Reckless." The edge was gone from his voice. The casual grasp back of the slur made the dimples indent on his face, the worry seeping out.

Another droplet landed on her cheek. When she lifted her hand to wipe it away, her jaw fell open. Her hands were coated in blood. She sat up with a start, swaying slightly as the cavern warbled and spun once more. Mud stuck to her arms in clumps from the cavern floor, contrasting with the visceral red. The front of her tunic was splattered just as badly. The rest of her body was a mix of dirt and blood, dislodged with the wave of water.

"Your nose and mouth," Quinn said, gesturing towards the blood. "That was a lot of power to push out in one go."

She pulled her bloodied, muddied shirt away from her body, scowling at the wet mess. A few more drops of blood fell from her nose, a fresh starburst blooming where it landed. She lifted her shirt over her head. The labyrinth of bloody capillaries had seeped deep into it, colouring her strophium below. Before the blood had a chance to dry, she splashed some of the heated water against her face, the droplets coming away pink, then dissipating into the lighter blues.

"Perfect," she muttered, staring at the ruined shirt. She wrung the fabric out in her fists, knuckles white. The stains only spread further, inky red water dribbling into the pool.

"I look like I crawled out of a grave." Her voice dipped, not quite joking. "Don't even know what half of this is." She tossed the shirt over her shoulder and forced a weak smirk towards Quinn. "Bet this isn't quite how you pictured the 'Great vollmagi'."

The water sloshed as Quinn pulled his legs out of the pool, drops clinging to his calves. Sybil stared at them, watching them trace the lines of scars and runes along his flesh before he stepped away, disappearing behind her. For a second, she expected him to reach down. Make some comment about how her chaos didn't matter. One that would undoubtedly fall on deaf ears. But then she heard buckles clicking and clothing shift.

Before she had a chance to turn around, a shadow passed over her head. The water cascaded up from the pool, the serene glass surface broken once more. Quinn resurfaced, pushing his dark hair back on his head, strands of it lying on his bare shoulders. His vibrant orange eyes glowed above the water's edge as he sunk down, peering up at her.

When she glanced behind and saw the trousers and tunic left behind, her face burned. Quinn swam over to her, treading water at her feet. The light reflected on the surface obscured her view, helping her keep her gaze fixed on his face.

"It's warmer the deeper you go." He crossed his arms over her legs, resting his cheek on them to stare up at her. His weight on her like this felt... right. So familiar and comforting, she almost leaned into him. The fear that had knotted tight in her ribs was unravelling. Like none of the pain, none of the terror had happened.

Sybil exhaled. Maybe, just for right now, she could pretend it hadn't.

"Why is it so warm?" Her nerves started to coil with every one of his soft breaths against her thigh.

"Must be those underground rivers of fire. I think it's what brings all the life to this cave too. Growing towards warmth."

"You seriously still believe those dumb myths? Fire isn't a liquid, it doesn't flow beneath the ground." The faintest smile tugged at her lips even as she berated him.

Quinn just shrugged, shifting to float away from her. "It explains why the northern shore of Losweau is so damn cold if all the rivers flow to the Peaks. Whatever it is, it feels amazing. But do what you please." He narrowed his eyes. "You can keep looking like you crawled from a grave." The sharp challenge in his expression sent a different warmth through her chest. A different river of fire beneath her skin.

She chewed on the corners of her lips, glancing back towards her soiled tunic. It sat in a messy clump near the doubly filthy mantle. A fresh set of laundered clothing would be a blessing from some unknown deity right now. Barring that, the warmth of the waters could suffice. Except, their current intruder, tempting as he was, still made her wary.

"Turn around." Sybil stood up from the edge of the water, grabbing the hem of her pants. The fabric felt coarse against her skin as it slid to her ankles. A polar opposite to the heavy gaze Quinn levelled on her as she stood. The tiniest flicker of a smile crawled up his face. It vanished from view as he turned to face the wall. She was thankful it came with no resistance, though she could feel the snide superiority that lingered after. It wasn't hard to pick apart what he was thinking. It wouldn't be the first time he had seen her so vulnerable. Still, something about it being so far removed from the last time made her skin bristle.

The strophium came next. Though, with both it and her underwear, she felt a mental battle waging in her head as she deliberated whether to remove both. Logic won over for a change; the anxious energy too thick for her to be so exposed. She could deal with the soaked underwear.

The water crested over her as she plummeted down. He was right, it was quite a bit warmer as she plunged, blessedly hot at her feet. A swift kick, and her head burst back out into the humid air of the cavern.

Quinn grabbed hold of her hand once she surfaced, pulling her towards him. He was standing on a small ledge under the water. Shallow enough for his shoulders to breach the surface, but hers only barely peaked above. Their bodies disappeared into the darkness below them, only the faintest blues lighting up their torsos. From the edge of the pool, it had seemed as though the lichen's light reached into the depths. Only now it was apparent just how much deeper it was than what it appeared.

"Thanks," she muttered, brushing the hair off her face. She felt around with her feet, shifting back from him, reopening the space between them.

The small ledge gave her a modicum of freedom, but even with the extra gap of their skin, the proximity seemed too much.

"Better?" he asked, shifting slightly to lean away from her.

She nodded, crossing her arms tightly over her chest. Even with the darkened waters, she felt too open. The heat did little to calm the prickles that had spread across her skin.

"So... Killian Bauer," he said, the sinister curve of his lips like ice through her veins.

The comment seemed to have been strung on the tip of his tongue like a nocked arrow. Just waiting to let it loose. Sybil groaned. The oppressive unease that followed twisted about in her torso like eels fighting for space against one another.

The water rippled around her, tiny waves floating past her skin as Quinn moved closer. "He was a snot-nosed, whiny little shit warden when I went to Hazel Gryph for that year." The barest space between his torso and her arms, the gap she had created being decimated with every movement.

"He was my partner during my first year and was quite a bit less... 'snot-nosed' by then."

"Partner? That's all?" An innocent enough question, though the tightening in his jaw said otherwise.

"He was *nice* to me. It was refreshing when you're surrounded by twits that push you around because of your family name." Killian had betrayed her. Had been the instigator that led to her attempted execution. Yet, she couldn't stop herself from defending him. As though the attack on him was a direct attack on her. On her choices.

A soft rumble tremored through the water as Quinn chuckled, the sound almost forced. "Oh, I'm aware he knows a lot about family names. I'm sure he was... nice."

"He was. Not that it's any of your business."

He paused, squinting at her for a moment. "I guess I just didn't think pretty boys were your type."

"*You* were a pretty boy," she snarled at him.

"'*Were?*'" Quinn clutched at his heart.

Sybil rolled her eyes, pulling on the back of her lids. "Sorry. You're right." She turned her back to him. "You're still a *boy.*" She let as much venom drip off her tongue as she could, throwing a sideways smirk over her shoulder.

There was another ripple in the water. She inhaled sharply as he slid his arms around her waist, tight below her ribs. He dipped down to press his chin to the crook of her neck. His breath on her ear amplifying the shivers that ran down her spine.

She wanted to pull away, but the unexpected contact locked her muscles. Electricity coasted beneath her flesh, emanating from where his cheek softly scraped below her jaw. A tightness wrapped around her throat, and she couldn't stop herself from swallowing against it. She felt him smile against her cheek, the tightening of the muscles slow and controlled.

"I can live with someone touching you," he whispered in her ear, his lips skating against the thin flesh. "I just can't bear the thought of someone making you feel what we used to feel." She tried not to press back into the heat of him, not to notice the way his body answered to hers. The touch of his skin was a warm fire after trudging through ice for days.

Another hard swallow. She licked her lips to bring back the moisture, though her tongue was drying in her mouth. "And you've been abstinent for a decade?"

"There were others. But it was never like this." He trailed his hand along the curve of her hip, slow and deliberate. "It was all just bodies, friction, and noise. Not this ache. Not this pull." He dipped his mouth to her neck, voice rough at the edges. "You make me remember what it's like to want. To need."

A soft noise escaped her throat before she could catch it and drag it back, making her cheeks flush with heat.

"Did Killian ever get to hear that little sound you used to make when you were right on the edge? Or was that only ever for me?" His hands slid higher on her torso, squeezing her tighter to his body. The water muted his callouses and softened the edges of his scars, but not the hunger behind his touch.

"You don't get to ask that," she said, though her voice fractured at the memory.

Warnings started to flare up through her thoughts. Flashes of the pain that he had caused her, mixed in a disorienting, muddled cacophony of all the times his hands had touched her skin. Soft, inkless hands, not tainted by whatever malice he went through. Two opposing struggles, each grabbing tightly to her mind and pulling in either direction. She knew she should push from his grip, knew that whatever she did, she couldn't let herself be swayed. He had shown her what a monster he could become, but she found herself being lulled by his touch, his voice. Even after it so recently broke her.

He'd reminded her just how alone and helpless she truly was. Once they stepped back from this brief fantasy, she would be right back there again. It had taken her years to stop staring into the shadows, waiting for him to step out. If she really had to leave and be on her own again, would she ever be able to look at the darkness and not see his silhouette haunting her?

"Quinn, please…" she felt him shudder, his fingers curling, gripping tightly to her flesh. But he didn't let go, his breath making her hair rise. She could barely hear the sound of the water dripping from above, her heart drowning it out. The rhythm pulsed through her, centring low in her body, demanding attention.

"Say that again," he whispered, his teeth against her ear. His hand started to slide south, the movement sending sparks up her spine. Fear screamed at her to stop it, but every touch made her relax further into him.

"Quinn… please…" she whispered back, her breath hitching in tandem with every movement of his mouth.

A deep rumbling vibrated through his torso. His hands slid from her stomach to grip her hips, pulling them to his. A harsh heat burned in her cheeks as he pressed into her back.

Then, slowly, he slid his hands along her sides and urged her to turn, his touch firm but gentle. Like he wasn't sure she'd let him.

He tucked his thumbs under her jaw, tilting her face to his. That same movement that had been so familiar years ago, yet so foreign under his new, haunting gaze. He rested his forehead on hers, his still dripping hair hanging between them. The orange glow of his eyes no longer eerie, but darkly tempting. They darted between hers, searching for what she could only assume was the same hesitation she sought from him. The storm hovered just out of sight, but she knew they could both feel the thunder coming. Fools to ignore it, but the tense tether between them blocked it out.

Though the suspension in time lasted seconds, lifetimes passed as every 'what if' tore across her thoughts. None of them outweighed the burning heat that had spread from her chest out through her nerves. A potent pulse between her legs that screamed out louder than any hypothetical her head tried to blind her with.

This was a second in her life. A second that, no matter what happened, she would never get back. For once, she let the voice that whispered from the darkness come forward and share its venom.

Would I rather think 'what if' for the rest of my life, or take one more reckless chance?

Sybil lowered her head, staring up through narrowed lids. The challenge was easy, and after a few moments, she found her voice again. No longer hitching in her throat but strong. Level.

"Quinn. Please."

The reaction was quick, barely seen as he let go of her jaw, crashing his lips to hers. He shoved her back against the edge of the water. She prepared for the sharp rock to dig into her back, but her skin only met smooth stone. A hand went to the base of her spine, the other to the nape of her neck, pulling himself against her. She tried not to think about how similarly he had grabbed her before, seething his threats into her ears. The hard length beneath him brushed against her, heat rolling through her like lava, slow and consuming, snuffing the trembling fear out in an instant.

A flicker of pain pricked across her scalp as his hand tangled in her hair and angled her head towards him. Quick and sharp. The kind of pain that should have made her recoil. But she didn't flinch. The pain wasn't cruel, it wasn't chaos or fury. It was controlled and she could feel the restraint in his hands.

He pulled back from the kiss, his eyes meeting hers. Dark. Hungry. No viciousness, no hatred. Just want. He was giving her every chance to say stop. With the patient stare, she knew, this time he would listen.

When she didn't shift away, his shoulders relaxed, whatever he'd been holding on to leaving him. "I missed you so fucking much." His lips skated against hers with every word, punctuated by once more enveloping hers in his kiss. His tongue slid between them, tasting and tangling. A hungry need as he angled her head to his.

She laced her arms around his back, flinching when she felt the raised edges of the scars beneath her palms. It vanished as his hips pressed into hers, her fingers acting of their own will to dig into his skin. A groan rumbling up his throat, a twisted grin pulling at the corners of his mouth.

He pulled her leg up around his hip, the tip of his cock dragging against the thin cotton barrier. A soft noise drifted past her lips as he tilted his hips once more, the tip now pressed against her apex. He cursed into her mouth, tangling his tongue once more with hers before gently taking her lip between his teeth.

Something in her shifted. Blood rushing against her control, heat rising beneath her skin. The feeling of his magic threaded beneath her flesh and burned through her veins. Sharp and sudden. Her body tensed, bracing for the anguish that would follow the loss of control.

But instead of pain, she felt warmth. It pulsed, and built, wrapping her in heat instead of tearing her apart. A growing, intense pressure that centred entirely between her legs.

"What... are you doing?" She managed to stutter out, breathless. Her arms and legs began to tremble in his grip. Every nerve felt exposed, raw and electric. Like her skin had thinned and the water was touching straight through her. Her thoughts clouded, but her body was lightning. Charged and impossibly awake.

"Agony isn't the only thing bloodweaving is good for," he whispered, drowned out almost immediately as another wave of pleasure washed over her.

She couldn't answer, all she could do was feel. If this was what giving into him could be, she would gladly do it all over again.

Quinn's hand slipped from her back to her thigh. He dragged the thin fabric out of the way, hands ravenous and unrelenting. The water rippled as her back arched. She rolled her hips in a silent plea for more. Her eyes instinctively closed, her head rocking back.

When the grip on her hair tightened, the pain once again reared its head. Quinn's eyes were on her, narrowed and intense, measuring her every move.

"Eyes on me. I want to watch you." He pressed his palm hard between her thighs. She wanted to disobey, to immediately look elsewhere. Fight him with inaction, but the rotating motions of his hand coaxed airy moans from her mouth, betraying her. He took the invitation, sliding a finger into her, then another, eliciting a sharp breath from her lips.

She pulled her hands away from his back, her fingers aching from how tightly they'd clung to him. One went to his neck to pull him back to her lips. The other drifted down his torso, her hand curling around the hard heat of him before he flinched out of her grasp.

"No. Fuck—just... no," he groaned, pressing his forehead to hers. His inhale was heavy and hitched in his throat, each breath shuddering past his teeth. "This needs to last, I need to... feel you. All of you. Touch every fucking inch of your skin."

Sybil groaned, grinding her hips against his, eliciting more sharp, coarse breaths from his throat. She narrowed her eyes at him, seething through clenched teeth. "You don't get to break me and then deny me." Her voice was sharp, edging with challenge.

"No," he growled, the vibration shifting through his chest and reverberating through her skin. "No, Sybil. I've thought about this for far too long. I'm not going to fuck this up by making it quick." He dragged her lips back to his.

He curled his fingers, dropping his shoulder to deepen his hold on her. He smiled against her mouth as a moan hissed past her lips. "There it is, that fucking noise," he whispered. "I missed that noise."

She tried to spit a retort, but it was interrupted by another gasp. "I will light you on fire..."

"I'd happily let you burn me alive just to hear you make that sound again." He silenced her with his mouth, his fingers curling deep as his palm ground harder against her.

This time, the unraveling felt like something she owned.

He pulled his hand free from between her legs and she let out a sharp, breathless curse. Her body arched towards him, the coil that had been slowly tightening inside her unspooled. Without his weight pressing her to the rock, pins and needles flared down her muscles, awakening the numbness left behind. He hoisted himself onto the ledge above the water. The muscles in his back flexed, droplets cascading off his hair and down his inked skin. She didn't move, just stared. The damage to his skin faded, eclipsed by the sheer presence of him. Hard, flushed and so intimidating. His body still slender, but every ridge and muscle carved through years of harsh movement.

Her teeth raked against her lip, fingers absently slipping between her legs to chase the pulse he'd left behind. But he caught her hand before it could reach her centre. In one smooth pull, he lifted her from the water and laid her beside him on the stone. The air was cooler out here, but his body pressed against hers melted the chill. He braced his arms on either side of her head as his mouth found hers again, wet and hungry. Her legs wrapped around his hips like they belonged there. His cock still hovered just out of reach, the head brushing against her. So close it hurt.

That nagging voice still told her she should be afraid, that he could still be the monster from before. But here, with his body above hers and his breath on her lips, all she felt was want.

With a few teasing shifts of his pelvis, he broke away from her kiss and brought his mouth to her neck, his teeth digging into her tender flesh. She clawed her nails once more into his back, a groan spilled against her throat from between his lips. He shifted his weight to his knees, slowly working his way across her chest with teeth, tongue, and lips.

She tried to mimic him, wrapping his hair in her fist to dictate his movements. Urge him lower, where the ache was spreading fast. He either didn't notice, or didn't care, continuing his tantalizing slow progress down her torso.

His teeth bit into her hip, just above the wound she'd carved into her skin. A reminder of the haunted version of herself she was leaving behind. The pain sent lightning through her core once again, followed immediately by frantic elation blooming in her chest. Like a scream held just beneath her ribs. His tongue slid over the bite, licking the sting away. It traced another line along her hip just above the line of her underwear, her pelvis driving upwards while her hand tightened in his hair, desperate to move him where the ache pooled. He only slowed his pace, the sharp tip of his tongue moving just enough to drive her mad.

Not taking his mouth from the tantalizingly close line on her hips, he slid his hands up her thighs. They tucked into the band of her underwear, fingers tightening around the fabric. She lifted her head, catching his eyes on her as he started to pull them down. Her head dropped back, a heavy sigh escaping as the fabric slid past her hips.

His stillness felt like yet another cruel tease. But when his voice rattled in the cavern, it shook her, snapping her out of the foggy reverie.

The warmth, the heat. Just like that. It all froze.

"What is that?" His arms dropped to either side of her hips, lifting his body up from between her legs. A horrifying pause. A thousand things flashed through her mind. Each one worse than the last. The anxiety flooding her body with an icy cold that dampened and extinguished the fire that had been growing inside her.

Sybil pushed up on her elbows and followed his gaze, only to see him staring at the rune on her hip with a frown that carved shadows across his face. A heavy breath of relief flooded out between her lips. "It's the rune I got the day you were taken, the one that gave me my magic." She sat up further, her hand cupping his jaw. She tried to pull him back to her, press her lips to his and draw the tension away.

He moved out of her grasp, shifting back to his knees, and dragged her roughly along the rocks to bring her hip closer. His fingers ran along the inks, tracing lightly against the radiating star. He pulled the skin taut to inspect it. "You got your magic from the Void. Who gave you this?"

She cocked her head, frowning at him. "What do you mean? It was the Void who gave it to me."

The last thing she had expected was for the colour to drain from his skin as he stared at the ink. Even in the dim blues she could see the way his hand shock as it continued to trace almost methodically around the thin, ragged tattoo.

His eyes darted to hers, his voice dropping an octave, almost accusatory. "This isn't a Void rune, Sybil. Who the fuck gave it to you?"

Twenty-Four

Though every nerve in his body felt like it had been stabbed by the sharp needles of his masters, Raekin still managed to buckle his pants with trembling fingers. Sybil was shouting, trying to grab his attention, but her words sounded as though somebody had locked them in a box and buried them. Trapped underground, muffled, incoherent, and leagues away. He was vaguely aware of the ruffling of her own clothing as she tried to dress and jog after him, but there was little he could do to turn his focus back outwards.

The symbol was Void. He'd see it enough times to know it, burned into the backs of his lids. Carved viciously into the bodies of the captured and tortured masses under their thumbs.

But the rest...

The crooked, shaky lines. Not a glyph of tradition like those below the ground, but cruder. Sloppy. Almost modern. Even the inks: a sheer black that stayed black under every twist of light and shadow. The shallow *depth*...

Memories were ripped out of the darkest corners of his mind, unfolded and plastered at the forefront. Pain in his shoulders seared through him. Jarring flares of lights and blood cascaded in front of his eyes before he snapped them shut, gently tapping his fingers against his temples until the world cleared beyond his ears.

"Quinn, stop," Sybil called behind him. Without thinking, he obeyed. His mind not fully connecting to the fact that it wasn't an order, working entirely against his will. When her hand rested on his, the sounds cleared, the muffled roar thinning in his ears. His tiny ritual shoving the darkness into the shadowy recesses of his mind. His given name once more sending painful shocks through his body. As though seeing those ragged lines on her had righted his head, reminding him exactly who he was.

Naz'Tak's blighted pull had started shortly after he sunk his feet into the water, but it had been nothing more than a frustrating itch. Now it was burgeoning on a painful tear against his spine. He'd barely felt it when he let himself get enthralled by her, and that just scared him more.

Her breath. Her skin. Her taste.

That fucking *sound.*

Raekin shook his head hard, drowning the heated pulse that started to spread through his chest. The acidic terror gripped him once more. There was no sense in holding on to anything other than that. Anything else would only put her in more danger than she already was. With that thing on her...

"How are you so sure it isn't from the Void?" Her light touch didn't halt his progress in tying the bags back to Trotter's saddle. The molhund was yawning, waking up to the commotion that surrounded him. His nose tendrils reaching wide as his front paws dug into the dirt to arch his back into a deep stretch.

He couldn't stop the sharp laugh that shot from his nose. "I have some experience with Void runes."

"But it's the same as yours. The same pentagram." Sybil stepped forward, trying again to tear his attention from the beast. He shrugged her off and tightened the saddle on Trotter.

"It's not the same. What the Void use for inks, what they use for symbols, what they do to..." He swallowed hard, hoping she didn't see it. "What they do to carve them. It's all different. The radiating pentagram is the same, but everything else is wrong."

"Can you stop for five minutes and explain it to me? *Before* you run off."

He'd made the decision the second he saw the crooked ink. Even if it wasn't the right decision. "I'm not running off. You're coming with me," Raekin said. He didn't slow, still throwing bags onto the saddle and cinching them tight.

The words left his lips, and dread carved a sharp knot between his shoulder blades. They'd no longer be hidden behind his rock barrier. He'd made a promise to himself to keep her safe and he was about to ride with her right into the belly of the beast. Right to the teeth that would devour her the second they tasted her flesh.

Someone above ground knew something about the Void runes. They knew enough to ink one onto her skin. If this person could emulate that enchantment, what else could they know? The Hag should have her stolen book by now, no doubt thumbing greedily through its thick, ancient pages. If there was anybody that could tell him about the rune's origins or at the very least what it meant, it was her.

"What? Where?!"

"We're going to the Nether Peaks. Someone there knows more than we do."

Sybil was more awake atop Trotter this time. She no longer needed to lace her hands in the straps of Raekin's armor. He barely noticed her body held against his as they traversed the tunnels. His mind was connected to the walls around him, feeling for any disturbance. Gauging any shift in weight that might indicate somebody else on this side of the Peaks. The glowing of the lichen had faded a while ago, only a few flickers of light contrasting the growing blackness. Raekin could have opted to relight the torches, but the darkness was a blessed covering. One he needed if he was putting all his focus into his magic.

The pulsing headache started about an hour back, the intense concentration of both his powers like a hammer to either side of his skull. He couldn't ease off the magic though. One wrong move, one fluctuation and they would have her. He'd have to manage.

Once they were closing in on the outskirts of Ktharheim, he eased Trotter to a stop, and hoisted himself off the saddle, turning after to help Sybil down. He had started feeling the growing number of heartbeats in the distance, the city blinking to life under the digits of his magic. Few liked to wander this far from the centre, but it wasn't unheard of. Regardless of his status among the Etched, he couldn't trust that their eyes would stay downcast and blind to a girl wearing un-shredded clothing, her skin untouched. This was the closest he could let her get in the open.

Raekin pressed his palms to the tunnel wall. The stone warmed quickly under his touch as his magic worked. The rock split and reformed with a groan. The noise was deafening, a wild contrast to the cautious way they had ridden towards the city, but it was the only way. He'd just have to hope that those that heard it would falsely assume the usual shifting and cracking of the fissures nearby.

His magic reformed the rock wall, first with a small alcove, then growing inwards. The rock folded away into shadow, contorting into a narrow path in the dark. The noise was almost unbearable in his ears, an earthquake by his hands. Tension coiled so tightly within him he felt seconds away from snapping. The pain in his skull raged against the one at the nape of his neck. Each of them battling for control with their vicious, clawed grip on his psyche.

With a quick glance backwards to see Sybil and Trotter following, he lifted his other hand, sealing the wall in behind them. They were surrounded by nothingness, the ripping and tearing of the stone in front of them circling through the darkness like a hurricane.

He barely heard the crack of the flint before their small tunnel lit up. A flame danced on the tips of Sybil's fingers. "Are you seriously going to build an entire tunnel just to get us there?" Her voice was barely heard above the stone shearing against itself.

"Yes," Raekin grunted. He didn't look away from the wall, his focus already pulled taut. One sense on the flow of blood around him, the other on the wall in front, both dragging sharp daggers through his muscles.

"You're going to kill yourself."

"No." He couldn't expend the energy to string more words together, sentences blurring to pictures and inane, fractured thoughts. It wasn't until the mass of stress and tension lifted the smallest bit that he realized Sybil had pressed one of her hands to the stone. The rock rippled and bent beneath her skin. It was slow and messy, but it was something. The tiniest twist flickered on Raekin's lips as he turned his attention away from her. The help was minimal, barely effective, but having her there and trying sent a swirl of emotion through his chest, the tiniest added burst of energy.

The hold on his magic wavered. The splintering and cracking of stones falling silent. Something moved in the rocks. Small twitches, barely shivers at first. But then the shadows started to take form. Fingers crawled from between the cracks, then hands. Blackened tendrils and horrific limbs, clawing and grasping their way out of the stones. Twisting and writhing, reaching for them.

For *her.*

For a horrifying moment, the only thing he could think was, *they're here, they know.*

A blink, and the nightmare was gone. Just stone.

Sybil stopped. Turning to question the hesitation, but he started to work again, drowning out anything she could voice. He didn't have time to dwell on it, could only refocus his magic and hope it burned out whatever madness was trying to eat away at his mind. This had happened before, but only when he was still chained in the Alpstraum, on the brink of shattering under the malice of his masters. That relation didn't bode well, but he bit down hard on his cheek until the taste of copper drowned the phantoms.

He had no way of knowing how far they got, could only use the heartbeats in the distance to gauge the city. It would have been pointless to count the minutes as they passed, everything inside his head shattered and crushed with the effort until there was nothing left. The tunnel creation had gone from an open walkway to a narrow crumble, to a grinding halt. Almost completely draining him of anything he might have still had left inside.

The dimming light at Sybil's fingertips started to flare into fractured starbursts as Raekin took his hands off the tunnel wall. He narrowed his eyes at it, trying to get the shifting image to refocus, but his vision only clouded at the edges. His gaze snapped skyward before everything went black. Pain shot through his back as it struck the rocks behind him, his breath knocked from his lungs in one hard burst. He was vaguely aware of Sybil's hands on his face, the cool touch of her skin a blessing to the intense burning that seemed to radiate through him.

"It's fine," he mumbled, though it was barely audible, the two words slurring together to become one. With a grunt, he pushed himself upwards, his hands bracing him as their tiny tunnel started to spin. For a moment, he thought it would drag him back under again, but his foggy, fading vision slowly cleared. Enough for the sharp, dangerous pull in his spine to become more visceral.

Raekin wiped his face with the back of his hand, only to look at it and pinch his lips in a tight line. Blood. Lots of it. He winced, trying and failing to hide the expression on his face.

"You're not fine. What is happening to you?" Sybil's frantic voice sounded so far away.

With her hands on his face, he didn't feel like Raekin. Or Quinn. He felt like something else, wrapped in their skin, patched together by chains and failure. One misstep away from coming undone.

"It's the Void. They're calling me back." He rubbed his eyes with his thumb and finger, then blinked the stars back out. "I need to leave you here." She opened her mouth, but he held up his hand. "I'll be back. Just stay in the tunnel and keep quiet."

Sybil's expression shifted, whatever inner thoughts she had battling silently behind her eyes. A flicker of sparks snapped over her knuckles.

With a sharp shake of her head, they vanished. She brought the sleeve of her mantle up and wiped off his face. "I'll be fine. Just promise me you'll be alright." He tried to turn, but she wrapped her fist in his tunic, pressing her lips to his. "And you better come back this time."

A short nod was all he could muster as he turned his attention to the wall at his back. The smallest smile still pulled his cheeks from the kiss. The tunnel groaned and crumbled, the stone folding away in front of him. Thin and jagged, but just wide enough for the molhund to squeeze through. The makeshift pathway broke through to the main walkway, bathing them in light. Torches that lined the tunnels burned his eyes for a moment as they adjusted.

With a tug on Trotter's reins, he pulled the beast out into the light. He would have liked to close the wall to prying eyes with just a flick of his wrist, but his exhaustion made him fumble and fall forward into the rock, catching himself with a sharp breath. His body shook as he sealed the wall behind him, leaving narrow vents in the stone.

Every fibre of his being screamed at him as he turned to leave her. He had to remind himself it was a necessity. He couldn't get her to The Hag if he was barely able to stand on his own without the flaring pain debilitating him. He'd get to Naz'tak, and take whatever punishment waited for him. That, at least, would eliminate one thing from this swirling, oppressive cacophony of nightmares.

He'd spent so much energy trying to hide her from the monsters. Now he had to go back to pretending he was one, barely able to stand on his feet.

After a few failed attempts, he hoisted himself onto the saddle, his arms shaking with the effort. Once seated, they felt like dead weight hanging off the sides of his torso. His heart was racing in his chest, his blood feeling cold as it surged through his body. There was no point staying upright, his body falling heavily onto the neck of the molhund. He could lie there and let the tunnels pass him. Trotter knew the way better than he did, Raekin just had to stay on the saddle long enough to get there. Hopefully with enough time to regain a modicum of strength.

His blinks started to lag. The soft, monotonous rumble of Trotter's paws lulling him into a dangerous calm. When the beat slowed, his eyes sprang open, the molhund passing below the makeshift stone arch of the stables outside Ktharheim. There was barely enough time for him to jolt up before Gunzik, the taker, grabbed hold of Trotter's reins.

His heavy set, red-rimmed eyes met with Raekin's for a split second before he dropped them to the ground. A common response from other Etched. It had stung at first, but by now, it was almost a relief to not be stared at with distaste. Or at least, not that he had to witness.

Raekin was able to swing his leg over the saddle, but even that was a struggle. He slid awkwardly off the beast, landing with a soft grunt on the hard stone. A wince slid through his teeth as his hands scraped roughly against the stone wall, catching himself from falling the rest of the way. He started to thank Gunzik, but the taker was already leading Trotter away. His limp had gotten worse even in the short time since Raekin last came to the stables. He had to turn away as the memories of Gunzik's hobbling came back to him. The sound, the screaming. While all Raekin could do was watch. A fresh wave of nausea twisted his already tightly clenched stomach.

Raekin lingered only a moment before starting down the winding stone path that cut through the outer edge of Ktharheim. The city loomed around him, harsh angles of obsidian architecture lit by veins of pale flame, the air thick with the ever-present hum of the dark Void runes, ash, and the burning cinnamon reek of the fissures.

No one stopped him. Not even the Etched that eyed the bloodstain on his shirt and the bruises on his arms. A common sight, barely eliciting second glances. Every step sent another wave of pain down his spine, a grinding burn that pulsed in time with Naz'Tak's call.

By the time he reached the outer tier of the Uldspire, he was drenched in sweat and clenching his jaw so hard it felt like his teeth might crack. The stabbing sensation in his back didn't falter. Didn't even dip in intensity for a moment. That didn't bode well. When Naz'Tak sensed his approach, he usually eased off the call, knowing it was being answered. Whatever waited for him in the hall was bad, and he cursed himself once more for letting himself get distracted. Even now, through the pain, he could still feel her lips on his.

And he *fucking hated it.*

"How do you suppose I should view this, Raekinblod? That maggot-filled imp walks his scabby, rotten carcass through my door and hands me the book my loyal pet was supposed to fetch for me." Naz'Tak had his back to Raekin, his clawed hands clasped behind him. The purple of his fins was vibrant under the torchlight. "And you were where exactly? Chasing down some degenerate blight? I expect better of you. I can only hope that you made their last moments agony."

Raekin barely made it two steps into the master chamber of the Uldspire before the paralyzing pain gripped his spine, locking him in place with the runic command. His breath was already starting to waver, coming out in chokes and gasps as the anguish lanced through his body. He'd expected it, could practically feel the intense heat of his master's rage emanating throughout the hall.

"You got yourself damaged by that sarco slut, and then you have the audacity to show up late. If you were in my position, what would you do?"

The hold released, and Raekin did everything he could to stay upright, not letting the anger flare on his face. "Whatever punishment you see fit." Though his body warbled with the effort, his words came out calm and level.

Naz'tak rolled his shoulders, slowly turning around. He regarded him with a disassociated hatred. The look so often plastered on his scaled face when Raekin screwed up. "The old bitch has her book, and I am one step closer to freedom, Raekinblod. This has put me in an exceptionally good mood."

Raekin had seen Naz'tak's good moods. At least they didn't leave as much lasting damage as the bad. "I'm glad to hear it," Raekin said, though he couldn't stop the poison from leeching out.

With the pain of the pull gone, Raekin was able to think a little more clearly. He'd been reckless bringing Sybil so close to Ktharheim. He should have spoken with The Hag first, made a plan. Too late now. She was already too close to the jaws of the beasts. He'd just have to think quicker on his feet, find a way to get her from the cave to The Hag's room safely.

Naz'Tak slapped his clawed hand against the wall, jerking Raekin's attention back. His master narrowed his eyes, the slits thinning to razors. "Am I keeping you from something?"

"No, sir." Raekin shifted his shoulders back. Now was not the time to distract himself, not when the monster was watching every twitch as though gauging it for attack.

"You've been drifting, pet. Distant. Sloppy. If this were any other day, you'd be on the post with needles in your joints. Lucky for you, I already got my frustration out," his crooked, reptile smile made Raekin's chest constrict. "You should visit your neuro friend. I'm sure he has lots to share."

"What did you do?!" The panicked words were out of his mouth before Raekin could think twice. Too exhausted to remind himself to keep his mouth shut. A surge of lightning shot through his back and across his shoulders. He let out a gasp, but it was everything in his power to not crumble to his knees. He could see the flare in Naz'tak's eyes, though it was quickly fogged over, agony distorting his vision. "Naz—"

"Do you think I enjoy explaining to Tolrin'ar why his property is damaged?" Naz'tak bellowed, another wave of pain following it. Raekin groaned, overwhelmed. He barely felt the hard stone connect with the sharp bones of his knees, the razors of his rune shearing his mind from his body. "Do you think I am happy about owing that lowly, weak-backed, matronly bastard a favor? I should string you up by your ankles and slice you with obsidian until you stop kicking. How many times do I have to remind you what it means when I call?"

"I—" Raekin choked, blood coating the inside of his mouth, though he couldn't be sure where it came from.

He hadn't noticed Naz'tak walking over to him until his sharp claws dug into the sides of his jaw, forcing his head up. His voice was low, quiet. Whispered like a knife drawn slow. "How long do you think you could hold in your blood if I tore out your throat?"

Naz'Tak's grip tightened, as though testing how far he could puncture before the bones snapped. With a sneer, he shoved Raekin's head downwards, claws tearing deep gouges through his skin. The pain that laced through his rune ebbed, allowing him a shaky breath. Raekin hit the stone on all fours, blood dripping off his jaw.

"As I said, I'm in a good mood."

Be useful.

It had seemed like such a pointless mantra when one of the older Etched said it after the nightmares of the Alpstraum. He'd told Raekin to repeat it in his head over and over. Remember that no matter what happens, don't break. That was weeks before Raekin watched the man be eviscerated when he was found stealing extra food. The man held his tongue throughout the process. It was horrifying to witness, but Raekin had held on to it like a beacon. The Void enjoyed the process, and once you were broken, you become lower than the dirt beneath their claws. So, stay whole, stay upright. Don't let them know that inside you are crumbling apart, so long as you are still able to look them in the eye.

Because of him, as Raekin gasped for breath, his blood pooling beneath him, he made no noise. He needed to see just what Naz'Tak's frustration had cost Hirn. It wouldn't help either of them for Naz'tak to turn his full fury to his pet. He needed to stay strong. He needed to stay whole. Useful.

Alive.

He took the time he needed on the ground, but the second his lungs were able to fill, he got to his feet. The shaking in his hands couldn't be stopped completely but knotting them behind his back hid the worst of the trembling from view. He could feel the blood running down his jaw, his face throbbing with every breath. All it would take was a thought to stave off the worst of the bleeding, but Naz'Tak's wrath was too precarious to test.

Naz'tak ran his hand down Raekin's face, the gesture so soft compared to the claws that were still tainted red. "You are my favorite, Raekinblod. My weapon and my partner. Once The Hag removes this curse from us, you'll be free. *We'll* be free. Don't make me kill you before you get to taste that freedom." His voice was gentle, coated with that noxious honey. "Go see your sarco bitch. You've been gone long enough. You need to get back to your duties and put a disgusting brood in her. I'll call on you once The Hag has gone through the tome."

"Yes, sir."

Varena and their *brood* were the last of his worries. Not with the vaguely veiled boast about his friend. The barracks where Hirn lived were several tunnels west of the Uldspire, tucked against the opening of one of the fissures. Said to be held there to make disposal of insolent Etched quick and easy, a constant threat just outside their doors. These accommodations were only slightly better than the mine shacks that actually teetered on the massive cracks in the ground. Some of the luckier Etched fell to their death in their sleep, rolling just far enough to tumble into the chasms. A quiet, painless escape from their waking nightmare.

Raekin had wanted to move Hirn to the Uldspire nearer him and Varena. Get him something nice to lie on. Have his own area. But he couldn't bring himself to burden Hirn with the horrors that dangled from the strings of those luxuries.

Hirn's rackhouse was already one of the betters along the western edge of Ktharheim. Most of the others had one large room for all the Etched to collapse in. Hirn's at least had their sleeping quarters separated into smaller rooms, a curtain giving them a modicum of privacy. Something Raekin was thankful for when they had to share hushed whispers within the confines of the city. As the only neuroweaver below ground able to grasp thoughts instead of just share them, they didn't have to worry too much about stray minds listening in.

Raekin let out a heavy breath of relief when he tore back the faded, threadbare chunk of fabric that acted as Hirn's door. His friend was still in one piece, sitting atop his 'bed'. He'd scavenged a few blankets and fabrics on their trips outside Ktharheim but had opted to give most of them away. All that remained was a bare, uncomfortable pallet with a small wisp of stolen straw across the top.

Hirn's head hung low, drooping over the splayed book on his lap. "Was it worth it?" Hirn asked, not lifting his head as Raekin entered.

"She's safe."

Hirn looked up and Raekin's heart shattered. Gauze was haphazardly adhered to Hirn's face, covering his right eye. A line of reddish yellow slid from the bottom of the bandage like a putrid tear. Beneath it, black lines criss-crossed his cheek, the ink still fresh, outlined in a feverish red.

"So, it was worth it?" Hirn asked again, lacing every word with venom. He slammed the book shut, hurling it as hard as he could. Raekin only shifted, letting the hard spine strike his arm. "You piece of shit."

"When did he take the eye?" Raekin asked, not bothering with the plethora of apologies that would fall on deaf ears. He curled his hands into fists to quell the tremor. They'd begun to rattle as soon as he laid eyes on the still healing ink, the skin already burgeoning on yellows as the bruising bloomed beneath.

"A few hours," he muttered. *When Sybil's legs were wrapped around you.* "But this was only twenty minutes ago." He lifted his arm, two more of his fingers missing from his hand. The stumps were lazily wrapped, and the gauze was already swelling with colour.

"All because I was late?" Raekin scoffed. "He's getting pettier."

"No, because he had been calling on you for hours and you didn't so much as step in the right direction. What the fuck were you doing?" Raekin opened his mouth, but Hirn held up his hand. "You know what? I don't give a shit, it doesn't matter." A barely noticed, soft smile curled up Hirn's face. The lackadaisical tone returning. "Where did you take her? The Losweau tunnels?"

"She's safe." Raekin did everything he could to keep his tone steady, to stay blank and unreadable. He should have lied. The second the words left his mouth, Hirn's face paled, his one eye opening wide.

"She's still down here?!" Hirn yelled, immediately slamming his hand over his mouth as the noise echoed through the rackhouse. "Have you lost your mind!?"

"It's temporary. I couldn't just shove her into the dark and hope she made it out alive. Besides, there's—"

Hirn leapt up from the bed. "You *have* lost your mind. Shit, Raekin. They're going to flay your skin when they find out about this." He chewed his lip. "They're going to flay *her* skin when they find out about this. And mine. And Varena's."

"Is Varena okay?"

The muscles in Hirn's jaw flexed, his voice seething through his teeth. "Are you sure you give a shit?"

"Is she okay?" Raekin repeated, ignoring the stab.

"She'll be fine. Tore out some of her hair, gave her a few more scars." Hirn let out a heavy breath, his shoulders slumping. "Raekin, can we trust that you still have your head on straight?"

"This won't impede anything. It's a small deviation, but the book is still here. The Hag can start working on the next steps. Sybil being down here does not stop that."

"That isn't what I meant."

"I know what's at stake, Hirn. I'm not—"

"Do you?" Hirn shouted, his voice ringing in the halls, no longer flinching at his own reverberated tone. "I *fucking* told you. You were so sure that you wouldn't sacrifice everything for her."

"And I'm not—"

Hirn stepped forward, jamming his finger into Raekin's chest, shoving him backwards. "We have all suffered right beside you. Don't put that at risk because you can't control yourself. She's one person, there are hundreds counting on you. Don't act like this is nothing. This is selfish, and disgusting. If it becomes us or her, don't fuck it up." Hirn glanced down, his lip sneering as he took in Raekin's torso. "Look at yourself. Naz'Tak has never gotten mad enough to mark you so openly. You're already slipping."

Raekin followed his gaze, seeing the disastrous state of his tunic. In his panic, he'd forgotten to staunch the bleeding of his face, letting it pour down the front of the tunic. Now it was dried and caked into the fabric. Even as he pulled the shirt over his head, he knew the thought was wrong. He didn't want her to see it, didn't want to scare her. And that should have been the last of his concerns.

Raekin had known since he pulled her through the dirt. That raking ache that sat in the back of his head. Though he had screamed it in her face, he was the one that needed a reminder. This was bigger than them. The scowling looks, the curses spat at his shadow as he traversed Ktharheim. He'd accepted that reality long ago when he started on this path. The hatred he could handle. He could even handle convincing himself that every horrific thing he did was for something better. But only if he had the end still in sight. Their salvation.

Would he still be able to be blind to that if it was her wrists and ankles wrapped by razor wire to the post? Would he be able to quiet out her screams when they split open her flesh and carved out her soul? How long before he tore his own blood out of his chest to silence that agony forever?

"I already told you, Hirn. If it comes to that, I will kill her myself."

"You better. If you don't, there will be a long line of people willing to do it for you," Hirn sneered. "And I can guarantee we won't be gentle."

Raekin held steady, not flinching, not dropping his levelled gaze. He knew the threat, had seen the knives poised at his back. He just wished he didn't have to hear it from the person he had to trust right now.

He took in a steady breath, already dreading what he had to ask. "Hirn, I need a favor."

TWENTY-FIVE

The silence was oppressive. At times, it felt as though the tunnel was collapsing inwards. It overcame Sybil, letting her thoughts run wild in the eerie echo of nothingness. Then worse moments would come, when the quiet broke. Distant footsteps or faraway shouts. Close enough to raise the hairs on her neck. She'd snap her hand over her mouth, terrified to make the slightest noise until the oppressive emptiness of sound returned.

Whether it was the suffocating quiet, or the raw fear of being found, Sybil's heart refused to still.

When the walls had first closed, she snuffed out the light that danced in her palm. The shadows that moved and twisted from the flame had set her teeth on edge. Too familiar. Without the fire, they didn't cease, only shifted their dance. With a snap, she finally tore her mantle from her arms, shoving it against the holes Quinn had left to block the last of the light. Trapping the shadows together and out of her sight.

The darkness offered a false comfort. She felt unseen fingers drumming a discordant rhythm down her spine. Exasperated, she collapsed against the wall, snapping her flint once more. She watched the flames dance between her fingers, drifting above and below each digit, flowing like water. Fire could be so easy, so calming. The flickering flames chasing the cold dread away.

Several times she had pulled the hem of her pants down, peering in the wavering light at the ink. Desperate as she turned this way and that, adjusting the lighting just so until each and every angle had been investigated. Hoping, above all else, to see what had crawled under Quinn's skin and burrowed that fear in him. Something she could name, something that might appear on her skin. But nothing changed. It was the same as it had always been, no deep-seated meaning, no hidden secrets twisting in the crooked, warped lines.

In the quiet, she kept thinking back to the way her heartbeat had felt under her magic. If she could only do it again, could she grasp the level of control that he had? No matter how many times she tried, she couldn't capture her pulse under her skin again. Every time she thought she'd get close, a flare of panic would knot around her quickening heart and the magic would warp or fizzle out. No Quinn here to catch her this time if she paused its beating, and definitely nobody here if she stopped it for good. But she still tried to feel it again, pressing the palms of her hands against the pulse at her throat and closing her eyes. Letting only the rhythmic thump enter her head.

There was a part of her that couldn't ignore the fact that she had grasped a new magic so quickly with his help. How many tutors had she sought out to guide her, only for her practice to leave a trail of destruction in its wake? But with Quinn, it was easy. Simple. Even now, thinking of him made her magic come without excessive calling, slipping off her fingertips, like oil over stone. A calming peace settled beneath her sternum, muffling the fear that had engulfed her.

A rotten pit of a reminder nestled beside the peace beneath her ribs. His rage, the sharp poisoned words. Watching how quickly he had flicked from Quinn to... that *thing*. Like the snap of her flint, instantaneous, and so loaded with the potential to destroy.

Never in her lifetime had she thought she would lay her eyes on him, let alone feel his touch. Now, it seemed the craving for that was a tangible thing, like a monster that rattled in its cage. The eerie, unnerving sensation of his scars didn't make her flinch away with her arms around him. His rough calloused hands no longer filling her with nostalgic yearning, but nervous anticipation.

"—tear out his intestines. I'd happily spend a day in the Alpstraum to watch that," a voice said, muffled, but drawing closer in tandem with the crunching of boots. Sybil jolted up with a start, ruffling the mantle still precariously hiding the light balanced on her fingers. She slammed her hands together, snuffing her little fire ball, returning herself to the darkness.

"Tsst," another voice hissed. "Say that any louder and they'll have you strung up." Stones thudded along the wall that served as her protector, kicked up by the ever-nearing footsteps.

"The smarmy shit stain is probably still on his knees at Naz'tak's feet. You saw him running," the first voice said, its tenor gravelly and raw. She heard someone spit, then the footsteps came to a halt. Her hand clamped over her mouth, stifling the sound of her breath. "Did you get a good look at Sarcovarena though? Haggard whore is probably bawling her eyes out in her cushy bed. Bet she wishes she'd never been mated with that prick."

"Ksch. I'd take a beating like that every day if it meant I got to take a load off my back once in a while."

Snickering echoed through the rocks, making Sybil's teeth itch. "I bet she takes lots of loads off on her back." The laughter swelled. "Raekinblod, Naz'tak, and the rest of the Void."

Sybil's brows pressed together as she listened, the names they spoke were grated, strange and unfamiliar. As cautiously as she could, she pulled back on the mantle, peering through the hole to the firelit pathway. A few metres away stood the owners of the voices. One leaned against the opposing rock, his arms crossed lazily over his chest. He had thick black lines running across his lips like stitches and sharp scars running from the corners of his eyes.

The other curled in on himself, his shoulders drooping low as his head darted back and forth. Sybil caught quick glimpses of the dark inks marring his face. The upper half of his head was inked pitch-black, scars radiating down his cheeks like cracks in glass. It only took one quick glance for her to understand what they were. The disconcerting array of oranges and yellows in their eyes, the inks and scars that littered their bodies. Albeit their faces quite a bit more damaged than Quinn's.

Captured mages.

"Do you remember—" the hunched one started, abruptly silencing his stifled laughter before frantically glancing around. "Do you remember that idiot botanomancer? The one who accidentally planted... what was that? What was that, what was that, what was that?"

"Hensfern?"

"Yes! Hensfern! Hensfern." Croaked, frantic bursts of laughter. "Hensfern. Remember? Made the entire field rot? Got dragged away by the masters kicking and screaming?"

"I heard Raekinblod was the one that tortured him after. Naz'tak's orders," the stitch-lipped one said, his manic glee draining from his voice.

"Ripped his blood out of his skin one drop at a time. Heard there was barely any skin left when he was done."

Sybil's chest flooded with ice as she listened. They couldn't possibly be talking about him. It was another bloodweaver, or a sarcomancer with… unusual skills. She swallowed hard against the growing pit in her throat and leaned closer to the opening.

"Naz'tak didn't order shit. That was all Raekinblod." The twitching one rolled his neck, shoulders shuddering. "Psycho gets off on killing us."

"Yeah, well, maybe if the Void liked our faces that much, we wouldn't be walking corpses while 'pretty boy' plays executioner."

The dank cave air suddenly felt as though it was filled with poison and Sybil's lungs refused to inhale anymore. She reeled back from the hole as though the truth had lashed her across the face. The mantle shifted back into place and once more surrounded her in the suffocating darkness. Her feet skidded loudly against the rocks, the noise grating in her ears, but she could barely hear anything over the pounding in her head as her chest collapsed in on itself.

It was impossible. Impossible. Impossible. Impossible.

The word kept ricocheting around in her head. Whenever she tried to get traction, something else would buffet it back away.

You don't know him.

He isn't Quinn anymore.

He's a monster.

The sharp pangs that radiated through her heart felt like crudely crafted arrows, twisted and gnarled as they splintered through her rib cage. The mysteries of this underground world were still shrouded in a thick coat of fog. She was grasping into the ether, taking the only things she knew about beneath the crust and tying them together. Easy assumptions that fit together with the right amount of distortion. Quinn had said it himself: this city was crawling with Void and their subservient mages. Subservient and likely corrupted.

Right?

He was *Quinn*. Boy who held her, boy who saved her. Boy who *loved her*. They could carve apart his flesh, but could they really carve away his heart, his soul? Who he was?

"He's a monster," she whispered into the dark, voice trembling as her fingers fumbled over her heartbeat.

Even as she said the words, she couldn't stop remembering how gently he'd held her.

TWENTY-SIX

Sybil barely noticed the fading crunch of footsteps and laughter. Whatever else they had to say never passed through the rock to where she curled her arms around her legs. Even the sharp rock that dug in her back hardly registered.

The courage to ask Quinn if any of their spewed venom was true shouldn't have been this difficult to muster. He'd been deflective, but he was still *Quinn*. She used to be able to talk to him about anything. All she had to do was ask for the truth, ask who Raekinblod was. For all she knew, she was panicking for no reason. There was some other monstrous being below the earth.

The memory that lingered of his eyes dark with want had twisted back to fury. The snap between soft and vicious was so quick. As though it hadn't been the first time he had to slip into the skin of something so malevolent. Would her accusations only bring forth the being she still feared?

When the shuddering and cracking of rock sounded, a fresh gust of air hit her face, cooling the wet streaks that trailed down it. She was quick to wipe them away, leaping to her feet. Orange eyes stared back at her as the wall split in two, the torchlight flooding through and briefly blinding her. A few sharp blinks and her eyes focused.

"It's just me," Quinn said.

Just me. As though that was such an easy concept. As though she even knew what that meant anymore.

Her breath caught, somewhere between an inhale and a scream. The side of his face was gouged, deep-looking wounds tracing from his cheekbone down under his jawline. His tunic was gone. Blood coated and dried along his neck. Time had cracked it, leaving drought lines across his skin.

How long had he been gone? She couldn't be sure. Time had folded in on itself in the darkness. Her imagination went wild as she tried to comprehend what could have possibly happened to him in that time. Or, worse, what he had done to elicit such a violent response. She couldn't help thinking of the way the other mages had spat 'pretty boy' like it was an insult. The damage was a cruel contradiction to their biting words. One nail being pulled out of the coffin she was building of the hope she still had in him.

Quinn caught her horrified stare, his hand hovering over the fresh wound. She tried to keep herself from staring at his hands, as though she could see whether they were stained in blood. Whether they were truly the hands of a barbaric murderer.

He cocked an eyebrow at her mantle once again crumpled in the dirt, but instead of questioning it, he produced a tattered, black cloak. Without words, he held it towards her, urging her out of her sanctuary.

Sybil opened her mouth, ready to ask verbatim about the mages and their rumors. But once her lips parted, the question vanished, replaced with, "Is it safe?" Her hitching voice made her cringe. As though keeping herself in the dark was keeping her fears from solidifying. Hiding in her memories of his softness.

"It will be." He handed her the cloak and stepped out of view.

The wind whistled through the tunnel, so high-pitched it almost screamed. Like someone begging. Maybe it was just the air. Maybe it wasn't. She didn't react. Could barely tell what was real anymore.

She wrapped the cloak around her shoulders to stifle the chill. The covering did little to stop the shivers that had started to rattle her spine.

When her feet passed the edge of her tiny sanctuary, something gleamed in the dim light, catching her off guard. A yellow eye watched her step into the tunnel. Her body moved before her mind did, shoulder colliding with stone as the pain bloomed. No sound escaped her lips, but her mouth was agape, breath stalling in her lungs.

"This is Hirn." Quinn gestured towards the dark-haired man leaning lazily against the tunnel wall. Her focus darted from the stained bandage across his eye to the fresh rune on his cheek, down to the sharp, gnarled scars that ran along the length of his neck in perfect parallel to one another.

The man said nothing as his eye narrowed, the bandage crinkling beside it. The tiniest twitch of his lip suggested an attempt at a smile, though it never quite formed on his face. His hands shifted nervously at his sides, closing and opening. Two more bandages wrapped around what was left of his fingers.

"He's going to get you into the city," Quinn continued, filling the sudden gaping silence.

Sybil brought her attention back to him, though the glaring man stayed fixed in her periphery. "You're not... coming?"

Quinn shook his head, stepping around the other man to start back the way he had come. "You'll wait five minutes, then follow. Keep the hood up."

"Quinn—" Sybil started. She flinched as Hirn moved. He only crossed his arms over his chest, but the sudden movement from someone so still made her skin prickle. His twitching lip now almost curved fully as he stared at her from under his brow.

"It can't be me. You'll be seen. Hirn can get you there quietly." He gestured towards the other mage. A gesture Hirn must have understood, as he wrapped his own cloak up around his head. Quinn turned to leave again, but hesitated, his eyes fixed on Hirn as his jaw worked, the muscles flexing. Whatever conflict was brewing in his head, he shook it off, turning his back to them. Before Sybil could argue again, he picked up his pace, jogging out of sight.

"Don't worry. I promised *Raekin* I'd get you there in one piece," Hirn said, his voice cool and calm, but with the sharp edge of a razor tied into it.

Raekin.

That name sent ice once more through her veins as she slowly turned under the hood to face him. A twisted smile had stretched across his face, missing teeth like open wounds in his mouth. She tried to keep the shock off her face, but it only made his eye crinkle deeper, like he had won something. He nodded in the direction Quinn had run off, the words not needing to be said.

She opened her mouth, the questions sitting at the back of her throat ready to boil up and pour out. With a sharp clack of her molars, she snapped them back away. She tightened the hood around her face, obscuring her from the disturbing man still grinning at her. His eerie stare she could handle, but she couldn't let him see the way her emotions burned across her face.

He's a monster.

He's still Quinn.

She could spend another lifetime trying to tell herself that everything she was hearing was a coincidence. An unlucky collection of rumor and her own fear clouding her thoughts. Tainting them into something darker than reality. But the name, the magic, the years: they lined up too easily.

When they bend you to the brink, how far can they push before you can no longer rebound? And where is the line where you finally snap?

"It's Raekinblod, isn't it?" Sybil asked, a sharp hitch in her throat. It was impossible to tell if it was courage or fear that had drawn the words out, but something forced them into the air between her and the twisted shape of a man beside her.

"Only the Void or the people that want to slit his throat call him that," Hirn said, shifting on the wall. "Where'd you hear that?"

"Is it true that he killed a man by bleeding him dry one drop at a time?" She angled her face just enough to catch his expression past the hood. She'd expected some sort of shock, or calculated confusion in his face, but he only narrowed his eye. His mouth stayed pressed in a thin line as he worked his tongue along his teeth.

The silence built to a crescendo between them, only dulled by the distant shrill cries of the wind. This wasn't Plaitius, it wasn't Hazel Gryph. Forced politeness and quick rebuttals to debunk crass, vicious rumors were a standard above ground. This wasn't her world. She could see it in the way Hirn eyed her. She supposed that she had wanted him to spread his hands out in surrender, the 'nos' spilling out of him like a wine vinegar as he frantically tried to quell her nerves.

Instead, he tilted his head towards the tunnel. "That should be enough time. We can go now." He adjusted his hood once more, the tails of the cloak kicking up as he turned on his heel, grinding dirt into the ground.

It wasn't a blatant omission, but it spoke volumes. The silence felt like stones in her boots, weighing them down as Hirn slowly got further and further away. With a quick twist of her neck, she stepped forward, quickening her pace to fall in behind him.

Dark twisted images that her own traitorous mind came up with started to flood through her brain. A wicked smile on Quinn's—Raekin's—face. In her mind's eye, she saw it. The screaming. The begging. Masses of people clawing at the ground as he stood over them, power surging from his fingertips. Blood flowing around him in a ceaseless tide of red. The high-pitched wind seemed to permeate her ears, expanding the nightmares that she tried so hard to dispel. Its screaming echoed back at her and through the mouths of the faceless people she pictured grovelling at Quinn's feet.

Hirn's footsteps were quick and deliberate, each one striking the ground in perfect intervals, his stride so much wider than hers. She made a point to mimic the way his head hung low, the hood wrapping his face in shadows away from the touch of the torchlight.

The flickering of light started to become less and less distant. The ceiling of the tunnel opened, slowly growing upwards and branching out to encapsulate the enormity of the city. Torchlight couldn't reach the farthest stones, leaving a yawning mass above them that bore down like a starless sky. Giant pillars of blackened, shining stone reached up towards the expanse, their tips sharp like fangs.

As they grew closer, the smell she had so easily associated with cinnamon had started to twist into something acrid and rotten. The common spice still lingered, but it brought with it a sharp stinging that burned her sinuses, forcing a thin sheen of tears to her eyes. Sybil had to choke down the coughing that was trying to claw its way up her throat, choking out her breath as she fought past the smell.

Buildings made of stone and wood formed themselves out of the shapeless haze as they approached, shifting silhouettes slowly resolving into people. Torches lit up everything and their light reflected odd purples and whites off the stones, glittering in an almost peaceful way. It was oddly beautiful.

Until she saw the monsters that walked amongst the cloaked figures.

Towering creatures, their muscular forms dotted with scales on their necks, backs, and arms. They glowed iridescent hues of purple and blue. Fins of shifting colour climbed up their arms and flared behind their ears. Some wore their long hair beaded and bound against skin that ranged in shades of deep violet. Eyes like molten ember and sulfur, slitted and watchful beneath the greasy strands of black hair.

She knew what they were immediately, their sharp claws making a hard lump form in her throat.

The Void Born.

The nightmarish children's stories did nothing to prepare Sybil to be so close to the monsters themselves. She fought herself as her eyes darted from one beast to the next, unable to look away. Her tongue felt heavy and dry in her mouth, jaw agape. Horrifying in their size and brutality, but the flux of colours drew her in, encapsulating her and contrasting the fear.

As they grew closer to the seemingly structured chaos of the populace, the noises around her started to blend into a drone, every sound clashing and colliding into nothingness. Most of the people wore their cloaks like masks shrouding their faces, though their black hair cascaded out from the tattered fabric.

Some people hurried down the streets, others meandering as though they had nowhere to be, some getting so close that they brushed against her shoulder, jostling her. No apologies, no quick shouts or curses. Continuing on as though she was nothing more than the stone the city was carved from. Not even the horrifying beasts turned their attention towards them. However, their clawed hands would lash out at any unlucky human that stepped too close to their path.

Carved into the wall of the far edge of the dome was an immense door, the front of which was covered in intricate details etched into the stone. Spreading out from either side were columns formed into wicked beasts and complex humanoids, scaled and sharp-toothed scowls aimed down at the buildings below. Each one carved with a delicate, detailed hand.

Sybil hadn't realized she had stopped to gawk until a voice called out in her direction. Her head snapped to the noise, the hood slipping back. When the light touched her hair, the shout slammed into her ears again, closer this time. She dropped her head down as quickly as she could, once more absorbing the shadows, but the thundering footsteps had already started towards her.

Frozen in place, she felt the lightning starting to crackle at her fingertips as the fear knit across her chest. It was limited now, but any further and it would be vibrant beneath the light fabric of the cloak. Fractals of ice had started beneath her feet, splintering outwards in tiny capillaries.

In Plaitius, magic was always in periphery. A spark of air, a quick flare of fire. Down here, that pungent storm smell was non-existent, only the visceral odor of burning and spice. Not a single touch of magic had passed through the fingers of any of the people with their downcast faces.

So, when Sybil saw her magic sputtering out from her skin, tainting the ground with its sudden flare, the twitching, snapping of heads in her direction was a visceral feeling.

A hand wrapped around hers, the grip far too hard, nails tight into her skin. A quiet wince scraped through her throat. She was pulled at a jolt around the corner of a nearby building, Hirn guiding her, wrenching her arm forward. Periodic flares of fire light would wrap Hirn in vibrant, glowing orange as he led her further away, his silhouette flashing underneath the cloak.

Hirn veered into a narrow gap, the space between the buildings bordering on claustrophobic. Her shoulders struck the wall hard as he shoved her against it. He pressed his palms to either side of her head, his tattered linen slightly shielding them both in its shroud. His chin was only a hair's width away from the tip of her nose as he leaned in close. She tried not to notice the sharp smell of rot wafting off him, nor the vicious gouges that trailed along his neck and disappeared into his tunic.

The quickening steps behind them hit harder now, thudding through the stone like war drums. She felt each one climb her spine, vibrating up through her boots, rattling her bones. Her lungs ached with the need to inhale, but she didn't dare. The boots were close enough she could hear the scrape of their heels, the hiss of breathless murmurs. Or maybe it was the rasp of Hirn's exhale, hot and fetid against her cheek. Her fingers curled into fists at her sides, nails biting through skin, doing anything she could not to scream.

When the boots finally faded into the distance, their echoes trailing off like ghosts, she still couldn't move. Her breath returned in shallow, shaky bursts, more instinct than choice. Every muscle in her body screamed from holding still, her knees weak, her back clammy with sweat. Hirn hadn't shifted, his hands still braced on either side of her face, and she couldn't bring herself to look at him. Couldn't risk what might still be lurking in his expression.

She had expected Him to back up, let her step away. But he held steady, the only movement the oddly slow raising and lowering of his chest. For a moment, she didn't know what to do. Could only stand between his arms, her eyes darting across his tunic as she tried to listen to the unheard noise that was keeping his attention. But when she looked up, it clicked into place.

The yellows of his irises had been replaced with chalky whites, slithering lines of veins running through them and breaking up the monotonous colouring.

Neuroweaver.

Horrifying flashes of blood and carnage started to ripple through her thoughts as she stared at the unsettling whites of his eyes. That nightmare crawlspace felt ages ago, yet the smell was still there, curling in her throat. She swore she could hear a faraway voice calling to her, begging for help from the far reaches of her memories.

The seconds that ticked by started to feel like minutes, dragging along like a muddy weed through the undergrowth. Should she shake him? Strike him? Slide down the wall and slip out from the shroud of his cloak? She ran her teeth along the bottom corner of her lip, weighing her options. They were hidden, and she couldn't see or hear anybody. But she couldn't understand why he would use his magic like this while they were being actively hunted.

Yellow slid down from his upper eyelids, and after a few chaotically rhythmic blinks, his pupils focused back on her. A good shake of his head and he backed off, dropping his arms from beside her head.

"They saw you. Your stupid light hair," he groaned, wiping his face on his sleeve. He wasn't quick enough to hide the tiny bead of blood that had drifted from his nose. "Fuck."

"What do we do?" she asked, keeping her voice deceptively calm. Even her hands stopped their shaking, the crackling electricity of her magic still lingering beneath her skin but tempered back.

Whoever he was to Quinn, he was trusted enough to lead her. She hadn't wanted to believe it, seeing this horrific visage of a man before her, but it was cemented the second he grabbed her hand and pulled her away from the shouting voice. That would have been a perfect moment to slip into the darkness, leaving her to be grabbed by whatever Void Born spotted her, but he had risked himself to drag her along. Quinn trusted him. Now she did too.

She could see his jaw working back and forth under his skin, the soft grinding making her teeth ache. "Get you to Raekin. Nothing changes, except now we don't just get to hide beneath our cloaks."

"Did they see you?" she asked.

Hirn's gaze flicked towards her, sharp. "Why?" His voice cut through the dark like broken glass.

"The Void don't strike me as forgiving, especially not something like this. I'd rather not be the cause of..." she trailed off as her eyes unwillingly drifted towards the bandage across his face. He seemed almost taken aback at the comment, his brows creasing heavy lines between them. As though the concept of his own safety was such a farfetched idea, she never should have even considered it.

His eyebrows furrowed, twitching with something unreadable, and though it could have been a trick of the darkness, she swore his lip trembled. With a swift turn, he started back off towards the pathway they had come from. His gait slowed considerably as they progressed forward, the wall with the monolithic statues looming ever closer to them over the tops of the crooked and decrepit stone buildings.

At every corner he would pause, taking a quick look in either direction, occasionally stopping altogether. Though she couldn't see his eyes, she didn't doubt that he was using his magic. When he stepped forward again, she took it as a sign that their path was, for the moment at least, safe. As though he could hear the thoughts around him, not just transmit them. A skill not entirely foreign to neuroweavers, but one that was rare, and considered dangerous above ground.

Not unlike the bloodweavers.

When the colossal spires towered above them, Hirn led her down another pathway away from the large door she could only assume was the main entrance. He picked up his pace, striking into a light jog parallel to the monuments. Sybil picked up her own pace, following him towards the edge of the wall where the lights had either been snuffed out, or never lit to begin with. When Hirn stepped into the shadows he practically vanished in the darkness. Sybil stepped quickly to fall in behind before she lost sight of him.

She slammed into his back, her nose striking hard into his spine. The pain was minimal, easily removed with a quick twisting of her face. She lifted her hands to the darkness, feeling blindly for him. Not wanting to collide with him again, or anything else that might be waiting there.

He stood in front of her, her hands trailing along his chest, no longer facing away from her. She recoiled, thankful for the darkness and hoping he didn't notice. Before she could fully tear her hands back away, he gripped her wrists, wrapping tight around them until her joints ground together. She let out a small cry but caught it quickly between her teeth.

"What—" she started, her voice barely audible above the pounding in her chest.

"Shut up," Hirn said. He was closer to her, his breath on her face, his voice so low she almost leaned in to hear it. "Just shut up." There was a tremor to his voice, broken briefly by a catch in his throat.

"Where's Quinn?" she hissed out, trying and failing to pull her wrists free. Her fingertips had started to go numb. All it would take was enough power and she could unleash a torrent of... something. Just how much of her magic could she loose before it lit up the darkened corner?

"*Quinn*," he snarled at her, the mocking tone wavering with the tremors in his hands, "isn't the same person you remember."

"I'm not stupid, I know—"

"Shut up!" His hold tightened again on her wrists, the grinding reverberating through her forearms. She bit back the yelp, tasting copper. "It has taken Raekin *years* to crawl to where he is. He's been degraded and mutilated, forced to do things you couldn't even imagine. That botanomancer? That was child's play for *Quinn*." She felt his nails dig into the flesh, pain radiating down her arms.

Lightning started to crackle at her fingers, and Hirn didn't so much as flinch as the sparks licked across his skin. The flashes briefly illuminated his face. She almost wished it hadn't. Now she could see the rage that burned in his one eye, his teeth bared as his words sheared through them.

"You had him for a decade? Well, so did I." His fingers relaxed just enough to lean in. "You got the part of him that was still whole. Still human. I got the broken pieces. I helped him put them back together. You have no idea what that turned him into. If I didn't trust that every decision he ever made was for the best, I would have torn out your throat the *second* I had you alone."

"Then why didn't you?" Sybil snarled back, curling her fingers into fists to stem the sparks. She bit down on her tongue to keep the light small, the darkness the only thing shielding them from the beasts.

"Because I owe Raekin more than your pathetic life. If that changes, you won't get a warning." Sybil tried to break from his hold again, but he shoved her, making her stumble. "You need to remember something." He leaned in, voice cold. "Every time you look at him like he's still yours?"

A pause, but she didn't dare answer. His gaze burned through her under the flickering light.

"He's not. He's theirs. And when they tell him to use you or end you, he won't even blink." Sybil felt the words like needles in her ribs. "And you'll beg him to stop like he still knows what *mercy* is."

TWENTY-SEVEN

With a shove, Hirn released Sybil's wrists. Pain spiked down her arms as feeling rushed back into her fingers. She barely had time to catch her breath before his shoulder slammed into hers, knocking her off balance as he stomped past. The echo of his footsteps disappeared around the corner, but Sybil didn't move. Her pulse battered against her ribs. Her hands ached. Her throat burned with everything she hadn't said.

Then came the crack.

Stone behind her split with a sharp, grinding groan. Light bled through the fracture, and her heart froze. For one horrible second, she thought the Void had found her again. Ice lanced out from her fingers, racing like a stampede towards the light. Its crystals curled up the ragged boots that stood in the broken opening.

Quinn didn't so much as twitch as the ice wrapped around his legs, locking tight against the frayed leather of his pants. He barely moved, more irritated than injured. The ice melted quickly, her magic dying out as she took in his sweat-marked face.

"You made it," he whispered, breathing in quick, razor-thin bursts. "Somebody saw you?"

She glanced behind her. "My hair," she muttered. "We were chased."

Quinn's jaw twitched. "But you're okay." Not a question.

He reached for her. Just a hand, nothing more, but her body recoiled on instinct. The sudden cold between them hit harder than any of Hirn's threats.

Quinn hesitated, brows tightening. She grabbed his hand quickly, forcing a tight grip before he could ask anything.

She didn't trust Hirn anymore. She wasn't sure if she even trusted Quinn. But he was the only thing down here that still resembled safety.

More torches had been set in sconces along this narrow, claustrophobic cleft, their path lit up ahead until it curved out of sight. She craned her neck around him. There was no divergence on either side of the winding path. Knowing the only exit was the dead end behind her sent spikes of cold through her neck.

"We're safe?" Sybil asked. She stuttered when he shot a look over his shoulder. "I mean, the Void can't find us?"

"Nobody knows this tunnel exists except for me, Hirn and... Varena." Quinn said, the added pause only making the name stand out further. She pretended not to notice it, but it grated on her like a serrated blade against her skin. The first mention of a third mage that Quinn had trusted. It was getting increasingly difficult for her to build up the wall she had bricked around the growing mound that was his new identity. Every moment that passed seemed to add another rotting, putrid growth to the *thing* that now lived in the softer places she kept the memories of him. A thing that told her over and over that he was... *wrong*.

There had been time for her to inspect his skin, but when his gaze levelled on her, it felt perverse, like she was invading whatever shield he had borne around himself. But now, with the regularly spaced light, and his attention focused ahead, she was able to look. Really look.

The inks and scars contorted and shaped themselves into a map beneath Sybil's eyes. A detailed path of the malicious decade that Quinn had suffered through. As she traced the lines, horrific visions seared her thoughts in tandem with the tortuous path.

Her mind was screaming over images she concocted, begging them to stop. Begging her imagination to stop recreating the horrors etched on his flesh. Rips and tears, slices and gouges. The inks were an intricate work across his skin, some touched with the fading of time, others still sharp and vivid. Scripture and runic markings wrapped around his biceps before curling across his shoulders and down his spine and ribs. A flicker of torchlight caught on his shoulder, throwing the rune at the nape of his neck into sharper relief. She looked away, but it lingered behind her eyes

The scars were their opposites. Varying in depth, length and shape. Thick and gnarled or thin and sharp. Some expertly curved around the runes that marked his body, others slashing directly through them. Her free hand twitched towards his spine, almost running along the coarse ridge of a scar that crookedly followed the path. She locked the hand in a fist, dropping it back to her side. For a second, she thought of asking, but better judgement won over. She didn't want to know, not really. Just a morbid curiosity that she didn't need to satisfy. Especially not if it would only further the sympathy she felt for someone so callous.

Telltale marks of destroyed runes followed the path some of the wounds cut, the ink spreading out as though dipped in water. Others appeared to have been redrawn, the sharp edges of the scars a ghostly pink peeking through the runes. Fewer still had been slashed, the tattoo split in two by the wound, the ink not dissipating. Ornamental markings, not etched with enchantment. Though decorative didn't fit the barbaric way they were carved.

The word 'torture' abruptly stabbed through her skull.

She stole a glance down at her own arm, the cloak riding up enough that the runes peeked out from under the linen. The pain of the enchanted inks hadn't been enough to tip her over to nausea or unconsciousness, but it was excruciating compared to the magicless ones that laced up her own biceps or the ones on her legs. What he went through must have been...

A sharp shake of her head to remove the thought.

She'd always been in awe of the higher-up wardens who had runic inks spread across their backs, some even daring to get them across their torso and stomach. The skin there was thin. Tender. The acidic sting of magic made the needle feel like a knife.

That was supposed to be you.

So far removed from her old life now, and it all still felt as though she was incapable of mourning it yet. Going back would never be a possibility. Still, there lingered that tiny flare of hope in the back of her head that kept her from accepting that everything she had strived for was no more. A mental wall built up to hide her from the corpse of her warden self that rotted just out of sight.

Instead of glory and duty, she was being pulled quickly through a tight, ominous tunnel towards an unknown enchanter by a man who was supposed to be dead. A man that had apparently ripped the blood from another's skin. A man who stood at the side of the beasts that had taken him, blending in with the monsters a little too seamlessly.

Though there was no blood between their hands, his tight grip still sent shivers through her skin. What was once a lifeline now felt like a noose that grew tighter with every step. The touch of his magic had felt cold and left a heavy dread in its wake. Every twinge of her heart made her skin bristle with panic. Unable to differentiate the icy hands of fear, or the harsh agony of his power.

She'd had his hands, lips, and teeth all over her body. Craved him, begged for him. But before that, she'd felt an agony so much more excruciating than any pain she had ever felt. Now, her hand in his, she couldn't even be sure he wouldn't turn that fury on her again.

"The tunnel walls are thick enough that no sounds will make it past them. We're alone, you don't have to worry about being silent anymore," Quinn said, breaking the quiet that had settled between them, only interrupted briefly by scuffs of his boots.

"I'm not—I didn't..." Sybil chewed her lip, trying to work through just what she was trying to say.

"You've stopped asking questions."

Sybil's throat tightened. Her mind scrambled for a retort, something dismissive or sarcastic. Anything to deflect.

Nothing came.

"Either you're scared of the answers," Quinn said, still not looking at her, "or you think you already know them."

She stared at the floor between them, a sudden roaring in her ears.

His grip shifted slightly, just enough to remind her she was still tethered. "Whatever you think you've learned," he said, voice low, "won't change what I came here to do. I'm getting you out. After that..." A beat, the passing torches casting twisted shadows along his scars. "You can decide who I am."

Opposing forces worked behind her eyes. One screamed at her to let go of his hand, flee to the Bastion, drop to her knees and beg for sanctuary.

Years of service, her father's accolades and the captain's support might just be enough to protect her. The Baters may be corrupt, but the Portcullis had led the country for decades with the faith of the people. They had to see reason. Had to listen when she warned them of the impending horror that was at their doorstep, hundreds of feet below the ground.

But the other voice didn't shout. It whispered. Its voice was soft, but not sweet. Heady, but not overwhelming. It sang of the way Quinn's lips had felt against hers, his hard flesh pressed against hers as his hands explored her body. Teeth grazing across her skin, tantalizing with just enough pain to awaken the senses she had long left dormant. Each movement of his muscles while her legs clamped around his waist. It sent a heat thrumming back through her to the tune of the lapping water dancing in tandem with the expert choreography of his fingers.

A mild pulsation drew her attention back to the rune etched on her hip. The reason he now dragged her through the confining veins of the Nether city. What had been sketched on his face at the sight was so close to fear, but that lingering anger that chased it couldn't be mistaken for anything else. He didn't seem to fully believe that she was as clueless to its origin as he was. All she had to go on was the smallest tether of trust still holding on between them, though it was growing weaker by the minute.

But there was still a shroud of mystery around the rune. Whether she had to hold the hand of a monster or not, she needed to unravel it.

Round a sharp corner, Quinn stopped suddenly, and Sybil stumbled, catching herself on his back. Her hand remained a second too long, just enough to feel his back tense under her touch. She pulled it away, too quick. Though he didn't look back, she could see the way his muscles shifted, as though missing the warmth.

In front of him was a wooden board, framed by the tunnel stones. An oddity in its cleanliness amidst the dirt. Drawn across its surface was a complex rune. One she had never set eyes on before, but it was decidedly Crae Vostian. No sharp, ugly angles like the Void, only smooth shapes and slick lines. Vastly different to any she had seen Ethissa weave, and wildly more complicated.

Quinn put his hand up to the board, his fingers spread evenly across the centre of the rune. He leaned close to it, his voice dropping low. "Durhaz," he whispered.

Sybil blinked and the board was gone.

No noise, no slow dematerialization, no flash of spell work. It simply *wasn't* anymore. Vanished into the ether, the only remnant of the magic was an almost imperceptible corporeal image of the rune beneath Quinn's hand.

Just like all schools of magic, enchanting had a cost. Something like this should have created some sort of energy transfer, some sort of ripple or flash as the physical body of the board was sent to whatever pocket realm.

That didn't take into account the immense amount of skill it required to enchant something with a vocal call. It was a dead art, once exciting and tantalizing at its first discovery, but it was quick to die off as a fringe magic when it was determined how wildly impractical it was. Ethissa had gone on long-winded rants about its pointlessness and all the qualms that came with it. Inflection, dialect, accent, pitch, enunciation. The list could go on with all the things that hampered an enchanter's ability to recreate something to react to voice. Even if it had been created to match Quinn's voice exactly, there was still a chance of the sound not matching beat by beat at every attempt, which could only result in...

Sybil had images of Ethissa's former apprentice flash through her mind. His scarred skin, the burns and gouges that littered his arms. Those were the consequence of nothing more than a simple focusing rune. This would have been catastrophic in its testing era. Burns would be the more positive outcome. Quinn would be lucky to not have been transported to the ether instead of the board.

Yet the ease at which he rested his palm on the wood only made her curiosity blossom. Such calm demeanor, so quick to speak. Either he didn't understand the repercussions, or he trusted the enchanter more than she trusted even Ethissa.

Past the board hung several long dresses, most of them shaggy and bugbitten. There was a decent amount of variation between them, their fabrics ranging from silken to rough cotton or linen. The layer of dust that clung to them only serving to enhance the decrepit state.

Quinn pushed through the clothing. Sybil's eyes widened further. Where she expected his disturbance to cause the dust to burst into a cloud around him, it held steady, not moving from its firm grip on the fibres. Even as he spread the dresses apart, some pushed far enough to threaten to be torn off their hangers, they stayed unchanged.

Ethissa would be absolutely riddled with envy.

She passed through the hanging dresses like parting a veil, and emerged into what must have once been a living space, though time had all but devoured it. The room was as decrepit as the clothing. What they had passed through had been disguised as a wardrobe, though the doors had either been torn off or rotted with time. A cot had been thrown haphazardly to their right. Several blankets were crumpled on top of it, though their surfaces were covered in sheets of paper and empty ink vials. The spilled ink creating a patchwork of capillaries across the ragged surface.

The dim candlelight barely lit up the far end of the room, vanishing into darkness beyond an archway. A desk was next to the archway, books teetering precariously atop it, creating a makeshift barrier around their occupant: an old woman. She sat in a crooked chair, her spine curved, and her head rested in one of her hands while the other scribbled furiously on more parchment. Even seated she towered over the desk. The faded blue robe she wore was tied tightly around her gaunt waist, the tails of the belt shredded and worn, no doubt from scraping over the floor in her hunched position.

Her hair was long and grey, most of it tangled and dreaded. Some was pulled back into a knot, two more quills struck through to hold it in place. The feathers were skeletal, stripped nearly clean save for a stubborn tuft of barbs at the crown. The small flames of the candles danced over the creases in her face; her brows etched into a frown as her foggy eyes darted across the paper in time with her frantic scribbles.

"It is not Whynstag," she said, her accent thick and coarse. A true Frew Braxian. Her pronunciation of Whynstag prefixed with a harsh rolling 'v' sound. It was the first Sybil had heard outside the mocking voices of her fellow wardens, though their imitations had been close. Their country's paranoid neighbours were an easy target, a joke she chose not to participate in. Now hearing the woman's voice brought forth an unnecessary guilt for not voicing her displeasure louder.

"You cannot come by at any hour. I do not host a—" she paused, staring at the wall in front of her. Her hand mimicked circles in the air, as though whatever word she was searching for would appear across the rock. "—a dirty party house." She finally finished, returning her attention to her papers.

"Brothel," Quinn offered.

"Yes, a brothel," the woman clicked her tongue, seemingly pleased with the new word.

She finally looked over at them, her frown deepening the creases on her brows. She could see now that the woman's eyes were not completely glassy, the mirror-like blues almost blending into the greying whites that surrounded them. The woman's sharp nose lifted up, then down, sweeping along Sybil as she took her in.

"Ah, Raekinblod," she cooed, her thick accent rolling out the 'r'. "I see Sarcovarena has finally hit your head against the stones enough times to knock the last bit of sense out of you, yeah?"

Cold hands trailed up Sybil's back at Quinn's alternate name, but that wasn't the one that stalled her breath in her lungs. This new one curled through her veins with such a painful dredge of ice she had to bite her cheek to keep from visibly cringing. The added prefix to *Varena* only made air in the tiny room suddenly feel far too cold, her last memory of a sarcomancer still haunting her thoughts.

Blood. Blood. Blood.

Quinn's voice pulled her back out of the darkness of her memories. Away from the manically screaming neuroweaver. "This is Sybil Wyntres." He turned towards her. "Sybil, I'd like to formally introduce you to Krebivyldinia Bolorick."

"Oh, kssh with formalities. Kreb is fine."

TWENTY-EIGHT

R aekin got a perverse sense of enjoyment as he watched Sybil's face fluctuate. It was so rare he got to witness the expressions as those that knew of her history try to piece what they were hearing together. Even as Sybil's initial confusion faded to a lighthearted amusement, he couldn't strip the grin that had started to spread across his face.

Sybil finally let out a half-hearted burst of a laugh, before pressing her palm to her torso in salute. "Pleasure."

"You laugh? Is this a new custom in Plaitius?" Kreb asked, her pronunciation of Plaitius exaggerated to four syllables.

"I'm sorry, it's just..." she turned to look at Raekin, a pleading in her eyes to step in and save her.

"*The* Kreb Bolorick," he whispered, leaning into her, his chest brushing against her shoulder. She flinched slightly at the touch. It soured the smirk curling at his lips.

Sybil let out another laugh, this one more choked and forced. "Okay, but you see how that's—" she glanced between the two of them, their heads cocking as they waited for her to finish. "Kreb Bolorick died more than a century ago." Her words were tumbling out of her, blending into one another as she tried to fill the space with noise. "You'd have to be over two hundred years old."

"Well, two hundred and sixteen, but the last forty years have just—" she mimicked her hand flapping across the room. The wrinkles around her eyes crinkled, spreading a pleasant light to their hazy depths.

"You know that isn't a problem for enchanters," Raekin scoffed.

"Kreb is a man." The sharp declaration left Sybil before she could catch it, the horror crossing her face as the words tumbled from her lips. She started to sputter, makeshift apologies and incomprehensible sounds leaping off the cliff of her voice.

Kreb's eyes flicked to Raekin, the confusion replaced quickly by a visceral fury. He could only shrug, knowing this same thought had tumbled in his own skull when he met her years ago. "They erected a statue shortly after the war to honour your sacrifice. I guess I just forgot to mention." He couldn't stop the twist of his lips. "You have quite the impressive beard."

Kreb hurled the quill she had clutched in her ink-stained fingers at him, though it sailed wide, stabbing into a pile of rags. With a surprising agility from her ancient bones she snapped to her feet, her arms raised in the air as she huffed and floundered about.

"A beard!?" she cried out. "A *beard!?*" She kicked a nearby pile of scrap papers, sending them airborne before they slowly crashed back down to their piles.

"Nobody knew—" Sybil started, but Kreb let out another yell, her throat croaking with the effort.

"*Lugiesse,*" Kreb spat. "Those *selblazen* in the Portcullis knew." She kicked another pile of papers, spewing out more Frew Braxian curses, only a few of which Raekin recognized.

"Kreb—"

"Do not 'Kreb' me, whelpling," she hissed, whirling around to face them, her tattered robe kicking dust around the room. "Those *selblazen* would do anything to crush whatever matriarch tried to stand. Always *hated* the cunt between my legs. I don't know why it even surprises me that they twisted my legacy to a... a... a penis!"

"Kreb, we don't have time—"

"Twelve men, cowering in the Bastion, only to be saved by an old woman. Bah! Weakness, bred between every one of them. Nobody should be governed by pathetic beasts carrying their most fragile parts outside their bodies."

"They're split now," Sybil said. The second her voice carried across the room, Kreb focused her rage on its source. Sybil's throat bobbed as Kreb veered on her. "Both the matriarchs and patriarchs of the families head the Portcullis."

Kreb narrowed her eyes, all six feet of her suddenly creaking upright. "They have equal say, then, yes?"

Sybil opened her mouth, but with a quick downcast of her eyes, her brows narrowing, she shut it again, the clacking of her teeth ringing out in the room.

"Is what I thought," Kreb murmured, her body once more curling in on itself. She let out a heavy breath and dropped her arms to the sides. "Is not your fault, *tochdel*." Her lips twisted up briefly as she clasped her hands together. "Now, Raekinblod. You have some reason for risking all of our lives by bringing her here?"

"Show her the rune," Raekin said, resting his hand on Sybil's arm. Her head swung towards it as though some grotesque creature was there and not him. A reaction he was so sure he had pulled out of her skin one moan at a time, never to come back. Hirn's name immediately ricocheted through his thoughts, the only outlier in Sybil and his brief separation.

Kreb crossed her arms and leered at Sybil as she pulled the edge of her pants down and lifted her shirt. "A rune? That is all? You risk all this for—" But Kreb stopped. She leaned over, snatching her glass off the desk and holding it up to her eyes as she squinted at the ink. "Where did you get this?"

"We were hoping you could tell us," Raekin said.

"I was told that it was given to me by the Void. That it was what gave me my magic. The magic I traded... for Quinn's life."

Kreb's brow flicked up at the name, but she didn't respond, only nodded. Kreb could ignore the past like a passing breeze, but Raekin felt it like a knife twisting in his scars. Sybil had used to speak about the ritual like it had hollowed her out, like the grief had eaten parts of her away. Now, it was almost said with disdain. As though the memory was scrubbed clean of the horror and only resentment remained. It may have been his own deep-seated fears, but it almost sounded as though she didn't mourn the loss anymore. Like she almost wished it was true.

"It's odd," Kreb said, tearing Raekin out of his dark thoughts, though it was said more to herself than them. A habit Raekin had noticed early. He slowly learned to stop replying when her voice took on the low lull. "The voided pentagram, yes, but these other symbols. They're..." she didn't finish her thought as she stood, her feet shuffling in her ragged slippers as she disappeared through the archway.

Another normalcy for the enchanter. One minute, you couldn't get her to shut up, the next, she would keep everything tightly closed, expecting you to read her mind. It was infuriating to say the least, but Raekin had learned long ago to ignore it and just let the woman be. He could spend a lifetime trying to unravel Kreb's chaotic mind, and he would be no closer to understanding a lick of what rattled between her ears. Whatever it was, it was far beyond anything he would have been able to decipher, even if he was also granted another two centuries of life.

Sybil had wrapped her arms around herself, her cloak once more shrouding her. He'd been too exhausted to reach out with his magic, but he opted to use what little he could to thread those tendrils through her. An invasion, but he needed to know.

Magic unspooled from him, seeking her pulse. A chaotic thrum thundered beneath her ribs. He stepped into her line of sight. Her eyes met his and the rhythm jumped. He didn't move, couldn't. Not when her heartbeat hammered like that. It wasn't just fear. It was fear of *him*.

"What did Hirn say to you?" He tried to keep his tone calm and level, but the grating that rattled his throat made it seem all the more vicious. Her gaze dipped low again, resting against his chest.

"Nothing," she said, but her hands drifted together, her thumb running lines along the scar on her palm. Heat flared through him again, pain stabbing through his jaw as his teeth clenched tight.

Hirn had gotten her through Ktharheim, Raekin owed him that much. But loyalty had limits, especially within the Void's talons. Whatever words were spewed while Hirn and Sybil were alone, Raekin knew Hirn wouldn't hold back. Not if they facilitated driving the wedge harder between them.

Raekin wanted to disagree with him, wanted to twist his blood to razors and force him to understand. She wasn't a threat. Not to Hirn, not to himself, and certainly not to what they needed to do. Except, every time he was this close to her, the rest of the world quieted down around them. Those raging conflicts that always lived at his periphery became dull and muted. Everything fading except for her. The way her skin felt, the way her lips tasted. Dangerous feelings that Hirn was right to fear.

Until now, the only forgiving deviation in Raekin's darkening world was a tryst away with a woman carved from cruelty. Each forced moment between them permeated with their loathing for each other. Sybil was his bright light. A warm fire. He never should have let himself stray, never should have put his lips on hers. He'd tasted that brief elation and now, it wasn't what he had done that would haunt him. It was knowing he never would again.

Nightmares don't seem so daunting when you forget dreams exist.

He'd poured fear into the hearts of men and women alike under the rocks of the Nether Peaks, never batting an eye to their screams. He'd heard echoes of those screams in the way she begged him to stop. Felt the horror as she clutched at him as though he was her survival even though he was dragging her down. So quick to turn on her as she spouted all the things he feared of himself. He despised whatever monstrous thing had come over him. But fear had always ruled over the Etched, and now it seemed to be the only truth he had left to show her. To remind her that the things down here were far worse than she could ever imagine.

So why, now, did seeing her look so petrified by his existence suddenly feel as though it wasn't right? As if it wasn't the emotion he had been trying to drag out of her in the first place?

"What did he say?" he repeated. He went to grab hold of her shoulders, but she took a step back, her eyes narrowing on his. Defiance. A look he knew better from her than fear. Her chin lifted, the tremble she had been failing to hide beneath her teeth stilling.

"How many people have you killed for them?" Her voice was strong, only the barest crack as she spat the words out at him.

Raekin hadn't expected the words to sting. It burned him alive that she caught a glimpse of that part of him. "What did he tell you?" He dropped his voice, no longer bothering to coat his tongue with the softness he had held for her.

"That the only reason he didn't rip out my throat was because he trusts you. Yet apparently that trust only goes so far. But that isn't what I'm asking. You've killed people for the Void, right? How many?"

He stepped closer to her, expecting her to flinch back again, but she held her ground, even straightening. No matter how hard she tried to stand tall, her heart gave her away as the rapid thrumming of it sent adrenaline coursing through her.

"What did he tell you?" Raekin hissed through his teeth, trying to keep his tone level.

"You'd be surprised what people will whisper about when they think they're alone. Something about 'tearing the blood from someone's flesh'? Sound familiar, *Raekinblod?*"

The sound of his voided name, seething from her lips, slashed across his mind like razors. She'd stepped closer as she spat the venom. Her rage burned off her like a visceral thing, a fire erupting in the small space between them. It took everything in him not to look back down at her lips again, but he didn't need to. The pulse between his legs reminded him how easily that feeling could come flooding back. He clamped his teeth down on the conflicting emotions that barrelled through him, their polar ideologies tearing his mind apart.

Both of those feelings wanted to shove her against the wall. One wanted to press himself to her, grind his hips to hers, make her scream his name as though it was the only thing tethering her to this world. Yet the other wanted to wrap his hands around her throat, tear that defiance from her, silence his voided name from ever escaping her soft mouth again. Just the passing thought made him want to tear out his own heart, silencing that violence forever.

Every second that passed with her in his presence, he felt Hirn's caustic remarks at the back of his mind. Maybe her being here would be his downfall, but only if he let one of those burgeoning rivals in his head burn out the other. Hirn would be only too pleased to let the visceral, rage-filled one take over.

"Who have you become? Really?" Sybil kept her tone level, her chin raised. Spoken as though asking the simplest question in the world.

The impulses won over and his hands gripped her shoulders. She winced, but didn't falter, only held his gaze. He immediately regretted it as he sensed the seeping wound beneath his hand. The scent pulled his head back out of the foggy ichor that was his rage.

"You have no idea what I have had to do to get where I am. To fight for what I believe in."

"Are you still... you?" The soft soothing of her tenor melted him.

Only long enough for him to take his hands off her, raking them through his dark hair. "The second we have answers about your rune, we are going to the surface." Before she could argue, he held up his hand. "You can't be here, and every second that you are, you risk being taken."

"But you—"

"I found it," Kreb sang from the doorway as she strutted back towards them. She was focused on the book in her hands, not noticing as the two of them stepped back from each other. The tension still swirled heavily in the room, but was invisible to the woman.

She stepped around Raekin, completely unperturbed by his clenched hands, only getting close enough to him that he instinctively shifted out of her way. The woman rarely asked nicely for anything, using her lanky body as its own forceful request. When she looked up at Sybil, she flicked her hand in the direction of the rune, her focus once more dropping to the pages. Sybil stared blankly at her, but a sharp nod from Raekin and she understood Kreb's faint, half-hearted pantomime. She pulled back the fabric that covered the ink on her hip.

"This here, this is the voided pentagram," Kreb said, tracing the star and its wavy lines. Sybil flinched once more under her touch, but only briefly as she leaned down over Kreb's shoulder. "This symbol here? Is protection." She spun the book around so Sybil could see, turning it too quickly for Raekin to catch much beyond ink. Sybil narrowed her eyes at the book, but nodded.

"It's a protection against the void? That doesn't make sen—" Raekin started, trying to step around to look.

"Hush, I am not finished." Kreb said, casting a hateful look over her shoulder. She pulled the other book from beneath her arm, the first dropping haphazardly to her feet. "There! Under chapter twelve, *Sycophants and the Hidden.*" She spun the book around once more, rewarding Raekin with only the briefest glance of the contents of the pages.

"What is... *Verhaimm?*" Sybil asked, leaning closer to the book, her hold on her shirt faltering as it fell back into place.

"Secret," Kreb said, turning briefly to Raekin. "Well, hidden secret, but that is... repugnant? Yes?"

"Redundant," Sybil corrected, but Raekin couldn't let Kreb get distracted.

"So, they branded her as the Void's secret?" Raekin laced his arms together over his chest.

Kreb stepped back, snapping the book closed in a plume of dust. She flicked his forehead. "Of course not, *bazten*. Is the opposite. Void. Protection. Secret. If I were to make such a mark, it would be to *hide* her from the Void."

Raekin watched Sybil's face twitch and shift under the news. Cogs whirling away beneath her skin, thoughts struggling to land. She had always been more clever than he was. Always able to sort through the chaos just a bit faster. So, when her eyes widened, the realization dawning on her, Raekin was still working through just what Kreb meant.

"Somebody gave this to me to hide me. Did they think I would try the ritual again? Or..." she paused, her brows once more pinching together. Her trembling hands dropped the cloak back over her body. "Somebody once told me that they may have other ways of finding mages. Is this true?"

Kreb didn't answer the question, just darted her eyes between the two of them for a moment, clucking her tongue. Raekin knew the look. The old woman and her cryptic secrets weren't new to him. Before he could call her on it, she said, "A rune such as this doesn't come easily. Whomever gave you this, sacrificed an awful lot to ink it in your skin."

"Who could even..." Raekin started, but his eyes immediately met with Sybil's as they both widened.

"Ethissa," Sybil whispered.

"She must have been—"

"Ethissa!?" Kreb shouted, tearing their attention back to her. "She is—" Kreb stopped, clearing her throat, the volume dropping from the shriek. "She is still in Hazel Gryph?" Raekin watched Sybil chew her lip, the uncomfortable air permeating the small room. A shadow of sadness crossed Kreb before it was quickly snuffed out. Her face pursed together like the name was suddenly sour. "And she didn't stop them from making me a bearded man?!" Kreb scoffed, once more raising her hands to the sky and groaning from deep within her gut. She snatched up her books, stomping back towards her reading room. Her angry curses could be heard for a brief moment before they faded in the distance.

"All this time, I'd thought this stupid thing was a reminder of what you did for me," Sybil whispered, wrapping the cloak more tightly around her torso. "Really, it was just another one of Ethissa's protections." There was the faintest glint of a tear in the corner of her eye, but she wiped it away on her sleeve before it could tumble down. She turned back to face Raekin, her nose already turning red. "It was the last fucking piece I had of you, Quinn. The last thing that still lingered from when you were still... you. Now, what do I have left? Darkness and blood? Ink and scars?"

Raekin crossed the room in a breath, holding her face in his hands. "Then forget about me, like I asked. Go back to when I was dead. Do whatever you need to, but please, don't grieve me again."

For a moment, she only stared at him, stiff and unyielding. She met his eyes, that crass attitude he loved in her flickering across her face as she pressed her lips to a thin line. He could beg her as much as he wanted, but it would be impossible for her to pretend he was dead. Just like it was impossible for him to pretend he didn't want to lock her away in his hidden cavern to keep her close. Just to hold on to the thing he hadn't realized he'd been so starved for. As long as he loved her, he wouldn't forget her. And he never stopped loving her.

"It killed me to grieve you ten years ago. Do you really think I *want* to go through that again?" A shimmer settled over her eyes for a moment before she let out a soft laugh. "I thought for a stupidly long time that it would be better if we had never met. Then, when you were suddenly *there* again, I... I didn't want to think it, but I even wished you'd stayed dead." Raekin felt a heavy weight fall on his heart, the confession a crushing reality, but she continued. "Then I remember just how incredible it was to have your arms around me again when I thought I was the one that was dying, and that all goes away."

His whole body screamed to stay away. To spare her. To spare himself. But the taste of her, even if it was poisoned now, was something he couldn't refuse. He dropped his head, and the kiss broke like a crashing wave. She didn't flinch, didn't hesitate. She should have pulled away. Should have spat every broken thing between them back in his face. But for now, maybe she was pretending he was Quinn again, one last time. If just for her own sake. He took the invitation as it was, wrapping his arms around her, pulling her into him as though he could make them one.

He would hold on to this for as long as he lived, the feeling of her lips on his, the soft smell of the water of the cavern still clinging to her hair. He wished so strongly to go back to there. To wrap her back up in his arms, to not stop as he buried the darkest parts away. If he spent another millennium in the Alpstraum, this would be the one thing that would hold his mind together as the Void hammered it into pieces.

I never should have brought you here.

His magic laced through her chest once more, wrapping around her heart as he fed off the quickening beat of it. As he deepened the kiss, he revelled in the speed, the hammering as her excitement rose.

But then, he reached out just a bit further and he felt another start to drum through his head. He tried to grasp on to it, but he was still weak, his hold like half asleep fingers brushing across the faint thrum. He broke away from Sybil, whirling around.

The faintest glimpse of black hair vanished through the doorway.

"Varena," he choked.

The scattered books across the room almost tripped him as tore himself from Sybil and charged towards the door. The warmth of Sybil's lips still lingered on his, a stark contrast to the icy claws of panic that tore through his chest. Varena had seen them. That image in her head was now the most dangerous thing within Ktharheim.

Kreb's quarters were hidden in a labyrinth of twisted tunnels in the Uldspire. Designed to keep errant Etched away, but the myriad of paths now crippled his chase.

His power was waning with every step, her heartbeat only brief flickers in the distance, far enough to be out of the bounds of his magic. In desperation, he glanced up at the ceiling. He could pull the walls down around them, trap her within the maze. A frantic burst like that could tear the entire wing down, burying all of them. Varena would be stopped, but so would he. Catching her was his only option.

The dirt scraped beneath his heels as he gained on her, the sharp pains in his legs doing little to slow him. He skidded around corners, the walls raking his flesh as he propelled off them. The punishment for the damaged skin barely flickered in his mind.

Alarms drilled their way through his head as he ran. She'd go to Naz'tak first. Spill everything before he could stop her. Anything to get herself firmly seated in his favor. Whisper poison is his ear about the Un-Etched mage that had touched his property.

Would he order Raekin to bleed her dry? Hirn to burn her mind up inside her skull? Or worse, would he take her, throw her into the Alpstraum, and make her another pet?

Varena's dark hair flashed into view as he gained ground. She was running hard, her pulse frantic and faltering with the outburst. But still too far ahead to grab. They were closing in on the main hall, the last stretch before it would be too late. He ignored the screaming in his lungs, the burning in his legs as he pushed harder, faster.

With a final burst that made his muscles scream, he leapt forward, his magic wrapping tightly to her blood and yanking her backwards. She slammed hard against the rock wall, her breath strangled in her throat.

"Rae—" She started, but he was on her, his hold on her blood so limited and weak, she still struggled under his grip.

"Why the fuck are you down here?" he snarled at her, hauling her upright. He tried so hard not to let the exhaustion show, but his breath was ragged and forced, burning his throat with every breath.

The fear that lit up Varena's eyes sent electricity through his body. He had won. He would always win. He shifted his magic upwards, grabbing hold of her lungs and squeezing, her air ceasing before it could crest her lips. Varena coughed and choked.

But, he hesitated.

That sound. That fucking sound.

So horrifyingly similar to *hers.* Her begging through sputtered breaths in the Arcaneum. That pleading gaze.

His hold fell, his hands shaking as he let go of Varena's shoulders.

Then the fear changed, shimmering and flickering across Varena's face before she narrowed her eyes at him. It wasn't until he felt the searing pain in his wrist that he realized her fingers were wrapped tightly around the skin, the sizzling sounds visceral. He roared, stumbling backwards and wrenching his arm out of her grip. The flesh melted, the muscles beneath twisting under the ruined skin.

He stared at the damage for a beat too long. The pain momentarily fogging his mind away from its source. The hesitation vanished and he lunged back towards Varena.

Or where she should have been.

She'd gotten to her feet in seconds, already disappearing around a nearby corner. Only a few turns until...

He tore through the tunnels anyways, the voice in the back of his head already telling him it was a waste. When he stumbled through into the main hallway, her dark hair disappearing further towards their master's wing, he knew.

He was too late.

Ten years. Ten years he had succumbed to the nightmares that had been harbored underground. Not once had he hesitated.

And now, that brief lapse would cost him everything.

TWENTY-NINE

Varena.

Nothing else before Quinn suddenly tore himself away from Sybil. Just that name. She didn't want to believe there was any connection between the name and how softly his lips were pressed to hers, but the sharp ache in her chest said otherwise. The stricken terror that had been plastered on his face was contagious, mutating in her skull. The warmth of his body was quickly cooling on her skin. She instinctively brought her fingers back down to her hip, though she quickly reminded herself otherwise.

It's not for him. Not anymore.

Instead, they laced together in front of her, her thumb absently stroking against her palm. He would be back. He had to be. That couldn't be his goodbye to her. Not this time.

He hadn't denied the poison that Hirn and the other mages had spewed. Only promised some altruistic reasoning and then immediately deflected. She'd hold on to that and remind herself every time she missed the taste of his lips, or the rough touch of his hands. It wouldn't change the way she felt, but maybe, just maybe, she could use it to remind her not to fall into that spiral.

Kreb stepped back into the room, a book spread open on her palm, another two tucked precariously under her arm. Their spines were torn and the covers sagged heavily against the pages, the glue stretched and crusted. She stopped almost mechanically, as though the room was depicted in the pages. A sudden shock parting her lips.

"Raekinblod?" She looked around, like he was somehow hiding beneath the piles of papers.

"He said 'Varena' and ran out." Sybil shifted to lean back against the wall, trying to feign a calm she didn't feel. Kreb only scrunched up her face. With a pop and a crack, Kreb sat down in the desk chair. A harsh exhale groaned from her chest as the wood struck her rear.

"Pity. Duty calls, I suppose," Kreb muttered, once more burying her face into the book.

"What duty? Who is Varena?" Her voice broke, betraying the casual tone.

"Sarcovarena?" Sybil shuddered again as Kreb spoke the name. "Raekinblod's assigned mate."

A heavy weight settled in Sybil's gut. Mate sounded so clinical, so forced. Yet it brought on a disgust that churned deep in her torso. "His what?"

"Assigned mate," Kreb said. She glanced over her shoulder at Sybil. Whatever she saw there made her click her tongue, rotating in her seat. "Their master has bonded them together to make a child. A mix of their powers. No rituals, no magic, just... breeding. Leaves out the messy *lugiesse.*" She paused, correcting herself. "Cow poop."

The sharp pangs beneath Sybil's ribs shifted, digging deeper into the tender tissue. He'd made the crass comment about there being others, and a decade is a long time. This shouldn't have exactly been shocking.

And there were a plethora of more important things at hand. That didn't stop the aching in her jaw as her teeth ground together.

Assigned to breed.

Like dogs. Cattle. Not lovers, not even people. Just bloodlines and magic, twisted together by force. If that's all it was, why did Sybil feel that nauseous anger boiling in her gut?

"It's just a—" Sybil cleared the hard lump from her throat, "transactional thing?"

Kreb let out a heavy sigh as she snapped the book shut, the spine straining from the sudden movement. She dropped it heavily on the desk, the noise shuddering around the tiny room. She turned to let a sardonic grin stretch across her face. "I am a wealth of knowledge, dear *tochdel*. But you need to tell me what information you want first. The rune or whom Raekinblod beds? *Twaheind, ab ain mod toil.*"

"Two hands, but one mind works," Sybil whispered, a sharp vice tightening around her chest. A Frew Braxian phrase, taught to her from the lips of a woman born across the seas and far from that country. Sybil twisted the threads together. Frew Braxian phrase, from a Frew Braxian woman. Her throat squeezed as the memory of Ethissa's bitter smile flooded her. The one she wore whenever she chastised the small girl that asked too many questions.

Kreb beamed. "You speak Brax?"

Sybil frowned, taking a beat to understand the slang, the shortened form not heard this side of the border. "Just something I heard growing up." She could explain, but she worried if she spoke further, whatever pent-up memories she had been cramming back into her spine would finally spew out.

"Tell me about the Void." Sybil changed the subject, seeing the sadness start to etch on the woman. No use digging up her ghosts today too. Sybil's were already crowding them enough. "They take powerful mages, right?"

"The Void may not breach the surface, but if one calls to them, they are theirs for the taking."

"So then why would Ethissa need to protect me from them? Did she think I was going to be a target, or that I'd reach out? Are you sure that was what this means? What if it's something else? What if it wasn't even Ethissa—"

"Slow, *tochdel*. Asking panic questions is not going to get them answered." Kreb let out another heavy breath. "I am certain this is what your rune means, whether or not you like it. I do not know why she gave you this, or if it even was her. The only certainty I can give is the meaning of the rune. You would have to ask her the rest yourself."

"But I can't—" Quinn burst back into the room, his skin pale and coated with a sheen of sweat. The arm that rested against the frame of the arch had small rivulets of blood flowing down it, pooling at his elbow. His wrist was mangled, red and swollen, the skin looking as though it had liquefied.

"And did you catch our Miss Sarco?" Kreb cooed, swivelling slightly in her chair. Her eyes rested on the wound, and her lips went tight. "This is not good then."

"We have to leave. Now." He stepped forward, reaching out to Sybil. A revulsion rose in her throat as she got a clearer look of the damage on his arm. She'd seen something similar to this, an accident at Maex's shop. A chemical they used to clean the forges had gotten on one of the smith's legs, effectively melting through his pants and down to his bone. Damage that wasn't completely foreign in the darker sides of flesh magic.

Before she could ask, Quinn gripped her arm and pulled her back towards the closet.

"This is very bad, yes?" Kreb called after him, standing from her desk.

"I need to get Sybil out of here as soon as possible. You know what to do if I can't," Quinn shouted back at her before they disappeared into the closet. He pressed his hand to the corporeal rune still hanging in the air and called back the board from whatever plane it had disappeared to.

"What is she supposed to do if you can't get me out?" Sybil asked, stumbling to keep up to Quinn's quick, long gait.

"Hopefully, save all three of us," he muttered back. She watched the beads of sweat travel through the shaved nape of his neck, tracing lines along his spine. Whether fear or pain, he was hiding it well, but not well enough that his body refused to give away his tells.

When they reached the end of the narrow tunnel, he pressed his hands to the rock and closed his eyes. Sybil felt the rumbling around them, a sharp cracking from within the stone under his touch.

But the rock didn't move. She could see the strain on his face, the muscles in his hand flexing, tendons taut to the flesh. It still only shuddered under his skin.

Sybil didn't hesitate, just brought her own hands next to his, throwing her power into it. The rock rumbled louder, fracturing and flaking off, showering them both in dust. She closed her eyes and willed the rock to move. To split, to shatter, to crumble away, anything to get it out of their way. An ear-bursting crack sounded beneath her feet. She opened her eyes in time to see rock crashing down around them as the ground split open underneath her boots.

A wind whipped up from her magic, swirling more dust around them, choking and blinding the small passageway. Through the mayhem, she felt Quinn's arm on hers, pulling it away from the wall with a bruising force.

The wall had cracked and splintered but stayed in place.

"Fuck!" Quinn yelled, slamming his hand against the stone once more, another low rumble ricocheting from where his fist struck.

"Let me try again, I can—" Sybil started. Her heart was hammering, a frantic energy vibrating her body as the chaos she had torn loose cleared under the dust. More cracks ran their way up the walls around them, stones coming loose and clattering at their feet. Her fingers still danced with sparks, but they ebbed, their light barely noticeable.

"No," Quinn said, not taking his hold off her aching wrist. "You'll take the tunnel down, you're too unstable." His voice was monotone, steady, nothing like the violent curse he had flung towards the stone. That didn't stop the words from stinging like acid as they threaded through her ears. Her face started to burn, her jaw aching with the pressure. She wanted to snap at him, or shove him away and try again anyways. But there was another cracking sound above them as the stone shifted dangerously.

He was right. She may have grasped the rock and been able to use her magic, but that didn't mean she would be able to direct it. Not like he could.

"What do we do?" Sybil asked through clenched teeth. "How long until you get your strength back?"

"There isn't enough time. We have to..." He glanced back behind them, another slew of curses slipping past his lips. "We have to go back. I think... I think I can get you out of here. If we get really lucky."

She didn't have time to get any more clarity, he'd already started staggering back. She picked up her pace, not letting him disappear too far out of sight.

When they reached the wooden board, Quinn barely got the word out before it shifted and stuttered out of existence, the closet reappearing beyond it.

"Where's Kreb?" she asked, glancing around the now empty room.

"Hopefully working on a miracle." Quinn reached over her head and drew the hood of her cloak up tightly around her face. "Stay right behind me and keep your head down."

"What if we—"

He pressed his lips to hers, holding himself there, breathing her in. "We won't. We can't." He turned away from her, heading out the door he had chased Varena through.

He walked with his head held high, his arms loose, footsteps assured, striking one after another. That didn't stop the tension she could see on his shoulders, both of them held tight to his neck, the slightest tremble to them. Sybil tried not to let her fear get to her, tried not to think about what would happen if they were caught. Tried desperately not to level her gaze on the violent, massacred state of the back of his neck. But her eyes kept landing on the harsh, malicious lines.

Ripped open. Carved apart.

She dropped her gaze to her feet, watching each step with a newfound purpose. Focus on what she can do now, one at a time. One thing left that she can control.

The hall was long. Too long. She wanted to talk, to fill the silence with questions, but every errant sound that seemed to permeate their advance made her heart race and her mouth go dry.

The tunnel opened into a large hall, the noise billowing around her the second they entered. Voices upon voices, a smattering of footsteps and scuffs. Even with her head down, she could see an influx of beings walking past the tunnel, only some of them human. Scales shone out from under ripped pants and torn boots, their iridescent blues and purples drawing her eyes every which way as they passed. Her breath started to come out in heavy gasps, but she held steady, focusing on Quinn and keeping her steps as close to his as possible.

She slammed into Quinn's back when the noises around her became overwhelming, not hearing the regular crunch of his boots halting. She wanted to look up, to see what had stopped him, but her head screamed at her to keep her curiosity to a minimum. She dared a quick glance upward, tracing along Quinn's thigh to his hand.

Her lungs cinched tight.

His hand was shaking, the tremors visible and rattling through him, the colour draining from it. She reached her hand out to grab it, squeeze it or something to still it, but before she could, he dropped to his knees.

She rushed to kneel in front of him. His face was pale, etched with pain, his jaw muscles tight under his flesh. His eyes were wild, wide and open. Terrified.

"I should have killed her. Fuck, why didn't I...?" he whispered. Her back seized with another wave of panic and dread, locking her spine.

"Raekinblod," Like bones on stone, a crooked, ragged voice growled behind them. "What are you dragging through my halls?"

THIRTY

"This wasn't supposed to happen," Quinn gasped out, still on his knees at Sybil's feet. "I love you. I'm—I'm sorry."

Whatever had forced him to his knees faded, the tension in his body tempering as he dropped forward. It lasted only a second and he was on his feet. He grabbed the sides of her hood, tearing it off her head. She opened her mouth to question it, but her jaw snapped shut with a crack as his fingers raked through her hair. He tightened his hand into a fist and yanked her backwards. She cried out, grasping at his hold, desperate to dig her fingers into his flesh, but he ignored every rip, only balling his fist up tighter and pulling her along beside him.

"What are you doing? Let go!" she shouted, but he only pulled harder. Her frantic clawing had dwindled now to holding tight to his wrist. Static flared to her fingers, quickly replaced by ice, then thawing and dripping down her arm. She could feel her lips cracking as her magic sucked the water out of her body. Her control on it was fluctuating and failing as she tried to focus on one power, all of them fighting for a spot at the front.

She had to breathe, had to take it as slowly as she could. She was no use if she was just flinging a collection of magic wildly into the air. If she was going to fight back, she needed to concentrate on one.

The static. She could bring it up hard enough to send the electricity through his arm, stun him long enough to slack his grip on her. The energy spread through her fingertips, that familiar burning dust smell circling around her as she let the sparks build in her fingers.

The crackling started to become audible, just a bare crinkle over the scraping and dragging of her boots on the ground as she fought to stay upright under his pull.

Just as she got a solid grasp on the magic, her hand went cold.

Pins and needles spread through her skin from the tips of her fingers to her wrist. It nullified the magic she had conjured, breaking it apart to nothing. Like her hand had been cut off. Her grip on Quinn's wrist failed, her arm dropping to her side. To her horror, the skin of her hand was turning a bluish grey, as though an invisible rope was tied tightly around her wrist. She shook the limb hard, willing the feeling back to it.

Blood magic.

"Well? What do you have?" That grating voice again. Quinn finally stopped, Sybil stumbling behind him, her face still wrenched down by his hip, but the grip lessened just enough to look up and narrow in on the voice.

Six Void Born stood across from them, though one of them stood at the head. His scales were a pearlescent purple that burgeoned on blues as they dipped around the fire light. Large obsidian plates were strung along his shoulders, some trailing down his broad chest. An odd thought crossed Sybil's mind as she stared at the rare stone. How easy it would be for her to shatter the ridiculous armor.

Then her eyes slid up to his face. The sneer that stretched across his wide, fanged mouth made Sybil's skin crawl as he studied her curled body.

"Whatever Varena told you, she's lying." Quinn snarled, drawing Sybil's attention momentarily from the monsters in front of her.

The Void at the head of the group didn't look at Quinn at first. He just stared down at Sybil, letting the words hang like smoke. Then, slowly, he turned his head. "I haven't spoken to Varena."

The silence that followed hit like a blow.

Quinn didn't move. Didn't drop his hand from Sybil's hair. His body frozen beside her. But Sybil could feel it: a tightening. Not of his grip, but of something deeper. Something colder.

The beast's head tilted just slightly, reptilian curiosity rippling through his brow. "Interesting that you'd bring her up." He took a single step forward, the obsidian plates clacking against his chest. "Have you done something I should know about?" He cocked his head, every second dragging on for an eternity.

"No," Quinn said flatly.

The Void let the silence stretch, then chuckled and waved a clawed hand through the air like clearing dust. "Good. Focus, then, Raekinblod. What is this thing that you dirty my halls with?" He tapped his claws along the stone, the sharp click absurdly loud in the large hall. "And do keep in mind, there have been an excessive number of rumors about an unmarked woman flitting about."

Quinn trembled for a moment, then stiffened, his hold tightening. He grabbed hold of Sybil's shoulder, tearing at her hair as he tossed her forward. Sybil barely caught herself, skidding on her hands and sending dirt and debris up. The coarse floor raked through her palms. She tried to stand, but a boot was pressed into her ribs, shoving her back over into the dirt. "Warden scum from Hazel Gryph. A gift, Naz'Tak."

Sybil spat out dirt, her chin raw from where it collided into the ground. She ignored the pain, calling on her magic, ready to flare it out. The moment it kissed the tips of her fingers, her hands quickly went cold again, the feeling being sucked right back out into the Nether. She cranked her neck, the muscles screaming as she twisted to look at the monster contorting her blood.

Quinn stood over her, his arms crossed over his chest, his boot resting on her side. She could see the strain in his hands as he used whatever little magic he had left in him to dampen her own. He wasn't looking at her, though, he was staring across the now cleared space in the large hall. Humans and Void alike surrounded them, stopping in their tracks. Their eyes darted excitedly between her and him, then to the Void that held his attention.

"Now, why would you bring me this?" the Void, Naz'tak, said. His hairless, spiked brow raised.

"Quinn—" Sybil started, but the sharp point of his heel cut her off with a jagged wince. She looked up, just in time to see Quinn's face pale.

Naz'tak started towards her, his heavy metal-lined boots kicking up plumes of dust as he walked. The plethora of onlookers started to whisper further, their voices rising to a crescendo of inane words that all ran together. He stopped in front to her, his hands laced behind his back. Sybil was sure she was imagining it, but she could almost feel a shaking that rattled through Quinn's leg and into her spine.

The hot stink of the Void's breath burned her sinuses as he squatted to her level. He sniffed the air around her, his wide nostrils flaring into black holes. "Quinn?" he sneered, the slightest laugh drifting past his fangs. "You didn't say this one was yours, Raekinblod." The obsidian clacked against itself as he moved, tiny shards raining down over Sybil's skin.

"Because she isn't. Not anymore." Quinn shoved his foot into her harder, another cry escaping her lips.

"So, you taint my halls with her reek for...sentimental value?" Naz'tak chuckled.

"I gave everything for her. My name, my body, my freedom. She gave me nothing. She was a *leertek* when I left her and that's all she will ever be."

Sybil fought the urge to twist around again, to question what he was saying. The slitted orange eyes of the beast too frightening to turn away from. Her fingers twitched, the feeling returning to them. If she could capture the flames of the torches, maybe she could engulf the monster in them. Grow them beyond the confines of the hall and shroud the entire congregation in fire. Push through the pain. Burning alive seemed easier than whatever nightmare Quinn had been through.

But he wouldn't let her. The second that acidic burn coursed through her veins, it was immediately followed by the icy touch of Quinn's magic. If only she could scream at him. Tell him to trust her.

"She let me die." Quinn's tone dropped, his voice low, grating. He spat, as though the words were bitter. "Whatever prize you gave her in exchange wasn't worth that."

"Exchange? What exchange?" Naz'tak asked, slowly stepping around them, keeping his eyes levelled on Sybil.

"My life in servitude for magical gifts that she must have foolishly wasted on something else."

"But—" Sybil tried again, Quinn silencing her once more with sharp pain. She thought it had been a ploy. But he was handing her to them. He wasn't letting her run, wasn't letting her unleash the chaos of her powers. Uncontrolled as it was, that was what they needed right now.

Just let me fight.

Naz'tak burst into laughter, the voice shaking the walls around them as he stretched his mouth wide. "Raekinblod, *you* are the fool, I thought you were better than this. There was no bargain." Sybil followed the scaled beast as it stalked around her, its wicked sneer carved into his face. "You think we act as magic dealers? Why would we claim magic only to gift it right back?"

The weight of Quinn's leg felt miniscule compared to the dread that was settling over her at the monster's words.

That's impossible.

"You summoned us. You gave yourself freely, a fool spilling his blood to the Void." Naz'Tak clicked his tongue. "If you thought we'd reward *her* for your sacrifice, you're more idiotic than I had hopes for." His gaze slid lazily over Sybil. "But there's always time to collect a debt."

Lying. He's lying. Lying, lying, lying.

She screamed it in her head over and over again, but the words wouldn't sink in beyond the surface. Said so matter-of-factly, so quickly and calmly. Like it wasn't a thought brought to his lips from crafted ideas but something tangible that was always there. She was a vollmagus now. It came from somewhere, and it certainly didn't come from the rune that burned into her hip.

Which meant...

I always was...

Quinn died for...

Sybil's head whipped backwards to stare at Quinn. His face fluctuated, twisting and contorting as his brain fought with what he was hearing. She could see the storm brewing behind his eyes, confusion and horror taking turns assuming control of his expression. But when his head turned to Sybil, only rage remained.

"All this time... I thought I had done something noble. Something selfless. And it was for *nothing!?*" He roared, tearing his boot off her side. She rolled away, only barely missing as he slammed his heel into the dirt. "The torture I suffered, the things I had to do? Meaningless?"

"Quinn—" Sybil started, but a rock came loose from the wall, sailing towards her, whistling past her ears. He went to strike out again but froze in place. Agony twisted on his face as his muscles locked tight, that same petrifying look from before.

"Not meaningless," Naz'tak said, crossing his arms as he watched Quinn struggle under the pain. "You've been a loyal, hardworking pet these last years and I am grateful for your patronage." Whatever hold the Void had on Quinn released and he hunched in on himself, his breath coming in ragged gasps. He levelled his eyes on Sybil, the fury emanating like a living, breathing thing.

"However, now you are wasting *my time*. Kill her, and be done with it." Naz'tak flapped his hand back towards them. The murmuring within the onlookers started to grow again, filling the large hall with venom. The Void leader only narrowed his eyes, fangs flashing in the dim light.

"With pleasure," Quinn seethed, his hands already curled in claws as the ground beneath him cracked and crumbled. He'd barely been able to move the wall of the tunnel, yet now the earth rumbled without a touch. Had he really been so exhausted? Or was that just another ploy to get her into the open?

She didn't have time to question it. A crack rushed through the ground towards her, splitting and fracturing the stone. With a quick push of her arms, she was up, leaping out of the way of the fissure tearing towards her. She brought her hands up, pulling at the water still left in her body and readying it to freeze into something sharp she could throw. Just as the water filled her palms, her arms dropped numbly to her sides.

In a breath, he was in front of her, the back of his hand already raised and ready to strike. The feeling rushed back to her arms. She caught the strike with her forearm, the momentum sending sharp vibrations through her bone and up through her elbow. The muscles in her jaw ached as she bit down, minimizing the rattling pain. She took the momentum of the block, twisting slightly to drive her knee into his gut, the breath leaving his lungs in a burst.

She raised her hands again, letting the air whirl around her and trying to focus it into a heavy wave towards him. He wasn't quick enough to freeze her blood in her veins and stop her. But he was quick enough to grab hold of a tiny capillary of it, tearing it through her skin. She cried out as she clutched the wound, her shirt slowly darkening with red. Barely enough to stop her, only the barest pain felt, but that was child's play compared to what she had witnessed already.

Was he toying with her?

There was a beat, one that seemed to be frozen in place between them as she glanced up from her wound and met his gaze. That unbridled rage peeling back the sneer on his lips. Behind that, though, she could see the strain. His skin was losing its pallor, his lips pale and cracked. Even under the faint firelight she could see the fresh beads of sweat on his forehead. He had clenched his hands tight, but the faintest tremor could be seen.

That was it. That strike. That show of force. It was all he had left. The last of his magic's strength now flowing down her arm. This wasn't a game. He was weakened. He might not be letting her use magic, but she'd been without it for years. The two of them had even been here before, facing one another with their fists raised. This wouldn't be the first time she would have to put him on his ass. Though Maiten wasn't there now, coaching them through, shouting his encouragement. And they'd never ended it with bloodshed.

Sybil feigned running to the right, only to duck and slide on the slippery dirt of the hall, coming up on him just as he swung out for her. Rock dug into her thigh as she twisted around, ready to throw her boot into the side of his knee, hobbling him as best she could. A sharp pain sliced through her cheek, then another through her shoulder, another just above her collarbones. The pain distracted her, her boot missing the centre of his leg.

Poised on the tips of his fingers were small red shards, each of them barely bigger than a moth. Solidified liquid, they almost looked like ice. She watched in horror as he pulled one of the shards from the fabric of her shirt, her own blood molding to a razor point.

The shard flung out, narrowly missing her face again as she ducked out of its way. The Void Born that had surrounded them flinched at the projectiles, the circle they had formed growing bigger as their fight escalated.

Another flurry of shards and stones rocketed towards her. She leapt out of the way, her ankle rolling uncomfortably as she stumbled. The pain flashed white hot through her skull, blinding her momentarily. She couldn't put weight on it, sharp lightning bursting up her leg with every step. The creatures surrounding her started to call out menacing taunts. Muted and empty by the time they reached her ears.

"Raekinblood, you are testing my patience," Naz'tak called from somewhere among the now spinning, morphing and merging flux of bodies. She could barely focus on the inked man before her, let alone the ones that all twitched and shuddered in the mass behind him. "Be done with this." His vague, towering shape warbling at the top of the circle, arms crossing as he watched them.

Quinn slowly nodded, raising his hands towards her. Sybil raised her own, though the movements were slow and lagging. Just the weight of them made her muscles shake. Eating scraps, sleeping on the ground: they'd softened her. She'd become soft long before that though, all the hard edges slowly chipped away by the cozy life in the Bastion. She chased after people, used her magic to defend the city, but this was different. This was... *animalistic.*

A sharp pain flared through her chest, the last strength holding her upright fleeing from her. She crumpled to her knees. The pain radiated outwards, stabbing shocks through her skin. *Under* her skin. A heavy weight followed, shoving her backwards to land hard on the stone, her head barely missing striking it. Everything spun and started to dip in and out of the fog. She could hear the screaming and yelling, the tormenting, callous remarks from all around, but they bled into her ears like a muddy river.

Someone straddled her, their heavy weight over her hips, pinning her torso to the ground. A few quick blinks and the haze cleared, details refocusing. Bright orange eyes peered down at her, wild and ferocious.

"Quinn..." she sputtered though she could barely hear her own voice over the drumming in her head. He didn't speak, just pressed his lips into a thin line. His hands hovered over her chest, the tendons casting sharp shadows. "Please..."

And you'll beg him to stop like he still knows what mercy is.

For a split second, his hands hesitated above her chest, a slight tremor up his arms. He didn't move, but didn't soften. Only met her with that pause, the fury still burning on his face. It lasted long enough for her to catch one last breath.

Then the pain burned through her again.

She uselessly clawed at his arms, weak and pathetic. Though her nails dug into his flesh, he didn't falter. The agony in her chest intensified, the pinpricks morphing to razors under her flesh. She tried to scream but she could barely breathe. She struggled harder, but it only made the pain in her chest flare to life. With a twist of his wrist, three red pins burst through the fabric of her shirt, hovering in the air for a moment, before they collapsed in on themselves. They splashed into red, starburst drops on the backs of his hands and across her torso.

The pain lanced again, the realization tearing through her as her own blood was ripped from her chest.

Bled dry one drop at a time.

She was finally able to scream, her voice tearing loose from her throat as Quinn crafted another set of needles beneath her skin.

Everything was flashing before her. Every mistake she ever made, one after another. She should have listened to her father and left the book alone. She shouldn't have gone to Trelusk in the first place. She shouldn't have left her celebration. She shouldn't have gone to that sarcomancer's house. She shouldn't have disobeyed the rules. She shouldn't have let Quinn read that fucking book.

She never should have talked to him that day outside the barracks.

The phantom memory of the Trelusk tower bells started to sound in the distance. The dank cave dampening their high-pitched ring, making it heady and dull. But it was there, ringing in the back of her head like a taunt.

The past hit her, and it was as though he was standing in front of her. Eight years old. That stupid smile on his face as he stacked his rocks. She should have turned away. Should have gone to her father, never talking to the orphaned ward. Stayed a *leertek*. Stayed useless.

"Quinn, stop," she whispered once more, her voice barely audible in her own ears over the ringing of the tower bells. The bells rung for another beat, the world seeming to stop and shudder, holding its breath in time with hers.

Then, the softest whisper. "I never stopped."

She wasn't sure she had heard it, wasn't sure if it was just another panicked hallucination. Too placid to come from the enraged sneer that bore down on her.

Then the pain ebbed. Disappearing back into her chest, fading to a muted roar. She blinked the tears that had welled up heavily behind her lids, clearing the watered view. Quinn was still on top of her. No longer the face of that eight-year-old boy, but the inked, scarred face of the monster he grew into.

But it had softened, the harsh edges of rage smoothed out.

With the pain no longer dragging every synapse to the surface and rubbing her face in sharp stones, things became clearer. The Trelusk bells were out of tune, yet they were there. Vivid and loud, echoing off the stone walls. These weren't the same bells. This was an alarm. A rattling that she now saw was causing their audience to dart their heads around in panic.

Quinn leaned down, his nose almost touching hers, the softest smile spreading to his lips. "You need to hate me for the both of us. If you forgive me, all of this will be for nothing."

His eyes rolled into the back of his head, his body going limp before he was tossed backwards off her, his head striking the stone behind him. The Void jumped out of the way, the rest of them frantically looking around as they searched for the source of the bells. Naz'tak wasn't swayed as he took several hurried steps towards her, his thin mouth pressed tight.

A cloaked figure darted out from between the Void, a flash of light as it tossed something. Smoke and sparks erupted around Naz'Tak at the sound of shattered glass. He stopped in his tracks, his arm going up to protect him from the sudden onslaught. He vanished into the smoke, disappearing as it flooded through the hall. The rest of the onlookers were too focused on the sudden flash to notice as the figure ran over to Sybil, peeling back the cloak from her head. Her white, knotted hair falling limply around her aged face.

"We are getting out of here," Kreb said, rolling the sleeves of her cloak up.

"Quinn—" Sybil started.

"Will be just fine. But we won't if you don't grab hold of my hand." Sybil had barely noticed the spot-flecked hand held out to her, the back of it scribbled in runes. She didn't think as she reached forward and took it. Kreb pulled another flask out from the robe, this one inky and dark, flecks of muddy green catching the light as it swirled in the glass. "Hold on tight, *tochdel.*"

Kreb slammed the glass against the rock below them, its contents spilling out around their feet. The liquid defied logic and started to spread out faster than it should have, like tiny fingers were dragging it along the ground. It separated and spread, split and reformed as it travelled around them, forming into a circle on the rock. Runes formed in the stone, the black liquid bending itself into shape.

Everything started to shake around them. It seemed to be centred to the circle. The rest of the Void that were still scrambling didn't seem to notice the world shifting and rumbling. Her sight focused for a moment in the smoke. A single figure was still visible amidst the encroaching darkness.

A line of blood traced down from the rock behind him, his head lolled awkwardly to one side. Before the smoke finished curling around his head, she saw the slightest twitch of his lips, his eyes briefly opening to the world. Sybil reached out, almost instinctively, as if she could reach him through the haze.

Then, a vicious pain lanced into her spine, tearing through her senses. It burned into her brain, white hot light flashing at the corners of her eyes as she screamed out. Her hand dropped, limp and useless, onto the ground. The pain faded, just as she saw the sharpest smile flicker up Quinn's lips.

Then, darkness.

THIRTY-ONE

The darkness only lasted a second, though Sybil could have sworn the world stayed dark for a millennium. Long enough for her to contemplate everything in her life a thousand times over. Each pass of the past flung around her like a wheel, the spokes driven into her and vibrating with the memories of every decision she made. All of them hurtling her towards this moment, surrounded by dust and black.

Cold stone was no longer digging into her knees, now replaced with a smoother, flatter surface. At some point Kreb's hand had slipped from hers, the woman's light grip no longer grinding her joints. Instead, her rough, raw knuckles were pressed into the floor, the sharp points of the bones crushed under her weight. With a heady coughing fit, and a few heavy blinks to clear her eyes, she glanced around.

Robes surrounded her, many of them rubbing up against the back of her head, their fabrics sending sparks through her hair. Panic flared its ugly head again as she frantically looked around for the runed board that led to the tunnel. But when she stood, nausea flooding her with the motion, the dust and debris that clung to the robes shook and burst into the air around her.

"Quinn?" she called to the faint darkness, though, deep down, she knew he wouldn't answer. Her hand pressed to her mouth. She tried to convince herself it was to stifle a coughing fit, but she could feel the gasping cry crawling up her throat. "Quinn…" She whispered it, choking back the crushing in her neck. A hand clamped around her shoulder, issuing a wince from her lips.

"You are a very loud guest," Kreb whispered from behind her. The woman was crouched low in the closet, her head brushing the gnarled hooks that suspended the robes.

"Guest?" Sybil asked, catching her breath, still trying to get a bearing of the towering figure of the woman.

Kreb flapped her hand again in the air. "Passenger? *Eghil,*" she muttered, shoving Sybil to the side as she stepped around her. The old woman had more strength than she should have for her age, and Sybil had to catch herself against the wall to stop from slamming into it.

"Where are we?" Sybil asked, but her words were lost behind a creak and a sharp flare of light that encapsulated the small space. Sybil's eyes immediately burned, and she fought them instinctively closing as tears started to well up. In the dark for so long, brightened only by the bare flickering of torches, her eyes took their time adjusting to the harsh invasion of light that seared them.

By the time they cleared, Kreb had vanished. A door gaped open in front of her, spilling the brightness into the tiny room.

She stumbled forward through the door, her eyes still adjusting. The source was finally clear: A massive window, the light pouring in from the sun above. It took Sybil longer than she would have expected to recognize it. The intricate filigree of metal that was shaped and bent to curl around the delicately cut windowpanes was one of a kind. Fashioned by a master mineralist. She'd stared up at it just about every day for the last few years, albeit from a different angle entirely, its mirror image almost more beautiful at this angle than from the ground.

"We're in the Bastion," Sybil gasped in awe as she turned slowly around the room.

Dust littered every surface. Everything held back in time, a stasis of the last day the room was occupied. A purple robe, once more vibrant than its faded grey tones, was laid over the post of a canopy bed. Valances hung down in swooping bolts of fabric, their surfaces sun-damaged. Scattered about the room were stacks of books, most of them so faded their titles were barely legible, the covers cracked and splitting, curled up from whatever moisture drifted in from the nearby washroom.

The candelabra that hung over the room had been runed, though the candles had long since burned out. Their dripping wax leaving puddles on the floor as they poured out of the catches. Though sun-damaged and faded, the room was kept in immaculate condition, every piece of furniture clinging to life under the weight of time.

She hadn't noticed that she had kicked through a few piles of papers as she surveyed her surroundings. They burst into fibres as soon as her foot connected with them, littering the ground with more debris. The inks that would have dotted them had either disappeared long ago, or never given the chance to populate the pages.

"Whose room is this?" Sybil asked, turning to where Kreb stood near the bed. A book was perched on her hand, fingers already carefully flipping through the delicate pages. Though she had asked, Sybil already knew the answer, the history that lingered here telling its age.

"I wasn't sure that would work," Kreb said, lazily throwing a finger towards the closet door. "After all this talk of 'men' and 'beards' I assumed they would have razed my quarters," she scoffed, flipping through a few more pages. "I doubt it was done for me. Probably scared of the wards on the door."

Her shoulders shuddered with a silent laugh. "But if the room wasn't still here? Imagine: I throw down the draught, and '*pop*'! We reappear halfway through a wall, our insides ripped apart by lumber and wood chips. Or worse. Appear in front of a *selblazen*, some poor girl perched on his cock." Kreb chuckled to herself, but shrugged. "I suppose it'd be more likely we would have just been stuck in the Peaks, looking foolish as the smoke cleared."

"We're in the *Bastion*," Sybil repeated, stepping cautiously over to the window, peering down at the courtyard. White mantles scurried below, some in pairs doing their rounds, other clumped in groups. Few she didn't recognize. It'd barely been a week, but she still wondered. Did they ask where she went, or what happened? What clever story did they spin about her death on the journey back from Trelusk? Did that really matter anymore?

"Yes, yes, it's very exciting coming home," Kreb muttered, disappearing back into the closet for a moment before emerging holding a dirty satchel, which she promptly slapped the dust off. She dropped a book into the flap, then strutted back towards the end table. With a heavy pull, the drawer came loose, though not without a loud complaint through the ancient wood.

"Quinn," Sybil swallowed hard. "Is he dead?"

Kreb tutted again, pulling another bound book out of the drawer, this one in much better repair than the others. "Of course not. That scaly *kretin* wouldn't kill his favorite pet. Though I'm sure he has some clever punishment in mind."

Punishment. She didn't need to imagine what that meant, she'd seen it. *Felt it.* The sharp ridges on his skin, the deep gouges filled with ink. Latticework of scars and tattoos that riddled his skin. Seemingly endless, but now she knew it for certain. Fresh wounds would dot his body soon enough. She couldn't be sure anymore that the last ten years of his suffering had been her fault, but any that came next would be.

Her mind felt as though claws dug in on either side, yanking it apart. The slices across her skin and the dark bruises blooming on her flesh by his hand. Her chest ached, the needles still feeling as though they were lingering, *waiting* beneath her skin.

"Why did he do that? Why did he try to kill me?" A flare of heat raced up her back as she spat out the words, only tearing her eyes from the window to stare at the splotches of blood that decorated the front of her shirt. Beneath, the wounds were barely seen, small red dots along her flesh. But the yellows and purples were already spreading in erratic, dark circles around them.

Don't ever do that to me again.

He'd never agreed to that, had he? The monster once more showing his teeth while he wore his sheep's clothing. She was a fool, and she deserved every second of the pain for believing, even for a second, that he was still that boy.

Kreb burst out laughing, the bells of her voice raking lines through Sybil's ears. "Tried to kill you? Goodness. If that's his trying, Naz'tak needs to find a new weapon." Sybil turned, coaxing another flourished hand gesture from Kreb. "He was buying me time. Boy could have torn out your heart in a flash."

"He was weak, he was—he couldn't do it."

"Bah! No excuse. He took his time with you. Though it was getting close. Any longer and he would have had to stop pretending," she muttered, turning her attention back to the small drawer by the bed, the clinking of metal and wood as her hand sorted through it.

"It was so *real*." Sybil muttered, Kreb barely grunting out a response. "Can we... can we do anything?" Sybil knew the words were meaningless, even as she tried to strangle meaning into them.

Kreb let out a heavy, exasperated sigh. "No, *tochdel*. I get us out, he stays there."

There was a pause, the only noise Kreb's hands rummaging through the drawers. The realization crawled across her skull slowly, the limbs of it digging in to each thought as it emerged. "You could leave at any time?" Kreb shrugged. Static cracked at Sybil's fingers. "Why the fuck *didn't* you?"

The room seemed to shudder with the outburst. A living thing that flinched at her rage. Kreb only straightened, her shoulders dropping.

"You could have come back and warned the Portcullis about what was happening under there, what they were doing to their people. *Your people.* You could have prevented Quinn from ever ending up there!"

"Oh? These same people who twist the history to match their..." she flapped her hand again. "They do not care about this. If they did, do you think mages would keep vanishing?"

"You could have told them!" Sybil jolted her hand towards the window. "You're Kreb Bolorick! There's an academy named after you, a town. You ended a decades-long war. They would have listened."

Kreb finally turned to her, her brows back in surrender. "*Tochdel*, they do not care. The people have forgotten me, forgotten the war. All they know is they are prosperous and the Portcullis saved them. Statues may be erected, but they will never tell the story. Just the fantasy people want to believe."

"That can't be the end of it. You're here now, we can go to the Portcullis. Tell them everything. We just have to avoid the Bauers, but the others must—"

"Enough!" Kreb stepped forward, her gaunt frame towering over Sybil. "Do you think the Bauers are alone? Do you think they are the only ones twisting things?"

The Haixens flashed through her mind, their glares and resounding pushes to remove her from the wardens. "What do we do?"

"We? We do nothing. *You* will go to Tabrasia, you will start a new life, you will mother many children and... churn butter." She tipped a small wooden container upside down, pouring the contents into her satchel before snapping the metal clasp. "I lost my bloodweaver and, in turn, my ability to collect books. So, I will go to Losweau and pray to their gods that I am able to continue my work."

"What work? Destroying the runes on their necks?"

"Aye."

"I'm coming with you."

"Ha! *Tochdel*, Tabrasia will take you in with open palms. Losweau will burn you alive when they find out you're Vollmagus. Stay safe and protect yourself. Is what Raekinblod would want, no?"

"I don't give a shit what he wants," Sybil snarled, revelling in the twitch of Kreb's brow. "I spent the last ten years of my life making up for his 'death' and it was all for nothing. Now I'm just supposed to abandon everything I worked for and... churn butter?"

The quick, crass words that spat from her lips shocked even herself. Tainted and coarse, but full of every ounce of fury she felt in her chest.

Every pain in her body amplified, finally fully felt as the world slowed. Every pain *he* had been the cause of thrumming through her bones. "Fuck that, I'm not hiding my head in the sand. If you're so afraid of the Portcullis, fine, we won't go to them. But I'm coming with you to Losweau. Whatever the Void is doing has to be stopped."

"Ah, is that it? She fights for love," Kreb cooed, following it with more laughter as she spun on her slippered heel. "I did that once too. It leads nowhere. Don't let the pathetic pulls of your heart be your reason for living."

"No. I wish he'd stayed dead." She didn't flinch, just held Kreb's gaze. "At least that would've meant something. Now he's one of them, pretending he isn't rotting in a cage."

Her hand curled, stilling her rapid heart.

"He made his choice. He bled for them. Killed for them. He made me choke on my own blood. Watched the light fade from my eyes. *Twice.*" Sybil narrowed her gaze. "I'm not here for him. I'm here to make sure no one else gets dragged down there and decides that nightmare is worth surviving."

Kreb regarded her from atop her sharp nose, one brow clocked high. "A noble lie," she said. "The kind worth dying for." She finally raised her hands in surrender, adjusting the bag higher on her shoulder. "You have to follow me to Tabrasia anyways. There are a few tomes I want to grab on the way through, some people I need to see. When you change your mind, you can stay there."

"If."

"No, *tochdel*. When. Road travel is dangerous and harsh, and that is when you have stores of supplies. We have nothing. You'll be begging for a nice bed by the time we reach the border. Is fine with me."

Sybil couldn't believe she was being berated about the hardships of the roads by a two-centuries-old woman who would topple under the weight of her own tangled hair. It certainly wasn't the first time she had been underestimated. She held her hand out with confidence, though the unfamiliar gesture felt awkward.

"Fine," she said, letting the old woman wrap her gnarled, ink-soaked hands in hers. "But *when* I want to keep going, you will not abandon me."

As she held the old woman's hand in hers, the old gesture of an older world, it grounded her. Steadied her on her lie: that this wasn't about him, that she could let him go. That whatever part of him still clung to life in that pit was already buried. If she had to tear through the Void to keep others from becoming what he did, she would. And if he stood in her way again, whatever was left of Quinn, she'd bury herself.

THIRTY-TWO

Everything hurt. His head, his arms, his legs. Pain clung to him like a second skin. It felt as though his head was under water. Weightless, lagging, drifting on an invisible current. He tried to open his eyes but could barely tell if they were open or not. Nothing quite seeming real yet. The shift of coarse fabric against his lids finally answered the question for him.

He tried to pull down whatever rested over his face, but his arm was stuck tight, a sharp, stabbing pain glancing through his wrist. He shifted once more, trying to move his body, but that shooting pain now stabbed through his other wrist and through his ankles. His mind spun. Slow at first, like a heavy fog rolling in. Then, the jarring awareness hit:

The wire.

It bit into his flesh, too tight to shift, humming with that sick heat of spell-forged metal. It dug into the melted flesh of his wrists, already slick with blood from struggling beneath the binds. The tips of his fingers were cold, static burning them as they went numb.

Out of instinct, he reached out with his magic, desperate to grab onto anything.

Rock, stone, dirt.

Blood.

Nothing responded. The tether was gone, severed clean. Not just bound by metal, but tied *and* broken.

Icy cold panic started to thread through him. He could hear the malicious voices that called to him in the dark, their cooing torments zipping past his ears. Shrill, fractured curses screaming through his skull.

No. No, no, no, no, no.

His mind screamed in protest, the dark voices of his tormentors clouding his thoughts.

That stench. The rot of blood left too long, the oily smoke of flesh burned wrong. It had haunted his worst nights. Etched into his sinuses when he woke up screaming. Yet here it was, surrounding him once more.

The Alpstraum.

Acknowledgements

I cannot express how amazing it is to finally see this in print. I am incredibly grateful to all the folks that were there with me along the journey. My sister, who read it in its earliest drafts when it was unreadable. My partner, dealing with the fluctuating ups and downs of my process. My editor who was able to limit the amount of eyerolling when I regularly, incorrectly used 'simmered'. The cover designers who accepted my plethora of changes.

And to you, dear reader! Thank you for following Sybil and Raekin along on *their* journey. More darkness and nightmares to come!

Corinne Price is an Alberta based author and Red Seal industrial mechanic with a love for dark and twisted tales. Whether fantasy, horror, or the strange realms between, she writes stories where the monsters and the humans traverse the same knife-edge. Wrought in Flesh is her debut novel.

For more information, updates, and news visit:
www.corinneprice.ca